Praise for the  es

"A welcome addition to this tough genre."
—*New York Times Book Review* on *Kindred Crimes*

"Dawson writes believable dialogue, creates quickly realized and appealing characters, and has a particularly nice atmospheric touch."
—*San Francisco Examiner* on *Till the Old Men Die*

"Intelligent and determined, Jeri holds her own among the ranks of impressive female detectives."
—*Publishers Weekly* on *Take a Number*

"Mother/daughter feuds, family solidarity, an ecological mystery: Dawson blends these familiar ingredients with a chef's elan."
—*Kirkus Reviews* on *Don't Turn Your Back on the Ocean*

"A rich plum pudding of a story sprinkled throughout with memorable characters."
—*Washington Post Book World* on *Nobody's Child*

"Thoroughly satisfying... As usual, Dawson offers a well-constructed plot and smoothly polished writing."
—*Booklist* on *A Credible Threat*

"Jeri combines V.I. Warshawski's social conscience with Kinsey Millhone's bad-ass attitude and snappy narrative voice."
—*Washington Post Book World* on *Witness to Evil*

~ Bit Player

Bit Player

A Jeri Howard Mystery

~

Janet Dawson

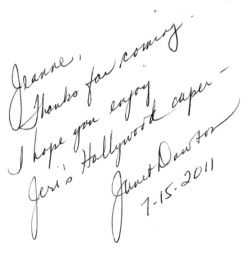

Jeanne,
Thanks for coming.
I hope you enjoy
Jeri's Hollywood caper —
Janet Dawson
7·15·2011

2011 · PALO ALTO / MCKINLEYVILLE, CALIFORNIA
PERSEVERANCE PRESS / JOHN DANIEL & COMPANY

Copyright © 2011 by Janet Dawson
All rights reserved
Printed in the United States of America

A Perseverance Press Book
Published by John Daniel & Company
A division of Daniel & Daniel, Publishers, Inc.
Post Office Box 2790
McKinleyville, California 95519
www.danielpublishing.com/perseverance

Distributed by SCB Distributors (800) 729-6423

Book design: Studio E Books, Santa Barbara, www.studio-e-books.com
Cover photo by Ross Parsons, hand tinted by Linda Lewis

10 9 8 7 6 5 4 3 2 1

LIBRARY OF CONGRESS CATALOGING-IN-PUBLICATION DATA
Dawson, Janet.
Bit player : a Jeri Howard mystery / by Janet Dawson.
    p.   cm.
ISBN 978-1-56474-494-4 (pbk. : alk. paper)
1. Howard, Jeri (Fictitious character)—Fiction.
2. Women private investigators—
Fiction. 3. California—Fiction.
I. Title.
PS3554.A949B58 2010
813'.54--dc22
2010040565

For my mother, Thelma Metcalf Dawson,
who was selling tickets in her family's movie theater
in Purcell, Oklahoma when she met Don Dawson, a handsome
young sailor. They married in March 1944. When Dad shipped
out with the Navy, Mom worked at a defense plant.
They were married for 61 years. I have the greatest
love and appreciation for both of them.

~

I gratefully acknowledge the assistance of
Thelma Dawson and
former LAPD Detective Thomas G. Hays

~ Bit Player

$$\sim \mid \sim$$

"GRANDMA SAID John Barrymore made a pass at her." I nudged my friend Cassie and pointed at the framed poster from *Rasputin and the Empress*, displaying the famous profiles of John, Ethel, and Lionel in the 1932 film, the only movie the three Barrymores ever made together.

Cassie chuckled. "From what I've heard about John Barrymore, he made passes at anything in skirts."

On this sunny Saturday afternoon, the last weekend in May, Cassie and I were in downtown Alameda, where we'd gone to a movie at the city's newly restored Art Deco movie palace, glittering anew like the jewel it had been when it opened back in the 1930s. After the movie, we crossed Central Avenue to the produce market on the corner. After making a few purchases, I suggested a visit to the ice cream parlor around the corner, on Park Street. Cassie heartily concurred and we strolled back up Central. Just opposite the theater I stopped, lured by the display of old movie magazines and posters in the window of a shop that hadn't been here the last time I'd been downtown, just a few weeks earlier. The sign above the door looked like a movie marquee, mirroring the real one across the street. The shop was called Matinee—Classic Hollywood Memorabilia. We decided to take a look. On the left, shelves held books about the movies and the stars, emphasizing the golden years of the thirties and forties. On the right, I saw movie memorabilia—the ephemera of Tinseltown, dating from the early part of the twentieth century up through the early 1960s. Posters and inserts hung on the walls. In the shallow bins along the wall, protected by clear plastic sleeves, were lobby and title cards, programs, and photographs, as well as old movie magazines, and publicity files containing yellowed clippings from newspapers and magazines.

The *Rasputin and the Empress* poster, with big red letters on a cream background, had the patina of age, with faded colors. At one edge the paper was cracked and brittle. The poster was an original, the real deal, with a high price to match. Most movie memorabilia of the pre–World War II era had answered the call to duty and wound up in paper drives for the war effort. Much of what was available from that time period was reprints. The vintage stuff was harder to get, and priced accordingly.

I really like movie memorabilia, but I have to be picky and buy only what I can afford. I'm Jeri Howard, self-employed private investigator, with a slim profit margin, a mortgage payment to make, and not much room in my budget for frills.

"When did your grandmother encounter John Barrymore?" Cassie asked.

"On the set of *Marie Antoinette*. Barrymore was playing King Louis the Fifteenth."

Grandma was thrilled to be an extra in the lavish costume drama, in production at Metro-Goldwyn-Mayer in the spring of 1938, especially because she was in a scene with her favorite actress, Norma Shearer, who starred as the doomed queen. The movie also featured handsome young Tyrone Power and a panoply of Hollywood names, including Barrymore.

My grandmother, Jerusha Layne, went to Hollywood in the fall of 1937. She was eighteen, just out of high school. Ever since she was old enough to stand on a box behind the counter, she'd worked in her family's theater in Jackson, California, selling tickets and popcorn, enthralled by the movies spinning from the huge reels her father wrestled onto the projector upstairs in the booth. She wanted more from life than she could find in that small Gold Rush–era mining town. The new gold rush, for pretty young women like Jerusha, was to Hollywood. Visions of movie stardom beckoned, as ethereal as El Dorado's glittering dust. Lightning could strike. She could climb the ladder to the top. After all, she sang, she danced, and she'd played the lead in several high school plays.

Except it didn't work out that way. Pretty and talented as she was, Jerusha discovered lots of young women just like her, scrabbling at the bottom of that Hollywood ladder, trying to get their feet on the first rung. She worked in the movies, all right, first as an extra, a silent face in the crowd, walking down a sidewalk or sitting at a table at a restaurant, filling in the background while the cameras focused on the stars. Then she worked as a bit player, or day player, as they were sometimes called. Bit players were different from extras, because they had a few lines of dialogue, or they did *bits*, specific pieces of business. Jerusha played telephone operators, hat check girls, waitresses. She was the shop clerk, chatting while she waited on the star, or the neighbor who witnessed the gangland shooting and gave a statement to the cops. She got jobs through agents, but often bit players weren't under contract like actors who worked steadily in larger roles. As she sat in the background, Jerusha dreamed of the day when the parts would get bigger, when someone at a studio would notice her and offer her a contract.

It didn't happen. But Jerusha stuck it out for nearly five years, working primarily at Metro-Goldwyn-Mayer. Then she left Hollywood, realizing her future wasn't written in lights on a movie palace marquee. Besides, she'd met a young man named Ted Howard. They married in the spring of 1942, like so many young couples in those war years, full of hopes and fears for the future. Later that year, Ted Howard, United States Navy, left to fight battles in the remote islands of the Pacific. But he came back, and my father, Timothy, was their firstborn. Grandma never had any regrets, but she certainly had some great Hollywood stories to tell her grandchildren. And I—the granddaughter named after her—relished every tale.

"I've always wanted something from one of Grandma's movies," I told Cassie. "A one-sheet, an insert, a title or lobby card—that would be great."

Cassie looked up from a bin of black-and-white photos, a still of Cary Grant in her hand. "What are all those things? I'm not familiar with the terms."

"This is a lobby card." I pulled one from a nearby bin. Encased in a clear plastic sleeve, the eleven-by-fourteen-inch card displayed a color photo of Marilyn Monroe, Tony Curtis and Jack Lemmon in the Billy Wilder masterpiece, *Some Like It Hot.*

"Lobby cards showed colored photos of scenes from the movie," I explained, "even if the film itself was shot in black-and-white, like this one. The cards usually came in sets of eight. They were displayed in theater lobbies. You don't see lobby cards for movies made after the early sixties. I guess they stopped making them. Sometimes there was a ninth card in the set, a title card. Instead of photographs, title cards showed the title, names of the cast, and an image, usually the same as on the one-sheet."

I gestured at the posters ranked along the walls—William Powell and Irene Dunne in *Life with Father,* Robert Mitchum and Deborah Kerr in *Heaven Knows, Mr. Allison,* Audrey Hepburn in *Breakfast at Tiffany's.* "These are one-sheets. A one-sheet is a full-size movie poster, twenty-seven inches wide and forty-one inches high. There's a larger size poster called a three-sheet, which is forty-one inches wide by eighty-one inches. Got to have a lot of wall space for one of those. But an insert is a good size for display, thirty-six inches high, but narrower, about fourteen inches."

"So the ones you have at home are inserts," Cassie said.

"That's right." The inserts hanging on my bedroom wall were from two of my favorite movies from the fifties—*The Journey,* a 1959 movie with Yul Brynner and Deborah Kerr, and *Picnic,* the 1956 classic, starring William Holden and Kim Novak.

A lobby or title card from one of Jerusha's movies would be a great addition to my small collection. Did the shop have anything from one of Norma Shearer's movies? Maybe the shop's proprietor could steer me in the right direction. Come to think of it, where was the proprietor?

I hadn't seen anyone behind the counter when Cassie and I had walked into the shop, though a tinkling bell above the door had announced our entry. But I'd been focused on the shop's wares. Now I tuned in my surroundings. We were the only customers in the place. The overhead lights were dim and the walls were a shade of bland somewhere between beige and brown. Music played softly. The tune was sweet and mellow, with that Big Band swing. Glenn Miller's "Moonlight Serenade." As I looked toward the counter, I smiled. The poster on the wall behind it showed James Stewart and June Allyson in *The Glenn Miller Story.*

The music segued into "String of Pearls." Someone was there after all, a man perched on a stool, partly hidden by the cash register and the old issue of *Life* magazine he'd been reading. He cleared his throat. His voice sounded rusty and disused.

"I couldn't help overhearing," he said, setting aside the magazine. "Your grandmother worked in Hollywood?"

"She was a bit player, from nineteen thirty-seven to nineteen forty-two."

"Ah, I remember," he said. "Those were golden years."

"Were you there?" I asked.

"Physically? Or in spirit? I might have been."

I walked back for a closer look, intrigued by his response. My grandmother had been past eighty when she'd died, her Hollywood years a long time ago. Even if the man who ran the shop was younger than Grandma, he'd have to be well over eighty.

Indeed, he could have been that old. He was a colorless, wizened little elf, ancient and musty, as though he'd been stored in a film vault for half a century. He had papery white skin and opaque brown eyes. A frieze of cropped white hair formed a half circle at the back of his polished bald skull. From his half-open mouth came a sound that might have been a laugh or a cough, the rustle of old celluloid running through a projector.

"What was your grandmother's name?" he asked.

"Jerusha Layne."

His thin lips curved into the ghost of a smile. It didn't fit his face, making it look instead like one of those masks. Comedy or tragedy, I couldn't tell which. "Jerusha Layne," he repeated, tasting the vowels and consonants. "An unusual name, very pretty. I imagine she was pretty. They all were. Where did she work? At what studios?"

"She worked mostly at Metro, though she did a few films at Warner, RKO, and Columbia. She was in the last six films Norma Shearer made before she retired. Well, before they both retired, Norma and Grandma."

The man behind the counter ticked off the titles of those last six Norma Shearer movies. "*Marie Antoinette, Idiot's Delight, The Women, Escape, We Were Dancing,* and *Her Cardboard Lover.* The divine Norma. What a wonderful actress she was. They don't make them like that anymore. These pictures today—" He cast a deprecating glance at the movie theater across the street. "A collection of car chases, explosions and sex scenes, starring people I never heard of—and don't want to."

I was inclined to agree with him. For me, movies today just don't have the same panache they did back in Hollywood's Golden Era. I'd grown up with my grandmother's tales of stars and studios. She and I had spent many afternoons watching the classics at the UC Theatre in Berkeley and the Castro in San Francisco. With the advent of videos and DVDs, we'd had our own film festivals at her Alameda home. Plenty of popcorn, of course.

"This shop is new. When did you open?"

"The first week of May," he said. "We do sell over the Internet, of course. Our website is listed on the business card."

"Do you own the shop? What's your name?" I asked. But he didn't answer either question. In fact, he acted as though he hadn't heard me, instead tapping a few keys on the computer at the counter. I wondered if he was hard of hearing. I plucked a card from the holder next to the cash register. But the card simply listed the shop's name, address, phone number and URL of the website.

He looked up from the computer. "Is there something special you have in mind?"

"Do you have lobby or title cards from any of those Shearer movies?" I asked, tucking the business card into my pocket.

"Let me check our inventory. I believe we do have some stock from *The Women.* I'm not sure what other Norma Shearer memorabilia we have."

The man consulted the computer on the counter. Then he hopped down from his stool and walked around the end of the counter, surprisingly spry in view of his evident age. I revised my assessment from frail to dapper. He was short, about five feet six, a little stoop-shouldered, wearing a pair of well-cut charcoal gray slacks. At his throat was a bow tie, with a busy pattern in gray and red. I hadn't seen a man wear a bow tie in years. His long-sleeved linen shirt was fastened at the wrists by a pair of square gold cufflinks that matched the ring he wore on his left hand. Both the ring and the cufflinks were decorated with the Celtic cross, the symbol that traditionally combined a cross with a circle surrounding the intersection. The arms of the cross were slightly wider at the ends, and inside were engravings of the Celtic knot, interlaced patterns commonly used for decoration.

He stopped at one of the bins. His age-mottled hands quickly flipped through the unframed, plastic-covered cards. He pulled out two title cards and handed them to me.

"Voilà," he said. "*The Women*, released September nineteen thirty-nine. And *We Were Dancing*, released in nineteen forty-two. Both of these cards are vintage."

They had prices to match. But I wanted them. I was already thinking how great they'd look in matching frames. Both title cards had yellow backgrounds and red lettering. The card from *The Women* had the names and photos of the three stars whose names appeared above the title—Norma Shearer, Joan Crawford, and Rosalind Russell—and the legend IT'S ALL ABOUT MEN! The card from *We Were Dancing* showed Shearer in a slinky red satin gown, leaning back and gazing into the eyes of her debonair dancing partner, Melvyn Douglas.

"Lovely, aren't they?" The man looked at me as though he knew he had a live one on the hook. "And in great condition."

Not that I needed much convincing. "I'll take both of them."

The proprietor moved slowly now as he walked back behind the counter, as though he'd expended his day's ration of energy. He rang up the sale, ran my credit card through the machine, slipped the title cards into a bag and handed them to me. Then he placed his right index finger next to his mouth and tilted his head to one side. It was a little too studied, a parody of a natural movement. The broad gesture, I thought, of an actor from the silent era, miming a man who was searching his memory.

"Jerusha Layne," he said, with a dramatic wave of his hand. "I remember now. She was involved in that business with Ralph Tarrant, in 'forty-two."

"Who was Ralph Tarrant?"

"A British actor who came to Hollywood in nineteen thirty-six. He was in *Lloyd's of London*, with Tyrone Power. Had a marvelous voice. Quite handsome as well." Something odd flickered in the man's dark eyes. "Of course, I never met the man. I just saw the movies he was in."

"What was this business with Ralph Tarrant that my grandmother was supposedly involved in?" I asked.

"I don't know all the details," he said. "Just what I read in the papers and heard on the grapevine. Probably nothing more than gossip. Hollywood simply thrives on gossip." A malicious smile teased the corner of the old man's mouth.

"The story was that Jerusha Layne and Ralph Tarrant were, shall we say, an item. Then they broke up. Not a friendly parting of the ways. So the police were rather interested in her whereabouts the night Tarrant was murdered. Rumors about who did it were flying all over town." He fluttered his hands, miming the wings of a bird. "It was quite the Hollywood mystery, you see. Still is. The murder was never solved."

~ 2 ~

"I THOUGHT you were going to come unglued," Cassie told me when we left the shop. I'd lost my appetite for ice cream and so we walked back to Oak Street, where I'd parked my car.

"I don't know about unglued, but I'm fuming," I said. "None of it is true. It couldn't be. Grandma and Grandpa met in 'forty-one and married in 'forty-two, before he shipped out to the Pacific. There's no way she could have been involved with some actor named Tarrant. She never mentioned anything like that when she talked about her Hollywood years."

"If she was involved with Tarrant..." Cassie began.

I shook my head and repeated, "No way."

"Hey, I'm only playing devil's advocate here. My point is that if she had dated Tarrant while she was engaged to your grandfather, it's hardly something she'd have told her fiancé, let alone her grandchildren."

"Dated? Hell, that old man implied they were lovers. He said they were 'an item.' I didn't like the way he said it, either. What nonsense. I don't believe it. And he claimed the cops questioned Grandma about Tarrant's murder."

"I'm sure he was just dramatizing," Cassie said. "Did you see the look on his face, when he called it a Hollywood mystery?"

I recalled the avid expression in the man's eyes as he'd told us about Tarrant's murder and implied that my grandmother had had some involvement in the crime. "Yeah. He was really getting a buzz out of it."

We reached my car and I unlocked it, setting the title cards on the floor behind the driver's seat. Cassie levered herself into the passenger seat and fastened the safety harness over her burgeoning belly. She and her husband, Eric, were expecting their first child in three months. I fastened my own seat belt, started the Toyota and maneuvered out of the parking space.

"So he was embellishing, having fun at your expense," Cassie declared as I turned right off Oak Street onto Encinal Avenue, driving away from the downtown area. "Just because you told him about your grandmother, the actress. The more I think about it, his story sounds like complete fiction. For all we know, he made the whole thing up. Was there really a Ralph Tarrant? I've never heard of him."

"Presumably because he wasn't famous," I said. "There were— and are—a lot of people like Grandma in Hollywood. People you never heard of, working as extras and bit players, trying to break in."

"Or maybe he was famous, but not for long," Cassie said. "That old man said Tarrant came to Hollywood in nineteen thirty-six. If he was killed in 'forty-two, he didn't have time to build much of a career."

"Maybe. How many people today—besides old movie buffs— have heard of Miriam Hopkins or Kay Francis?"

Cassie chuckled. "I've never heard of either of them. But then, you're the old-movie buff, not me. Anyway, even if there was a Ralph Tarrant, how do we know he was murdered? Or that the crime was never solved."

I didn't answer. I was thinking about a couple of other un-solved Hollywood mysteries. Thelma Todd was an actress who'd worked in Hollywood from the mid-twenties through the early thir-ties. Known as Hot Toddy because of her hard-playing social life, she'd been found dead in her car in 1935. The death, due to car-bon monoxide poisoning, was labeled accidental. But rumors she'd been murdered persisted to this day.

Equally intriguing was the 1922 slaying of director William Desmond Taylor, detailed in a book by Sidney D. Kirkpatrick, called *A Cast of Killers*. Among the suspects questioned by the police in that homicide were silent-era actresses Mabel Normand and Mary Miles Minter. That murder had never been officially solved either, though several authors had theorized that Minter's mother was responsible.

I stopped at a red light, turned right onto Chestnut Street, then left at Alameda Avenue. Cassie and Eric had bought their house, a Victorian-era fixer-upper, last year. I pulled up at the curb in front. "Whether Ralph Tarrant existed is easy enough to find out. As for his murder, when it comes to Hollywood mysteries, the man in the store picked the wrong audience for his yarn."

"A private investigator, you mean?" Cassie smiled as she unhooked the harness and opened the passenger door. "Don't tell me you're going to investigate your grandmother's purported involvement in a murder that might have happened more than sixty years ago."

"I just might," I said.

~

I headed home. I had a fixer-upper of my own, in Oakland's Rockridge neighborhood. The truism about owning a house or a condo is that there's always something that needs doing, and it's usually expensive. I'd been saving up for a kitchen remodel, new appliances and countertops. Then a plumbing situation became a crisis and moved to the top of the priority list. I'd get to the kitchen one of these days, when I had enough money. Business had been slow this last month. I had more time on my hands, but that was affecting my bank account. Right now I had a flash of buyer's remorse about my impulse to purchase those title cards from *The Women* and *We Were Dancing*. Then I took them from the bag, and propped them up, side by side, admiring them. They would look great in matching frames with red and yellow mats, to highlight the colors. What's done is done, I told myself.

I carried the title cards to my home office, where I already had a spot picked out to hang the cards when they were framed. I switched on my computer and moved my tabby cat, Abigail, off my chair. She grumped at me and stalked off to join Black Bart, the

other cat, who was curled up on my bed doing what cats do best—
sleeping.

The Internet Movie Database and the Turner Classic Movies
websites are great tools for movie buffs. Key in the name of an actor, a director or any other human being associated with a film, and
both sites will provide a list of films that person worked on, as well
as a short biography. Frequently there are photos, images of movie
posters, and sometimes even a link to play an old movie trailer. The
TCM site will even tell you when the film was in production and
when it was released.

My grandmother worked in Hollywood for nearly five years.
During that time Jerusha Layne appeared in many films. In all of
these movies, her name is down at the bottom of the cast list. There
is no photograph on the IMDB or TCM websites. The biography
section simply states the date and place of her birth, and the date
she died.

Jerusha's first job was as an extra in an Andy Hardy movie with
Mickey Rooney, called *You're Only Young Once.* Her penultimate
movie was *We Were Dancing,* starring Norma Shearer and Melvyn
Douglas. Now, on the TCM site, I typed in the title *We Were
Dancing* and clicked on the button labeled "Search." The page
that came up had a graphic, the same image on the title card I'd
just purchased. I scrolled down the cast list and found Grandma's
name: Jerusha Layne, her role listed simply as "bit part (uncredited)."

Now I typed in Ralph Tarrant's name and clicked my mouse.
A few seconds later I had a photograph. So Tarrant was real. He'd
lived and died. He had a lean, wolfish face. His dark hair was
slicked back from his forehead, and his hooded eyes reminded me
of George Raft. He didn't have Raft's Hell's Kitchen background,
though. What I read about Tarrant reminded more of his better-
known countryman, the elegant and urbane Leslie Howard.

According to the brief bio, Tarrant had been born in London,
England, in August 1906, too young to serve in the army during the
First World War but old enough to serve in the Second—though it
appeared he hadn't done so. He went on the stage in the late 1920s,

appearing in several plays. Then he turned to the movies, first in England. Like Howard, Tarrant had migrated to the United States. Unlike Howard, who returned to England in 1939 to aid in the war effort, Tarrant stayed in Hollywood. He was thirty-six years old when he'd died on February 21, 1942. As the result of a homicide, read the biographical note. Tarrant had indeed been murdered.

I glanced through the list of films Tarrant had appeared in and recognized a few of the later titles. Then I sent the search-engine spider crawling across the World Wide Web, looking for hits. These days there's a website for everything. William Desmond Taylor and Thelma Todd even have sites dedicated to their deaths. Tarrant was mentioned on a number of web pages. One of these, devoted to Hollywood mysteries, gave me some background on Tarrant's Hollywood career and a brief account of the actor's murder.

Tarrant had arrived in Hollywood in 1936. He had a minor role in *Lloyd's of London,* at Twentieth Century Fox. It was evidently on this film set that Tarrant had met another cast member, George Sanders. The two Britons became friends.

Many of Tarrant's movies had been made at Fox, but studios had the habit of loaning out actors who were under contract to them. So Tarrant's filmography showed movies made at several studios, including Columbia, Warner Brothers and Metro-Goldwyn-Mayer, moving gradually up the cast list as he got bigger parts. But he'd never achieved top or even second or third billing. Since Jerusha had made most of her movies at Metro, I checked to see if she and Tarrant had ever worked on the same film. But they hadn't. After examining cast lists, I didn't see any career intersection between my grandmother and the British actor. Had they met because they were working on the same lot at the same time?

Tarrant was filming a movie at Metro in early 1941, I discovered. He was listed in the cast of *They Met in Bombay,* starring Clark Gable and Rosalind Russell, in production February through April and released in June 1941. At the same time Jerusha was working in the Hitchcock movie *Suspicion* at RKO. Then she had a part in a George Raft picture, *Manpower,* at Warner Brothers. No connection there. But she'd had a small role in *The Feminine Touch,* which was the next movie Russell had made at Metro, shot during the month of July 1941, a tenuous connection at best. Jerusha had appeared in another movie at Metro, *When Ladies Meet,* a movie featuring Greer Garson and Joan Crawford. That film was in production June through August of 1941. Tarrant was also at Metro in August 1941. He had appeared in *H.M. Pulham, Esq.,* directed by the great King Vidor. That film, starring Hedy Lamarr and Robert Young, had been shot during August and September of 1941, then released in December 1941.

So they could have met at some point, I reluctantly conceded.

I turned my attention to Tarrant's murder, described briefly on the Hollywood mysteries website on the screen in front of me, reading the short account of Tarrant's death, then I went to a database of historic newspapers that included the *Los Angeles Times* and searched on a range of dates from February 21, 1942, the date of Tarrant's demise, to the end of the year. The search returned several hits and I clicked on the links that led to the scanned articles.

Ralph Tarrant was killed sometime Saturday evening at his rented Hollywood bungalow. He was supposed to meet friends for dinner at eight that evening, at a restaurant in nearby Beverly Hills, but he never showed up. A next-door neighbor saw the shadowy figure of a woman get into a car and drive away. A short time later, the neighbor saw an orange glow, flames dancing in Tarrant's windows, and called the fire department.

Tarrant's body was discovered sprawled on the living room rug, with five slugs in the corpse. LAPD's subsequent investigation into the actor's murder evidently hadn't come up with any leads. As I read through the articles I saw that coverage went from the front page to small columns on the inside pages of the *Times,* and ultimately out of the public consciousness altogether. The last article was dated August of 1942. I checked an Internet timeline for World War II and saw that there were more pressing matters occupying the attentions of newspaper readers in the spring of 1942. Tarrant was killed right after the British surrendered Singapore to the Japanese invasion force on February 15, 1942. The murder of a little-known actor didn't mean much when it competed with headlines about a Japanese sub shelling an oil refinery off Santa Barbara; the creation of the War Relocation Authority that ultimately sent over a hundred thousand Japanese American civilians to internment camps; the attack on, invasion, and surrender of Bataan; and the Doolittle Raid on Tokyo.

Nobody knew who killed Ralph Tarrant. I guessed the case got colder and colder, with no more evidence, only speculation. I pictured the case file, stuffed with documents and the investigating officer's notes, pushed farther back on the detective's desk, as other cases demanded precedence, then finally transferred to an anonymous shelf somewhere at LAPD, gathering dust.

Where was that case file now? And could I get my hands on it? I frowned at the computer screen, itching to get more details about Tarrant's death, such as a list of people interviewed in the course of the investigation, to see if my grandmother's name was on that list. I was betting that list was in the Tarrant case file.

What if I went down to LA?

Wait a minute, Jeri, I told myself, putting on the brakes. A crime that happened during World War II? You've got to be kidding. Why was I so irked by the old man in the movie memorabilia shop and his innuendo about my grandmother and Tarrant? Most people would call it ancient history and leave it at that. But it was my grandmother he was implicating in Tarrant's murder. And I'm the kind of person who likes to get to the bottom of things, no matter how old the case. I had a few resources here in the Bay Area, ones I should use before getting on a plane to Los Angeles.

~ 3 ~

THE ROOMMATES, I thought, later that evening after I'd had dinner.

When Jerusha arrived in Hollywood, she rented a room in a boarding house, living there for a couple of years. In 1939 or 1940, she moved into a bungalow court, sharing a house with a series of roommates, all of them aspiring actresses. I remembered her stories of how small the place was for the four of them. It was a cottage really, originally with two bedrooms and one full bathroom. The tiny back porch had been enclosed and converted into a third bedroom. The master bedroom, a decent size, was partitioned and occupied by two of the roommates. The second bedroom, much smaller, had room for one person. The most recent arrival always got stuck with the back porch. Though it had the benefit of proximity to a tiny half bath with toilet and sink, the porch was cold, damp and drafty in the winter, and it didn't have a closet, just a makeshift rod and some hooks, hidden by a curtain. Grandma chuckled as she described how elated she felt when she'd been promoted from the porch to a real bedroom. It was warmer, she said, and it had a closet.

Jerusha had lots of roommates during her Hollywood years, first in the boarding house and later in the bungalow. But she'd kept in touch with some of them. Every now and then she'd talk about receiving letters from the girls who'd shared her quarters. That would lead to the stories I enjoyed so much as Grandma reminisced about those Hollywood years. But who were they? What were their names? Try as I might, I could not dredge them from my memory.

Now I wished I could get my hands on those letters. But they were probably long gone. Grandma had been dead for several years now. I recalled my father and his siblings clearing out her house in Alameda. Those possessions that Grandma had not already given to her children and grandchildren had been divided among family members and the house had been sold. Had anyone kept Grandma's personal papers and correspondence?

I called my father at his condo in Castro Valley. He had been a history professor at California State University in Hayward. Now he was retired and enthusiastically enjoying a new passion, birding. While walking for exercise, he became interested in the birds he was seeing and bought a book. That led to more books and a beginning birding class. Then he joined the local chapter of the Audubon Society, going on their field trips. I had accompanied him on several of his own excursions to East Bay parks and a bird walk at Abbott's Lagoon in the Point Reyes National Seashore in Marin County. Now he was planning to attend a birding festival later in June, the Mono Basin Bird Chautauqua in Lee Vining, the site of Mono Lake in the Eastern Sierra Nevada. I envied him his trip. The most direct route was over Tioga Pass Road, which wound through the beautiful high country of Yosemite National Park.

"You should come with me," Dad said. "I rented a cabin at the Lakeview Lodge in Lee Vining. I know you like hiking in Yosemite and it's not that far from Lee Vining to the east entrance of the park. You could go tramping around Tuolumne Meadows."

"It's tempting," I said, and it was. "I'll check my calendar. Say, Dad, what do you know about Grandma's time in Hollywood?"

"Only what I remember from the stories she used to tell. She worked with some big stars and a lot of people we'd never heard of. She really enjoyed those years, but after she met Dad, she was ready to give it up and settle down."

Unless something had happened, something darker, like a murder. Something that propelled her to leave Hollywood. I pushed away that thought as my father asked why I was interested in Grandma's years as a bit player.

"Just curious," I told him. "There's a new movie memorabilia shop in Alameda. Cassie and I stopped for a look. I bought a couple of title cards from two of Grandma's old movies, *The Women* and *We Were Dancing*. Both starred Norma Shearer."

"Norma Shearer," Dad said. "Mom thought the world of Norma Shearer. Said she was a real lady."

"I know. I wished I'd recorded some of Grandma's Hollywood yarns while she was still alive."

"Water under the bridge," he said. "You did record her oral history about working at the Kaiser Shipyard in Richmond during the war, and that was important."

I'd made the recording about the time they were building the Rosie the Riveter National Monument up in Richmond. Digital versions of the oral history recordings were now available through the Oral History office at the University of California's Bancroft Library. "Here I am in my welder togs," Grandma used to say when she showed off the picture that now stands framed on my desk at home. The photograph was taken in 1944 at Kaiser. Grandma's welder togs were a pair of coveralls that hung on her slender frame. She also wore a mask pushed back to show her short blond hair and a big smile. That was her life after she'd married Grandpa. It was the Hollywood years that nagged at me now.

"She kept corresponding with a couple of her roommates. Maybe they're still alive. But I don't remember their names. Did anyone save any of Grandma's letters?"

"I don't know," Dad said. "You should check with your Aunt Caro. She took a lot of Mom's personal papers."

Dad and I chatted awhile longer. After I hung up, I looked up the phone number for Aunt Caro, my father's younger sister Caroline. She and her husband, Neil, lived in Santa Rosa, up in Sonoma County.

"I kept a lot of the letters," Caro told me. "Mostly the letters Mom and Dad wrote to each other when he was overseas during World War Two. She kept his, of course, and Dad carried a packet of her letters with him all through the war. I thought that was so romantic."

What we keep and what we throw away. It was logical that Caro would preserve her parents' wartime correspondence. And just as logical that she would winnow out what looked like chaff, the letters from people who were not family members. These days we're drowning in paper and clutter. We can't keep everything. So we make those choices of what to keep and what to throw away.

I wondered what this would mean to future historians, the people who rely on personal correspondence to reveal the lives and characters of historic figures. Somehow scrolling through e-mails doesn't have the same cachet. And electronic communication is so easily disposed of, gone in the click of a mouse, dumped into a symbolic trash can.

"She could have mentioned her roommates in those letters to Grandpa," I said.

"It wouldn't surprise me," Caro said. "Mom wrote really newsy letters. I enjoy reading them. They're such a time machine, back to the United States of the forties. Come on up to Santa Rosa. You're welcome to look through them."

I looked at my calendar and Caro looked at hers. We set a date for getting together, the following Saturday. We were about to end the call when Caro said, "You should go see Aunt Dulcie, too. She and Mom were always close. They wrote each other lots of letters and I did keep some of those. But I know Dulcie keeps everything. After Uncle Fred died and Pat moved Dulcie in with her and Bruce, I remember Pat saying her mother refused to throw out any of her letters. I'll bet Dulcie remembers things from Mom's Hollywood days. And her letters would be a treasure trove."

"That's a great idea." My grandmother was one of four siblings. Her older brother, Woodrow, stayed in Jackson and became a mining engineer. Her younger brother, Jacob, had been a Central Valley farmer. Dulcie, the youngest, had also been a Rosie, working at the Kaiser Shipyard. On a blind date she met a guy in the Army Air Forces, Fred Pedroza, home on leave before going overseas. One thing led to another, letters were exchanged, and when the boys came marching home from that war, Dulcie and Fred got married and began contributing to the postwar baby boom. Fred decided to stay in the Army. Then in 1947 the Army Air Forces became the Air Force, a separate branch of the service. Fred spent thirty years in the service, moving his family all over the United States, Europe and Asia. Great-uncle Fred's last duty station had been Hamilton Air Force Base, in Novato, at the northern end of Marin County. He and Great-aunt Dulcie had retired there, surrounded by children and grandchildren.

When Fred died, Dulcie stayed in her house for several years, then age and medical problems led to her decision to stop driving and change her living situation. She'd moved in with her daughter and son-in-law in Graton, in western Sonoma County.

Caro was right. Aunt Dulcie would be a great resource. I looked up the number and reached for the phone. A few seconds later my cousin Pat answered. When I explained my mission, she said, "Come on up. We'd love to see you. How about brunch on Saturday?"

~ 4 ~

OTHER WORK, the kind that paid the bills, kept me busy in Oakland on Monday. I did take the time to search the Alameda County online database for fictitious business names, looking for the particulars on Matinee, the movie memorabilia shop on Central Avenue. The names on the business license were Charles Lowell Makellar and Raina Simms Makellar. Was Charles the man who had sold me the title cards? Or did the old man just work there? Either way, he was the one who started me on this quest, when he brought up Ralph Tarrant's murder and mentioned my grandmother's supposed connection to it.

Further investigation into the shop revealed that the Makellars had leased the space in March. The man behind the counter at Matinee had told me the shop opened the first week in May. So it had taken the Makellars two months to ready the interior—painting, buying or leasing the fixtures that displayed the merchandise, and setting up the shop. The owners had access to a large stock of movie memorabilia; the business card I'd picked up at the shop listed a website and I had already checked that out, browsing through the online searchable inventory. Some of the items for sale were vintage, even rare. I didn't know much about the movie memorabilia business, but there appeared to be a lot of money involved in these collectibles. How did the Makellars acquire such items? From the studios themselves? From collectors?

I set the wheels in motion to find out more about the Makellars. My background search didn't take long to bear fruit. They were husband and wife, former residents of Los Angeles, married just five years. Charles was forty-six, nine years older than Raina, his spouse, who was thirty-seven. So Charles was too young to be the man behind the counter, who had to be past eighty. As the old man had dangled the story about the murdered actor Ralph Tarrant and my grandmother, he'd looked as though he himself had been in Hollywood in 1942. I dug deeper and learned that the Makellars had previously owned a movie memorabilia shop in Hollywood, along with a man named Wallace Simms, presumably, due to the last name, a relative of Raina Simms Makellar. Was the old man in the shop Raina's father or uncle? But Wallace could have been a brother or a cousin, and his name wasn't on the business license of the Alameda shop. The old man was an employee, then. Or did he have another connection to the Makellars and their memorabilia business?

The Makellars had two vehicles, a brown Ford SUV registered to Charles and a maroon Lexus sedan registered to Raina, with vanity plates that read RNAMAK. They were renting a house in Alameda. Late Tuesday afternoon, I drove past the house, located near the corner of Lafayette Street and Central Avenue, walking distance to the shop. It was a one-story stucco bungalow on a deep, narrow lot. I peered up the driveway and saw that the detached garage had been turned into an apartment.

I checked my watch. It was five-thirty. The business card I'd picked up earlier indicated the shop was open from ten A.M. until six P.M. I circled back to downtown Alameda, parked near the shop, and waited. At six o'clock the elderly man closed and locked the front door. Then he set off on foot, carrying a canvas bag with shoulder straps. He stopped at the produce market on the corner of Oak Street and Central Avenue and purchased a few items, placing them in the bag. He continued walking up Central Avenue, moving briskly for a man of his age. I started my car, pulled out of the curbside parking space and followed him at a discreet distance. At Lafayette Street he turned left. Then he walked up the driveway of the Makellars' house, unlocked the apartment door, and went inside.

On Wednesday morning I checked the telephone and utility records and discovered that all the services for both the house and the apartment were in the Makellars' names. The man behind the counter must be more than an employee, if the Makellars were providing him with a place to live and paying his expenses, though he could be paying rent. During my visit to the shop on Saturday, I'd asked the man for his name. He had avoided answering the question. At the time I'd thought he might not have heard me. Now I wasn't so sure. I needed his name in order to run a background check.

I went back to the shop on Wednesday afternoon. The old man wasn't there. Someone else was behind the counter, working at the computer. I went inside and took a good look at the woman I guessed was Raina Makellar. She was medium height and slender, with blue eyes in a round face and full red lips. Her black hair was sleek and straight, showing a few threads of silver at the temples, in a stylish chin-length cut. She wore a deep purple blouse, setting off the heavy silver chain around her neck and the silver hoops in her pierced ears. I strolled to the shelves arrayed on the left wall, scanning the titles of the books displayed there. She glanced up from the computer and smiled. "Good afternoon. Please let me know if there's anything I can help you find."

"Just looking, thanks." I reached for a fat hardback biography of Cecil B. DeMille and leafed through the pages, reading passages about the director amid photographs from his movies. I set the book back on the shelf and examined the cover of another, this one about Hollywood tough guy George Raft. Then I picked up a biography of Grandma's favorite actress, Norma Shearer. The book was used, in good condition. I decided to buy it, not only because I wanted to read it, but also as a way of engaging Raina Makellar in conversation. I took a step toward the counter. Then the bell above the door rang. I detoured to one of the bins on the opposite side of the shop and flipped through plastic-covered lobby cards. The man who'd just entered wore a U.S. Postal Service uniform. He had a bag slung over his shoulder and a bundle of mail in his hand.

"Afternoon, Ms. Makellar," the carrier said. "Where's Mr. Calhoun today?"

"He's taking a few days off," Raina Makellar said.

Now I had a name for the man who was usually behind the counter. Mr. Calhoun.

The mail carrier handed the bundle to Raina Makellar and departed. She removed the rubber band and glanced at the envelopes, then stepped through the doorway to the back of the shop, where I saw her deposit the mail on a desk. As she returned to the counter, the front door opened again, admitting a short, frizzy-haired woman in a green dress, carrying a cardboard box containing two disposable cups and a paper sack. "Hey, Raina. Here's your afternoon pick-me-up, direct from Peet's Coffee. A latte with a double shot of espresso for you, and a mocha with extra whipped cream for me."

"Oh, thank you, Marge," Raina said. She reached for the cup marked with an L, took a sip of her latte and sighed contentedly. "I really need my caffeine fix in the middle of the afternoon."

"I couldn't resist getting a caramel chocolate bar." Marge tore open the sack. "Want to split it with me?"

"It looks positively decadent." Raina examined the treat. "I shouldn't. Oh, what the hell, I'll have a bite."

Marge broke the bar in half. Raina took a napkin and picked up one piece, nibbling at the end. "I was surprised to see you in the shop alone," Marge said, around a mouthful of crumbs. "Where's Henry?"

Henry Calhoun. Now that I had his full name, I could do a background check. I edged closer to the counter, eavesdropping on the conversation between the two women.

Raina sipped her latte. "I'll be working here for next few days. Chaz and Henry are making the rounds, talking to prospects. Chaz found out someone in Placer County has a big collection of posters and lobby cards from musicals of the forties and fifties. And Henry says there's another collection up in Sonoma County that sounds interesting, with lots of Hitchcock memorabilia."

"So they're buying merchandise?" Marge asked. She drank some of her mocha and the whipped cream left a trail on her lip.

Raina shrugged. "Making contacts, handing out business

cards, and just maybe buying merchandise. It would be great to get some items from either collection. Musicals are always good sellers. I understand this particular collection has lots of Judy Garland stuff. There's always a market for Garland. And Hitchcock. But not everyone wants to sell. Collectors like to have things that reflect their passion. That's why they accumulate the stuff."

"So they collect just to have it?" Marge asked.

"That's right," Raina said. "Just for the joy of collecting, which means that often collectors don't want to let go of it. Or they won't sell if they know how valuable items are. Or maybe they will sell, but they want an inflated price. Collectors can be quite knowledgeable about what they have and what it's worth. Chaz is great at bargaining, though. And Henry has a nose for locating merchandise. He worked for my father for years when we were down in LA. So Chaz and Henry make a good team. They've had some good luck in Sonoma County. Earlier this year Henry heard about a great collection up there. The elderly woman who owned wasn't interested in selling. Later she died and Henry saw her obituary. So Chaz went looking for her heirs. There was a son, and he didn't know or care about the value of the collection. He just wanted to get rid of her things so he could sell his mother's house. Chaz gave him a lowball offer to take it off his hands. Maybe that sounds opportunistic."

Marge brushed her hands together, shaking off the pastry crumbs. "No, it just sounds like good business. So you're settling in a little better."

"I guess so." Raina sounded unconvinced. "Alameda seems like such a small town after Los Angeles."

"It's not small," Marge protested. "The population's seventy-five thousand plus, I think. And the whole Bay Area is huge."

"I know, I know." Raina rolled her eyes. "But it feels like a small town to me after LA. And it feels so different. I'm a lifelong Angeleno. I practically grew up in Hollywood, helping my father with his shop on Melrose. My aunt worked in publicity at the studios. They'd throw the posters and lobby cards away, and she'd grab the stuff for Dad's shop. I really wanted to stay in LA. But after

Dad died, the landlord raised the rent on the shop so high that we couldn't afford it. So we had to relocate anyway. Chaz wanted to get out of Southern California, come up here and make a fresh start. But it's all so new. Oh, don't mind me. I'm feeling a little lonesome, that's all."

"You'll be fine," Marge said. "It takes time to adjust after you move. Once you get used to it you'll like Alameda as much as I do. And you'll meet people. Anyway, I'd better get back to my shop." She picked up her cup and left Matinee.

Raina used the napkin to sweep a few errant crumbs from the counter. Then she looked up, as though she'd forgotten I was there. "Oh, I'm sorry. I've been ignoring you. You said you were browsing. Is there a particular actor or picture that interests you?"

I said the first name that came to mind. "George Raft. I've always liked him. Do you have any lobby cards from his movies?"

"Let me check our inventory," she said, turning to the computer.

I left the bin of lobby cards I'd been examining and walked to the counter. "The last time I was here, there was an elderly man behind the counter. Your father?"

"Oh, no." She smiled. "My father's gone. Henry's a friend. He just works here."

He was more than a friend, and scout, if he was living on the Makellars' dime. "He was very knowledgeable about old Hollywood."

"That's why we hired him." She glanced up from the computer screen. "We do have a few lobby cards from George Raft movies—*Johnny Allegro*, *Race Street*, and *Rogue Cop*."

I shook my head. "No, thank you. *Nocturne* is the movie I'm interested in. That, or *They Drive by Night*."

She smiled. "Sorry, nothing right now. I can keep an eye out for some memorabilia from those two, if you like."

"That won't be necessary. I'll just check the store from time to time." I turned to leave. Then I remembered the Norma Shearer biography I'd left on top of a bin of lobby cards. I picked it up and returned to the counter. "I will take this, though."

I paid cash for the book, for anonymity. Then I left the shop, mulling over the few facts I'd gleaned. The man I'd spoken with on Saturday was Henry Calhoun, and he'd worked for Raina Makellar's father in a similar business in Los Angeles. In addition to working behind the counter at the shop, he also seemed to function as a scout, locating merchandise. I wanted to get a closer look at him, and Charles Makellar as well.

My background check kicked out some more information on Thursday. I learned that Raina Makellar's father, Wallace Simms, had died a year earlier, leaving the inventory of the shop on Melrose Avenue to Raina, not to Charles. I found that interesting. Even more interesting was information that Charles Makellar, aka Chaz, had a police record. Back in his early twenties he'd passed some bad checks, resulting in a conviction and probation. Another arrest for petty theft in his late twenties led to some jail time. These incidents had occurred more than twenty years back. Had he been a law-abiding citizen ever since? Or did he still have a streak of larceny combined with more skill at eluding the law?

Chaz had been sued twice. The first lawsuit dated back seven years and involved plans to open a restaurant in Hollywood. That venture had gone awry in a dispute between the partners. That could happen to anyone, I thought. But the most recent lawsuit, two years ago, involved a collector alleging fraud over some memorabilia he'd purchased from Chaz Makellar. Both lawsuits had been settled out of court. But it made me wonder. What had led the Makellars to leave Hollywood and come north to the Bay Area? Was there a need for Chaz Makellar to get out of town?

As for Henry Calhoun, my background check hadn't found much of a past at all. It was as though Calhoun didn't exist before the 1980s. That set off alarm bells in my head. A man as old as that ought to leave a much longer record of his passage through life. Unless Calhoun wasn't his real name. I suspected that was the case. Henry Calhoun, or whoever he was, must be hiding his past.

On Friday afternoon I went back to Alameda. I grabbed a parking space a few doors down from the shop, got out of my car, and dropped coins into a meter. Then I saw Henry Calhoun on the sidewalk in front of the shop, dressed casually in khaki pants and a long-sleeved blue shirt that must have been warm on this June afternoon. He was feeding coins into a parking meter as a brown Ford SUV backed into the parking space.

Just under the SUV's rearview mirror, affixed to the windshield, I saw a Fas Trak device, the toll tag that would be read by the electronic toll collection system on the various Bay Area bridges. The driver—I guessed he was Chaz Makellar—straightened the wheel, cut the engine and got out of the vehicle. He was tall, over six feet, with an angular frame in khaki pants and a red T-shirt. His face was long and narrow, and his brown hair, streaked liberally with gray, was worn long, curling around his ears and touching his collar.

Chaz walked to the back of the SUV and opened the door. I had taken up a position in front of the restaurant next to the shop, pretending to examine the menu displayed in the window as I flipped open my cell phone and hit the button that activated the device's camera. I took a photo of Raina standing in the shop doorway, then the old man standing near the SUV. Inside the vehicle were some medium-sized boxes and several large flat items covered with a stained beige blanket. Chaz pushed the blanket aside and grabbed one end of a framed one-sheet poster from *The Pirate*, a movie musical with Judy Garland and Gene Kelly. Henry took the other end of the poster. Raina held open the door as the two men carried the poster into the shop. Then she moved to the back of the SUV and opened one of the boxes, peering inside. "What else did you buy?" Raina asked when the two men came out to the sidewalk.

"Got a good haul from that woman who collects musical stuff," Chaz said. "This other one-sheet is Judy Garland, too, from *In the Good Old Summertime*. Two inserts, one from *Weekend in Havana* with Alice Faye. That's a find. The other insert is from *Gigi*. Some lobby cards from a couple of Doris Day movies. And a title card from *Royal Wedding* with Fred Astaire. The woman who sold me the stuff gave me the name of another Garland collector who has a poster from *Meet Me in St. Louis*."

As they stood together on the sidewalk, I shifted position and took several more photos of the trio with my cell phone, working the buttons as though I was sending a text message. Luckily none of them noticed me. They were intent on their conversation, and the merchandise in the back of the vehicle.

"What about the Hitchcock collection?" Raina asked. "I was hoping you'd get some of that."

"Struck out." Chaz picked up the Alice Faye insert. "The guy didn't want to sell."

"There's a problem with that," Henry said. He picked up one of the boxes and disappeared into the shop.

Present tense, I noticed. As though the problem, whatever it was, still existed. Henry and the Makellars finished unloading. Then Raina put a hand on her husband's arm. "Middle of the afternoon. I need my caffeine fix."

"Same here. I'll make a Peet's run. The usual?" She nodded and Chaz glanced at Henry, who stood in the shop doorway, looking preoccupied. "Hey, Henry, I'm going for coffee. Want anything?"

Henry shook his head. Then he went back into the shop, followed by Raina. As Chaz started down the street toward the Peet's on the corner I quickly retrieved a book from the front seat of my car, the Norma Shearer biography I'd bought at the store on Wednesday. It might be good camouflage. When I entered the corner shop Chaz was looking at the pastry offerings. I got into line behind him and bumped him slightly, making sure the cover of the book I held was visible.

"Oh, I'm sorry," I said.

He turned and gave me a full-wattage smile that extended to his hazel eyes. Up close he was good-looking in a roguish, frayed-around-the-edges way. "No problem," he said. He glanced at the book I was carrying. "Hey, Norma Shearer. One of the greats."

"I love old movies," I said. "And I just adore *The Women* with Norma Shearer and Joan Crawford."

"Oh, yeah. What a cast. Rosalind Russell, Paulette Goddard, Joan Fontaine."

"Don't forget Marjorie Main," I added. "I'm really interested in old Hollywood, that Golden Era of the thirties and forties. There's this new shop down the street that has books and posters from those years. That's where I picked up this Shearer biography."

Chaz gave me a twinkly smile, turning up the charm. "You're talking to the right guy. I own the shop."

I noticed he didn't mention his wife. He wasn't wearing a wedding ring either. "What a great location. Across the street from the movie theater. The city did such a wonderful job of restoring it. So many of the old movie palaces from the thirties have been torn down. I'm glad this one is still here."

"Yeah, the theater's beautiful. And the location, well, it can't be beat. Lots of street traffic. That's what you need in retail. Plus, the theater is showing classics as well as current movies, so that helps business." He offered his hand. "I'm Chaz, by the way."

"Jeri." I shook his hand.

The woman in front of him moved away from the counter. Chaz stepped up, ordering a latte with a double shot, a cappuccino, and two brownies. He paid for the items, then stuck his wallet into his pocket and moved aside to wait for his coffee order.

It was my turn at the counter, so I ordered a latte and paid for it. Then I joined Chaz. "What else do you recommend? Books, I mean? I recently read a really interesting book about the studio system, *The Glamour Factory* by Ronald Davis."

The young woman behind the counter called Chaz's name and he picked up his order. "Try *The Star Machine* by Jeanine Basinger. That's more recent and it's really good. I think we may have a copy in the shop. If you'll stop by, I'll look for it."

"Thanks," I said, not committing myself. The smile he gave me as he left bordered on flirtatious. Raina must have her hands full with this guy, I thought.

~ 5 ~

SEEING AUNT DULCIE was like seeing a very good copy—though not quite the same—of my grandmother. They were sisters, after all. Dulcie, the youngest of Grandma's siblings, was now the same age Grandma had been when she died. My great-aunt had aged since the last time I'd seen her. Wrinkles furrowed her sweet-natured face and her soft, gently curling hair was white and thin. Dulcie's blue eyes were just as sharp as they'd ever been, though. I greeted her with a hug and admonished myself for letting so much time lapse between visits. It's best to go and see people while they're alive, rather than wait and find yourself attending their funerals.

Pat and Bruce Foxworth, Dulcie's daughter and son-in-law, had both retired from their professions. Now they grew apples and pears on their farm near Graton, a small community in western Sonoma County. As I left the nearby town of Sebastopol and drove north on Highway 116, I saw orchards stretching on either side of the road. I looked forward to the harvest of sweet, crunchy apples. The first to ripen would be Gravensteins, then an array of varieties through the fall until the season ended in December. I was partial to Northern Spies and Rome Beauties myself.

I turned left and headed west on Graton Road, past homes and then a three-block cluster of businesses, then into a landscape of gently rolling hills. I turned right onto a gravel driveway, parked at the side of the two-story house, and got out of the car. Mabel, a dog of indeterminate parentage, barked a greeting as she walked up and gave me an olfactory once-over. I scratched her floppy ears and she wagged her tail.

"Hey, there," my cousin Pat said, coming out the front door onto the porch. She was the youngest of Aunt Dulcie's three children, now in her sixties, short and trim, with salt-and-pepper curls springing out around her head. She hugged me and ushered me into the house. "I hope you brought an appetite. Bruce and I fixed a sumptuous brunch, if I do say so myself."

"Sounds great," I said. "All I had before leaving home was coffee."

Out on the patio, we savored the food, the fine June morning, and the view of the coastal hills to the west. As we talked about family, hummingbirds darted around the roses in the garden. We worked our way through omelets stuffed with cheese and vegetables, thick crisp slices of bacon, and a coffee cake with a crumbly topping of cinnamon, sugar and walnuts. The coffee cake tasted a lot like the one Grandma used to bake. Must have been the same recipe, I thought, or the coffee cake was flavored with nostalgia.

When we finished our meal, we lingered over coffee. Mabel stretched out in a sunny spot and woofed softly, twitching her paws as she chased rabbits in her dreams. Then Pat and Bruce gathered dishes onto a tray and carried them into the kitchen, leaving me to talk with Dulcie. I poured myself another cup of coffee and steered the conversation in the direction of old-time Hollywood and Grandma's small role in the movie business.

Dulcie smiled, remembering. "Jerusha enjoyed herself so much. She was excited about being in the movies, even if they were little parts. I enjoyed it all vicariously, in her letters. Why, she was in *Marie Antoinette*. It was a big, prestige production at MGM, with a huge cast and lots of gorgeous costumes. And the stars were Norma Shearer and John Barrymore. Oh, I was impressed. We all were."

I smiled, remembering Grandma's story about Barrymore making a pass at her on the set of that movie, back in 1938.

"Her first movie was in nineteen thirty-seven," Aunt Dulcie said. "An Andy Hardy picture, with Mickey Rooney. She used to tell stories about what a cut-up that boy was. After that, Jerusha was in all sorts of movies: comedies, dramas, Westerns, musicals. She could sing and dance, you know. First she was an extra, then she had speaking roles, bits, they call them. She was in several Norma Shearer movies. We both were big fans of Norma Shearer, the queen of the MGM lot. So you can imagine how thrilling it was when Jerusha wrote and told me that she was working at MGM, with Norma Shearer. When I think of the stars your grandma saw in Hollywood during those five years, people like Clark Gable, Irene Dunne, Tyrone Power, Greer Garson."

"What do you recall about the last couple of years Grandma was in Hollywood?" I asked. "The years right before she left to marry Grandpa? That would be nineteen forty-one and nineteen forty-two."

Dulcie thought for a moment. "Well, Jerusha met your Grandpa Ted in the summer of 'forty-one. He knew right away that she was the girl for him. But she wasn't quite ready to leave Hollywood. I know they argued about it. They even broke up at one point, in the fall, I think. But they got together again, in December. After Pearl Harbor. A lot of men joined up right after that. Your Uncle Fred joined the Army then, and your Grandpa Ted joined the Navy, December of 'forty-one, right after Pearl Harbor. Early in 'forty-two he was in training down in San Diego. They wanted to get married before he shipped out. I think by then Jerusha was ready to chuck Hollywood and settle down. She'd had her fun, but five years was enough."

Or something had happened, I thought. Like Ralph Tarrant's murder. I wanted to push away that thought, but I didn't. Instead I asked, "Had something happened, other than the war, to take the bloom off the rose?"

"I think it was mostly the war." Aunt Dulcie's face looked pensive. "Pearl Harbor was such a shock. When I look back, I guess it shouldn't have been. The war in Europe had been going on for more than two years. It was in the newspapers and on the newsreels, what with Hitler invading Poland and France. And even before that, when the Japanese invaded China, all the reports of that horrible massacre at Nanking. I remember hearing people say they hoped we'd stay out of the war. We couldn't, though. We should have known what was coming. But even so, Pearl Harbor was a shock. We were finally at war, and our boys were dying overseas. The news was all bad that first part of nineteen forty-two. Being an actress in Hollywood must have seemed unimportant to your grandma, what with Ted in the Navy and ready to go to the Pacific. I remember he gave her an engagement ring for Christmas." She smiled. "But there was something else about those last few months in Hollywood. I had the impression something was troubling your grandma, something on the home front. But I just don't remember. Maybe when you start reading the letters you'll figure it out."

"Shall we go look at the letters, then?" I stood and held out my hand, helping Dulcie up from her chair. She moved slowly, troubled with arthritis in her joints, but she didn't need the assistance of a cane or a walker. The house was large, two stories. Pat and Bruce's bedroom was on the second floor, but Dulcie had a big suite of her own on the first floor. Her bedroom held a double bed, dresser and chest of drawers, the tops crowded with photos of her family. Just past the bathroom was a door leading to a smaller room, where I saw a sewing machine and shelves holding baskets of colorful fabric. Dulcie was a longtime quilter. I had always admired the craftsmanship of the bright red-and-yellow Sunbonnet Sue quilt on her bed. Even now she was piecing a quilt top, triangles of blue and purple floral-print cloth.

Dulcie settled into a low, wide-bottomed oak rocking chair near the window and waved her hand at a closed door near the bed. "The letters are in that walk-in closet. When I moved out of my house in Novato, some of my grandkids helped me organize them by year into storage boxes. In fact, my great-grandson Trevor did a school report using your Uncle Fred's letters from the front. Of course I have every single letter he ever wrote me." She smiled and her blue eyes looked a bit moist. "I do miss that man. We had a good life together. Anyway, Jerusha wrote me such nice long, newsy letters. I'm glad I kept my letters, even if they do take up space. They're a link to the past. Sometimes I read your grandma's letters. It's just like being in the same room with her."

I opened the door to the roomy walk-in closet. One wall held a rail where Dulcie's clothes hung, with shelves below holding her shoes. Floor-to-ceiling shelves had been installed on the other three walls, holding photo albums and boxes, the kind used to store photographs, sturdy cardboard with colorful printed designs on the exterior and a place for a label in front. I read a few of the labels, hand-printed with names and dates. One section of boxes had Uncle Fred's name on them, starting with 1942, the year he'd met Dulcie. I scanned the boxes until I found several with Grandma's name, starting from 1937, the year Jerusha Layne went to Hollywood, and going on till the year my grandmother died.

Early this morning, driving north from Oakland to Graton, I'd told myself I was only going to read those letters Grandma had written to her sister in 1941 and 1942. This was an investigation, after all. I was looking for any mention of Ralph Tarrant, the actor murdered early in 1942. But now I opened the lid to the box labeled JERUSHA 1937 and pulled out the first letter. The envelope was faded and yellowed, with a three-cent stamp in the upper right corner, a faint postmark dated July 1937, and my grandmother's handwriting addressed to Miss Dulcie Layne in Jackson, California. Waves of nostalgia and loss washed over me. I missed Grandma, our visits to the race track, our forays out to Brentwood during the summer to get produce for canning, our long talks about anything and everything. I opened the envelope flap and pulled out the letter. I read the words Grandma had written to her sister that long-ago summer, and I knew exactly what Aunt Dulcie meant. It was like having young Jerusha Layne in the same room with me.

I had to read all the letters. I carried all the boxes containing Jerusha's correspondence with her sister out of the closet, stacked them on the floor in the middle of the bedroom, and sat down cross-legged on the carpet. I opened the lightweight laptop computer I'd brought with me, to take notes, and turned it on. When I removed the lids from the boxes, I gently fanned the tops of the envelopes inside. The dates on the postmarks were faded but readable. The letters had been filed in chronological order, which suited my purpose, and I thanked Dulcie's grandchildren for their organizing job.

Jerusha wrote long, newsy letters, the kind to be savored, the sort of letters people don't write anymore, since the advent of e-mail. She had an eye for detail and great skill at describing what was going on in her life. Her handwritten words provided me with a glimpse of what life was like back then, as the country edged slowly out of the economic hardships of the Great Depression toward the trauma and devastation of World War II.

I read Jerusha's accounts of her arrival in Hollywood, where she got a small room in a boarding house. Then there was a detailed and amusing description of her very first, and very brief, role as an extra on the set of *You're Only Young Once*, part of the Andy Hardy series. The amusing part of the letter dealt with some of the antics of MGM's young star, Mickey Rooney.

I glanced up at Aunt Dulcie. She dozed in her rocking chair, her blue eyes closed, her wrinkled old face tilted to one side, the skin furrowed into little hills and valleys. I smiled and went back to the letters. Over the next hour or so, I read steadily, taking notes, moving through the correspondence written in the summer and autumn of 1937, through 1938 and into 1939, the year of *Gone with the Wind* and other great movies such as *Stagecoach*, *The Wizard of Oz*, *Mr. Smith Goes to Washington*, and *The Women* with Norma Shearer. Jerusha had worked as an extra and bit player in some of these, including the Shearer film. She sometimes had to take temporary jobs, clerking in a store or typing in an office, just to keep money coming in. But her movie work at various studios steadily increased, feeding her hopes of a career as an actress. I enjoyed her accounts of her day-to-day life. Jerusha commented on everything from the cost of living to the beautiful dress Marion Davies wore the day Jerusha saw her at Metro, posing for pictures outside a soundstage, with L. B. Mayer on one side and William Randolph Hearst on the other.

Nineteen thirty-nine was also the year World War II officially started, and in the months leading up to Hitler's invasion of Poland in September of that year, Jerusha also commented on politics and news of the day. She always read the newspapers and listened to the radio news, I recalled, and watched TV news in her later years. I'd had many long discussions with her about current events and politics. I looked up from a letter Jerusha had written in early September, mentioning the newly declared war in Europe. I remembered what Aunt Dulcie had said about the shock of Pearl Harbor.

The boarding house where Jerusha lived seemed to have a revolving door as hopeful young girls like Jerusha Layne came to Hollywood to try for movie stardom. Her comments about her fellow roomers were, depending on the circumstances, poignant and amusing. And Jerusha's description of her boarding house landlady made me laugh out loud. The woman was a salty dame who'd worked in silent movies back in the early days, doing slapstick comedies for director Mack Sennett at Keystone Studios.

I'd been making notes as I read Jerusha's letters, looking for information about her roommates. Finally I found a familiar name— Pearl Bishop. It was at the boarding house, in the fall of 1938, that Jerusha met Pearl, her future roommate at the bungalow. The first time I saw Pearl mentioned in one of the letters, she was working steadily as an extra and bit player at Republic Pictures, one of the leading studios on Poverty Row, a collection of small, mostly short-lived B-movie studios producing low-budget films, although Republic went on to bigger movies after the war. When Jerusha met her, Pearl was working on a movie I'd never heard of, though with *Outlaw* in the title I guess it was a Western.

Jerusha liked Pearl immediately, and so did I. From her descriptions, Pearl sounded down-to-earth, a real good-time gal, the kind of friend who'd give you the shirt off her back, or five bucks to see you through till payday.

It was through Pearl that Jerusha met Anne Hayes, a sensible and forthright young woman from Colorado. Anne lived in another boarding house down the street and worked as an extra and bit player at some of the larger studios, including Metro. Soon Jerusha and Anne became good friends. It was early in 1939 that Anne and a friend of hers, Ellie Snyder, broached the subject of leaving their boarding house and renting a bungalow Anne had her eye on. They needed more roommates to afford the rent. The figure Jerusha mentioned in her letter sounded like a pittance to me now, but by the standards of the late thirties it was a big sum. And I knew Jerusha never made a fortune in Hollywood. The four women finally moved in together in April of 1939. The cottage had two bedrooms, and the larger of these was partitioned, providing space for two twin beds. The smaller bedroom had one bed, and the back porch had been enclosed and turned into a makeshift bedroom. The four roommates drew straws for the sleeping accommodations. Ellie and Pearl wound up sharing the larger bedroom, Anne got the small bedroom all to herself, and Jerusha got the back porch, along with a promise that if anyone moved out, she could graduate to an actual bedroom.

I didn't get much of a sense of Ellie, but soon she was gone, back to Washington State. Jerusha moved from the porch to the large bedroom, sharing the space with Pearl. The new roommate stayed only a few months, leaving at the end of 1939, and was replaced in January 1940 by another Colorado girl, Mildred Peretti. Jerusha wrote that Mildred was a friendly girl who liked to bake and kept the household supplied with cakes and cookies. In the past they'd used the cookie jar as a stash for the grocery money, Jerusha added, but since Mildred kept the jar filled with cookies, they'd transferred the funds to an old coffee tin. All the roommates pitched in for food and other essentials. In her letters Jerusha sometimes referred to the price of groceries. A loaf of bread cost eight cents back in 1940, mere pennies to me now.

Most of the time the roommates used public transportation, but Pearl had acquired a car, purchased from her cousin, a fisherman in the port community of San Pedro. It was a 1931 Model A Ford, its formerly black finish weathered to a murky gray, and more dings than paint, according to Jerusha. Anne dubbed the car the Gasper, because it always seems to be gasping its last, but it kept running, despite its disreputable appearance, Jerusha wrote, and all four young women chipped in to buy gas, at nineteen cents a gallon. I shook my head at that. Those gas prices were long gone.

In addition to the cost of living, my grandmother's letters to her sister mentioned current events, such as Franklin Roosevelt running for a third term as president, and the war now raging in Europe. Closer to home, in February 1940, she and Pearl had gone to the racetrack at Santa Anita, to watch the fabled horse Seabiscuit's comeback run in the Handicap, known as the Hundred Grander. I knew this because my grandmother had told me many times. But it was so much more vivid reading the description she'd written to her sister that very evening.

I read through the letters from 1940 and the early months of 1941, more slowly now, looking for any mention of Ralph Tarrant. I saw nothing. Then I opened an envelope with a May 1941 postmark. The first few lines brought a smile to my face. On a sunny Saturday morning, my grandmother and her roommate Pearl had gone on an outing, to buy produce and other supplies at the Farmers Market on Third and Fairfax. Jerusha met someone there, a young man who came from a town in the Sierra Nevada just like her.

His name is Ted, she wrote, and I like him a lot.

~ 6 ~

Los Angeles, California, May 1941

IT WAS A FINE Saturday morning in May, with a glorious blue sky. Too pretty a morning to stay in bed. Jerusha and Pearl took the Gasper, Pearl's old Model A Ford, to the Farmers Market.

"I guess I'm still a small-town girl in that way," Pearl said as she slowed and signaled a turn. "I'm used to buying produce direct from the farmers."

"We always did, back home in Jackson," Jerusha said. "It just tastes better."

The market was seven years old now, started in 1934, with stalls set up at the corner of Third and Fairfax. Pearl angled the Ford into a parking space and cut the engine. They got out of the car and strolled toward the first row of stands, both carrying baskets. Jerusha had the list and the coin purse with the money from the grocery kitty. They made their way down the aisles, carefully selecting their purchases, checking items off the list, as Pearl told Jerusha about her latest part in a movie at Warner Brothers.

"We start shooting in June. It's a remake of *Satan Met a Lady,* that movie with Bette Davis, back in 'thirty-six."

Jerusha looked over a bin of oranges. "I saw that picture. It was awful, a remake of something with Ricardo Cortez in 'thirty-one."

"I think this one will be good," Pearl said. "It's got a great cast, Humphrey Bogart and Mary Astor."

"Who's directing?" Jerusha squeezed an orange and set it aside.

"John Huston. He worked on the script for *High Sierra*. He was hitting on all six with that script. But this is his first time out as a director."

Jerusha selected four oranges and paid for them. "What's it called?"

"They've got a couple of working titles—*The Gent from Frisco* and *The Knight of Malta*. They should just use the title of the book it's based on. *The Maltese Falcon*. The guy that wrote that, Hammett, he wrote *The Thin Man*, too. I like Bogart. He was such a nice guy when we were making *High Sierra*."

"Yes, he is. I worked with him and Raft last year in *They Drive by Night*." Jerusha moved toward a display of snap beans and spinach. Early tomatoes, too, but they didn't look ripe enough to suit her. "I'll be at Warner Brothers next month, too. I have a bit in a picture with Raft, Edward G. Robinson, and Marlene Dietrich. Raoul Walsh is directing."

"Raft, can that man dance! What a pepper shaker." Pearl pointed at a stand. "We need eggs, right? That's a good price."

"Yes, it is." Jerusha opened the coin purse and doled money into Pearl's waiting hand. While Pearl bought the eggs, Jerusha walked on, then stopped to look at bins of apricots and cherries, first of the season. She bought both, then strolled to the next stall, where boxes of fat red strawberries beckoned.

Inside the stall a young man sat on a stool, head tilted back as he drained a bottle of Coca-Cola. When he saw Jerusha, he discarded the empty bottle and stood, moving toward her. He was tall, with a lanky frame and a head of curly red hair. His face was tanned but that didn't disguise a liberal dusting of freckles. His eyes were as green as glass, with a roguish twinkle as he picked up a bowl of strawberries. "Sweetest strawberries in California. Almost as sweet as you."

What a line. Jerusha smiled in spite of herself. She liked his looks, those green eyes and the smile that curved his lips. "How would you know how sweet I am?"

"I can tell just by looking at you," he said. "Here, taste one."

"Don't mind if I do." Jerusha plucked a strawberry from the bowl and bit into the luscious red fruit. "Oh, they are good."

"Grown in Ventura County. Picked this morning. I ought to know, I drove 'em down here."

"Is that where you're from?" she asked. "Ventura County?"

"Nah. I just drive a truck for my Uncle Walt. He owns this stall." He gestured at the stacked boxes of produce around them. "I pick up loads of fruits and vegetables and bring them here to sell at the market. I stay with my uncle, too, in Chatsworth, out in the San Fernando Valley. But I'm originally from Oakhurst. You know where Oakhurst is?"

"I should hope so," Jerusha said. "It's on the south end of the Mother Lode Highway. I'm from Jackson, farther north. But I live here now."

"So you're a Los Angeles girl now. You sure are pretty," he said, still holding the bowl as he stared at her.

Jerusha felt herself blush. She reached for another strawberry. He set down the bowl. She felt a little tingle as his fingers brushed her palm, picking up the strawberry hulls. He discarded them in a nearby box.

"What's your name?" he asked.

"Jerusha Layne."

"I'm Ted Howard." He stuck out his hand. "It's nice to meet you, Jerusha Layne. That's a pretty name. Sounds old-fashioned."

"It's a family name, passed on through the years. I have a great-aunt named Jerusha." She shook his hand. "It's nice to meet you, too."

"Jerusha," he said, still holding her hand. "I'd sure like to buy you a cup of coffee."

"I'm…I'm here with someone."

"Don't let me get in the way if you've got a better offer." Pearl appeared at Jerusha's side. She looked up at Ted and beamed. "Who's this?"

"Ted Howard." He released Jerusha's hand and shook Pearl's. "From Oakhurst. But I live in Chatsworth now, with my uncle who owns this stall."

"Hello, Ted. I'm Pearl Bishop." With a sidelong glance at Jerusha, Pearl chuckled. "I see you've already met Miss Jerusha Layne. I think you've made an impression on her."

"Pearl..." Jerusha felt her cheeks redden. She looked down at her hand, stained by the juice from the strawberries.

"I hope so," Ted said. "I hope she'll go out with me. What do you two ladies do here in Los Angeles?"

"We're actresses," Pearl said.

"Wow. I never met an actress before," Ted said. "And now I've met two. Would I have seen you in any movies?"

"Maybe." Jerusha tilted her head and looked up at him. "I was in *The Women* with Norma Shearer. I've been in lots of movies, and so has Pearl. I just finished a picture at RKO, called *Suspicion*."

"You say you're living in Chatsworth," Pearl told Ted. "I did a couple of Westerns that were filmed on location out there, at the Iverson Movie Ranch."

"Yeah, I know where that is," Ted said.

"I'm working on a picture at Paramount," Pearl added. "With Veronica Lake and Joel McCrea, directed by Preston Sturges. They're calling it *Sullivan's Travels*."

"You ever work with that guy Frank Capra?" Ted asked. "I like his pictures. *Lady for a Day*, *Mr. Smith Goes to Washington*, and *You Can't Take It with You*."

Jerusha shook her head. "Not me. I'd like to, though. I think he's a good director."

"I had a bit in *Mr. Smith Goes to Washington*," Pearl said. Ted looked mystified at the term. "We're what they call bit players. That means you have to look really hard to see us on the screen."

"I've heard of extras," he said, "but not bit players."

"We do bits," Jerusha explained. "Small parts, a little bit of dialogue and action. Let's say we're making a movie about the Farmers Market, starring Norma Shearer as the woman searching for..."

"Strawberries," Pearl said, helping herself to a berry from the bowl. "With Tyrone Power as the young man in the produce stall."

Ted grinned. "Oh, I see Jimmy Stewart in that part. Or maybe Gary Cooper."

Jerusha laughed. "So the customer who keeps interrupting the stars while they're trying to have a conversation—"

"Flirting with one another." Pearl winked at Ted.

"The customer would be the bit player," Jerusha finished.

"I get it," Ted said. "What about Uncle Walt?" He pointed a thumb at the older man who was walking toward them.

"He could be a bit player," Jerusha said. "Or a character actor."

"I see Frank McHugh in that role," Pearl said, popping another strawberry into her mouth.

"Too short." Jerusha looked up at Uncle Walt, who was nearly as tall as his nephew. His hair was going gray, but it had a hint of red and he, too, had freckles on his weather-beaten face.

Ted made the introductions, then he glanced at his uncle as he stepped out of the produce stall. "Hey, Walt. Is it okay if I buy these ladies a cuppa joe and some pie?"

Walt smiled, nodding. "Go ahead. Take your time."

"I'm gonna amscray and let you two beat your gums," Pearl said. "I see a fella I know down there who owes me five simoleons, and I'm gonna remind him." She winked at Jerusha. "I'll meet you at the car in about an hour."

"You know, I like that Pearl," Ted said. He took Jerusha's arm and escorted her to a stall where a woman was selling coffee and homemade pie. They shared a wedge of buttermilk pie and Ted asked if Jerusha was free for dinner.

She shook her head. "I have a date tonight."

"How about tomorrow night?"

"I don't go out on Sunday nights. Particularly this Sunday. I'm auditioning for a part in a Fred Astaire picture on Monday. I have to work on my song-and-dance routine."

"How about coffee again, tomorrow afternoon?"

She laughed. "You don't take no for an answer."

"I'm not going to. You just name the place and the time, and I'll be there."

She considered for a moment, then she nodded. "Okay. Coffee tomorrow afternoon. There's a little café on the corner of Sunset and La Brea. I'll meet you there at two."

She didn't get the part in the Fred Astaire picture, *You'll Never Get Rich*. But coffee with Ted led to lunch the following Saturday, and dinner the weekend after that. Jerusha enjoyed Ted Howard's company. He was easy to talk with. He listened to her as she told him of all her dreams and aspirations, and he told her about his.

"Some day I want to go to college, train to be a teacher," he said one Saturday evening at the bungalow. Her other housemates were out on dates and Jerusha had cooked dinner for the two of them. "But I don't have much money. I've been working ever since I was a kid. When I got out of high school back in 'thirty-five, I did some work in the north part of the state with the Civilian Conservation Corps. Last year I came down here to work for Uncle Walt."

"If you keep working for your uncle, maybe you could save some money and go to school." Jerusha gathered up the plates and began washing them in the sink.

Ted got up and grabbed a dish towel, drying the plates and cutlery as she stacked them in the drainer. "Maybe. I'm thinking about joining the Navy."

Jerusha stopped, a fork and the dishrag in midair. "The Navy? Why?"

"Get out of California for a while, see the rest of the world." He took the fork from her and dried it. "My older brother, Tim, he's in the Navy. He joined up six years ago. He really likes it. He's been all over the Far East. China, the Philippines, a place called Guam. Now he's on one of those big battleships in Hawaii."

"My Uncle John was in the Philippines during the Insurrection, back at the turn of the century," Jerusha said, rinsing the rest of the cutlery. "He was in the Army."

"Besides…" Ted frowned. "I think we're going to wind up in this war."

"In Europe? You think it will spread?"

"Yeah. Hitler needs taking down. And the Japs sure are making a lot of noise in the Pacific. What they've done in China, it's just wrong."

"Yes, it is." Jerusha nodded, remembering those horrible stories in the newspaper, about Nanking. "But it's not our fight yet."

"It will be," Ted said. "Sooner or later."

Jerusha shivered, as though something had crept up her back. She shook off the feeling and looked up at the man next to her. His presence warmed her. "I baked a pound cake. It should taste good with those strawberries you brought."

~ 7 ~

GRANDMA HAD written so many letters to Aunt Dulcie that there wasn't enough time to read all them today. I had another appointment, in Santa Rosa, where Aunt Caro also had a collection of letters.

I'd read Grandma's correspondence through July of 1941, caught up in the blossoming romance between Jerusha Layne and Ted Howard, charmed at my grandmother's discovery of the man she would marry the following year. But that didn't get me any closer to solving the mystery that had brought me here in the first place, my grandmother's connection—if any existed at all—with Ralph Tarrant, the British-expatriate actor she was supposedly involved with before his murder.

Not that I believed that for a minute. But still, I wanted to know. I *had* to know.

I gathered up the letters I'd taken from the storage box labeled JERUSHA 1941 and put them back in chronological order. I set the lid on the box and stacked it with the rest, then I got to my feet and carried the storage boxes back to the walk-in closet, arranging them on the shelves.

Dulcie had been dozing while I read. As I shut the closet door, she woke and rocked her chair back and forth with refreshed vigor. "I wonder," she said.

"About what?"

"Jerusha's roommates. Maybe one of them is still alive. It's possible."

"I was wondering the same thing."

"There were two of them she kept in touch with after she got married and left Hollywood," Dulcie said. "Anne and Pearl."

"Anne Hayes and Pearl Bishop."

"That's right. They were the original roommates in that little bungalow they rented. Pearl had a car, I remember. Anyway, Anne, Pearl and Jerusha lived together for several years and they were good friends. There was always a fourth girl, though, to help with the rent. It seems to me there was a problem with one of them. Not paying her rent or being messy. Or maybe it was more serious." Dulcie furrowed her brow, then shook her head. "I can't remember. But Jerusha mentioned it in her letters."

"If they were having roommate problems, it's not in anything I've read so far," I said. "In addition to Anne and Pearl, I found names for two other roommates, Ellie Snyder and Mildred Peretti. When I get home I'll look on the Internet to see if I can locate any information on those four names."

Aunt Dulcie smiled. "Your grandmother always said Pearl Bishop was a character. She stayed in Hollywood and worked in movies and television for years. I remember Jerusha saying she'd seen Pearl on TV from time to time, in an episode of *Dragnet* or *Gunsmoke* or *The Fugitive*, one of those old classic TV shows. If Pearl is alive, surely she must have retired by now."

"If she's alive I'll find her. After reading Grandma's letters, I'd like to meet her." I bent over and kissed Aunt Dulcie. "I have to leave now. I'm due over at Aunt Caro's. But I want to come back and read more of your letters."

"You come see me any time," Aunt Dulcie said. "I enjoy visiting with you."

Pat sent me off with jars of homemade apple butter and apple chutney, made from last year's crop, decorated with labels that read FOXWORTH ORCHARDS and showed a picture of her and Bruce filling jars from a kettle in their kitchen. "Private reserve," Pat said, "made from first-crop Gravensteins and stirred with mine own hand."

"Thanks," I said. "Can't wait to try both of them."

"They're good right out of the jar." Pat walked with me out to my car. "I enjoy visiting with you, too. So don't be a stranger. Did you find what you were looking for?"

"No, not yet. The letters are fascinating, just from a historical standpoint. Primary sources about life in the late thirties and early forties."

"Now you sound like your father the history professor," Pat said. "Does this have something to do with one of your private investigator cases?"

"Not really a formal case. Let's just say it's a mystery that took place in old-time Hollywood. I thought Grandma's letters from the era would give me some insights."

"Well, I'm intrigued," Pat said. "You're welcome to come and read the letters any time. On the condition that I get the scoop when you're ready to dish it out."

"That's a deal."

After leaving Graton, I drove east through the rural landscape of rolling hills dotted with apple trees and wine grapes. Nature gave way to buildings as I reached Santa Rosa, the Sonoma County seat. I headed north on Highway 101 and took the College Avenue exit. My aunt and uncle lived northeast of downtown, in the St. Rose district, a neighborhood of old homes and commercial and institutional buildings that had grown up around St. Rose Church, a Gothic Revival stone structure built by local Italian stone masons in 1900. Many of the homes in the district dated from the 1870s to the 1940s, including several grand nineteenth-century homes and a number of well-maintained twenties-era bungalows, like the one I parked in front of, on Washington Street near Tenth. I walked to the front porch and rang the doorbell.

Caroline Howard, known to the family as Caro, is my father's younger sister. Her nickname results from Dad's inability, as a toddler, to pronounce all three syllables of his baby sister's name. Like Dad, she was born in the forties after Grandpa Ted returned from the war and went to college on the GI Bill. Dad got his father's red hair, freckles and green eyes. So did I, although in my case, the freckles are faint and fewer in number. Caro resembles her mother,

Grandma Jerusha, in her willowy figure and dark blond hair, now streaked with gray and worn chin-length.

On this warm June afternoon, Caro wore khaki shorts and a short-sleeved shirt with a tropical print of pink and purple hibiscus. She greeted me with a kiss and ushered me through the kitchen into the family room, where a Puccini aria, "O Mio Babbino Caro," poured from a portable CD player. She lowered the volume and waved me toward a chair. French windows at the back of the house opened onto a deep, narrow backyard. Red, yellow and pink roses ranged along the fence. A square patch of garden held neat rows of vegetables, with tomatoes and green beans growing up inside their metal cages.

Caro's laptop computer was on the coffee table in front of the sofa. Next to it was a thick pile of papers, a manuscript, the pages festooned with yellow Post-its covered with notes in red ink. My aunt is a fiction writer. Her novels are big fat ones, chockful of impeccable historical research, fascinating characters, intrigue — altogether good reads, the kind of books I savor while sitting on the sofa with a cat on my lap and a cup of tea at my side.

"I enjoyed your latest book," I told her. "The most recent published one, that is."

She laughed. "Music to writers' ears. We never tire of hearing it. That means I've managed to pull it off one more time. It's the current opus that's occupying me this afternoon, the California Gold Rush book." She pointed at the stack of pages. "That's the copyedited manuscript, which I got in the mail two days ago. Of course the publisher wants me to review it and get it back to New York as soon as possible, preferably yesterday. Neil is off playing tennis so I've had the house to myself all morning. I'm making progress. Want some iced tea? I just brewed a batch of sun tea."

"Yes, that sounds great."

"Coming up." She went out to the deck at the back of the house and came back a moment later carrying a big jar of water and tea bags that had been left to brew in the sun. In the kitchen she filled a couple of glass tumblers with ice and tea, with a wedge of lemon for garnish. She returned to the family room, handed a glass to me, then sat down on the sofa.

"I've been reading this manuscript all morning. You know, I finished this book nearly a year ago. Took me over three years to research and write it. I sent it off to my agent, who then took several months to sell it and negotiate the contract with the publisher. In the meantime I've been making notes and doing research for other projects. Now here comes this manuscript I thought was finished. But it's not quite done. It never is, until the book's in print and on the shelves. I have to answer the copyeditor's questions and I suspect I need to tweak a couple of chapters in the middle. It's rather like a kid who's left home and moves back again."

I smiled and set my glass on a nearby coaster. "Speaking of kids, how are yours? Where is Daria these days?"

"At Fort Bliss in El Paso, Texas, thank goodness, and not Afghanistan or Iraq."

My cousin Daria, a few years younger than me, had joined the Army ROTC while in college and she'd been commissioned as a second lieutenant after graduation. She had just been promoted to major and had already done a couple of tours of duty in Iraq. I knew that her parents worried about her. Caro and her husband Neil Lowry, who had recently retired from his job as a city planner for Santa Rosa, had two sons as well. Alex was my age. Keith was younger than Daria, and like his sister, unmarried. Alex, who lived in Sacramento, had a wife and two children, one of them a three-month-old baby. Caro happily showed me the most recent photos of her grandchildren.

"Are you going to see Brian while you're up here?" she asked.

My younger brother, Brian, follows in the family tradition of being a teacher, like Dad and Grandpa Ted. He and his wife and children live in Sonoma, east of Santa Rosa. Normally I would have taken the opportunity to head southeast on Highway 12 and see him and his family, but not today. I shook my head. "I was, but when I called a few days ago to tell them I'd be in the area, Brian said they were heading up to Yosemite for the weekend. They left Thursday and won't be back till Tuesday."

We chatted awhile longer, catching up on family news about my divorced parents. Dad was enjoying his retirement. Mother still worked, running her restaurant in Monterey, where she was surrounded by an extended family mingling Irish with Italian.

Caro set aside her glass. "I dug out those letters after I talked with you. I've read through them several times since Mom died. I have thought about using them as the basis for a novel set during World War Two. Even made some notes and started developing a plot and characters. There I go, mining my own family for fiction, again. Hey, that's what writers do. Everything in our lives is grist for the mill. Our family does have a rich and varied history. In fact, it was an old family story that started me on the Gold Rush novel. You remember Uncle Woody, Mom's brother? He was a mining engineer up in Jackson and he had some yarns to tell about the Forty-niners and gold mining. Anyway, the World War Two homefront era was such an interesting time and Mom was a participant, right in the thick of it. Barriers were being broken all over the place, with women in the workforce, like Mom, operating a welder's torch at Kaiser Shipyard. And the breakdown of color barriers, with different races working together."

"I know," I said. "There was a huge influx of African Americans moving to the Bay Area from the South for war-related work. I got plenty of information when I interviewed Grandma for the oral history to submit to the Rosie the Riveter National Monument."

"I listened to that recording again," Caro said. "Mom really had an eye for detail."

"That's what I found while reading through Dulcie's letters. It's not the Rosie the Riveter period of Grandma's life I'm interested in right now, though. It's the years she spent in Hollywood."

"These letters are primarily correspondence between Mom and Dad while he was overseas," Caro said. "She saved all of his and he saved as many of hers as he could. But there are some letters from earlier in their relationship, while they were dating and engaged. So why are you interested in the Hollywood period?"

I told Caro about my conversation with Henry Calhoun, the old man behind the counter in the movie memorabilia shop.

"That's bizarre," Caro said, leaning forward. "Mom having a fling with an actor who was murdered? I'm sure she must have had relationships with other guys before she met Dad, but after? I don't believe it."

"I don't either. But there was an actor named Ralph Tarrant, and he was murdered. If Grandma did know the guy, even in passing, she may have mentioned it in one of her letters. Although it's more likely in one of the letters she wrote to Dulcie than in her correspondence with Grandpa. I'm hoping the letters you have will give me more details on her roommates."

"Let's get to work, then. The letters are in my office." Caro led the way to the bedroom she'd converted into a workspace. The letters were in plastic storage bins. She left me to return to the family room and her copyedited manuscript. I sat down on the floor and booted up my laptop. Then I opened the first bin and delved into the letters. The postmarks on the envelopes were roughly chronological by year, and the slim bundle I held was dated 1941.

I took out the notes I'd started earlier. At the time Ted Howard met Jerusha Layne, he'd been working for his Uncle Walt, the man who ran the produce stand at the Farmers Market. He'd lived with his uncle as well, so that was the address on the envelope, Chatsworth out in the San Fernando Valley. The community was part of the vast urban sprawl that was Los Angeles, but before World War II and its postwar boom, Chatsworth had been agricultural, its scenery a backdrop for Western movies.

I opened the first envelope, with a May 1941 postmark. Jerusha had written to Ted Howard shortly after their first dinner date, thanking him for a wonderful evening. I smiled as I read it, then moved on to the next letter.

A letter dated July 1941 caught my attention. It mentioned Mildred Peretti, the young woman who'd moved into the rented bungalow in January 1940. Like the roommate before her, Mildred gave up on Hollywood and returned home to Colorado. They were looking for a new roommate, Jerusha wrote. Pearl knew someone, a woman she'd met while working on her latest movie at Metro. Sylvia Jasper was from Mobile, Alabama. The roommates planned to invite her over to look at the house—and to look at Sylvia before making a decision. The next letter told me that Sylvia had moved into the space Mildred had vacated, the converted back porch. It appeared Sylvia had passed muster. Or had she?

"She seems nice enough," Jerusha had written. There was a "but" in there, I thought. I read through the letter again, wondering what I detected between the lines. Maybe Jerusha hadn't liked Sylvia at all. Perhaps she'd been overruled by Anne and Pearl. Or it could be that the financial need for a fourth rent contributor had trumped any doubts about Sylvia. Dulcie had told me that at some point there was a problem with one of the roommates. Not paying the rent or being messy, Dulcie had said, or something more serious. She didn't remember which roommate. Was Sylvia the problem?

The next few letters, written in August 1941, hinted at what I'd already surmised, that Sylvia had her faults. Jerusha painted the picture of a flighty Southern belle who liked to party and was promiscuous. It was clear that Jerusha Layne didn't much care for Sylvia Jasper. And finally, there was the name I'd been looking for—Ralph Tarrant.

~ 8 ~

Los Angeles, California, August 1941

"MAY I SIT down?" the man said.

The three young woman at the table glanced up from their lunches. "Suit yourself," Anne said, then she turned back to Pearl and Jerusha. The commissary at Metro was crowded that August afternoon as the employees ate their midday meals, a welcome break from their shooting schedules. When the studio was busy, as it was today, chairs and tables were at a premium. The stars mixed with the extras and bit players and everyone mixed with the crew.

Jerusha heard Marjorie Main's raucous laugh and looked over at a nearby table, where the well-known character actress sat with her co-star, Clark Gable. They were both in costume, Main in a high-collared black dress, Gable wearing a vest over his shirt and tie. He cut into a steak as he chuckled at something Main said. The stars were filming a Western called *Honky Tonk*, with young Lana Turner, whose terrific reviews in *Ziegfeld Girl* had elevated her to the A-list.

Pearl was playing a dance hall girl in *Honky Tonk*. She sat to Jerusha's left, wearing her costume, a low-cut, spangled red dress, a napkin spread over her bodice as she ate her ham sandwich. Earlier she'd been regaling her friends with the latest gossip from the set. It seemed Gable's wife, actress Carole Lombard, wasn't happy about Gable working with Turner, the young blonde who was getting such a build-up from the studio. Gable liked blondes, and he'd sent Lana flowers the first day of production. So Lombard showed up on set during the filming of a love scene. "That put the lid on anything Clark had in mind, and how!" Pearl added.

Anne was at the studio for a costume fitting for her role as a gangster's girlfriend in *Shadow of the Thin Man*, with William Powell and Myrna Loy. She was subdued, having just heard that a stuntman she knew had been killed on location while filming *They Died with their Boots On*, with Errol Flynn and Olivia de Havilland. The picture about Custer was shooting about forty miles north of Los Angeles, with Raoul Walsh directing, and this was the second death during production.

Then the man showed up and asked if he could join them. He sat down at Jerusha's right, his lunch on a tray. How could he eat roast chicken on such a hot summer day? She herself only had the appetite and money for a green salad. Frequently she brought her own lunch but since Pearl and Anne were at the studio today she'd agreed to meet them in the commissary.

He was dark and good-looking, dressed in a gray pinstriped suit. On his right hand was a wide gold ring engraved with some sort of repeating design. He smiled and opened his napkin with a flourish. "My name is Ralph Tarrant. And you ladies?"

British, Jerusha thought. His plummy accent reminded her of Leslie Howard or George Sanders. The housemates introduced themselves and went back to eating, but this Tarrant fellow wanted to talk. Jerusha picked at her salad, making polite conversation. She was finishing up a bit part in a movie called *When Ladies Meet*, starring Joan Crawford and Greer Garson. Tarrant said he had worked with Garson in a London stage production. He himself was currently filming something with Hedy Lamarr.

"These bit parts," he said, "they keep you busy here at the studio?"

"Busy enough," Jerusha said. "I've made several movies this year, here and at other studios."

She pushed away the plate that held her salad, thinking about the trajectory of her Hollywood career so far. She'd been an extra and a bit player. Featured roles were the next step on the ladder to stardom. They all hoped for stardom, didn't they? That one big break, when the director noticed what a terrific reading she was giving those few lines. That big part, the featured role that put her name on the poster. Surely it would come, someday. Soon, she hoped. Maybe her next picture, *Babes on Broadway*, with Mickey Rooney and Judy Garland, would provide that break.

But there were other roles for a young woman, and Ted had been hinting at that over the summer. They'd been seeing each other quite often since they met a few months ago. It was getting serious. Too fast, she thought. Ted wanted a wife and he wanted Jerusha to take that role. Marriage and children, yes, she was open to that. But not yet. Hollywood and its stardust still beckoned.

As he tucked into his roast chicken the Englishman kept talking. Then he touched Jerusha's hand and asked what she was doing Saturday night. What a wolf, she thought. He's on the make.

She shook her head and pulled her hand away from his. "I'm seeing someone."

He smiled. "Well, if you change your mind, you know where to find me."

A tray carrying a plate of fruit salad and a glass of iced tea landed on the table on the other side of Tarrant. "Lord have mercy, it's hot," Sylvia Jasper said in the Southern drawl that became more pronounced when Sylvia was directing her attention to a man. The new housemate unbuttoned the two top buttons on the sheer white blouse she wore, then fanned herself with her right hand. She stretched and arched her back, showing off the curve of her bosom, barely constrained in a wispy lace brassiere. Then she leaned forward, her blue eyes focusing on Tarrant. "And who is this handsome man?"

Ralph Tarrant laughed and introduced himself. What a floozy, Jerusha thought. Leave it to Sylvia to come on like gangbusters. Tarrant was staring at Sylvia's cleavage, evidently liking what he saw. Across the table, Anne rolled her eyes. Pearl looked amused as she undraped her own bosom, folding the napkin she'd used to protect her costume.

Sylvia ran her fingers through her curly blond hair and sat

down, pulling her chair very close to Tarrant. She launched into a story about her audition that morning for a new picture going into production in September. "It's called *Johnny Eager*, with Lana Turner and Robert Taylor. I just love Robert Taylor. He's such a he-man. I do like a he-man." Sylvia laughed and gave Tarrant a sidelong glance. Then she looked at the table. "My goodness, I don't see any sugar for my tea." She stood up, turned, and plucked a sugar bowl from the next table. Tarrant's gaze ranged over Sylvia's slim figure, encased in a tight blue skirt.

That's my skirt, Jerusha realized, annoyed, as Sylvia sat down again. The new girl had moved into the bungalow the first weekend in August and she had the most irritating habit of "borrowing" things that didn't belong to her. Jerusha really didn't like Sylvia. The Southern belle act wore thin. But at the time they hadn't found any other potential housemates. Pearl and Anne suggested giving the blonde from Alabama a try. But already Jerusha was wondering if this was a mistake.

~ 9 ~

I SAT FOR A MOMENT with the letter in my hand. So the roommates, all four of them, met Ralph Tarrant in August 1941, when the British-expatriate actor sat down at their table in the MGM commissary. Just a casual meeting, over lunch. But Sylvia had flirted with him, right from the start. I wondered if the flirtation had subsequently led to a relationship with the actor. So how did my grandmother fit into this equation?

I straightened my legs and stretched. I'd been reading letters all day and my eyes were tired. It was now late afternoon, time for a break. I shut down the laptop computer and went out to the family room, where Caro was gathering manuscript pages into a folder. "My brain is fried," she said. "I'll have to work on this tomorrow. Any luck?"

I nodded. "I found Ralph Tarrant's name. But it was more in the context of sharing a table at the MGM commissary. The guy sat down near Grandma and her roommates while they were eating lunch. That does not a relationship make. At least not at this point. Grandma does say that one of the roommates, a woman named Sylvia, flirted with him. Maybe something developed there. I need to keep reading, and go back over to Graton to read more of Dulcie's letters. But…" I rubbed the area around my eyes. "I don't think I can read any more today."

"You're welcome to spend the night here and take another whack at the letters tomorrow. Neil should be back from his tennis date soon. I'll start dinner. We have tickets to a concert at the

Luther Burbank Center, so you'll have the house to yourself. The guest room is all made up and I'll give you a key in case you want to go out."

"Thanks, that would be great." I always kept a small bag packed with a change of clothes and toiletries in the trunk of my car, just in case. I called Darcy Stefano, the tenant of my garage apartment, who had a key to my house. She agreed to feed the cats that evening.

Uncle Neil returned, in sweat-stained shorts and shirt, with a brace enclosing his left knee, a sun visor on his unruly gray hair, and a tote bag containing two tennis racquets and assorted paraphernalia. He greeted us with the news that he and his mixed doubles partner had won their tennis match in straight sets. He also played men's doubles, and he and his partners in both categories were planning to compete in the National Senior Games, he informed me, having qualified at the state games. Neil grabbed a tumbler of iced tea and headed for the shower.

I picked up Saturday's Santa Rosa *Press Democrat* and sifted through the newspaper sections, glancing at headlines. The front page of the entertainment section caught my attention: GALLERY SHOWCASES HITCHCOCK MEMORABILIA. I read the article that went with the headline. A gallery on the square in Healdsburg, the small town located some fifteen miles north of Santa Rosa, was exhibiting movie memorabilia from Alfred Hitchcock's films, with an opening reception this evening. The items on display were part of an extensive collection of Hitchcock-related memorabilia belonging to Healdsburg resident Michael Strickland, the white-haired man in the accompanying photograph. He stood next to a large poster from the movie *Shadow of a Doubt*, which was set in and largely filmed in Santa Rosa.

I sifted through my memory, going back to an overheard conversation. Earlier in the week, when I was in Matinee, the memorabilia shop in Alameda, I'd heard Raina Makellar say her husband, Chaz, and their employee, Henry Calhoun, had gone to Sonoma County in search of merchandise. She'd mentioned a man who collected Hitchcock memorabilia. Was this the man she'd been talking about? Surely there couldn't be that many collectors here in Sonoma County focusing on Hitchcock. On the other hand, it was a large county.

"Look," I told Caro, pointing at the newspaper article. "This Hitchcock exhibit in Healdsburg opens tonight. That's what I'll do after dinner."

"I read that. It does look interesting. I'll have to go another time."

I set the table while Caro cut up vegetables for a salad to go with the chicken cacciatore simmering in a pan on top of the stove. After we ate, I drove north to Healdsburg. The gallery reception was due to start at six o'clock. I arrived around six-thirty and found a parking space on a side street, a couple of blocks from the grassy square that is the centerpiece of downtown Healdsburg. My destination was on the south side of the square. On this warm summer evening, people spilled onto the sidewalk in front of the gallery, sipping wine as they talked. Soft jazzy music played in the background. I entered the gallery and stopped, looking up. A framed one-sheet poster hung from the ceiling, dominating the room. It was the *Vertigo* poster created by Saul Bass, the design as nerve-jangling as the movie itself—orange, black, and white, with the black-and-white figures of a man and woman caught in the middle of a spiral. Alfred Hitchcock's name was in jagged black letters in the upper left corner, along with the names of the stars, James Stewart and Kim Novak.

Memorabilia from the movies that defined Hitchcock's career as a director were displayed throughout the gallery, in a roughly chronological and clockwise fashion, beginning with a one-sheet poster from the 1934 original version of *The Man Who Knew Too Much*, with Peter Lorre. I snagged a glass of wine from a table near the entrance and strolled through the exhibit, looking first at posters from two Hitchcock films from the thirties, *The 39 Steps* and *The Lady Vanishes*.

Hitchcock was prolific in the forties. Here were posters and photographs from *Rebecca* and *Suspicion*, both starring Joan Fontaine. I saw a narrow insert from *Lifeboat* and a set of lobby cards from *Spellbound*. Rounding out the decade were posters, photos and lobby cards from *Notorious, The Paradine Case*, and *Rope*. The fifties brought an insert from *Stage Fright*, with Marlene Dietrich. Next to this poster I saw a one-sheet from *Strangers on a Train*, starring Robert Walker and Farley Granger. Then came a title card from *Dial M for Murder*, and a huge poster from one of my favorites, *Rear Window*, with James Stewart. A pair of framed one-sheet posters showcased Cary Grant, in *To Catch a Thief* and *North by Northwest*. James Stewart had also starred in *Vertigo* and the 1956 remake of *The Man Who Knew Too Much*.

Hitchcock's films from the sixties started with *Psycho* and its memorable shower scene. The film was represented here by a poster and lobby cards. The collection also featured memorabilia from *The Birds, Marnie, Torn Curtain, Topaz* and *Frenzy*. Rounding out Hitchcock's career was artwork from the director's two forays into television, the 1955–1961 series *Alfred Hitchcock Presents*, and *The Alfred Hitchcock Hour*, which ran from 1962 to 1965.

I'd never realized how orange and yellow predominated in the advertising artwork for Hitchcock's movies. Walking through the gallery, I saw those colors over and over again, in posters for the black-and-white films, *The 39 Steps, Notorious, The Paradine Case, Strangers on a Train*, and the later color films, *Rear Window, To Catch a Thief, North by Northwest*, and *Vertigo*, of course. The colors repeated, but it was interesting to see how styles of poster art had changed over the years.

Hitchcock's 1943 movie *Shadow of a Doubt* had a featured role in this exhibit, because much of the film had been shot in nearby Santa Rosa. The one-sheet poster showed the faces of stars Teresa Wright, Joseph Cotten and Macdonald Carey, caught in the vortex of a dark orange tornado rising from shadowed figures in the lower left corner. Clustered around the poster were framed stills from the movie, as well as photographs taken on the set during location filming. Here was a black-and-white shot of the old Santa Rosa train station, still standing today. It had played a key role in the movie's action. And another photo showed the house on Mc-Donald Avenue that had, in the film, served as the home of Teresa

Wright and her family. Several frames held articles from the local newspaper describing the invasion of the movie folks while the film was in production in the fall of 1942. In a nearby glass case I saw a program from the film's January 1943 premiere, signed by Teresa Wright and Joseph Cotten.

A man stood near the display case, a friendly smile on his face. I recognized him from the photograph in the newspaper—Michael Strickland, the collector. He was tall, a few inches over six feet, with close-cropped white hair, thinning at the top. Laugh lines crinkled the skin around his mouth and his eyes, hazel in his tanned face. He was casually dressed on this summer evening, in blue slacks and a lightweight beige linen jacket over a white shirt, open at the neck.

He put out his hand and greeted me. "Hi, I'm Mike Strickland. This is my collection."

"I'm Jeri Howard." I shook his hand. "I'm really impressed. You have a lot of great stuff. How did you get started collecting Hitchcock memorabilia?"

"Well, there's a personal connection," he said. "My older sister Molly was a bit player in Hollywood, back in the forties."

"Small world," I told him. "My grandmother was a bit player, too, in the late thirties and early forties. Her name was Jerusha Layne."

He laughed. "Small world indeed. What movies was she in?"

"She was in *Suspicion*." I pointed at a poster from that film. "And Norma Shearer's last six, including *The Women*. Your sister?"

"Molly was in several Hitchcock movies. In fact, she was in this one." He motioned me toward a still from *Shadow of a Doubt* and pointed at a tall brunette whose open, friendly face echoed his own. "That's Molly, there on the end. She played one of Teresa Wright's girlfriends. We grew up in Los Angeles. Our uncle was a stuntman, worked in the movies from the silents all the way into the talkies. He retired in the fifties. So Molly got bit by the acting bug. She worked at all the studios—Metro, Universal, RKO, Paramount, Warners, Columbia. First she was an extra, then she worked up to bit player."

"Same story with my grandmother, an extra first, then doing bits. She worked at Metro and other studios, too. She came to Hollywood in nineteen thirty-seven and left in nineteen forty-two. That's when she married my grandfather, before he shipped out for the Pacific."

"Nineteen forty-two," Strickland said. "That's the year Molly started, when she got out of high school. She was the oldest, eight years older than me. I was just eleven then, still a kid. She lived at home. When she was working, sometimes she'd bring some bit players and extras home for dinner. We always had a few of them around the table, some of them names you might recognize, because they went on to bigger and better parts. But back then, they were just bit players like Molly. She only worked in the movies until nineteen forty-six. In 'forty-three she started volunteering at the Hollywood Canteen and met her future husband there, while he was on leave from the Marines. When he got back from the war, she left the business and they got married. Never looked back."

I took a sip of wine and steered the conversation back to his Hitchcock collection. "It looks like you have some valuable items."

He nodded. "Yeah, some of the stuff is worth a lot. But like any collection, the value depends on what it is, what kind of shape it's in, and how much you want it. And how much somebody's willing to pay for it. I know a collector back east who just bought a one-sheet from *Bolero*, the nineteen thirty-four movie with George Raft and Carole Lombard—and Sally Rand, doing her fan dance! He paid eight thousand dollars because he just had to have it. Now, I wouldn't have shelled out that kind of dough for the poster, because I'm not interested in collecting Raft or Lombard. But it if had been *The Lodger*, the movie Hitchcock made in nineteen twenty-six with Ivor Novello, I would have been there with checkbook in hand."

"Eight thousand for a movie poster? Wow!" I shook my head. "I had no idea."

Strickland laughed. "Oh, that's pocket change. A poster from a nineteen thirty-four movie called *The Black Cat*, with Boris Karloff and Bela Lugosi, sold at auction several years ago for two hundred and eighty-six thousand bucks. A short time later, a poster from *The Bride of Frankenstein* went for three hundred and thirty-four thousand bucks. Now that's some serious money. I don't know that I'd shell out that much cash for anything. On the other hand, I've been looking for memorabilia from *The Lodger*, or any of Hitchcock's movies from the twenties, for years. I might pay big bucks for those items. But I haven't found much."

"Why is that?"

"Most of it is gone." Strickland gestured at the display. "These posters and lobby cards were advertising. Nobody ever thought they were art. When it was time to change the bill in the local theater and move on to the next picture, the old posters and cards got tossed in the trash. A lot of the stuff has turned to dust."

"So, much of the value is based on the rarity of the item," I said.

"Yes. But it's also based on the condition." He pointed at the nearby poster. "Now, I've had this one-sheet of *Shadow of a Doubt* since the movie came out in nineteen forty-three. It was Molly's first Hitchcock film. She got it for me, from the publicity department at Universal. I've taken good care of it, had it mounted and framed early on, so it's in excellent shape. That's why it's worth more than a poster that's been folded or taped to a wall."

"I'm sure you have a lot of collectors and dealers wanting to buy."

"I get approached by dealers all the time. Four this month. In fact, a couple of them stopped by my house earlier this week. You know, there was something about one of those guys. I can't put my finger on it. Maybe I'd seen him before. Don't know where." He shrugged. "It'll come to me, though. I never forget a face. Anyway, I'm not interested in selling my collection. I do this for the fun of it. And because of Molly," he added. "Molly's dead now. But it's nice to know I can watch one of the movies she was in and see her the way she was back in the forties, so young and pretty."

"I know what you mean," I said, thinking of Grandma. My own memories of my grandmother were of a woman who was first middle-aged and then elderly, with a face full of wrinkles and a crown of white hair. But the younger Jerusha Layne, fresh-faced, lovely, and full of promise, had been captured on film. All I had to do to see Grandma's earlier self was watch one of her movies. "I wonder, could you tell me the names of the dealers who've approached you recently?"

"I've got some business cards at home, if I haven't already tossed them. Names, let's see…"

For the past few minutes I'd noticed a woman hovering nearby, eavesdropping on my conversation with Strickland. Now, before he could answer my question about dealers, she walked over and put her hand on his arm. She was older than I, and nearly as tall as he was, slender in her pale green slacks and shirt. She had the same hazel eyes, and her short, gray-streaked brown hair was swept back from her face. "Dad, there are some people I'd like you to meet. You're monopolizing this lady." From the look she gave me, she meant I was monopolizing him.

"This is my daughter, Tory Ambrose." Strickland smiled and put his arm around her waist. "She lives down in Santa Rosa with my grandkids. This is… You said your name is Jeri?"

"Yes, Jeri Howard. I didn't mean to take up so much of your time. I'm just fascinated by your collection."

"Jeri's grandmother was a bit player," Strickland said. "Just like your Aunt Molly."

Tory Ambrose smiled at him affectionately. "You just get Dad talking about Aunt Molly and his collection, and away he goes."

"Your grandmother's name was Jerusha Layne, right?" he asked.

"Right. I'm named for her."

"I'll look her up on the Internet. Now I guess I'd better go circulate."

"It was a pleasure meeting you, Mr. Strickland."

~ 10 ~

I FOUND THE CLIPPING Sunday morning after breakfast. I was in Caro's office reading letters. After that one mention of Ralph Tarrant in August 1941, Jerusha had never mentioned him again, at least not in her letters to the man who would soon become her husband. I quickly read through the letters she'd written him while he was in basic training in San Diego, full of plans for their wedding. Jerusha Layne had married Ted Howard in her hometown of Jackson, California in April 1942. They'd gone to Yosemite for their honeymoon, staying four days in Stoneman Lodge at Camp Curry in the Valley. Then Grandpa left, shipping out on a carrier escort. And Grandma had left as well. She didn't want to spend the war in Jackson. In the summer of 1942 Grandma moved to the Bay Area, taking a job as a welder at Kaiser Shipyard in Richmond. She lived in a rooming house with another set of roommates and she wrote Grandpa frequently, care of a fleet post office, letters that probably took some time to reach him on his ship. But he'd eventually received the letters, perhaps not all, and those he kept.

The newspaper clipping, weathered yellow and crumbling at the edges, was tucked into a letter postmarked in September 1942. It was short, just a couple of column inches. Written in ink on the top were the words "LA Times" and a date, 8/23/42. One of Jerusha's Hollywood roommates was dead. Sylvia Jasper, the Southern belle from Mobile, Alabama, had been reported missing in May 1942, by her brother, Byron Jasper. Sylvia's decomposed body, buried in a shallow grave in the shifting sands of a Santa Monica beach, was found by some beachgoers.

Where did Grandma get the clipping? Why had she sent it to Grandpa? I quickly read the letter and answered the first question. Pearl, still working in Hollywood, had sent the article to Grandma. The answer to the second question was more elusive. Grandma wrote, "I guess this puts an end to it."

An end to what?

If I was correct in reading between the lines of the earlier letters, Grandma hadn't liked Sylvia Jasper. So why send the clipping about Sylvia's death to Grandpa? Had Ted Howard ever met the blue-eyed blonde from Mobile? Had there been some sort of clash or an incident between Grandma and Sylvia? Something was missing. I had more questions than answers.

As I was putting away the letters I saw handwriting that didn't look like Grandma's. It wasn't. The letter had a postmark dated April 12, 1947, and it had been mailed from Boulder, Colorado. The return address listed a last name only, Sanderson. I opened the envelope addressed to my grandmother and took out a folded letter. Inside was a black-and-white snapshot, showing a man and a woman. They were both tall. The woman had shoulder-length dark hair and her rounded belly indicated she was pregnant. The man had blond hair and a rugged frame. Mountains were visible in the background. I turned over the photograph and saw a penciled legend, ANNE AND LEMUEL SANDERSON, BOULDER, COLORADO, APRIL 1947. I examined the woman's image. So this was Anne. She had a practical, no-nonsense face. I liked her looks. More important, I had a last name and location. Boulder was the site of the University of Colorado. I was betting Anne's husband was going to college on the GI Bill, as had so many returning servicemen in the postwar years.

The letter Anne had written to Grandma confirmed my theory. Lemuel Sanderson, Anne's husband, was working on his master's degree in geology at the University of Colorado. They were living in married student housing, Quonset huts that had been converted into apartments, cold and drafty in the Colorado winter, and dust constantly blowing in with the Chinook winds. She was so glad that spring was finally coming to the Rockies. Lem was supposed to graduate the following year. She hoped that they'd be able to afford an apartment in a real building and move out of the Quonset hut by the time the baby, their first, arrived in August.

Mildred was fine, Anne wrote, and she, too, was pregnant, due later in the fall. So Anne had kept in touch with Mildred, the roommate who had moved back to Denver before Sylvia moved in, not surprising since Anne was also from Colorado.

Now that I had Anne's married name, maybe I could trace her through her husband. I jotted the pertinent information in my notes. Maybe Dulcie's letters would supply the information I sought. I said good-bye to Caro and Neil and went back to Graton, back to my great-aunt's room where she napped in her rocking chair while I looked through letters. I started where I'd left off, in the fall of 1941, and soon learned why my grandmother and the other housemates parted company with Sylvia Jasper.

~ || ~

Los Angeles, California, October 1941

"I WANT HER OUT!" Anne sputtered, indignation written on her face. "This is absolutely the last straw. I did not expect to come home tonight and find a naked man wrapped in a towel, eating cake here in the kitchen. What's more, it was my towel."

"It was my cake. The one I baked to take to a birthday party," Jerusha added, "with a note that clearly said, 'Do Not Touch.' It's not just the cake. And it's not just the man. It's everything that's happened since she moved in."

Pearl looked glum as she refilled all three coffee cups and resumed her place at the kitchen table. "This isn't the first time she's had a man in here at night. Three weeks ago I was parking the Gasper in the driveway and I saw a fellow leaving by the back door."

"You didn't say anything to us," Anne said.

"I should have, I know," Pearl said. "I talked with Sylvia and reminded her it was against the house rules that she agreed to when she moved in. She said it wouldn't happen again."

"She lied." Jerusha sipped her coffee. "She has to go. Since she moved in here in August she's been late with the rent twice. And I think she's been taking money out of the kitty." The grocery kitty was an old coffee tin kept on the kitchen counter. All four of the housemates—in theory—contributed money each week for expenses, primarily groceries and gas for the Gasper.

"I counted the money in the kitty a couple of days ago when I put in my share," Jerusha said. "And I counted it again this morning. It's short twenty bucks. That's stealing! From all of us. I just can't tolerate that. She's messy. She helps herself to my clothes without asking. I don't mind you girls borrowing my things but people should at least ask. Then she doesn't return them, or when she does, things are dirty or torn. That blue silk blouse she took is ruined. The seam is ripped under the arm and something was spilled down the front. Liquor, from the smell of it."

"Ditto," Anne said. "She took my hound's-tooth jacket. I had to ask for it back. Two buttons were gone, and there was a cigarette burn on the lapel."

Pearl shook her head. "I'm really sorry, girls. You've got every reason to be in a lather. I'm the one who suggested that she move in. I didn't know she was such a bimbo. She seemed okay when we worked together on that movie at Metro. I guess I was all wet."

"She puts on a good act, I'll give her that," Anne said. "She had me fooled, too. I thought she'd be all right."

"I was willing to give her a chance," Jerusha said. "But no more. I'm tired of her Tallulah Bankhead routine."

Sylvia didn't come back until the following afternoon. She and the naked man had departed as soon as he'd put on some clothes, leaving Anne's towel in a crumpled heap on the kitchen floor, and a mound of crumbs from the purloined cake in the middle of the kitchen table. When the housemates confronted her in the kitchen, a look of waspish annoyance crossed her face, quickly masked by the lashes fluttering over her blue eyes. She ruffled her left hand through her blond curls. "Y'all are just a bunch of prudes. What's wrong with having a man around the place?"

"The house rules say no men staying overnight," Anne said. "When you moved in, you agreed to abide by the house rules."

"Oh, honey, don't be such a wet smack. Rules are meant to be broken." Sylvia reached for a pack of Luckies and shook out a cigarette. She struck a match, held it to the end and inhaled.

"Not here," Jerusha said. "It's a small house. It only works for four of us to live here if everyone plays by the rules. This isn't working out, and we want you to move out as soon as possible."

Sylvia shrugged. "Well, I was thinking about leaving anyway. You see, my kid brother Binky—his name's really Byron but the whole family calls him Binky—he's moving out here to Hollywood, gonna try his luck in the movies. He and I can get a place together. He said he'd be here by Halloween." Her Southern drawl broadened and took on a cajoling tone. "Now it's already the first week in October. So me moving out now, why that just doesn't work. It would be much better if I could stay here till the end of the month. I really don't have enough money to rent an apartment on my own, not right this minute. And I don't want to go back to one of those boarding houses for such a short time until Binky gets here. I'll start looking now, though, if I could just stay here till the end of the month. I promise I'll behave myself, truly I will."

The housemates traded looks, then they moved into the living room to confer. A moment later they returned, and Pearl told Sylvia, "All right. You can stay till the end of October. But no longer."

~ 12 ~

MONDAY AFTERNOON I had an urgent phone call from a client, an attorney in an insurance fraud case. "Jeri, can you possibly go to LA to interview a witness?" she asked. "I'm really sorry, this is short notice, but tomorrow is the only time this guy is available. You're the investigator who's familiar with the case and I don't want to have to find someone down there and explain it all over again."

I looked at my calendar. The next few days were relatively light. "Sure. I can move a few things around. What time and where?"

"One o'clock tomorrow afternoon, at a law firm in Century City. Here's the address. Thanks, Jeri, I owe you."

"Yes, and I'll send you a bill." I laughed and copied down the address she recited. Then I rescheduled several appointments, phone tucked under my chin as I checked the flight schedule on the Southwest Airlines website. I could leave Oakland Airport as early as six in the morning, and fly back from LAX as late as nine o'clock at night. It would make for a long day. Ordinarily I would have considered such a short-fused, drop-everything-and-go trip a pain but right now it was an opportunity. I made one more phone call, hoping the person I wanted to talk with was in his office. He was. Then I selected my flights, purchased my ticket and printed out my boarding pass.

Tuesday morning I stepped off my early-morning flight at LAX, made my way through the terminal and went outside to catch the shuttle to the off-site rental car lot. Once the paperwork-and-credit-card drill was over, I received the keys to a sedan and drove off the lot. I headed for the freeway, driving north on the 405. It was just after eight in the morning, but rush hour is never over in LA. Still the traffic flowed, so a short time later I took the exit for eastbound Santa Monica Boulevard.

LAPD's Hollywood Division is located on North Wilcox. I found a parking space a block or so away and fed quarters into the meter. Then I detoured to a nearby espresso joint, where I ordered a latte for myself and a mocha for Sergeant Liam Cleary, the homicide detective I was meeting at the station.

Liam looked great for a guy in his late fifties. He was Tyrone Power–handsome, packaged in a rugged frame over six feet tall with thick black hair going gray at the temples. He greeted me with a broad smile, his twinkling blue eyes focused on the coffee. "Is that for me?"

"I've got a coffee jones, but not so much I'd drink two at once." I handed him one of the containers. "Double mocha, extra whipped cream, chocolate sprinkled on top."

"Oh, you're a darlin' girl." He grinned at me and took a sip, then licked the residue of whipped cream from his upper lip. "Is this by way of a bribe?"

"It's by way of thanks, for letting me look at the Tarrant file," I said.

He opened the security door and beckoned me to follow him down a corridor. "This is quasi-official. Had to dance the dance with the chief's office and the currently assigned detective, Nacio Lopez. I told them what a wonderful and reliable investigator you are and implied that you might—emphasize might—have a lead. Old as the case is, Lopez would love to clear it. Even though there doesn't seem to be much chance of that, realistically speaking. Do you have a lead?"

Just hearsay, I thought, recalling Henry Calhoun's hint that my grandmother had something to do with the Tarrant murder. "I caught a whiff of a rumor, that's all."

"On a case this ancient?" Liam cut his sharp blue eyes in my direction. "Must be a ripe old whiff of a rumor to bring you down to LA to poke around in a murder that happened before either of us were born."

"I'm actually here on another case and I have to be in Century City at one o'clock, so I'm multi-tasking. Thanks for arranging this, Liam. I really appreciate it. What about the other file, on Sylvia Jasper?"

"I called a buddy of mine on the Santa Monica force," Liam said, handing me a slip of paper. "Here's his name and number. He says you can take a look at the Jasper file this afternoon. Now that's two old murders from the forties. I'm sure there's a story behind all of this. I hope you'll tell me what it's about."

"I will, as soon as I figure it out." I followed Liam into a small conference room, with a rectangular table in the middle and shelves on the far wall. There was a thick folder in the center of the table, exuding an aged, musty aroma. Or maybe that was just my imagination.

A wiry, dark man stood on the other side of the table. Liam made the introductions. "Detective Nacio Lopez, this is Jeri Howard, licensed private investigator out of Oakland, and a friend of mine."

Lopez and I exchanged handshakes. He gestured at the folder on the table. "There's the file. I have to be present while you review it."

"Fair enough," I said. "Some questions may come up while I look at it."

Liam left us alone with the file on Ralph Tarrant's murder. It looked much as I had imagined, a folder thick with paper that was old, yellowed, crisp with age around the edges. Dust, too. I hadn't imagined the musty smell.

I carefully opened the file. Stuck in the middle were two manila envelopes, one labeled CRIME SCENE PHOTOS and the other PRESS CLIPS. I set these aside and peered at the stack of papers affixed to the right side of the file. The first document was a typewritten report. At the bottom I saw a scrawled signature, so faded with time that I had trouble spelling out the name.

"Who were the initial investigators?" I asked Lopez.

"Sergeant Dick Mulvany was the lead man. His partner was Detective Frank Partin." Lopez cracked a smile. "After that... Well, that file's been passed to a lot of detectives over the years. I got it two years ago, when another guy retired. I read through the file then, and again when Liam told me you wanted to review it. There hasn't been a decent lead on the Tarrant murder since nineteen forty-two, the year it happened. No one's even written much about it. Every now and then some writer decides to do a piece on famous unsolved Hollywood murders. William Desmond Taylor, back in 'twenty-two, that one got a lot of ink. There's the Black Dahlia case from 'forty-seven and the Jean Spangler case from 'forty-nine. This case, not much interest. Tarrant was British, not well known to start with. These days I doubt most people have even heard of him."

"I know what you mean." I hadn't heard of Tarrant either, until that day in the memorabilia shop when Henry Calhoun had mentioned his name and implied my grandmother knew something about his murder.

I leafed through the documents, identifying crime reports, lab analysis, autopsy report, handwritten notes on lined paper, and lots of yellowing pages that had been typed on a manual typewriter. I began reading the preliminary crime report written by Sergeant Mulvany and Detective Partin.

It had been raining that Saturday night in February 1942, the kind of downpour that beat a steady rhythm on the roof. Maybe that's why Ralph Tarrant's next-door neighbor didn't hear any shots. Besides, he'd been listening to the radio, focused on a musical program and the war news. At some point—he thought it was around seven-thirty or a quarter to eight—he got up to go to the kitchen for a snack. On the way back to his easy chair, he looked out his front window. Someone in a raincoat and hat—the witness thought it was a woman—rushed from Tarrant's house and ran to a car parked at the curb. The figure got in on the passenger side and the car drove away. It wasn't Tarrant's car, a blue 1941 Packard Clipper that was still parked in the detached garage in back of his house. The car on the street was older, the witness said. It was under a streetlight so he got a good look at it. He was sure it was a Model A Ford.

That wasn't much help, I thought. In the forties Model A Fords must have been positively ubiquitous on the streets of Los Angeles, and everywhere else in the country.

The neighbor didn't give much thought to the car at the curb or the figure in the raincoat until a short time later, when he went back to his kitchen, glanced out that window and saw flames devouring the curtains of the house next door. He called the fire department. Whoever started the blaze must have hoped to make the actor's death look like an accident. But the firemen got to the house quickly. After they put out the fire, they looked at the body in the living room and saw bullet holes and blood. It was abundantly clear that Tarrant had been murdered. Enter Detectives Mulvany and Partin.

I read the autopsy report and the lab analysis. Ralph Tarrant was shot five times, at a range close enough to leave powder burns on the front of his shirt. The first two bullets entered Tarrant's heart while he was standing. The remaining three bullets were fired into his heart and abdomen after Tarrant collapsed onto the Oriental carpet.

The first two shots probably killed him. Both the medical examiner and I agreed on that point. It took a killing rage to keep pumping bullets into a man who was already mortally wounded. Whoever shot Tarrant must have been angry, furious. I pictured a shadowy figure in a raincoat and hat, a revolver in a gloved hand, spitting lead into the man who lay bleeding to death before…him? Her? Who?

Could I see my grandmother, Hollywood bit player, then in her early twenties, shooting a man at close range and leaving him to die?

I pictured the elderly white-haired woman I'd known. Jerusha Layne Howard, a woman who read a stack of library books every week, who crocheted, baked chocolate chip cookies and snickerdoodles, loved cats, grew roses and tulips, a dear companion who took me with her to movies and horse races.

Murder? Grandma? My imagination couldn't stretch far enough to connect those two dots. But who had killed Ralph Tarrant, and why?

I turned my attention back to the dry, utilitarian prose in front of me. Tarrant had died quickly—shock, trauma, massive loss of blood. The bullets recovered from the body came from a .32-caliber handgun, but the preliminary report said the weapon wasn't found at the scene.

I reached for the envelope that held the crime scene photographs, opened the flap and carefully removed a stack of black-and-white shots. I held the first picture lightly, my fingertips at the edges, and examined the image.

Ralph Tarrant was a handsome man, with somewhat wolfish looks, judging from the publicity photos I'd found on the Internet. But death offers no touch-ups or air brushes, no gauze filters, no soft lighting. The photographer's lights and flash were bright and harsh, revealing the corpse of a man lying flat on his back, eyes open and staring, sprawled in a pool of something that looked inky black in the old photo and had probably been deep red in real life.

Blood. Who would have thought he had so much blood in him? I thought, recalling the line from *Macbeth*. Tarrant was dressed in what appeared to be gray slacks and a long-sleeved shirt, both stained with his own blood. He wore a tie. According to what I'd read about the case, he was due to meet friends for dinner at eight o'clock that evening. So he was getting dressed when his killer arrived. He hadn't yet put on his jacket, or his shoes. Instead, on his feet were socks and bedroom slippers. I consulted Detective Mulvany's report. No sign of forced entry, so Tarrant evidently opened the door to whoever killed him. It was a good bet he knew his killer.

I looked up from the photos. "Why wasn't the body burned in the fire?"

"Something odd about that," Lopez said. "If I was trying to hide a murder, I'd have torched the body first. But the fire started near the fireplace, probably to make it look like an accident. It burned that section of the room and jumped to the curtains. That's when the neighbor spotted it and called the fire department, and they showed up and put it out. So the flames hadn't even reached the body."

Yes, it was odd. It was as though whoever started the blaze wanted to cover up the murder, but couldn't bear actually setting the victim on fire.

In subsequent shots, the photographer got close enough to detail the powder burns from each of the five bullets and the spots of gore at each entry wound. There were also close-ups of Tarrant from several angles, including his wrists and the cuffs of his shirt, now stained with blood.

"Why would the photographer have taken so many shots of Tarrant's wrists?" I asked Lopez. "I can see photographing the palms of the hands, to see if the killer had left any evidence in the murder victim's hands. But why the wrists?"

"I wondered that myself, when I got the file," Lopez said. "Mulvany and Partin wanted pictures of the shirt cuffs. If you'll look closer, you'll see why."

I took a small magnifying glass from my purse and held it to the photographs of the cuffs, both with dark smears of blood. On both cuffs, the slots where a cufflink would have been inserted looked frayed and torn. I glanced up at Lopez. "He was wearing cufflinks. But someone ripped them out, and tore the cuffs doing it."

"Yeah," Lopez said. "Mulvany and Partin were really curious about that. Everything else in Tarrant's closet was shipshape. He was always well-dressed, according to witnesses, so he didn't seem like a guy who'd put on a shirt with torn cuffs. Unless he'd just noticed it and hadn't taken off the shirt yet when the killer arrived. The detectives figured Tarrant was wearing cufflinks and that the killer took them and tore the cuffs in the process. A couple of people who were interviewed said Tarrant usually wore fancy gold cufflinks and he had several pairs. All of the victim's jewelry was stolen the night he was killed. So it could have been a murder in the course of a robbery."

"Robbery?" I shook my head. "Tarrant was shot five times at close range. That says personal to me. What if the killer was the person who gave him the cufflinks, and wanted them back?"

Lopez nodded in agreement. "It's possible. Mulvany and Partin explored that. But they never found out if someone had recently given him jewelry. Could be he'd had the cufflinks all along. Anyway, take a closer look at the right cuff. There are several strands of hair. Nowadays we could do DNA analysis and match the hair to a possible suspect. But back in the forties, they didn't have the kind of technology we use now."

I squinted through the magnifying glass, looking for the hair Lopez had mentioned. Indeed, there were three strands of hair on the right-hand shirt cuff, near the seam. The strands looked like gossamer filaments, about two inches long, pale against a bloody splotch. Tarrant had dark brown hair, but the hair on his right cuff was blond, curly and short. It could have come from a man or a woman.

I gathered up the crime scene photographs and slipped them back into the envelope. Then I burrowed deeper in the file, finding a batch of fingerprints with numbers, one over the other, so that it looked like fractions written over them. A notation told me that they were Tarrant's prints, taken for comparison purposes.

"Is this how they identified prints back then?" I asked Lopez.

"Yeah. No fingerprint computers. They visually identified the prints, looking at the loops, whorls, tented arches, that kind of thing. Then they'd assign numerical classifications for searching. That's what these numbers are. I've heard it was fairly accurate."

"But they didn't find any prints at the Tarrant crime scene that would point to the killer?" I said.

Lopez shook his head. "No. You'll see from the next batch of prints that they just found a partial here and there, not enough to classify. Most of the prints belonged to Tarrant. Plus, there was the fire. The firemen tromped all over that living room and probably destroyed some evidence. Mulvany says something about that in one of his reports."

I turned my attention back to the stack of papers in the Tarrant file. Mulvany and Partin had begun their investigation into Tarrant's murder by questioning the next-door neighbor. Then they had interviewed anyone who'd had any contact with the murdered man during the entire time he'd been in Hollywood, from his friends to his co-workers to the rest of his neighbors and the woman who cleaned his house once a week.

I thumbed through a couple of reports and found a list of dates, names and addresses—the people that Mulvany and Partin had interviewed in the course of their investigation. The names on the typewritten list weren't in alphabetical order. Instead, they were listed chronologically, by the dates on which people had been interviewed. I ran my finger down the list. A few of the names I recognized, actors mostly, names that evoked Hollywood in the forties. But most of the names were unfamiliar to me.

Then I saw a name that leapt off the page. Jerusha Layne, and an address in Hollywood. The police *had* interviewed my grandmother in conjunction with the Tarrant homicide, just as Henry Calhoun had said. The interview took place in late February, a week after Tarrant's death. Right below Jerusha's name were two other names, Anne Hayes and Pearl Bishop, listed as living at the same address. So Mulvany and Partin questioned all three roommates, on the same date. And the following day they had questioned Sylvia Jasper and her brother Byron Jasper.

I looked up at Lopez. "Are the interview statements in the same order as they are on this list?"

"They should be," Lopez told me. "The officers kept notebooks—still do—and during an interview, they'd make detailed notes. Then they would dictate the report to a record clerk who typed as the detective talked. Or the detective would write it out longhand, and then the record clerk would type it. But the first method was faster."

My fingers moved through the pages, looking for the statements given by Jerusha Layne and her housemates. Mixed in with the witness statements I saw what looked like old employment records from several movie studios—Metro, Columbia, Warner, RKO. When I found the statement Jerusha had given the police, I also found a note saying that that Detective Mulvany had received an anonymous phone tip from someone claiming that Ralph Tarrant was dating a girl named Jerusha Layne. The caller added that

Jerusha was at Tarrant's house the night of the murder, and that she'd driven there in a black Model A Ford owned by her room-mate Pearl Bishop.

Jerusha's statement was brief and matter-of-fact. Since it was raining, it was a good night to stay home, and that's what she did that evening. She'd listened to the radio while mending a dress. Then she had switched off the program and read a book before going to bed early. Her roommates had gone out. Perhaps her next-door neighbor could vouch for her, because Mrs. Ellison had stopped by the cottage around seven, to bring a letter for Anne that had been delivered by mistake to the Ellison bungalow. No, Jerusha told the police, she wasn't involved with Ralph Tarrant, romantically or in any other way. She barely knew the man. Of course, she knew who he was, and she saw him from time to time, because they both worked at Metro-Goldwyn-Mayer—with a lot of other people, Jerusha added. But a relationship with Tarrant? No, certainly not, never. In fact, she was engaged to be married, to a sailor named Ted Howard.

Pearl's statement said she'd been driving her car, the black Model A Ford known as the Gasper. She left the house at six-thirty that evening and had returned at ten, or thereabouts. She met her date at a restaurant and after dinner, they went dancing. Her companion was a soldier she'd met a few weeks earlier. As for tracking him down for corroboration, she thought the guy had shipped out. Yes, she knew who Ralph Tarrant was. She'd met him at Metro, and yes, she saw the actor now and then at the studio. But that was the extent of it. No relationship. But there *was* a relationship between Tarrant and their former roommate Sylvia Jasper, who had moved out of the bungalow in January. Moved out, Pearl added, because of a dispute. Well, to be perfectly frank about it, the housemates had made Sylvia leave, and there were some hard feelings about that. So they'd been on the outs with Sylvia since.

Anne's statement was similar. She had gone to a party with two other actresses and they'd picked her up at about six-thirty in a car belonging to one of them, just as Pearl was leaving. As far as she knew, Jerusha was planning to stay in that night. Anne had returned home between ten and eleven. And no, she didn't know Ralph Tarrant.

She told the detectives that the housemates had parted ways with Sylvia Jasper and told them why: that Sylvia was constantly late with the rent and took things that didn't belong to her. She'd also told her brother Byron that he could live there in the bungalow and that was unacceptable, so the housemates made them leave in January. There was some vandalism as a result, Anne said, and some jewelry and clothing had gone missing. Most of the property had been returned. However, hard feelings lingered on both sides.

The detectives had asked both the Jaspers about the allegations of vandalism and theft at the bungalow after they had moved out. The hard feelings Anne had mentioned in her statement were quite clear when this subject came up. Sylvia and Byron had portrayed themselves as the aggrieved parties. Their version of the dispute was that they'd simply asked if Byron could stay temporarily at the bungalow until he and Sylvia could locate an apartment of their own. When that request was refused, Sylvia had moved out hastily, without cleaning the back porch bedroom, but that wasn't vandalism, it was carelessness. And if she took anything that hadn't belonged to her, well, that was just carelessness, too. She certainly hadn't intended to take those items, which had of course been returned. It was just a trivial misunderstanding among roommates who'd fallen out.

And no, Sylvia added, she wasn't living with Ralph Tarrant, although she had dated the actor several times. She and her brother Byron were sharing an apartment in Hollywood.

I wondered what had really happened. If Jerusha had mentioned the incident in a letter to Dulcie, I hadn't found it yet.

The two homicide detectives decided Jerusha and the others were telling the truth. That appeared to be the extent of my grandmother's involvement in the Tarrant murder case.

So how did Henry Calhoun, working behind the counter at the movie memorabilia shop, know that my grandmother had been questioned? I was still troubled by the fact that he didn't have much of a history, at least not one that went back more than a couple of decades, according to my background check. Still, people talk. Gossip and rumors must have been making the rounds about Tarrant and his murder. I suppose that's how Calhoun could have known. He did imply he had been in Hollywood in the forties.

I found the statements given to the police by Sylvia and Byron Jasper. They had alibied each other, claiming they'd been together all evening in the apartment they shared in Hollywood. And there were no witnesses to prove this, or that they'd been anywhere else. They didn't have a car, couldn't afford one, Sylvia said. So how in the world could they have gotten over to Tarrant's house?

As for a relationship between Sylvia and Tarrant, she admitted that she'd dated him. But nothing more. Why, she hadn't even seen him since the end of January. Byron said he didn't know Tarrant, though he'd seen him at the studio.

I read quickly through the other witness statements. The investigating officers, Mulvany and Partin, had asked several of Tarrant's friends and co-workers if the actor had a set of valuable cufflinks and whether he'd purchased them or received them as a gift. Nobody knew for certain, but two witnesses mentioned cufflinks. One said Tarrant had a pair of diamond cufflinks in a round gold setting. Another described a pair of square gold cufflinks with a ring that matched, both decorated with a cross.

The door opened and I looked up, expecting to see Liam Cleary. Instead, it was a woman wearing a shoulder holster under her jacket. "We've got to roll," she told Lopez. "Shooting over on Sunset."

"I'm sorry." As Lopez got his feet he was already gathering up the Tarrant file. "I have to go. Which means I take the file with me. I have to be here while you look at it."

"May I come back later this afternoon?" I asked, giving him one of my business cards. "Just in case I have more questions?"

Lopez grinned and gave me his card. "Sure. Call me. Now you've got me intrigued all over again by the Tarrant murder, even if I do have a more current caseload."

~ 13 ~

I LEFT THE Hollywood Division, feeling as though the truth were there, somewhere, tantalizing me as it danced just out of my grasp. As I walked down the street, I reached for my cell phone and the slip of paper Liam had given me, and called his friend at the Santa Monica Police Department. We set up an appointment for later that afternoon. I grabbed a quick lunch at a nearby restaurant, then retrieved my rental car and drove to Century City. When I was finished interviewing the witness in the insurance fraud matter, I headed for Santa Monica and a look at another case file.

The last time anyone saw Sylvia Jasper alive was Friday, May 15, 1942. She was playing a bit part in a movie being filmed at the RKO lot. When she was finished for the day, she left, and was due to report back to the set Monday morning. Four days later, on Tuesday, May 19, 1942, Byron Jasper filed a missing persons report with the Los Angeles Police Department. A copy of that report was in the Santa Monica Police Department file and I looked through the statement Byron gave to LAPD. He told them he and his sister rented an apartment in Hollywood. He had last seen her on Friday morning, sharing a hasty breakfast before they both left for the day. He was working as an extra at Paramount. He got home late on Friday and Sylvia wasn't there. At the time he thought nothing of it, assuming she'd gone out.

When she didn't come home Friday night or Saturday, he decided she'd gone away for the weekend. She'd done it before, he said, without telling him until after the fact. By the time Sunday night came and went, he was getting concerned. When he learned she hadn't shown up on the set of the movie at RKO on Monday morning, his concern changed to worry. He reported her missing on Tuesday morning. No, he didn't have any idea where she could be. Although, he added, lately Sylvia had been involved with a rough crowd—heavy drinking, drugs, gambling. Maybe one of these new unsavory friends was responsible for her disappearance. No, Byron didn't know who these friends were. Sylvia had mentioned first names only, and talked about this nightclub or that, but she wasn't particularly informative. After all, they were both on their own, in Hollywood, and what his sister did on her own time was her business.

What was left of Sylvia's corpse had been found on a Saturday in August 1942, on a stretch of beach south of the Santa Monica Pier, the area known as Muscle Beach. The pier, a popular destination then and now, drew lots of soldiers and sailors during the war. A couple of sailors on leave, out for a stroll along the beach with their girls, spotted the hand uncovered by shifting sands and waves, and summoned the police.

According to the autopsy report, Sylvia Jasper had been bludgeoned to death, her skull crushed by a heavy object. Then her body had been buried in a grave scooped out of the sand. She must have been killed during the night, I thought, perhaps even the Friday she'd last been seen. I pictured that night on the pier, pulsing with lights, noise, and people. And several hundred yards south of the pier, where her body had been found, no lights at all, just darkness, the rhythmic rush of waves, the occasional amorous couple strolling along the shoreline where the Pacific Ocean kissed the sand. Nighttime, and away from the pier. Yes, that would have been a good spot to conceal a crime.

The detective in charge of the investigation of Sylvia's death interviewed her brother Byron, quizzing him on the information he'd given LAPD when Sylvia went missing. But his statement to the Santa Monica officer was vague, not particularly useful. Again he referred to her new and unsavory friends, but this time he implied Sylvia was involved with mobsters and that they had been responsible for her death. It was true that organized crime had moved to Hollywood in the thirties and forties. The Santa Monica detective had pursued that line of inquiry, to no avail. He had also interviewed the other bit players who'd been working on the movie at RKO. That, too, was a dead end.

Sylvia had few friends or confidantes, it appeared, except her brother Byron. She wasn't popular. In fact, her co-workers had little to say about her, and most of that unfavorable. A woman who worked in Makeup referred to Sylvia as a nasty, demanding bitch. A fellow actress, another bit player, said Sylvia had a reputation for sleeping around and using the casting couch to get parts. No one on the set of the film at RKO, either in front of or behind the cameras, knew or cared about her plans for the weekend. Only one person, a man who worked as an electrician, was sympathetic or concerned. Sylvia had seemed troubled, bothered by something, he told the detective, as though she were carrying the weight of the world. He hoped she hadn't committed suicide, he added.

Not unless she'd fractured her own skull, I thought.

Sylvia Jasper was a bit player, small fry, insignificant, her life and death mostly unremarked. End of story, I thought as I closed the file. Jerusha seemed to think so. "I guess this puts an end to it," she'd written on the newspaper clipping she sent to Ted Howard, her new husband. But there was a hint of unfinished business in the air. Who had killed Sylvia, and why?

I had several hours before I had to catch my flight back to Oakland, so I drove back to the Hollywood Division. Nacio Lopez was back, and he let me take another look at the Tarrant file. Then I reconnected with Liam Cleary and offered to buy him another cup of coffee. He insisted it was his turn. We left the division and walked to the coffee shop I'd visited earlier. I grabbed a corner table and Liam joined me a few minutes later, bearing our java jolts, a couple of plastic forks, and a plate containing a brownie and a lemon bar.

"Sugar and caffeine," I said. "You're a man after my own heart."

"I was feeling a bit peckish." He used a fork to split both the pastries and went for the brownie.

I took a bite of the lemon bar and my mouth puckered as sweet warred with tart. "What do you know about a guy named Charles Makellar? Otherwise known as Chaz. Tall, thin, dark hair, in his late forties. He's got a criminal record, most of it obtained down here."

"Chaz?" Liam laughed. "Don't tell me he's moved north."

"He has. He and his wife own a movie memorabilia business in Alameda, specializing in stuff from Hollywood's Golden Age. The classics, thirties up through the sixties, I'd say. They have a shop located right across the street from the Alameda Theatre, which has been restored to all its Art Deco glory. I take it you do know him. What's the scoop?"

"Well, well." Liam took a sip of his mocha. "That's quite a change for an Angeleno like Chaz. I wonder what prompted that move. He got married a few years back and the story was, he'd cleaned up his act. But I'm not sure whether to believe that. You know me, I'm a suspicious old cop."

"Middle-aged, surely," I said.

"Thank you, darlin'. I've still got most of my hair, even if it's turning gray. Anyway, I figure the leopard doesn't change his spots."

I sampled the brownie. It was so rich it made my teeth hurt. "Tell me about Chaz and what kind of spots he has on his record."

Liam took a bite of the lemon bar. "Whew, that'll make you pucker up. Well, now, I first ran into Chaz Makellar when I was working at the Wilshire Division, I guess it's about twenty years or more. He's a small-time hustler, always had some sort of a scam going. First time I encountered him he already had a record for passing bad paper."

"Yes, I saw that in the background check I did on him. He got probation. Then later he was arrested for petty theft and spent some time in jail."

"And in between the two, I arrested him," Liam said. "Also for theft. But the charges were dropped. Problems with the chain of evidence. Not my doing, I might add. I kept an eye on Chaz over the years. He got more sophisticated with his scams, good at avoiding the law. He works in some kind of legitimate business and then bends the rules until they almost break. Once a hustler, always a hustler, as far as I'm concerned."

"He's been sued a couple of times," I said. "The first was over some plans for a restaurant, the second time over some alleged fraud with some movie memorabilia. Both lawsuits settled out of court."

"So what prompts your interest in Chaz Makellar?" Liam asked.

"It's not so much him as it is an old man who works in the shop. His name is Henry Calhoun."

Liam nodded as he polished off the rest of the brownie. "Movie memorabilia, and files on a couple of unsolved murders of actors from way back in 'forty-two. I'm all ears, darlin'. What gives?"

I told Liam about my encounter with Henry Calhoun and how he linked my grandmother to the murder of Ralph Tarrant. "I couldn't resist investigating."

"Can't say as I blame you," Liam said. "It's piqued my interest, too."

"I've been itching to look at that Tarrant file ever since. And the file on Sylvia, ever since I found that clipping about her murder. When my client wanted me to come to LA on business, there was my opportunity. I confirmed that my grandmother was interviewed by the police, but they certainly didn't consider her a suspect."

Liam chuckled. "Now my Granny Cleary was a sweet old soul, wouldn't hurt a fly. But my Granny Hallinan, I could see her killing someone. She was a tough old broad, for sure."

"I'm not sure how Chaz Makellar figures into this," I said. "But something about the shop and the people feels a bit off. Particularly since I did a background check on Henry Calhoun and didn't find much of a background. That's unusual for someone who must be eighty-plus. I overheard Raina Makellar talking and she said Henry used to work for her father, whose name was Wallace Simms, who had a shop on Melrose Avenue, near La Brea. Evidently one thing that prompted the move from Los Angeles to the Bay Area was that the rent on the shop went up after Simms died. Henry scouted and bought merchandise for the Melrose shop, and he's doing the same thing for the Makellars, in addition to working behind the counter. He also lives in an apartment at the house they're renting in Alameda."

"Melrose has changed a lot over the years," Liam said. "It definitely skews to a younger crowd, and I'm not sure any of them would be interested in movie memorabilia, let alone anything older than they are."

"I'm just curious as to how Henry Calhoun, whoever he is, knew my grandmother had been interviewed by the police in connection with Ralph Tarrant's murder."

"Good question," Liam said. "Maybe he has firsthand knowledge."

"That's my theory. But right now I don't have anything to back it up."

Liam finished his coffee and looked at his watch. "I've got to get back to work. Tell you what, I'll nose around a little bit, see if Henry Calhoun has ever come onto the LAPD radar. He might not have a police record, but someone may remember him."

I thanked Liam and we parted outside the coffee shop. I had a couple hours before catching my flight back to Oakland, so I drove over to Melrose Avenue near the intersection of La Brea. Liam was right about the much-younger patrons of the shops and restaurants. I located the former site of Wallace Simms's movie memorabilia shop and starting asking questions. I didn't find anyone who remembered the shop, let alone Henry Calhoun or the Makellars. I was just about ready to leave for the airport when a shop on a side street caught my eye. It was a vintage clothing store with a window display of cocktail dresses from the forties and fifties. I went inside, past a twenty-something woman who was trying on a jacket, and saw on the back wall a large photo of Gloria Swanson as Norma Desmond in *Sunset Boulevard*. A display case full of costume jewelry served as a cash register counter, staffed by a middle-aged woman. I approached and showed her the photograph of Henry Calhoun.

She nodded. "Yeah, I know who he is. Henry something-or-other. He worked at that poster shop on Melrose. It's gone now. The owner died, I think, and his daughter and her husband closed it."

"His last name is Calhoun," I said. "What do you know about him?"

She ruminated for a moment. Then we were interrupted by the younger woman who had been trying on the jacket. Now she wanted to examine a bangle bracelet inside the display case. While I waited, I picked up the proprietor's business card and learned her name was Maria Cortez. Finally the customer left, after purchasing both the jacket and the bracelet.

"Henry was a strange little guy," Maria Cortez said, taking up our conversation where we'd left off. "I think he was off the grid, you know, paid under the table. Knew his Hollywood stuff, though. I'm always on the lookout for vintage clothes from the forties and fifties. Henry was good at finding things, steering me toward them. He had some sort of connection with the family, the man and his daughter who ran that movie shop. Wallace was the father's name. And her name was Raina. I always thought that was a pretty name. Let's see. Henry lived somewhere in Hollywood, in an apartment building they owned. No, wait a minute. It was the aunt that owned the apartment building. What was her name? Dorothy? Dolly?" She shrugged as two more customers entered the store. "Sorry, I'm not clear on the name, just that it started with a D."

I thanked her and consulted my watch. Past time for me to get on the road to LAX. I had to turn in my rental car and catch a plane.

~ 14 ~

ON WEDNESDAY I unlocked my office and tossed that morning's edition of the *San Francisco Chronicle* onto my desk. I made a pot of coffee, planning to glance at the front section while I drank my first cup, but I got a call from the attorney who'd sent me to LA to interview that witness. She was eager to get my notes so I sat down and wrote the report right away. After I e-mailed the document to her, I began digging for information about Jerusha's roommates in that Hollywood bungalow long ago. I knew from the letter and photo I'd found at Caro's house that Anne Hayes had married a man named Lemuel Sanderson. In 1947 they had been in Boulder, Colorado, where Sanderson attended the University of Colorado on the GI Bill, working on his master's degree in geology. I discovered that Sanderson eventually got his doctorate, specializing in sedimentology, and wound up on the CU faculty, at one time serving as chair of the Department of Geological Sciences.

I did a search on Anne Hayes Sanderson and discovered that she, too, taught at the University of Colorado. She had a doctorate in history, focusing on women and the West. In addition to teaching, she'd written books and won awards. She sounded like a thoroughly interesting woman. Unfortunately she had died three years earlier. I would have liked to talk with her.

Even so, I certainly wanted to talk with one of her children. I made some calls to the history department, where Anne had taught for so many years, but I came up empty. Either the people I talked with didn't have the information I sought, or because of privacy concerns they didn't want to part with it. Initially I had the same result in CU's Department of Geological Sciences, where Lemuel had taught.

Then the woman on the other end of the phone said, "Wait, I just remembered something. A woman named Campbell who works here on campus, at the Center of the American West. It seems to me she has some connection with Dr. Sanderson." In the background I heard another phone ringing. "I have to get that. You can find the center's phone number on the CU website."

I pointed my Internet browser to the Center of the American West, a research unit at the University of Colorado, devoted to the West, both past and present, with a publications program and an extensive roster of events and conferences. On the web page listing the center's staff I found a program administrator named Elisa Campbell. I reached for the phone. My call went into her voice mail. I left a message with both my office and cell phone numbers, explaining that I was seeking contact information for the family of Dr. Lemuel Sanderson and that I'd been referred by the geology department.

I turned my attention to finding Pearl Bishop, who was evidently still alive. The Internet Movie Database showed that Pearl had worked in movies and TV as late as the mid-eighties. Her last three credited performances were on the TV series *Cagney and Lacey, Hill Street Blues,* and *Remington Steele.* Unfortunately the database didn't include any biographical information that would help me trace her.

The Screen Actors Guild, I told myself. I should have thought of that the day before, when I was in Los Angeles. But the guild had a website, and they might know where Pearl Bishop was. I wasn't sure how it worked, but I knew that there were payments called residuals, and actors got them.

Through more detailed research I learned that residuals were paid to creators of performance art, or performers of the work, for subsequent showings or screenings of the work. So writers and actors got residuals when a movie was shown on television, or when a television program was rerun. Actors got residual payments as a result of a long fight by the Screen Actors Guild, which resulted in a 1960 agreement with movie studios that paid residuals for movies produced after that date. Initially television residuals were limited to six rebroadcasts, but in the mid-seventies the agreement was altered so that residuals were paid on an unlimited basis for programs produced after that date. The TV production company retained the lion's share, eighty percent, while the remaining twenty percent was divided among performers and crew. Now, with the advent of DVDs and streaming video, a new battle over residuals was looming.

But that wasn't my concern. All I knew was that Pearl Bishop had worked in TV during this period and was eligible for residual payments. If Pearl was getting residuals, those checks had to be mailed to a current address.

I explored the Screen Actors Guild website and finally found an 800 number for their "Actors to Locate" hotline. "Pearl Bishop," I said. "She's a bit player and extra, worked steadily from the late thirties through the mid-eighties."

"I can look her up and give you the name of her agent," said the woman on the other end of the line.

"Do bit players typically have agents?"

"Some do," she said. "And if she doesn't, it's up to her to keep her contact information current. Let's see…Bishop, Pearl. Yes, she has an agent."

She gave me the name of the agency that represented Pearl. I thanked her and ended the call. I looked up the agency online and reached for the phone. That's where I ran into a snag. The agent had died. I explained the situation to an administrative assistant. "I'm trying to locate someone he represented. Her name is Pearl Bishop. I believe she's retired, since the mid-eighties."

"I'll have to do some research on this, and get back to you," she said. I gave her my contact information and made a note to call her back in a few days.

I got up to pour myself another cup of coffee. My cell phone rang and I looked at the display. The caller was in the 303 area code. That was Colorado. I answered the call.

"Hi," said the voice on the other end. "I'm Elisa Campbell at the Center of the American West. You left me a message, asking about Dr. Lemuel Sanderson."

"Yes, I did. Thanks for getting back to me. I know that both Lemuel and Anne Sanderson are dead. But I'm trying to get in touch with their children. A woman I talked with in the geology department seemed to think you might be able to help me."

"What is this about?" Elisa Campbell asked, sounding intrigued.

"My grandmother," I told her. "Her name was Jerusha Layne. She and Anne Hayes Sanderson were roommates back in Hollywood in the early forties. I hope you can help me."

Elisa Campbell laughed. "Okay. You've got the right person. Anne was my grandma. You want to talk with my mother. She lives in Denver. But she and Dad are away right now. I'll call her on her cell phone and tell her what you've told me. I'm sure she'll get in touch with you. Will that work?"

"That works very well indeed. Thank you." I gave her my numbers, wondering how long it would be before I heard from Anne's daughter.

By now it was past noon and my stomach was growling. I left my office and walked to a nearby deli, ordering my usual pastrami on rye. I carried lunch back to the office and ate at my desk, reading the front section of the newspaper. I finished my sandwich and balled up the paper it had been wrapped in, tossing it into the wastebasket. Then I picked up the local news section and unfolded it. A headline just below the fold read NO LEADS IN HEALDSBURG SLAYING. With growing disbelief I read the article. Mike Strickland had been found murdered at his home on Monday, two days earlier—just two days after the opening of the gallery show displaying his Hitchcock memorabilia.

Damn, I thought, remembering the tall, amiable man with white hair, and how much I'd enjoyed talking with him Saturday evening.

There were few details in the *Chronicle*, so I went online to the Santa Rosa *Press Democrat* website and learned that Strickland had been shot twice in the chest. His body was discovered by his daughter, Victoria Ambrose, who lived in Santa Rosa. She'd been unable to contact him on either his home or cell phones. Concerned, she drove up to Healdsburg after work that Monday evening to check on her father at his home, located off Dry Creek Road, northwest of town. She found him dead in the foyer, lying in a pool of blood.

What had happened? I wondered. Was this a robbery gone sour? According to the article, Strickland's house was located outside the Healdsburg city limits, so the Sonoma County Sheriff's Department was investigating Strickland's murder. I had no contacts in that department. But an old friend of mine, Joe Kelso, was the police chief in Cloverdale, a town at the northern edge of Sonoma County. He could steer me in the right direction.

Joe was in his office. We spent a few minutes chatting about our respective lives, then I came to the point. "Hey, what do you know about a murder in Healdsburg on Monday? The victim's name was Michael Strickland, found dead at his home on Dry Creek Road. He'd been shot."

"Yeah, I heard about that," Joe said. "Two slugs in the chest, at close range. One of them went right to the heart. It's a county case. What's your angle? You got information?"

"Not sure at this point," I told him. "Possible connection to something I'm working on. Who's the investigating officer?"

"Detective Sergeant Marty Toland, Violent Crimes Investigations Unit at the Sonoma County Sheriff's Department. Mention my name."

"Thanks, I owe you one."

"Hey, next time you're in Cloverdale, I'll collect. Come on up. Brenda and I would love to see you."

I looked up the address and phone number for Sergeant Marty Toland. She was in her office and she wasn't very forthcoming when I identified myself as a private investigator. She warmed up a little when I told her Joe Kelso and I went way back. I found out the coroner estimated Mike Strickland had been killed four or five hours before his daughter found his body, which put the time of death in the early afternoon. At this point, Sergeant Toland didn't have any leads, and I assured her that if I turned up anything, I would be in touch.

Mike Strickland's funeral was scheduled on Saturday afternoon, at a local church. I noted the time and made plans to attend. I wanted to talk with his daughter.

Strickland's murder bothered me, and not only for the obvious reason. I'd first heard about his collection of Hitchcock items when I eavesdropped on a conversation between Raina Makellar and another woman, at the shop in Alameda. It sounded as though Chaz Makellar and Henry Calhoun were among the dealers who'd contacted Strickland to see if he was interested in selling items from his collection. Raina had also talked about a collection that had been owned by a Sonoma County collector who had died recently. Her son didn't know, or didn't care, how much the collection was worth. He wanted to get rid of it. So Chaz Makellar gave the son a lowball offer, as Raina put it, and purchased the collection at a fraction of its value.

The line of work I'm in gives me a suspicious nature. Now I wondered if the collector had died of natural causes. When had she died? Raina said earlier this year. It was June now, the sixth month, which gave me a range of five months from January to May. And where had the woman lived? Sonoma County was large, just north of Marin County, with towns ranging from the coast to the Napa County line. So which town was home to the woman who'd died? Santa Rosa, the county seat, was a good place to start, and so was the Santa Rosa *Press Democrat*. I'd have to do some serious digging to find out. But for the time being, I had an appointment with a paying client in Pleasanton, something that would keep me busy for the rest of the afternoon. I locked my office and headed for the garage where I kept my car.

I got home at six o'clock, after fighting my way through rush hour traffic. My cats, Abigail and Black Bart, met me at the door, loudly declaiming hunger and neglect. After I fed them, I dug through the DVDs in my collection until I found *Shadow of a Doubt*. Then I sat on the sofa, munching on a big bowl of buttered popcorn, and watched the movie, in honor of Mike Strickland and his sister Molly, who had a bit part in the Hitchcock picture.

~ 15 ~

THE PHONE was ringing as I unlocked my office Thursday morning. I grabbed the receiver and identified myself. On the other end of the line I heard a woman's voice. "My name is Noreen Campbell. I'm Anne Sanderson's daughter. My daughter Elisa says you want to talk with me."

"I do. Thank you so much for calling me. I'm Jerusha Layne's granddaughter. In fact, I'm named for her, but I prefer Jeri to Jerusha."

"Nice to meet, even if it's on the phone rather than face to face," she said. "How can I help you, Jeri?"

"I'm doing some background research into my grandmother's days in Hollywood. Your mother was one of her roommates."

"Yes, my daughter mentioned that," she said. "I do recognize your grandmother's name, because it's so unusual. I'm not sure how much I can help you, though. Mom didn't talk much about Hollywood. She enjoyed her stint as an actress, but once she left, that chapter of her life was closed."

"It's not so much Hollywood I'm interested in, but life back in the early forties, right before the war, sharing that bungalow with those other aspiring actresses."

"Well… She did talk about her roommates, and she corresponded with them later. Your grandmother, for one. I think Mom and Dad even visited your grandparents once, when they took a vacation in California. That same trip they visited another roommate, a woman who stayed in Hollywood and worked steadily for years. Mom used to see her on TV. Oh, what was her name? A jewel name. Ruby…no, it was Pearl."

"Pearl Bishop," I said.

"Mom used to say Pearl was a character."

"That's the impression I got from Grandma."

"And Mildred, of course," she added.

"Mildred Peretti, the roommate who moved back to Denver?"

"Mom and Mildred were really close friends. They were both from Colorado. And they lived together during the war. Mildred was like an aunt to all of us."

"Why did your mother leave Hollywood?" I asked. "Was it something to do with the war?"

"Definitely the war," she said. "Mom's older brother was killed in November of nineteen forty-two, at Guadalcanal. After that, her Hollywood career, such as it was, didn't seem important. Mom went back to Alamosa. That's where she was born and raised, down in the San Luis Valley, which is south-central Colorado. Her dad worked for the Denver and Rio Grande Railroad. She went home when the family got the news about her brother, and got a job in the railroad freight office there. But in the fall of nineteen forty-three she moved to Denver. She and Mildred got an apartment and they worked in civilian jobs at Buckley Air Force Base, at the Army Air Corps training school."

"How did she meet your father?" I asked. "Was he in the Army?"

Noreen Campbell laughed. "He was, but they met before the war. Dad was from the Valley, too, a town called Monte Vista. He was going to Adams State College in Alamosa and so was Mom. She had her freshman year there. He was a junior and he knew her brother, the one who got killed. They'd even gone out a couple of times, while Mom was a coed. Then she went off to Hollywood to be an actress. After he got his commission in the Army in 'forty-two, he was sent to some training camp in California. When he got to Los Angeles, he looked her up. So they reconnected and the relationship took off from there. He came back to the Valley in nineteen forty-three before he went overseas, to see his family and marry Mom. They were married over sixty years."

"That sounds like my grandparents," I said. "They met in nineteen forty-one and married in 'forty-two, before Grandpa shipped out. He was in the Navy. I'm trying to get more information about another roommate, a woman named Sylvia Jasper."

"Oh, her," Mrs. Campbell said. "The bitch. That's what Mom called her. And she must have been something, because if you knew my mother, well, she was very forthright, but she just didn't use language like that. My impression was that Sylvia was a pain in the butt from the start and then something happened that brought things to a head. I don't know what it was, but it must have been a doozy."

"I've been reading my grandmother's letters to her sister, and it looks like Sylvia was helping herself to the roommates' clothes and jewelry—and the money in the grocery kitty. I also get the impression she was sleeping around. Ultimately they asked her to move out, sometime in 'forty-two. The kicker is that Sylvia was murdered later that year."

"No kidding? Now you've got me curious. I wonder what happened."

"Me, too. I'm hoping to locate Pearl Bishop. I'll bet she could tell me a lot. As far as I know she's still alive. She worked in movies and TV up through the eighties, and I haven't found her obituary. By the way, did you save any of your mother's correspondence from that era, such as letters she wrote to family while she was in Hollywood, or to her roommates after she left?"

"Oh, no," Mrs. Campbell said. "There were some letters she'd kept, and when she died I read some of it, then tossed the whole lot. Mom wouldn't have approved, since she was a history professor. But you just can't keep everything."

"I know. But I'm really enjoying reading my grandmother's letters. She wrote to her sister frequently during the Hollywood years. And there's also some wartime correspondence between Grandma and Grandpa."

"Wait a minute," she said. "Same thing. Letters Mom and Dad

wrote each other while he was in the Army, while they were engaged and when he was overseas. There are some of those. My daughter Elisa took them."

"Great. Would you and Elisa do me a big favor? If there are any letters from nineteen forty-two, would you read through them and see if there's any information about Sylvia Jasper?"

"Why are you interested in her?" she asked. "Mom didn't even like her."

"Neither did my grandmother," I said. "But since she was murdered, I'm really curious about her."

"I see what you mean. Okay, my husband and I are visiting relatives in Wyoming right now, but we're heading home tomorrow. I'll call my daughter and we'll get together and read the letters. You know, my son did an oral history. He interviewed Mom a few years before she died. It was mostly about what she did during the war, but she did talk about working in Hollywood."

"I did the same thing with my grandmother," I said. "She was a welder at the Kaiser Shipyard during the war. I'd really like to listen to your mother's oral history. Is it an audiotape, or a digital file?"

"I think it's digital," she said. "I'll call my son and see. If it's a tape, he could make a copy, and if it's digital, he can e-mail it to you."

I gave her my e-mail address. "Can you think of anything else that might help?"

"Mildred might be able to help you."

"Mildred Peretti? She's still alive?"

"Oh, yes. Her married name is Roberson. She lives in Greeley, Colorado. She'd already left Hollywood before Sylvia moved in, of course. But she and Mom were such good friends. If something strange was going on, I'll bet Mom told her all about it."

"I hope so. Yes, I want to talk with her. Would you please give her my phone numbers?"

"I certainly will."

That was productive, I thought, as Mrs. Campbell and I ended the conversation. I pictured Anne Hayes and Mildred Peretti in their Denver apartment back in World War II, dishing the dirt after a day of work at Buckley Field. Surely Anne would have told Mildred about Sylvia.

I turned my attention to other matters and then left the office for an appointment with an attorney and some surveillance regarding an insurance case. When I returned I started researching deaths in Sonoma County during the first five months of the year, hoping to find information on the collector who had died suddenly, providing Chaz Makellar with the opportunity to purchase a collection of movie memorabilia from her son. I knew from the conversation I'd overheard that the collector was an elderly woman who'd lived in Sonoma County. I looked through news articles, obituaries and funeral notices in the online archives of the Santa Rosa *Press Democrat*, starting in January. It was a long and tedious process, but I found a likely prospect, when I clicked on a name next to a photo and the link took me to a longer and more detailed obituary. In early March, Mrs. Roberta Cook, aged eighty-three, a lifelong resident of the southern Sonoma County town of Petaluma, had died in an accident. Her survivors included a son, Lewis, of San Mateo; a daughter, Margaret Duggan, of Pismo Beach; five grandchildren and one great-granddaughter. The nugget I gleaned from the obituary was that Mrs. Cook collected movie posters.

What kind of accident? I stared at the photo that went with the obit. Mrs. Cook had been a pleasant, motherly-looking, white-haired woman, with a plump, smiling face. I looked through the archives of the website, which focused on Petaluma news, and found the answer. On a rainy afternoon Mrs. Cook evidently left her house and went down the front steps to check her mailbox. She slipped and fell, hitting her head on the porch railing. A neighbor found her and called 911. The death was deemed accidental.

I was going up to Healdsburg on Saturday, for Mike Strickland's funeral. I decided to leave early so I could make a stop in Petaluma as well.

~ 16 ~

ON SATURDAY morning I drove north on Highway 101 to Petaluma, in southern Sonoma County. The area, with its rolling hills, had first been settled by the coastal Miwok Indians. Then Alta California became an outpost of Spain. A huge land grant, Rancho Petaluma, was given to General Mariano Guadalupe Vallejo, the Commandant of the San Francisco Presidio. The adobe house he built in 1836 still stands near Petaluma, one of the best-preserved buildings of its era in Northern California.

I steered my Toyota into the right lane and drove across a bridge, glancing down at the Petaluma River, which flows into the upper reaches of San Francisco Bay and made the city, chartered in 1858, a center of trade as flat-bottomed boats called scows sailed between Petaluma and San Francisco, carrying agricultural produce and other materials. The chicken-and-egg business flourished here in the late nineteenth and early twentieth centuries. At one time the city was known as the "Egg Capital of the World" and one of the big local celebrations, called Butter and Egg Days, is in April.

I left the freeway, heading downtown, where iron-fronted Victorian commercial buildings line several streets, survivors of the 1906 earthquake that left Petaluma relatively unscathed. The older neighborhoods surrounding the downtown area are full of Victorian-era homes, Queen Anne, Eastlake and Stick Gothic.

Mrs. Roberta Cook had lived on Liberty Street, a few blocks northwest of the city's commercial center. The one-story Queen

Anne house was built high off the ground, with a driveway on the right leading to a detached garage at the back. The structure had the usual Victorian-style curlicues, including fishscale siding. It was painted pale blue with darker blue trim and bright yellow flourishes, the color nearly matching that of the yellow roses blooming in front of the porch railing. A FOR SALE sign stood in the front yard, with a Plexiglas pocket on the base, containing information sheets about the house. I parked my car and got out, plucking a sheet from the pocket. The house dated to 1902 and the asking price made me wince. It would probably sell for that, though. It was a lovely house, obviously well-kept.

I returned the sheet to the pocket and walked toward the porch, examining the front steps, eight of them. Someone had installed safety measures, applying non-skid strips to each step and adding grab bars to the original porch railings, so someone on the stairs could hold onto a bar with each hand. I saw another grab bar just outside the front door. At the bottom of the porch, the original railings ended in a couple of squat, pyramid-shaped ornaments. The mailbox was attached to a post, about six inches from the base of the steps, on the left as I faced the house. Mrs. Cook had supposedly slipped on these steps, wet from the rain, and tumbled down, hitting her head as she fell. I could see how it might have happened. The non-skid surface didn't extend the full width of the steps. If Mrs. Cook's foot had landed on one of the smooth portions, she could have slipped. I walked toward the house and ran my fingers over those pointy pyramids. They felt like solid wood and they could have caused some serious damage to a skull.

"Are you going to buy this house?" a voice demanded behind me.

I turned and looked at the woman who stood near the FOR SALE sign. She was elderly, but spry, short and wiry, with white hair and a determined expression. On this June morning she wore bright blue pants and a matching floral shirt. She carried a canvas shopping bag draped over her left shoulder and a bright pink fanny pack cinched around her middle.

I walked toward her. "I can't afford to buy this house."

She sniffed. "It's priced too high, in the middle of a recession. Lots of lookers, but no takers. It'll sell eventually, though. It's a really nice house. I just hope whoever buys it will be a good neighbor."

"Where do you live?" I asked.

"Next door." She pointed north, at a modest Stick Victorian house. "Fifty-two years I've lived here. Almost as long as the woman who lived in this house. She died. I found her."

"Did you?" Just the person I wanted to talk with.

"They said she fell down the steps." She sniffed again, a derisive sound.

"But you don't believe that?"

A pair of sharp brown eyes looked me up and down. "If you're not interested in buying a house, why are you here? Are you lurking?"

I smiled at the word. "I didn't think I was lurking." But I was.

"Listen, honey, I've been watching you all the time I walked up the street. I read lots of mysteries. I know lurking when I see it. Are you a cop?"

"No. Why do you think I'm lurking? Were you expecting a cop?"

"Because my friend was murdered. I want somebody to do something about it."

Bingo. I held out my business card. "I'm not a cop. I'm a private investigator. And I'd really like to talk with you."

Her eyes widened. "A private eye. Like Sharon McCone or Kinsey Millhone?"

"Yes, something like that."

"Well, Jeri Howard, I'm Sadie Espinosa. Come on over to my house and let's have us a talk."

I followed Mrs. Espinosa to her own house. She had the same sort of fall-prevention setup. She unlocked the front door. A pair of cats greeted us in the foyer. One, a calico, meowed softly, while the other, a big orange tom, gave my shoes a thorough examination. "That's Poppy," Mrs. Espinosa said, indicating the calico. "And the big orange boy is Ducks."

"Hey, Ducks." I knelt and scratched his ears. He purred loudly, left off sniffing my shoes and rubbed his head and body against my charcoal gray slacks, leaving a liberal coating of orange hair.

Mrs. Espinosa beckoned me to follow her into the kitchen. On the far side of the counter was a family room with a wide-screen flat-panel TV fastened to the wall. Below it shelves contained DVDs and videotapes. Opposite the TV were two recliners. A carpeted kitty gym stood in front of the window that looked out on the backyard.

She deposited her shopping bag and fanny pack on the counter. Then she poured a couple of glasses of iced tea, handed one to me, and lifted the lid on a plastic container of cookies on the kitchen counter. She put several on a plate and grabbed a fistful of paper napkins from a nearby holder. "Peanut butter–chocolate chip. I made 'em yesterday. Pretty good, if I do say so myself."

"Oh, my, yes," I said, after taking a bite. Now I had gooey dark chocolate smeared on my hands. I took one of the napkins and followed Mrs. Espinosa to her living room. She set the plate on the coffee table and put a cookie on a napkin, setting that and her glass on an end table. She settled into a wing chair to the left of the fireplace and Poppy, the calico cat, jumped onto her lap. I sat on the sofa opposite her. Ducks, my new best friend, plopped down next to me. He kneaded my thigh with his big paws and rumbled with his big purr. With every movement he shed more orange hair.

"Your clothes will be covered," she said, nibbling on her cookie.

"It's just cat hair. It'll brush off." I sipped my tea. "So tell me about Mrs. Cook."

She stroked the calico cat. "We were good friends. She was two years younger than me. I'm eighty-one. Both widows. My husband passed on six years ago and hers had been gone ten years. He was a lot older than she was. Anyway, she was getting on, but she wasn't doddery, if you know what I mean. Very independent, like me. We did lots of things together, playing Scrabble, going for walks, driving over to the library. She was a big mystery fan, too. We'd go to the Cinnabar Theater here in Petaluma, if they were showing something interesting. We both loved old movies. We'd have a DVD night, watching movies on my big screen, with a big bowl of buttered popcorn."

"What kind of movies did Mrs. Cook like?" I asked.

Mrs. Espinosa smiled. "Anything with Joan Crawford. Roberta liked film noir and those women's pictures from the forties. Barbara Stanwyck, Bette Davis, and Greer Garson: three-hankie pictures, you know. Now me, I love Westerns. Give me Randolph Scott, Joel McCrea, and Audie Murphy. So we'd mix and match. Oh, and we'd watch a lot of those BBC miniseries. *Upstairs, Downstairs* and *Poldark*, that sort of thing."

"Sounds like fun."

Mrs. Espinosa sighed. "Yes, I miss it. I still watch the movies and pop the corn, but it's not the same without her."

"Tell me what happened the day you found her body."

"It was cold and rainy. A big storm blew in early that morning and it rained like the dickens, coming down hard and sideways. It was a good day to stay indoors. I built a fire and sat here drinking tea and reading." Mrs. Espinosa indicated the fireplace between us. A wicker basket full of books sat at the base of her recliner, all mysteries, I saw, recognizing titles and authors' names.

"It rained off and on all afternoon, sometimes hard, then there'd be a lull. I had some stew cooking in the Crock-Pot, so I called Roberta about one o'clock, to invite her over for an early dinner and a movie. She said she'd come over at four. The mail comes around three, maybe a little before. I saw the carrier go by but I didn't notice the time. I went out to check my own mailbox. I didn't see Roberta then, so she must have been inside. It started raining again, not as hard as before, just sprinkling off and on. Four o'clock came and went and Roberta didn't come over. I called and she didn't answer the phone. So I went outside. There she was at the bottom of the porch steps."

Mrs. Espinosa compressed her lips into a tight line. "There was blood on her head. I had my cell phone with me. I always carry it in my pocket. So I called nine-one-one. The paramedics came, and the police. I told that detective it wasn't an accident, but nobody listens to little old ladies."

"What was the detective's name?"

She screwed up her face, trying to remember. "Harper, Hooper, something like that. He gave me his card but I don't know if I kept it. I'll look for it, and let you know."

"Thanks, that would be helpful. My cell phone number is on my business card. What makes you so sure Mrs. Cook's death wasn't an accident?"

"She was careful. You saw the fall-prevention stuff on her porch and mine. Grab bars and non-skid, inside the house, and out. We had that done several years ago, at the same time, both of us doing whatever we could to prevent falls. She wanted to stay in her own home as long as she could, just like me."

"Accidents do happen."

"Not to Roberta," she said stubbornly. "The steps weren't that wet. The porch overhangs them. She always held on with both hands whenever she went up and down those steps. I just don't see how she could fall and hit her head. I think somebody pushed her down the steps, or hit her on the head and tried to make it look like an accident. I told the policeman that, but he said I'd been reading too many mysteries."

"I understand Mrs. Cook collected movie memorabilia."

"Yes, and it was valuable, too," Mrs. Espinosa said. "She had a lot of things from Joan Crawford movies, including a poster from *Mildred Pierce*, in really good condition. And *Sudden Fear*, that movie from the fifties. The most valuable piece, I think, was the poster from a movie called *Rain*, because that one dated back to nineteen thirty-two, before the Hollywood Code. Roberta called that poster a three-sheet. It was pretty big. Anyway, she said the poster was in mint condition because it had never been folded and didn't have any tears. She also said it was linen-backed, whatever that means. Anyways, she told me that poster from *Rain* was worth ten thousand dollars."

"I imagine she had dealers contacting her all the time."

"Oh, yes," Mrs. Espinosa said. "Dealers were always after her to sell her stuff, either pieces or the whole collection. She'd turned down several offers over the years. I told her she really should make an inventory, get an estimate on the value from a reputable dealer, and put the inventory in her safe deposit box. She said that was a really good idea and she would do that. But I don't think she had when she died."

"So what happened to her collection?"

Mrs. Espinosa frowned. "Her son sold it to the first person that made him an offer. I'll bet he got taken. It serves him right. He's so greedy. All he could think about was the house. He couldn't wait to clear out her things and put that house on the market."

"Do you have any idea who bought Mrs. Cook's collection?" I asked.

"I do, because I saw them loading it into a rental truck," Mrs. Espinosa said. "It was the dealer who visited her earlier, back in February. She asked me to be at her house for the appointment, just to be on the safe side. She didn't want to be alone with the pair of them. In fact, she told me she didn't want to sell, but this dealer was very persistent. He kept calling her, asking to see the collection. She finally agreed to let him look. He made an offer, but she turned him down. That was the end of it, I thought."

"There were two men?"

"Yes. A younger man, maybe in his forties or fifties. But the other fellow, why, he was as old as me. Had to be eighty if he was a day. I saw them twice, when they looked at the collection, and later, when they took it away. And in between, before Roberta died, I saw the old man. Where was it? I know. It was in Copperfield's bookstore downtown. Roberta had ordered a book. I was with her the day she picked it up."

I asked Mrs. Espinosa to describe the men and the vehicle they'd been driving the day they made an offer to Mrs. Cook. The younger man was tall and skinny with dark hair, she said. The older man was short and slight of build. Her response left me no doubt that the dealer who'd visited Mrs. Cook was Chaz Makellar, accompanied by his elderly employee, Henry Calhoun. I had printed several photos of Chaz and Raina Makellar and Henry Calhoun, the pictures I'd taken with my cell phone camera that day in Alameda when they'd unloaded merchandise from the SUV. Now I took those from my purse and handed them to Mrs. Espinosa. "Would you please take a look at these photos and see if you recognize any of these three people?"

She examined the snapshots closely and then nodded. "Yes, that's them. The men, anyway. I've never seen that woman before. But the men, definitely. I particularly remember the old man, since I saw him in the bookstore." She returned the photos to me.

"When did the dealers come look at the collection?" I asked.

"Must have been early February. Yes, it was. Before President's Day weekend."

"And when did you see the older man in the bookstore?"

She had to think about that for a moment. "You know, I think it was a week before she died. Late February or early March. But I'm not completely sure."

Before I left Mrs. Espinosa's house, I asked if she had contact information for Mrs. Cook's son. She did. He lived in San Mateo, on the Peninsula south of San Francisco. I wrote down his name and phone numbers. I wanted to talk with him as well as the detective who'd investigated Mrs. Cook's death, but both interviews would have to wait. I had a funeral to attend. I thanked Mrs. Espinosa for her hospitality, brushed orange cat hair from my gray slacks, and left Petaluma, driving north towards Healdsburg.

~ 17 ~

MIKE STRICKLAND'S funeral was at two o'clock Saturday afternoon, at St. Paul's Episcopal Church in Healdsburg. It was a traditional white church with a steeple and it was very crowded when I arrived at one-thirty. The crowd skewed older, given Strickland's age, but I saw a smattering of middle-aged and younger people. A closed casket bedecked with flowers stood below the pulpit, with photographs of Strickland on a nearby table. I walked up the aisle and looked at the photos, one of them showing a very young Strickland in a Navy uniform. Given his age, that must have been the early fifties, the era of the Korean War.

The first few pews, on my right, were reserved for the family. I turned and walked back down the aisle, past groups of people who knew each other, talking quietly among themselves. I took a place on the aisle of a pew near the back, and studied the program for the service, as well as the obituary I'd found online. I'd met Strickland's daughter, Victoria—he'd called her Tory—Ambrose the night of the gallery opening. He also had a son and daughter-in-law, Dennis and Melinda Strickland, who lived in Carson City, Nevada. The surviving family members included six grandchildren and assorted nieces, nephews, and cousins.

A woman began playing Bach on the church organ. Conversations ceased as people sat down, waiting for the service to begin. Then the family filed into the church sanctuary. Tory Ambrose, somber in a black dress, was the first to walk up the aisle. As she neared the pew where I sat, she glanced to her left and saw me. She frowned, as though trying to place me. Then she continued up the aisle, followed by a teenaged girl, about fifteen, who dabbed at her tear-stained face with a tissue, and two younger boys, about ten and twelve, looking subdued in their suits. Then came the man I assumed was Dennis Strickland, accompanied by his wife and three children, two girls and a boy. Behind them was an assortment of relatives. Once the family was seated, the organist stopped playing and a minister in vestments stepped up to the pulpit.

After the service was over, I waited near the entrance to the church sanctuary, watching Mike Strickland's family as they stood in the building's foyer, accepting the condolences of the people who filed by. I needed to talk with Victoria Ambrose but now didn't seem like the time. I was pondering how best to approach her when she saved me the trouble. She walked up to me, a no-nonsense look on her face.

"I recognize you," she said. "You were at the gallery opening last Saturday, chatting with Dad about your grandmother, the bit player."

I had a feeling she didn't miss much. "Yes, I was."

Her voice turned icy. "You didn't know my father. You just met him that night, didn't you? Why did you come to his funeral?"

"To pay my respects. I really enjoyed talking with him at the gallery opening. But there's another reason." I took a business card from my purse and handed it to her.

She frowned as she looked it over. "A private investigator?"

"I don't normally come to funerals and hand out business cards," I said. "However, I wonder about the circumstances of his death. A random murder doesn't fit. There must be a connection."

"With what? One of your cases? Why did you come to the gallery opening? To meet my father?"

"Yes. Your father had a large collection of movie memorabilia. And a buyer approached him recently."

"He was always being approached by buyers," she said with a wave of her hand.

"This was a specific buyer, the week before the gallery opening."

"How do you know about this?"

"I overheard a conversation."

"Someone mentioned Dad's name?"

"No. The conversation concerned a man in Sonoma County who collected movie memorabilia and had some valuable Hitchcock items. When I saw the article in the *Press Democrat* about the gallery opening and the Hitchcock memorabilia, I figured it must be the same man. So I decided to check it out."

"And you met Dad and talked with him. That story about your grandmother being a bit player in Hollywood, is that phony?"

"No, it's true. That's what led to my own interest in movie memorabilia. Just like your father became interested in collecting because his sister was a bit player."

She frowned again but this time it was different. She was no longer annoyed with me, and my intrusion into a time of grief. She was putting the pieces together. "The collection? Or someone wanting to get their hands on the collection? Does this have something to do with my father's murder?"

"I'm not sure. There are threads but I'm not certain where they lead right now." One thread was Strickland and the other, I was sure, was Roberta Cook, the collector in Petaluma. "Right now I'm just operating on my gut, which tells me that your father's murder and another death are related."

"Is your gut usually accurate?"

"Frequently. I've been in this business for years and I have a good track record."

"Fine." Tory Ambrose tucked my business card into her pocket. "My gut tells me I want to hire you. We have to talk. But it can't be today. I have all these relatives here for the funeral. Even my ex-husband showed up. He always did like Dad." She sighed as her brother beckoned to her. "Anyway, they're all gathering at my house. I can't leave without getting a lot of questions. You know how it is when people die: Sit around, drink coffee, and eat. People bring food. I've got enough food to feed an army."

I nodded. "Yes, I know how it is. Is tomorrow a possibility?"

"My brother and his family are staying with me, and they're heading back to Carson City tomorrow morning. So late morning, let's say eleven o'clock. I'll meet you in Railroad Square in Santa Rosa, at Flying Goat Coffee."

"I know where it is. I'll see you there. My cell phone number is on my card, if you need to get in touch with me."

I left the church. The day before, I had called Sergeant Marty Toland, the Sonoma County sheriff's detective who was investigating the Strickland murder. She told me she'd be at the funeral and we agreed to meet after the service. Now I looked around and spotted a woman who fit the description Toland had given me on the phone. I walked over and introduced myself.

"What's your connection with all of this?" she asked. "Please tell me you're not trolling for clients."

"I'm not, although I will disclose that Tory Ambrose has expressed an interest in hiring me. She and I will be having coffee tomorrow morning."

"Just so you share information," she said. "I checked you out, and Joe Kelso vouches for you."

"If I find out anything that will help you clear this case, I'll be on the phone. As I told you yesterday, I'm curious about a movie memorabilia dealer named Charles Makellar. I believe he visited Mike Strickland the week before Strickland was killed, trying to purchase items from the Hitchcock collection. This morning I found out Makellar visited an elderly woman in Petaluma. She also collected movie memorabilia, and Makellar tried to buy her collection. Then she died." I outlined what I'd learned from my talk with Sadie Espinosa.

"That's a stretch," Toland said after I'd given her what details I had. "But if you can connect the dots and give me some evidence I can use, I'll take it."

We parted, and I walked back to my car. I had more than twenty hours until my appointment with Tory Ambrose. I'd made arrangements to spend the night in Graton, with Aunt Dulcie and Cousin Pat.

As soon as I arrived I changed from my gray slacks into something more comfortable, and sat on the floor in Dulcie's room, with boxes of letters around me. Up until now the correspondence

I'd read had been in chronological order, but this latest batch was mixed up, with letters from 1942 stuck in with those from 1941. I sorted them and then began reading letters postmarked in the fall of 1941. I hadn't found out anything more about Sylvia Jasper or Ralph Tarrant. But I did get a sense for the ups and downs of Jerusha's relationship with Ted Howard. They dated steadily during the summer and fall of 1941, sharing a love for long walks and Glenn Miller's music. Ted was sure Jerusha was the woman he loved and he wanted to get married. In fact, Ted had given her a sort of pre-engagement, I'm-serious-about-you present, a heart-shaped locket, gold set with a big amethyst. On the back it was engraved with their initials. I knew it well. That particular item was in my jewelry box at home, with pictures of Grandma and Grandpa inside. My grandmother had given it to me before she died.

But the road to marriage was strewn with obstacles, and one of them was big, labeled "Jerusha's career." She wasn't ready to give up on Hollywood, as so many others had before her. She was sure, even after four years of bit parts, that the next job would be that bigger part she hoped for, the role that would get her noticed and elevate her to the ranks of featured players.

After all, Jerusha argued in a letter to Dulcie, look at Susan Hayward, who had also arrived in Hollywood in 1937. She played bit parts, too. And now she was featured as the second lead in *Reap the Wild Wind*, with John Wayne and Paulette Goddard.

Between the lines she wrote, I sensed Jerusha's soul-searching. She had done so well in *Babes on Broadway*, in that scene with Mickey Rooney at the drugstore, and singing and dancing in the elaborate "Hoe-Down" number, hoping to come to the attention of director Busby Berkeley.

But… There's always a but. And Jerusha was asking herself questions. If her career was progressing, wouldn't she be getting those second-lead parts now? But no, she was back to bits, just one line of dialogue in a scene with Rosalind Russell, in a movie called *Design for Scandal*.

I understood Jerusha's aspirations, I thought, leafing through the pages of the letters. We all need our dreams. Many people who wind up successful must pursue those dreams despite naysayers and doubts. How many women have given up what they wanted to do to get married? But I also understood the feelings of urgency Ted felt. Their letters to one another mentioned the war in Europe and the darkening mood of the country that autumn.

Then they broke up. Specifically, during Thanksgiving dinner at his uncle's home in Chatsworth. Jerusha and Pearl had made the trek to the San Fernando Valley in Pearl's old car, the Gasper. They left before the pumpkin pie. Jerusha's subsequent letter to her sister said she'd tried to return the locket to Ted but he wouldn't take it.

I tucked that letter back into its envelope and reached for the next one. A chill crept up my back when I saw the postmark next to the three-cent stamp.

December 8, 1941.

I unfolded the letter and saw that it had been written the day before it was mailed. The date at the upper right corner was in Jerusha's handwriting. But the voice I heard in my head was that of President Franklin Delano Roosevelt, saying, as I had heard so many times on the preserved recordings, "Yesterday, December seventh, nineteen forty-one, a date which will live in infamy, the United States of America was suddenly and deliberately attacked by naval and air forces of the Empire of Japan."

Then, as I read the words written on paper, I heard my grand-mother's voice.

Dear Sis,
I don't know where to begin. So I'll start with breakfast. I didn't eat much, just a piece of toast. Everything else seemed to stick in my throat. Then I went for a walk. All I could think about was Ted. I don't know when I first noticed some-thing was wrong. But it was in the air, like vibrations. Maybe it was when I saw that man running down the sidewalk. Why would a man be running on such a quiet Sunday morning?

~ 18 ~

Los Angeles, California, Sunday, December 7, 1941

THE MAN looked agitated, his face red, as he ran down the sidewalk. He was too old and too fat to be running that hard, Jerusha thought. The man ran across the lawn of the house on the corner, up the steps onto the porch, and began pounding on the door. As a woman answered and pulled the man into the house, Jerusha felt a chill run down her back. She stopped, standing very still. Something was wrong. She could feel it in the air, vibrating. Then she whirled and headed back down the hill, quickening her pace until she, too, was running.

As she went up the court's sidewalk toward their bungalow, she heard the radio, blaring loud from the living room. Inside, Anne and Pearl had pulled up chairs on either side of the radio, both leaning toward it as though seeking warmth. Jerusha tried to make sense of the words pouring from the radio.

Pearl looked up, her face grim. "The Japs have bombed Pearl Harbor, in Hawaii. They sank a lot of ships."

"Pearl Harbor? That's where Ted's brother is stationed. On one those big battleships, named for a state." Jerusha felt cold as she searched her memory for the name of the ship. What was it? "The *Oklahoma*. What happened to the *Oklahoma*?"

Pearl shook her head. "I don't know which ships. They haven't said."

They listened to the radio in silence, as the news came over the wire. All eight of the battleships in the fleet were sunk or damaged. The announcer read the names of the ships, his voice tolling like a bell. The *Pennsylvania*, the *Maryland*, the *Tennessee*, the *Nevada*, all damaged. The *West Virginia* and the *California*, sunk. The *Arizona*, sunk, a total loss. And the *Oklahoma*, sunk, total loss.

Jerusha stood up, shaking. "Oh, God, I've got to talk to Ted."

"You need some privacy," Pearl said, switching off the radio. "And I need a stiff drink. I've got a bottle of Scotch in the bedroom."

"I'll join you. Get the bottle and meet me in my room." Anne collected a couple of glasses from the kitchen and followed Pearl out of the living room.

Jerusha reached for the phone and dialed the number. She knew it by heart. There was no answer at Uncle Walt's house. She hung up the receiver and stared into space as she thought about Ted, how they met back in May, and how they'd argued on Thanksgiving Day. The amethyst locket he'd given her was still in her jewelry box. He wouldn't take it back. Now she didn't want to give it back. I still love him, she realized.

She tried the number again. This time Uncle Walt answered. "He's on his way home to Oakhurst. Packed up as soon as we heard the news about the *Oklahoma*. He left an hour ago."

"When will he be back?" Jerusha asked.

Walt sighed. "I don't know that he will be back. He's going to join the Navy."

Jerusha felt tears starting in her eyes. "What's the address in Oakhurst? I'll write to him."

He gave it to her. As soon as she hung up the phone she went back to the bedroom she and Pearl shared. She took the amethyst locket from her jewelry box and hung it around her neck. Then she took out pen and writing paper and started her letter.

~ 19 ~

THE FLYING GOAT coffee shop was located in the old Western Hotel building, constructed around the time the nineteenth century gave way to the twentieth, by the same folks who'd built other still-standing buildings on the square, including the Santa Rosa railroad depot featured so prominently in Hitchcock's *Shadow of a Doubt*. I arrived at ten forty-five and joined the line of java junkies ordering coffees. I eyed the pastries but I certainly didn't need any, not after another one of Cousin Pat's sumptuous weekend breakfasts.

With latte in hand, I found a table near the front. As I sipped coffee I thought about the correspondence I'd been reading. Jerusha had written several letters to Dulcie after Pearl Harbor. One of them mentioned a letter she'd written to Ted after learning that the battleship *Oklahoma* had been sunk during the attack, killing Ted's older brother, Tim. I'd wondered if that letter was among those preserved in the correspondence kept by Aunt Caro, the letters Jerusha and Ted wrote to each other during their courtship and after they were married. So after that Sunday morning breakfast in Graton, I'd driven back over to Santa Rosa for a look at those letters.

Jerusha wrote to Ted on December 7, 1941. The envelope that had held that letter was long gone. Aunt Caro had put the single sheet of paper in a clear protective sleeve. I had not removed it, fearful of tearing it further. Through the clear plastic I read the lines written in now-faded blue ink, front and back of a single sheet of paper. Jerusha told Ted how sorry she was that his brother, Tim, had been killed at Pearl Harbor. Then she told him that she still loved him. "If there's a chance for the two of us, in spite of this war," she wrote, "I'd like to take that chance."

Ted kept that letter, folding it many times, until the creases were fragile and torn in places. I imagined him taking that letter from his wallet, reading it over and over again while his ship plowed through the restless waves out in the Pacific.

The next few letters were also in protective sleeves. Ted had responded to Jerusha's letter, telling her how much it meant to him. He had joined the Navy and he was going to basic training in San Diego. And yes, he still wanted to marry her. He wanted to ask her in person as soon as he could, and he did, en route from Oakhurst to San Diego right after Christmas. That was when he'd given her the engagement ring, the little gold circle with a diamond that she wore, along with her wedding ring, until the day she died. Ted and Jerusha agreed to marry as soon as he finished basic training in the spring of 1942.

Someone else got an engagement ring in December—Anne Hayes. Jerusha mentioned this in her letters to Ted. I had gleaned more detail last night while reading Grandma's letters to Dulcie. The young man Anne had dated in college, Lemuel Sanderson, was now an officer assigned to Camp Roberts, the big Army training base in central California. The two of them had been corresponding and Lemuel, en route to the camp in December, had marriage on his mind. He proposed and Anne accepted, making plans to marry in the spring or summer.

By February of 1942, Jerusha had already made her last movie, the Norma Shearer film *Her Cardboard Lover*. As I read through the correspondence, I learned that she and Anne had been cast as bit players in another film at Metro, one that had been shelved and never completed. Both Jerusha and Anne were finished with the movies. The old gang was breaking up, the war changing everything. Movie careers didn't seem as important as they once had. Real life had intruded on the fantasy. All that was left was cleaning up the details and finishing projects.

Nowhere in the letters I'd read last night and this morning did

Jerusha mention Ralph Tarrant, the actor who'd been murdered on February 21, 1942.

Tory Ambrose entered the coffee house at eleven o'clock, casually dressed in khaki slacks and a T-shirt, a leather purse hanging from one shoulder. She had dark smudges under her eyes, as though she hadn't slept well for several nights running.

"What can I get you?" I asked when she joined me at the table. I'd finished my latte and I wanted another.

"A double-shot latte," she said.

I walked to the counter and ordered. Then I carried the coffees back to the table and sat down. "How are you holding up?"

She sighed. "I found Dad's body, you know, in the entry hall. That's a picture I wish I could erase from my mind. But I can't. I called him from work that day, about two in the afternoon. He didn't answer the phone, so I left a message. I thought he was outside, or running errands. But he would have returned my call when he got home. I called later, around four. He still didn't answer the phone. I just knew something was wrong. So instead of going home after work, I drove up to Healdsburg. His car was in the driveway and he didn't answer the doorbell. I let myself in with my key. I thought maybe he'd had a heart attack. I didn't expect to see him lying on his back in a pool of blood."

I reached for Tory's hand and squeezed it. Words didn't seem adequate to assuage her feelings, or blot out the image imprinted in her brain.

She shrugged. "So how am I holding up? As well as can be expected, I guess. For the past week I've been dealing with the sheriff's department investigators, making funeral arrangements, notifying people about Dad's death, and coping with the family. We're all taking this hard, especially my kids. They loved their grandpa, and they spent a lot of time with him. My brother Dennis and his family left for home first thing this morning. But he'll be back later in the week. We have a meeting with the attorney. We have to deal with all that stuff around the will and the estate. Thank God, Dad put everything in a trust so it's all spelled out."

"A death in the family is rough under any circumstances, and it's worse when it's a murder. You look exhausted, Tory. You need to take care of yourself."

"I know. Or I won't be any good to anyone." She wrapped both hands around her latte, blinking back tears. "It takes a lot of effort to be strong and put on the capable, comforting front. I'm all wound up and running on adrenaline, and tired at the same time. I finally had to take some pills, a sleep aid, last night. I did sleep, but I felt dragged out when I woke up this morning. So now I'm ingesting caffeine to stay awake." She flashed a crooked smile as she raised the coffee cup to her lips.

"To lose Dad like that, it's devastating," she said. "Now I feel like an orphan. My mother died of cancer. That was tough, too. Because it was slow. But it was expected. We knew she was going to die. Mom and I had our problems, but I was Daddy's girl. He was like a rock, always there for me, so supportive. I never would have made it through my divorce without him. In the back of my mind I knew Dad would die eventually. That's something I thought about from time to time after Mom died. Dad was in his seventies, but he was so active and vigorous. I just can't believe he's gone. Especially like this. He was the nicest guy in the world. Why would anyone murder my father?"

I considered the mortality of my own parents and how much I still miss my grandmother. "I don't know. But I'd sure like to find out."

"How does this work, me hiring you?"

"You give me a retainer check. Then I'm working on your behalf." I explained the business details and gave her a copy of my standard contract and an overview of how I worked.

She reached for her purse and took out a pen and a checkbook wallet. "Let's do the business first. I'm not going to tell my brother about this, for now anyway. I know how he'll react. He'll say, let the cops handle it. But they don't have any leads."

"Your brother's reaction is common. I usually work in conjunction with the authorities. Believe me, if I turn up any leads, I'll go to the sheriff's investigator who is handling your father's murder." I took the check she'd written and tucked it in my own wallet.

Tory ran her hands through her hair. "So where do you start?

At the funeral, you told me you'd overheard a conversation, some-one talking about a collection of Hitchcock memorabilia in So-noma County. That must have been Dad's collection. A lot of people know about his stuff, because of the ties to Santa Rosa, with *Shadow of a Doubt* filmed in town. Right here at the depot." She glanced out the window at Railroad Square. "You also said another death might be connected."

I nodded. "That's where I start, with the possibility that your father's murder is somehow connected to his movie memorabil-ia collection. As for the other death, I learned of the death of an elderly woman who lived in Sonoma County. It happened a few months ago. She supposedly fell down her front steps, hit her head, and died as a result of the injury. She also collected memorabilia, primarily Joan Crawford items."

"That sounds like an accident," Tory said with a frown. "Dad was shot."

"Maybe the woman's death was an accident, maybe not. I'm looking into it. Not long after the woman died, her son was con-tacted by a dealer, wanting to buy her collection. It may be too soon after your father's death, but I'm sure you'll get calls from dealers wanting to buy his collection."

Tory grimaced. "It's not too soon. I've already gotten a few calls, right after Dad's death hit the news, because the stories mentioned the collection and that exhibit in the gallery. Ghouls. I just hung up on them."

"In the future, don't hang up," I said. "If anyone calls asking about the collection, I want to know who those people are, where they're located. Would your father have kept any business cards or notes about dealers who contacted him?"

"Possibly. If he did keep any cards, they'd be at his house." Tory sighed. "That's another big item on my to-do list. My brother and I have to go through his things. I haven't even been able to think about that. I'm working up to it."

"Takes time," I said. "For now, I'd like to look at the house, to see if I can find any cards or other information about dealers who may have contacted him."

"You think someone killed Dad to get the collection? That seems far-fetched."

"Maybe. But stranger things have happened. I have pieces that don't fit that theory. If it was just the collection, it would be better to make your father's death seem like an accident, like the elderly woman I told you about. But he was shot. Definitely murder. That seems personal. I wonder if there's another reason, something besides the collection. When I spoke with your father during the gallery opening a week ago, I asked him if he recalled the names of any of the dealers who approached him. He said he might have some business cards. He was trying to recall some names when you joined us."

"I remember," Tory said. "So now what?"

"I'd like to go to your father's house, take a look around, and see if I can find some of this information."

She nodded and pushed back her chair. "Let's go."

I followed Tory's silver Prius onto northbound Highway 101 and we drove to Healdsburg, taking the exit that led us onto Dry Creek Road, which angled north toward Lake Sonoma. The road wound through meadows and hillsides planted with rows of wine grapes. About three miles out of town, Tory signaled a right turn at an intersection. I followed her onto the side road, where blackberry bushes crowded a redwood fence and pines shed needles onto the blacktop. A hundred yards beyond the corner, she slowed and turned on her right blinker. Then she pulled over to the side of the road and stopped, just this side of a row of mailboxes on posts. I did the same. Tory got out of her car and approached one of the mailboxes, using a key to unlock it. She removed the mail and returned to her car. On the other side of the mailboxes were two driveways leading up a hill. Tory turned right into the first driveway. I followed her up the sloping driveway to a double garage, parked, and got out of my car.

The one-story ranch-style house, yellow with green trim, looked as though it had been built in the sixties. The front yard was landscaped with native plants and grasses. A weathered redwood bench sat under the mature oak tree that spread its branches and shaded the yard. Tory unlocked the front door, stepped inside, and disarmed the security system. A poster from *The Man Who Knew Too Much*—the Doris Day–Jimmy Stewart version—hung over a long narrow table in the hall. Framed lobby cards and title cards ranged along the walls on either side of the hall. In the living room, furnished with a comfortable sofa and chairs, were family photos of Mike's adult offspring and their spouses, with lots of pictures of the grandchildren. The living room walls had been decorated with Hitchcock posters, but now just one remained, a poster from *Lifeboat*. The rest were with the memorabilia on display at the gallery in Healdsburg.

"What will you do with his collection?" I asked.

Tory sighed and ran her hands through her hair. "I don't know. I just can't think about that right now. There's so much to do. The house, his safe deposit box. The collection is just part of it. Most of the larger posters are at the gallery. That's where they'll stay for the time being."

The kitchen was painted a cheery yellow. At one end of the oak trestle table a basket overflowed with unopened mail addressed to Mike Strickland. Tory tossed the mail she'd taken from the mailbox onto the pile.

A widescreen TV hung on the den wall, above a stand holding audio-visual equipment. Floor-to-ceiling shelves lined the walls on either side, full of DVDs, videotapes and books. French doors led from the den to the backyard.

"He really enjoyed this house, and living up here in Healdsburg." Tory hung her purse on the back of a kitchen chair. "My brother and I, we grew up on the Peninsula, in Palo Alto. Dad was a lawyer. After Mother died—that was eight years ago—he sold that house and moved up here. I'd just gotten divorced and he wanted to be near me and the kids. I've been living in Santa Rosa for fifteen years. I work for the city."

"So did my uncle," I said. "Neil Lowry. He retired recently from the Planning Division of the Community Development Department."

Tory laughed. "You're kidding. I'm in the Building Division, same department. I know Neil and his wife, have for years. What a small world."

"My Aunt Caro, Neil's wife, is my father's younger sister."

"Who knew they had a private investigator in the family," she said, then, "Dad's office is one of the bedrooms."

I followed her from the kitchen to the other section of the house. The bedroom that looked out on the backyard had been turned into an office. The walls in here were bare as well, save for the picture hangers that had held posters, and a framed diploma telling me that Mike Strickland had a Juris Doctor degree from Boalt School of Law at my alma mater, UC Berkeley. In one corner was a computer table, next to a four-drawer filing cabinet. To the right the computer setup was an old wooden office desk. The phone on the desk was also an answering machine. It blinked numbers, showing that there were eleven messages.

"I don't know where he would keep any business cards from dealers, if he kept them at all," Tory said. "He might not have, since he wasn't planning to sell any of his collection. But go ahead, look through the desk, the filing cabinet, for that matter. Maybe you'll find something that can help pin down his killer." She took a letter opener and picked up the blue recycling bin next to the wastebasket. "I'll leave you to it. I've got to deal with the mail."

After Tory left the office, I walked to the filing cabinet and opened the drawers, looking at file labels. I found the sort of things most people keep in filing cabinets—bank statements, insurance policies, investment paperwork, tax returns.

The bottom drawer of the cabinet, however, contained files on his Hitchcock collection. I scrutinized these more closely, looking at documents showing he'd insured the collection. There were also photocopies of sales receipts from purchases of memorabilia, from shops, galleries and dealers all over the U.S., and some from Europe. The invoice copies were in reverse chronological order, with the most recent purchases first. I flipped through the pages, wanting to know if Mike Strickland had ever purchased anything from the memorabilia shop on Melrose Avenue in Los Angeles, the one owned by Raina Makellar's father, Wallace Simms, and later by Raina and Chaz. Indeed, Mike had. I found two receipts for purchase from that shop, both fairly old. One was dated in April, nine years ago, when Mike bought a title card from Hitchcock's *Strangers on a Train*. Twelve years ago, in September, he bought an insert from *Psycho*.

A correspondence file contained recent letters about the gallery exhibition. Farther down the pile of papers I found letters from dealers offering Mike items for sale, and dealers inquiring about purchasing specific pieces from the collection. Clipped to these were Mike's responses. In the case of inquiries about selling, he'd written that he wasn't interested.

I moved to the old wooden desk and sat down in the gray office chair. There was a weekly desk calendar illustrated, appropriately enough, with art from old movies. I opened the desk drawer to the right of the knee hole and found a stash of letters that looked very much like the ones I'd been reading, only these were from Mike's wife, written to him while he was in the Navy during the Korean War. Another bundle contained letters from an address in San Diego. The name on the return address label was Molly Ransom—his sister Molly Strickland who'd been a bit player—and the letters ranged from the mid-forties, when she had married, up until a few years ago, presumably when she'd died. I was tempted to read the earlier letters, to find out if she said anything about her years in Hollywood, but I didn't want to look at them without Tory's permission.

I pulled out the shallow center drawer and smiled. This was the junk drawer. We all have one, the repository for everything else that doesn't fit anywhere else. In contrast with the neatness and order I'd found in the other drawers, this was a jumble. And here, at the back of the drawer, were business cards.

I spread the cards out on the desk, separating them into categories. Lawn services, plumbers, contractors, insurance brokers, wineries, restaurants, several galleries, an architect and a couple of attorneys—and people who dealt in antiques and collectibles, including a card from one Charles L. Makellar, who listed himself as a dealer in movie memorabilia, with the address and phone number of the shop in Alameda.

So Chaz had indeed paid a visit to Mike Strickland. I turned over the card and saw something written in blue ink—a large question mark and a date. Why the question mark? What did it mean? I consulted the desk calendar. The date was the Wednesday before the gallery opening, the Wednesday before Mike was murdered. That was the same day I'd gone to the shop in Alameda, where I'd overheard Raina Makellar tell her companion that her husband Chaz and their employee, Henry Calhoun, had gone to look for and possibly buy merchandise. That was the day I'd first heard about the man in Sonoma County who had a Hitchcock collection.

I got up from the desk and went to the kitchen. Tory sat, wielding the letter opener over the contents of the basket of mail, now dumped onto the table surface. She kept a steady rhythm, slitting envelopes and pulling out the contents for quick examination. Some papers she set aside for further action, but most she tossed into the recycling bin, already half full of paper, including catalogs and magazines.

"Did you find anything?" she asked.

I showed her the business card and the notation on the back. "This dealer visited your father the Wednesday before he was killed. I assume your father wrote the question mark and the date on the back. But that's just a guess."

"Wednesday, Wednesday." Tory frowned. Then she dropped the envelope and letter opener she held and reached into her purse. She took out a smart phone, the kind that keeps a calendar and a contact list. She punched buttons and consulted the screen. "You know, my kids spent the day with Dad that Wednesday. He came and picked them up in the morning and brought them back in time for all of us to go out to dinner. So my kids were here when that dealer visited Dad. Of course, the boys could have been roaming around, playing. And if I know my daughter, she was holed up somewhere with her nose in a book."

"Maybe they saw or heard something," I said. "I need to talk with them, ask them some questions about that day. Before we do that, though, there are eleven messages on the answering machine in your father's office. I'd like to listen to them."

We walked back to the office. She sat at the desk and grabbed a pencil from the mug and the notepad from the basket. Then she punched the button on the answering machine. The first call, date-stamped the day after Mike's murder, was from a friend of his in LA, saying he was going to be in San Francisco later in the week, and he wondered if Mike was available for lunch. Tory wrote down the number he left. "I'll have to call him and let him know Dad's dead."

The next call was from a roofing contractor, and after that were several hang-ups. The roofing contractor called again, wanting to discuss his estimate. Then there was a call from a memorabilia dealer in Chicago, saying he had a Hitchcock poster for sale, something that might interest Mike. A couple more hang-ups, then three messages from dealers expressing an interest in buying the Hitchcock collection, now that the owner was dead. The last message was from Chaz Makellar, saying he'd discussed a possible sale with Mr. Strickland before his death, and now he was interested in further discussion with Strickland's heirs.

Tory looked up, pencil paused over the notepad. "That's the guy whose name is on that card, the one who was here that Wednesday," Tory said.

I nodded. "Let's see if your kids remember anything about his visit."

~ 20 ~

AS WE LEFT Mike Strickland's house, Tory rearmed the security system. Outside on the front porch, she gave me directions to her home in Santa Rosa. Then we both headed back down Dry Creek Road toward Healdsburg and the freeway on-ramp for southbound U.S. 101. Half an hour later, I parked at the curb in front of a two-story house in an older residential neighborhood, just south of Guerneville Road. Tory led me into the living room, where flower arrangements with sympathy cards attached sat on the fireplace mantel and the end tables on either side of the high-backed sofa. A basket on the coffee table held more cards.

I followed Tory into the kitchen, where the counters held plastic containers of food. More containers were stacked on top of the refrigerator. Bringing food to bereaved families is an old custom, much appreciated. There is so much to do when someone dies that the surviving family members often forget to eat. And when they do need a meal, shopping, planning and cooking are the farthest things from mind.

A counter separated the kitchen from an area that served as dining room and family room. Next to the counter six chairs surrounded an oval table. On the opposite side were a sofa and two chairs. In the grassy backyard, a tree, its branches laden with little green apples, shaded one section of the lawn. Two boys were in the garden along the back fence, dressed in shorts and T-shirts, pulling weeds and lobbing them into a pail.

Tory opened the sliding door, stepped out onto the patio, and called to her sons. "Hey, guys, come here, please. There's someone I want you to meet."

The taller boy stripped off a pair of gardening gloves and tossed them on the grass. The younger boy hadn't bothered with gloves and his hands were stained from contact with the dark, wet soil. Both her sons had Tory's brown hair and slim, wiry build. She put an arm around each boy's shoulders.

"Thank you for pulling all those weeds," she said. "That was really nice of you and I appreciate it. Now, I'd like you to meet Jeri Howard. These are my sons. The older one is David. He'll be thirteen later this year."

"It's nice to meet you, David." I shook his hand.

"And this is Jason, who is ten," Tory said. "And who really needs to wash his hands." She pointed the younger boy in the direction of the kitchen sink and turned to her older son. "Where's Serena?"

David sounded subdued. "Upstairs. I tried to get her to come outside, but... She's been crying again."

Tory sighed. "Okay, thanks." She left the kitchen and I heard her footsteps going up the stairs. I engaged David in conversation, learning that he was in middle school. Jason joined us in the family room, drying his somewhat cleaner hands on a dish towel. He would be in the fifth grade come the fall, he informed me.

A big black-and-white tuxedo cat ambled into the kitchen and came over to inspect me. "That's Tux," David said.

"I can see that." I knelt and stroked Tux's back, and was rewarded with a big rumbling purr. Then the cat jumped onto one of the chairs and began washing himself.

Tory returned, accompanied by the teenaged girl I'd seen at the funeral on Saturday. She'd been crying again, as her brother said, her eyes red and swollen. Dressed in shorts and a flowered camp shirt, the girl was fair where her mother was dark. Perhaps she resembled her father. She looked me over, then turned to her mother, a question in her eyes as to who I was and why I was here.

"This is my daughter Serena. She's fifteen. Serena, this is Jeri Howard. I'd like all of you to talk with Jeri. It's very important and

I want you to answer all of her questions." Tory walked into the kitchen. "I'm hungry. I'm going to make us some lunch. Ham sandwiches all around. Does that sound good?"

The boys reacted enthusiastically and I chimed in. "Thanks, it sounds great."

"Lemonade first," Tory said, taking a pitcher from the refrigerator. She filled glasses with ice and lemonade and I handed them around. She pulled the lid off a plastic container on the counter that separated the kitchen from the family room, revealing a mound of chocolate chip cookies. "Here, help yourself. I'll make the sandwiches." She removed a platter of sliced ham and cheese from one of the shelves, then rummaged around for condiments and bread.

I offered the kids cookies. The boys each took one, but Serena shook her head. I sipped lemonade and set the glass on the table, pulling out one of the chairs. I sat down and looked at the curious faces of Tory's children. The boys were on the sofa. Serena picked up Tux and sat down cross-legged in the chair the cat had occupied. She settled him on her lap and stroked him under the chin. The cat purred loudly and rubbed his head against her hand.

"My name is Jeri. I'm a private investigator," I said.

"Cool." David's eyes widened, sparkling with interest. "Are you gonna find out who killed Grandpa?"

"If I find out any information that will help solve your grandfather's murder, I will turn it over to the sheriff's department investigator." Serena looked interested as well, but she didn't say anything. "I hope I can help. I met your grandfather at the gallery opening and I really liked him. For now I have some questions. Your mother tells me you spent the day with your grandfather, the week before he died. I'd like you to tell me about that day. It was a Wednesday."

"We went on a picnic," Jason said. "To Lake Sonoma."

"That wasn't the beginning," David said. "We should start at the beginning, right?" I nodded. "Okay. Grandpa picked us up early, before Mom left for work. Serena didn't want to go." David and Jason exchanged glances with their sister. She ducked her head and took a sip of her lemonade. "But Mom said she had to go. She didn't want Serena hanging out here by herself, because she'd be, like, going to the mall and all."

"David," Tory said from the kitchen counter, where she was constructing our sandwiches. "Just stick to the facts."

"Like *Dragnet*. That old TV show in Grandpa's DVDs." Jason laughed and gave his Jack Webb impersonation. "Just the facts, ma'am."

"We worked in Grandpa's garden," David said. "I like to garden. I think it's cool. You plant seeds and stuff and later in the summer you've got lettuce and cucumbers and tomatoes. And it was just fun to spend time with Grandpa." He frowned, as though remembering that his grandfather was gone now.

"We fixed our picnic," Jason said. "Sandwiches and cookies and fruit. We went to Lake Sonoma and ate, and hiked around and looked at birds and stuff. We saw an osprey flying over the lake with a fish in his claws. That was really cool."

"What happened when you came back to your grandfather's house?" I asked.

David swallowed a mouthful of cookie and brushed crumbs from his mouth. "We were hanging out with Bobby Miller. He lives next door to Grandpa. We were looking at pictures of ospreys and hawks in this bird book he has. Bobby told us all about this big vacation the Millers are going on and he showed us their tent camper. They'll be gone a couple of weeks. They're gonna visit all these great parks along the way. Glacier, Yellowstone, Grand Teton, Dinosaur, and they're coming back by the Great Salt Lake. What a cool trip. They were going to leave on Saturday."

"But they delayed their trip, just a day," Tory said. "So they could go to Dad's funeral. I think they left today."

That was too bad, I thought, because I probably needed to talk with the Miller boy as well, just in case he had seen anything.

My stomach growled. Tory handed each of us a plate and a napkin, but Serena shook her head. The boys bit into their sandwiches. I picked up mine, ham and Swiss on whole grain, took a bite, and wiped a stray bit of mustard from my mouth.

The cat on Serena's lap roused himself, jumped down, and

came over to rub against my legs, enticed by the prospect of food. "No, Tux," Tory said. "Leave Jeri alone. Here, I'll put some ham and cheese in your bowl. Come on, kitty." The cat perked up and headed for the kitchen. Then Tory came out to the family room, pulled up a chair and sat beside me.

"Is this about those men?" Serena asked. Up until now she'd been silent, but her body language told me she'd been hanging on every word. "Those two men who came to see Grandpa?"

I swallowed a mouthful of my sandwich and chased it with some lemonade. "Tell me about them. When was this?"

"It was the middle of the afternoon, about half an hour after we got back from the lake. I was in the tree, reading."

"The oak tree in the front yard? With the bench underneath?"

Serena nodded. "I like to climb up in the tree. I get on that bench and then there's a low branch. I can get up pretty high, and the afternoon sun makes it nice. And I can see the driveway and the front porch, or some of it anyway. The roof kind of hangs over."

"What did you see?"

"I heard a car come up the driveway," Serena said.

"It wasn't a car, it was an SUV," David said. "A brown one."

Serena looked annoyed at her brother's interruption. "Car, SUV, what does it matter. Anyway, it was brown."

I nodded and glanced at David and Jason. "So you boys saw it, too? Where were you when the SUV got there?"

"Yeah," David said. "We were by Bobby's garage. He was showing us the camper, 'cause it was parked in their driveway. We saw that SUV."

"It parked behind Grandpa's car," Jason added.

"There's those bushes between Grandpa's driveway and the Millers' driveway," David said. "But there's space between them and we could see the SUV and the guy on the driver's side that got out. I couldn't see the guy that got out of the passenger side."

"Well, I could," Serena said. "Because I was up in the tree. I saw two men get out. I got a good look at them."

"What did they look like?"

"One of them was really old," she said. "Older than Grandpa, even. He was short. The other one was about Dad's age, maybe. He was tall and skinny. He had brown hair but it was turning gray."

Chaz Makellar and Henry Calhoun, I thought. "What happened then?"

"The tall man got out of the driver's side," Serena said. "He stretched like he'd been driving for a while. The short man got out of the other side, the passenger side. They went to the porch and rang the bell. I heard it ring but I didn't see them at the front door. They were under the porch roof by then. But I heard them talking to Grandpa after he answered the door."

"Did you hear what they said?" I asked.

Serena shrugged and sipped her lemonade. "Some of it. They must have said something about buying the collection, because I heard Grandpa tell them he wasn't interested in selling anything. They talked a little bit longer. I saw those men step off the porch. They were getting ready to leave. Then Grandpa walked off the porch. I heard him say something. What was it? He said, 'I think I know you. I never forget a face.'"

I leaned forward. "Which of the men did he say that to?"

"I don't know," Serena said. "Where they were standing, there was a branch and leaves in my way. I could see Grandpa, but not those two men. Right after that, they got into the SUV and left."

I thought about what Mike Strickland said to me at the gallery opening, right before he was killed, and three days after his visit from the two men in the brown SUV. He talked about a couple of dealers who'd stopped by his house earlier that week.

You know, there was something about one of those guys, Mike said. *I can't put my finger on it. Maybe I'd seen him before. Don't know where. It'll come to me, though. I never forget a face.*

Whose face? Did Mike recognize Chaz Makellar? Or Henry Calhoun?

I set my plate on the counter and reached for my purse, removing the photos I'd taken of Chaz and Henry unloading the SUV in front of the shop. I showed them to the children. "Do these men look familiar?"

The two boys peered at the pictures and shook their heads. "I guess I didn't get a really good look at them," David said. "Just that one was tall and one was short."

Serena was slower to respond. She looked from one photo to the other. Then she nodded. "Yeah, that's them. They were dressed kinda like that, too. I remember the old man had on long sleeves. I thought that was strange because it was hot that afternoon."

"Sometimes older people get chilled easier," Tory said. "Your grandmother was like that, always cold."

"Thanks, you've been very helpful." I put the photos back in my purse.

"You can go outside now," Tory told them. "I need to talk with Jeri."

The boys erupted from the sofa, setting plates on the table and grabbing more cookies before heading out to the backyard. Serena got up from her chair. "I hope you find out who killed my grandpa."

I smiled. "I'll give it my best. If you remember anything else from that day, you call me. Your mother has my business card."

"Okay." She looked at Tory, then went back toward the stairs.

"She's taking Dad's death so hard. It's good to see her come out of her shell a bit." Tory took a bite of her sandwich. "So Charles Makellar is the dealer who visited Dad and then left that message on the answering machine. Do you think Dad recognized him from somewhere?"

"It's possible." I pondered this while I worked on my sandwich. "Charles is the younger man. He's from Los Angeles. He and his wife, Raina, had a movie memorabilia store down there. They recently set up shop in Alameda. The older man is Henry Calhoun. He works for them, behind the counter, and he also scouts memorabilia to buy. Charles and Henry were out on the road looking for merchandise the week before your father died. I took those pictures on Friday of that week, while they were unloading their purchases from the SUV. I overheard them say that they hadn't been able to buy any Hitchcock items because the owner didn't want to sell. The business card that I found at your father's house confirms that they visited Mike that Wednesday. All three of your children saw those two men, and so did the neighbor boy, Bobby Miller. I want to talk with him as soon as the Millers return from vacation."

"I don't know when they're due back," Tory said. "Maybe the end of next week. So that's why Dad wrote the question mark on the back of the business card. He recognized one of those men."

"That's my theory, anyway." I paused for a sip of lemonade. "While I was looking through your father's filing cabinet I found some invoice copies. He purchased two items from a memorabilia shop owned by Charles Makellar's father-in-law, on Melrose Avenue in Los Angeles. Those sales were nine and twelve years ago."

"Dad was back and forth to Los Angeles all the time," she said, "and not just on business. He grew up in Hollywood, remember. The uncle who was a stuntman back in the thirties had several children and one of his sons also worked as a stuntman. So we have lots of relatives in the LA area, and a lot of that side of the family lives in the San Fernando Valley. Plus my mother was from Pasadena, so there's another set of relatives in that area. Aunt Molly, the one who was the bit player, she and her husband lived in Santa Monica for a long time, then they moved to San Diego."

"Since your father collected movie memorabilia, I'm sure he visited all sorts of shops and dealers in Los Angeles."

Tory nodded. "He was always on the lookout for new things. Maybe he recognized this Makellar guy from that shop."

"Could be," I said. But my earlier background check on the Makellars indicated Raina and Chaz had been married for five years. Mike's purchases at the Melrose Avenue shop predated that by several years. He'd dealt with Wallace Simms, Raina's father. Though it was possible that Chaz had been in Raina's life before the couple tied the knot. Since the Makellars had inherited the memorabilia business, so to speak, it was logical that they would mine Wallace Simms's old contacts for current purchases and sales.

What if Mike had recognized Chaz from another aspect of Makellar's life, his encounters with the law? "What kind of law did your father practice?"

"Patent and trademark," Tory said as she finished off her sandwich. "He retired about ten years ago, when Mom got sick."

Well, that didn't work. At the moment I couldn't envision any scenarios in which Mike Strickland would have legal dealings with Chaz Makellar, the LA hustler who had a record of petty theft and passing bad checks. If I thought about it long enough, I might come up with something.

I finished my lunch and left Tory's house. I was spending Sunday night in Graton, for another session reading Aunt Dulcie's letters from Grandma. I drove west on Guerneville Road, leaving Santa Rosa for the rolling wooded hills of western Sonoma County. When I arrived at the house in Graton, I chatted with Pat and Dulcie, then I retired to Dulcie's room with my laptop computer.

On Thursday when I spoke with Noreen Campbell, Anne Hayes Sanderson's daughter, she told me that her son had recorded Anne talking about her wartime experiences working at Buckley Field in Denver. Noreen's son e-mailed the digital audio file to me on Friday. Now I listened to it again, the early part of the recording, where Anne talked about working in Hollywood as a bit player.

Anne certainly didn't like Sylvia Jasper. I knew from the letters I'd found so far that Sylvia had the habit of helping herself to her housemates' belongings. Instead of contributing to the grocery money stashed in the kitchen, Sylvia was more likely to help herself to the cash. She always said she'd pay it back, but she never seemed to do so. And I knew from reading the witness statements in the police file on Ralph Tarrant's murder that there had been a blow-up, an incident involving Sylvia and her brother Byron, that resulted in Sylvia moving out. Anne's digital interview didn't provide any more details. I closed the audio file and began reading Jerusha's letters to Dulcie. Last night I'd left off with Pearl Harbor and its aftermath. Now I read the letters for the rest of December 1941. War and the changes it wrought made for a subdued holiday season in the little Hollywood bungalow. Early in the new year of 1942, I discovered a letter containing the details about Sylvia's departure.

~ 21 ~

Los Angeles, California, January 1942

"BOTH OF YOU have to leave," Jerusha said. "I don't want to hear any more excuses. We've already asked you to move out. And now this. It's unacceptable. Your brother cannot live on the back porch."

"Don't be such a stick-in-the-mud. Y'all are fussing over nothing." Sylvia's Southern drawl had been grating on Jerusha's nerves ever since the woman moved into the bungalow. And the magnolia syrup got thicker when Sylvia was trying to cajole something out of someone, as she was now.

Sylvia shook a cigarette from a nearly empty green pack of Luckies and stuck it into her lipsticked mouth. She struck a match and touched it to the tip of the cigarette, then extinguished the flame and tossed the match in the chipped saucer that served as an ashtray. Smoke trailed from her nostrils as she looked at her three housemates, standing in a semicircle around the kitchen table. Sylvia shifted in the chair where she sat, one shapely leg crossed over another, stretched like a sleek cat and ruffled her wavy blond hair with her left hand. "Binky's just a little ol' boy, barely eighteen. Y'all have brothers. What's the big deal about him staying here just a spell?"

"He's not my brother," Jerusha said. "And I don't want him living here."

"How long is 'just a spell'?" Pearl asked.

"Too long," Anne said. "The two of you have to leave."

"Oh, come on now," Sylvia said in that wheedling tone. "There's plenty of room for Binky and me on the porch. If you're such shrinking violets about having a fella here, it's not like he's using the main bathroom. There's a toilet and a sink back there. He can shower at the studio. You'll barely see him, just here in the kitchen maybe, getting a cup of coffee in the morning. It's just temporary. Besides, I should think y'all would want someone else contributing to the rent."

Anne glared and put her hands on her hips. "Contributing to the rent. That's a laugh. You're a month behind with the rent."

"You've been taking money out of the grocery kitty again," Pearl added.

Sylvia took another drag on her cigarette. "I didn't take the money. Binky just borrowed a five to tide him over until he gets paid. Now look, it'll be fine. We're both working now and we'll square everything at the end of the month."

"We asked to you to leave in October," Jerusha said, exasperated. "And you're still here."

Sylvia had moved into the bungalow in August, and it didn't take long for the others to realize she wasn't working out as a housemate. Her messiness, her perpetual lateness with the rent, her raids on the grocery kitty, her habit of borrowing clothes and jewelry without asking—all of these got old in a short time. Then there was the day Anne had come home to find the naked man wrapped in a towel helping himself to food in the kitchen. As September gave way to October, there had been another confrontation around the kitchen table, with Anne, Pearl and Jerusha telling Sylvia it was time for her to move out, and soon.

Of course, Sylvia said. She was sorry it hadn't worked out. It would be better for all of them if she left. But she wanted to stay until the end of October, until her younger brother Byron, the one she called Binky, arrived in Hollywood. But he didn't show up until just before Thanksgiving. He got a room at a boarding house and the housemates assumed that Sylvia would be out by the end of November. They were wrong. Sylvia didn't leave. Her excuse was that she had to stay through December. She was working but she really needed to wait until Binky found work so the two of them could afford to rent an apartment. She certainly didn't have the funds to rent a place on her own.

That no-money excuse didn't wash well with Jerusha. Sylvia had plenty of cash to spend on Christmas presents, including a set of gold cufflinks. Jerusha saw Sylvia buying the cufflinks at a jewelry store in Hollywood. Jerusha went in one day in early December, looking for a present for Ted. She was surprised to see Sylvia at the counter, looking at cufflinks. Sylvia had waved Jerusha over to where she stood and asked her opinion. All the jewelry looked ornate and too busy to Jerusha—and expensive. Sylvia had finally selected a pair with a Celtic cross, the design similar to the ring Ralph Tarrant wore that day in the commissary, back in August. Later in December, at the studio, Jerusha saw Tarrant, wearing the cufflinks Sylvia had purchased with a wad of greenbacks.

So Sylvia was lying about having no money to rent an apartment. And Binky was working steadily, as an extra. Sylvia swore she'd be gone by the end of December. But she was lying about that, too.

But this was really the last straw. On this Saturday in January, Jerusha, Anne and Pearl had gone out to lunch with friends. When they came home in the middle of the afternoon, they discovered Binky camped out on the back porch. He'd made a pallet on the floor near Sylvia's single bed and his clothes hung in the makeshift closet next to the half bath with the toilet and sink. He made himself scarce, going out to buy cigarettes, or so he said, and leaving Sylvia to confront her angry housemates.

"Just give us a couple more weeks," Sylvia said now.

Jerusha shook her head as Anne said, "No, no, you have to leave now, and so does your brother."

"It's time for you to shove in your clutch," Pearl said. "We're out of patience and browned off."

The object of the rancor opened the exterior door leading from the backyard to the porch. Byron Jasper strolled into the kitchen, whistling as he tucked a house key into the pocket of his jacket. He was short and slender, about five feet five inches, and he had non-descript hair and a pale face. His eyes were a deep brown, hard like pebbles, and they flickered briefly as he looked from face to face. He stopped whistling and his thin mouth curved into a malicious smile.

"My, my," he said, his drawl a few tones lower than Sylvia's. "What have we here? The Inquisition?"

"We're discussing your imminent departure." Jerusha could barely control her anger. She didn't like Binky any more than she liked Sylvia, and at the moment she wanted to wipe that smile off his narrow face.

"I'm not going anywhere," Binky declared. "I'm tired of living in that boarding house, and you've got plenty of room."

Several voices boiled up at once. Even as she spoke, Jerusha saw Binky's smile mirrored on Sylvia's face. They were enjoying this, she realized. They must have been planning it ever since Binky arrived in Hollywood.

Anne drew herself up to her full height and stared down at the shorter Binky. "No, we don't have room. And we don't wish to share our quarters with a man."

"Not very broadminded of you," Binky said. He stared at the engagement ring Jerusha wore, the tiny diamond Ted had given her for Christmas. "Though you will soon enough. I understand both Miss Anne and Miss Jerusha are getting married."

"I'll share quarters with a man of my own choosing," Jerusha snapped, "and that's not you. We want you out, now, by the end of the day."

Binky touched the corner of his mouth with his right index finger and tilted his head to one side. "Oooh, I'm so scared. Well, I'm not leaving. You can't make me." He pulled out a kitchen chair and sat down next to Sylvia, tearing the wrapper from a new pack of Luckies. He shook out a cigarette and lighted it, his look insolent as he blew out smoke.

Jerusha stared, frustrated, then she turned and walked out of the kitchen, followed by Anne and Pearl. They went back to the room shared by Pearl and Jerusha.

"What the hell are we going to do?" Pearl asked, plopping down on her bed.

"If they won't move, we'll have to do it for them," Jerusha said.

Anne nodded. "You mean, pack up their stuff and put it outside. I suppose you're right. She's given him a key. The locks will have to be changed, so that means talking with Mr. Collier, the landlord. We need some backup, some big strong guys. I wish Lem was here but he's up at Camp Roberts."

"And Ted's in San Diego. But we do have some guys for backup," Jerusha said. "Ted's Uncle Walt in Chatsworth. And we know fellows from the studio, like that stuntman Pearl used to date."

"My cousin Floyd in San Pedro," Pearl added. "I'm sure he and his fishing crew will help."

"And the landlord's son is a nice, big, high school football player." Anne rubbed her chin. "We can't make phone calls from here, not with those two in the kitchen. I'll go down to the store on the corner and use the phone to call Mr. Collier. He's not going to like the idea of that nasty young man living here in his house, any better than we do."

Once the plans were made they came to fruition quickly. Sylvia and Binky left for Metro early Monday morning. Pearl was shooting a film at Paramount, but Anne and Jerusha weren't working, having recently completed projects. The two women quickly packed up all of the Jaspers' belongings. Mr. Collier, the landlord, arrived just before noon, accompanied by a locksmith. He changed the locks on the front and back doors, and gave Jerusha four new keys.

"Thanks," Jerusha said. "As soon as Sylvia's gone we'll find another woman to move in. I hope we have better luck this time."

"Me, too," Mr. Collier said. "So I'll be back tonight, with Albert."

"I'll be glad when this is over," Anne said when he'd gone. "I hate unpleasantness. But sometimes people have to stand up for themselves."

Jerusha sighed. "I agree. It'll be over soon and they'll be gone." She jingled the new keys in her hand. "How long do you plan on staying in Hollywood?"

Anne shook her head. "I don't know. I might take one more job. Lem and I haven't set the date yet. I don't think I want to move back to Colorado until spring or summer." She smiled. "I'll have to get used to all that snow again, after balmy Southern California."

"I'm ready to leave," Jerusha said. "As soon as Ted's finished with training down in San Diego, we're getting married. And once he ships out... I don't really want to go back to Jackson and wait out the war. I want to do something useful. Maybe I'll get a job in a defense plant, start saving money for when he comes back after this war is over."

They were both silent for a moment. Jerusha thought about Ted's brother, Tim, still entombed in the wreckage of the *Oklahoma* at the bottom of Pearl Harbor. She jingled the keys again. "I'm going to stash these in the bedroom. Looks like Pearl will have to get three new roommates before the year is out."

"I'm going to make cookies," Anne said. "I feel like making cookies."

Pearl returned from the studio late that afternoon, accompanied by her cousin Floyd and another strapping young fisherman from San Pedro. They'd picked her up at Paramount in Floyd's rattletrap old truck. They were followed shortly by Ted's uncle, Walt Howard, and Mr. Collier with his son Albert and three classmates. They loaded the boxes containing all the Jaspers' belongings into the truck. Jerusha made another pot of coffee and handed cups around to the assembly who filled the living room to capacity, eating most of the plateful of Anne's freshly baked oatmeal cookies.

It was nearly six o'clock that evening when Jerusha heard a key in the front door lock. The door didn't open. Then she heard Sylvia's voice swearing. "God damn it, they've changed the locks."

Jerusha opened the front door and stepped out onto the front porch. Sylvia stared. Binky was behind her, his face visible in the porch light. "That's right. Mr. Collier had the locks changed this morning. And we've packed your things. They're in that truck out there at the curb. You no longer live here."

"You can't do that," Sylvia spat out. "You can't just kick us out."

"We already have," Anne said. She and Pearl joined Jerusha on the porch. "I'd advise you to go quietly. We don't want any more trouble. If you do make trouble, we have some friends here to see that you leave."

Floyd stepped up behind Pearl. "I'll drive you anywhere you want to go," he said, "one-way trip. 'Course, if you act up, me and my buddies will take your stuff out and leave it on the curb."

Sylvia sputtered in frustration. Binky's face was a mask of cold anger. He took Sylvia by the elbow and pulled her away. Then he stared at the three young women on the porch. "This isn't over," he said. "You may think it is, but it's not."

~ 22 ~

I LEFT GRATON early Monday morning and drove south through Sebastopol and then to Petaluma. Sadie Espinosa had called late Sunday afternoon to let me know that she'd found the business card for the Petaluma detective who'd looked into Roberta Cook's death. His name was Kevin Harper and he was in the Investigations Unit. A short time later we exchanged handshakes and business cards as I explained why I was there.

"Roberta Cook," Detective Harper said. "I looked into it. Especially after the neighbor, Mrs. Espinosa, insisted Mrs. Cook was murdered. But the evidence pointed to an accident. I think Mrs. Espinosa fancies herself as Petaluma's Miss Marple."

I smiled. "Miss Marple was always right."

"Don't remind me," he said. "I have to say this movie memorabilia thing sounds interesting. If you do find a connection to that homicide up in Healdsburg, let me know."

"I will, thanks."

I got on the freeway, heading south toward the Bay Area. Back in Oakland I made a stop at my house and reassured my cats that, despite my many absences lately, I hadn't abandoned them. Then I drove downtown to my office. I kept a late-morning appointment, returned phone calls, wrote some reports, and then I surfed the Internet. I was looking for the poster from the 1932 movie, *Rain*, starring Joan Crawford and Walter Huston. According to Mrs. Espinosa, Roberta Cook had a poster from that movie. It was a three-sheet, a larger poster, measuring forty-one by eighty-one

inches, and Mrs. Espinosa said Mrs. Cook's poster was in mint condition, never folded and without any tears. For that reason, Mrs.
Cook told her friend the poster was worth a lot of money, ten thousand dollars, which made me think she'd had it appraised.

After Mrs. Cook's death last March, Chaz Makellar had
purchased her collection. I'd overheard Raina saying he'd made
a lowball offer to Mrs. Cook's son. I wondered how much Chaz
had paid, and how much the Makellars were selling the poster for
now. I checked the online inventory on the Matinee website, but
I didn't see the poster listed. The movie memorabilia shop was
closed on Mondays, so I had to wait until Tuesday to call. However, I did make another call. Lewis Cook, son of the late Roberta
Cook, was an insurance broker with an office on El Camino Real
in San Mateo. I scheduled an appointment with him on Tuesday
afternoon.

As soon as Matinee opened on Tuesday, I called and Raina answered the phone. I went into my spiel. "I collect Crawford memorabilia," I told her. "I'm particularly interested in pre-Code items
from the thirties. If it's the right item, I'm not concerned about
price."

Raina's voice perked up at the prospect of reeling in a live one
to whom money was no object. "Let me check our inventory," she
said. I turned up my nose at posters for *Grand Hotel*, which I'd
seen, and two movies I'd never heard of: *Dance, Fools, Dance* and
Montana Moon. Then she dangled *Rain* under my nose. "We have
a wonderful three-sheet in mint condition, priced at ten thousand
dollars."

I sniffed. "I've already got something from *Rain*." I resisted her
attempts to get my name and phone number so she could call me
with any hot items.

I worked on other matters until noon, when I left to drive to
San Mateo for my one o'clock appointment with Lewis Cook, son
of Roberta Cook. When the receptionist ushered me into his office, I saw a middle-aged man with thinning hair, a thickening
torso, and a florid face. He smiled as he shook my hand. I sat down
in the chair in front of his wide desk.

Cook settled into his own chair and tented his hands on the wide, uncluttered surface of his desk, preparing to sell me insurance products I didn't need. "Now, how can I help you, Ms. Howard?" I took out a business card and handed it to him. His smile disappeared, the corners of his mouth migrating downward to a frown. "You led my assistant to believe that you were here about an insurance matter."

"I simply made an appointment. Your assistant assumed. My visit concerns your mother, Mrs. Roberta Cook," I said. "She died recently, at her home in Petaluma."

"My mother's death is none of your business," he snapped. "Private investigator, for God's sake. I know who sent you. That old biddy next door, Mrs. Espinosa. She told the police some cockamamie story about my mother being murdered. She's been reading so many mystery books her brain is addled."

"Mrs. Espinosa did express some concerns about your mother's death."

"It was an accident. I'm not surprised she fell down the porch steps. She had osteoporosis and she wasn't very steady on her feet. And it was raining that day. That house was just too much for her." Lewis Cook sounded defensive, as though he was trying to convince himself. I wondered if someone else besides the neighbor had raised the issue of the manner of his mother's death. He had a sister, I recalled from the obituary. But he was his mother's executor.

"I was after her to sell the house and move into assisted living," he said. "But no, she didn't want to leave. Said she wouldn't have enough room for her collection. Collection! That's what she called all that movie crap. Clutter is what I call it. The house was crammed full of the stuff, posters, knick-knacks, programs."

"I'm interested in what happened to the collection, Mr. Cook. Your mother's collection of movie memorabilia."

"That junk? It's gone. I sold it."

"Can you tell me who bought it?"

"Hell, I don't remember. That was a couple of months ago. Is that what this is about? You want to buy some of that movie stuff?"

I let him think what he wanted. "I've been told your mother had some Joan Crawford posters that were collectible. Perhaps I could locate the dealer who purchased the collection. I'm wondering if you have his name in your files."

Lewis Cook thought for a moment. Now that he'd decided I wasn't here to accuse him of negligence concerning Mrs. Cook's death, he was a bit more accommodating. "I'd have to check. I think it was Charles something, with a funny spelling on the last name."

"Could it have been Chaz Makellar? He's a dealer I've heard of, in the East Bay. He has an assistant, an elderly man named Henry Calhoun."

"Maybe. Makellar sounds about right. He did have an old man with him, but I never caught the old guy's name. The younger man is the one I dealt with."

"Did he contact you, or vice versa?"

"He called me," Cook said. "I just wanted to get rid of that junk so I could put the house on the market. I sure as hell wasn't going to pay to store it. I was ready to toss it into a Dumpster. Then I got a call from this dealer. He told me he'd seen Mother's obituary, where it said she collected movie stuff. Said he could probably take it off my hands but he needed to have a look at it first. I told him to come on up to Petaluma. Which he did, him and the old guy. The dealer said it was mostly junk, which is what I figured all along. But he said he thought he could move some of it. He did an inventory and made me an offer I thought was reasonable, so I took it. He wrote me a check. Once it cleared the bank, which it did with no problem, I arranged to meet him at the house. He and the old man showed up in a rental truck, packed up the stuff and hauled it off."

"Do you still have that inventory? I would like to confirm whether your mother had those Joan Crawford posters."

"She did have a lot of Joan Crawford stuff. She always did like Joan Crawford." He swiveled his chair around to face the credenza behind his desk, opened a file drawer and removed a folder. He set the folder on the surface and riffled through some papers. "Here it is," he said. "I was right about the dealer's name. It's Charles Mackellar, in Alameda." He pulled out several sheets stapled together and turned, handing the inventory to me. "The dealer's name is on the top."

"Thanks," I said. I quickly read through the inventory of Roberta Cook's movie memorabilia collection. Makellar had listed the items in lots, such as assorted movie posters, lobby cards, and programs. A notation read, "Assorted Joan Crawford posters, eight." Presumably the poster from the 1932 movie *Rain* was included in that lot. It wasn't noted anywhere else. Makellar had estimated the value of Roberta Cook's entire collection at $5000. A copy of a check for that amount was attached to the inventory.

That was the lowball offer, a pittance compared to what the memorabilia was actually worth on the collectibles market. Lewis Cook, ripe for the taking, was convinced his mother's collection was junk, and happy to get that sum. I wondered how Cook would react if I told him the Makellars were marketing the poster from *Rain* for $10,000.

Caveat emptor, I thought. Or rather the other way around. In this case the seller had been taken. I was still left with the question of whether Roberta Cook had help falling down her porch steps.

~ 23 ~

I RETURNED to Oakland and spent the rest of Tuesday after-noon completing a report for a client. Then I called the office of Pearl Bishop's former agent, but got nowhere trying to find contact information for Pearl, at least not from that source. I powered up my laptop and looked at the notes I'd taken while reading Dulcie's letters from Jerusha.

Pearl Bishop had met her first husband while volunteering at the Hollywood Canteen. Spearheaded by Bette Davis, John Garfield and Jules Stein, the Canteen was a club offering free food and entertainment to men and women in the U.S. and Allied armed forces. It was open from October 1942 through November 1945 and was operated and staffed by volunteers, everyone from stars, directors, producers, writers and technicians to the secretaries who worked in studio offices. Pearl Bishop wasn't the only volunteer to meet a sweetheart at the Canteen. When I had talked with Mike Strickland at the gallery opening in Healdsburg, he'd told me his sister Molly had met her husband the same way.

Pearl Bishop's serviceman was a Marine corporal named Edward Galvin, and she married him in 1943, before he shipped out to fight the island war in the Pacific. During 1944 he fought in the Marshalls and the Carolines, and helped liberate Guam. Then in 1945, the corporal made it as far as Iwo Jima, a small volcanic island south of Japan. The hard-won battle for that island ran from mid-February until the end of March 1945, with heavy fighting and casualties on both sides—including Galvin. In a letter dated March first, 1945, Jerusha told Dulcie that Pearl was now a widow. She'd received the dreaded telegram in late February.

In the postwar years, Pearl dated several men but the relationships didn't last. Then, in 1948, Jerusha wrote to Dulcie with the news that Pearl had married a man named Steve who worked as a grip at Metro. Their son, Carl, was born in 1950. The couple divorced in 1955, with Pearl gaining sole custody of the boy. Unfortunately, Jerusha hadn't told Dulcie the last name of Pearl's husband.

By now it was after five. I drove home and fixed myself a salad for dinner. I was just cleaning up the kitchen when my cell phone rang. I looked at the readout and saw an area code I didn't recognize. I answered the call and heard a woman's voice on the other end of the line.

"This is Mildred Roberson," she said. "I got a call from Noreen Campbell, saying you want to talk with me."

"Yes, I do. I'm Jerusha Layne's granddaughter, Jeri Howard." And Mildred Peretti Roberson was the roommate whose departure had resulted in Sylvia Jasper's moving into the house.

"Hi, Jeri," Mildred said. "Nice to talk to you. Your grandmother wrote me that you're a private investigator. I'm sorry I haven't called you sooner. I wrote your number on a piece of paper when Noreen called, and then that note promptly got buried under some other papers. I unearthed it this afternoon and figured I'd better call. So what is it you want to know?"

"Tell me about your years in Hollywood."

"Oh, yes, Hollywood. I was going to be a big star." Mildred laughed, sounding wheezy over the telephone line. "We all felt that way. We were sure the next break was just around the corner. I was in some good movies, made enough to support myself and to send money home to my folks."

"Why did you leave?" I asked.

"Real life," she said. "More important than making movies and me wanting to be an actress. The war was coming. Anyone who could read a newspaper could see that. And we were still struggling out of the Depression. My dad was a farmer near Lamar, in Prowers

County down in the southeastern corner of Colorado. We were hit hard by the Dust Bowl. It would have made a lot more sense for me to stay in Lamar and work. But I won a talent contest, back in 'thirty-six. My prize was a ticket to Los Angeles and a bit part in a movie. So that's why I left. Me and a lot of other girls."

"Like my grandmother," I said. "Just one year later, in nineteen thirty-seven."

Mildred laughed again. "There were flocks of us, like pretty little birds with stars in our eyes. We lived in rooming houses and apartments, made the rounds of the studios, worked as extras and bit players. I worked steadily, but I never got past playing bits. People can make a living at it. Lord knows Pearl did, for a long time, and she eventually got bigger roles. But I'm a practical sort. When I got to Hollywood I gave myself a time line—five years."

"And the five years were up in nineteen forty-one." I thought of Jerusha's five years, from 1937 to 1942.

"That's right. I went back to Lamar in September of 'forty-one, lived at home, and clerked in a store until early in 'forty-two. I knew I could make more money in war work in Denver. So I moved up there, lived with my aunt, and found a job at Buckley Field. In 'forty-three Anne and Lem got married and later Anne came to Denver. She got a job at Buckley and we shared a tiny little apartment near the base. That's where I met my husband, Jack. He was in the Army Air Corps. We got married in 'forty-four."

I steered the conversation back to Pearl Bishop. "What can you tell me about Pearl? I know you moved into the bungalow in January of 'forty."

Mildred laughed. "Oh, that drafty old back porch bedroom. I wasn't sorry to see the last of that."

"Did you keep in touch with Pearl or my grandmother, after you left Hollywood, and after the war?"

"Your grandmother, definitely," she said. "Jerusha was quite the correspondent. I so enjoyed her letters. Pearl didn't hold a patch to Jerusha, but she did write now and again. All four of us had something in common, besides being bit players in Hollywood. We were from small Western towns. The Colorado contingent, me from

Lamar and Anne from Alamosa. Jerusha and Pearl were the Californians. Your grandmother was born and raised in a little town in the Gold Rush part of the state. She said it was right in the heart of the Mother Lode and her brother worked in a gold mine, the deepest gold mine in the country."

"Jackson. It's on the western side of the Sierra Nevada. Uncle Woodrow worked at the Kennedy Mine until the federal government closed down all gold mining operations in nineteen forty-two. Then he joined the Army."

"Yes, that's right. Her older brother. She had a picture of him. Nice-looking fella. Well, anyway, Pearl was from the other side of the mountains. I remember now, that town that was used as a location in so many movies."

"Lone Pine," I said. The town is at the southern end of the Sierra Nevada, on the eastern side, near Mount Whitney and the Owens Valley. Ever since the Silent Era, Lone Pine had been a favorite movie location. Generations of filmmakers shot movies in the nearby Alabama Hills, from Westerns featuring John Wayne, Gene Autry and Roy Rogers, to classics like Humphrey Bogart's *High Sierra* and Spencer Tracy's *Bad Day at Black Rock*. The area even subbed for frontier India in *Gunga Din*.

"Yes, that's the place. I was there once," Mildred added. "I was in a Western back in the late thirties, something called *The Cisco Kid and the Lady*, with Cesar Romero. We shot exteriors at Lone Pine. That's where Pearl was from."

Maybe she'd retired there, if she was still alive. "I understand Pearl married twice, and her first husband was killed during the war."

"Yes," Mildred said. "Eddie, the Marine. She met him while she was volunteering at the Hollywood Canteen. They weren't married very long. He was killed somewhere in the Pacific. She married again after the war, a man named Steve. He was a grip at one of the studios, Metro, I think. Pearl met him on the set and they started dating. I don't remember his last name, either. Pearl always used the last name Bishop professionally, so that's how I know her. That marriage lasted several years and ended in divorce in the mid-fifties. Pearl has a son from her second marriage. His name's Carl. If she's retired I'll bet she's living with him, or somewhere near him. I hope this helps you find her. I haven't had a letter from her in a long time."

"Thanks, you've been helpful," I said.

Mildred chuckled. "I'm at an age where I don't remember things. It's like my brain cells have gone south. Wait a minute, that's it. A direction."

"A direction?"

"Like north, south, east or west," Mildred said. "The first part of the name of Pearl's second husband, it's a direction. Northcote? No, that was an actor she dated right after the war. Westbrook! That's it. His name was Steve Westbrook."

By Wednesday afternoon, I knew that Steve Westbrook, the grip Pearl Bishop married in 1948, had continued working in the movie industry until his death in the late seventies. More important, I knew where to find his son Carl Westbrook. He worked for the United States Forest Service, at the Mono Basin Scenic Area Visitor Center, located near the town of Lee Vining in the Eastern Sierra. He lived there as well, with his wife.

I opened my Internet browser and sent a search engine looking for the visitor center website and a phone number. A woman answered and I asked if Ranger Westbrook was available.

"He's not here right now," she said. "He's leading a tour. Would you like to leave a message?"

"Actually I'm trying to locate his mother. Her name is Pearl Bishop." Was Pearl still alive? A leading question was one way to find out. "I wondered if she might live there in Lee Vining."

"Pearl?" The woman laughed. "Oh, Pearl is a hoot. Yes, she lives with Carl. I saw her just the other day at the Mono Lake Committee bookshop. Sometimes she helps out a couple of days a week."

I thanked the woman and hung up the phone, a big grin spreading across my face. Pearl Bishop was alive, living with her son in Lee Vining, and still spry enough to volunteer.

I pointed my web browser to the Mono Lake Committee website. I was a member of the committee, an organization dedicated to preserving the unique ecosystem of the lake. The committee's information center and bookstore was located on Highway 395, the main north-and-south route on the eastern side of the Sierra, which also served as Lee Vining's main street. I found the number and reached for the phone, then I replaced it in the cradle. This was a conversation I wanted to have in person.

My calendar for the rest of the week was light, and the weekend was clear. I made some phone calls and rearranged a few appointments. As soon as I got home that afternoon, I went up to the garage apartment and arranged for Darcy, my tenant, to feed the cats during my absence. Then I started packing.

~ 24 ~

THURSDAY MORNING I loaded a cooler of water and provisions into the trunk of my car, tucking it in next to my overnight bag. I carried some camping gear that included a sleeping bag, a deflated air mattress, and a folding chair and table. Just in case, I thought.

The worst of the morning rush-hour traffic had thinned as I headed out of the Bay Area. The road climbed up Altamont Pass, where huge windmills spun against a clear blue summer sky. On the other side of the pass, the highway dipped down into the haze of California's broad Central Valley. I made my way east, past fields, orchards and fruit stands, and stopped in Oakdale for gas, coffee and a bathroom break.

Farther east, the terrain changed, the elevation climbing gradually at first, with rolling hills and knobby outcroppings. Then the Sierra Nevada, the white mountains, loomed in the distance, rising through the summer haze, filling more of the sky as I drove closer. I turned south on California Highway 49, the Mother Lode route that ran from the northern mines up by Downieville, down through Grandma's home town of Jackson, all the way to Oakhurst, where Grandpa was born and raised.

South of the Don Pedro Reservoir I saw a mountainside cross-hatched by huge pipes transporting water to San Francisco from the reservoir behind O'Shaughnessy Dam, in the now-drowned Hetch Hetchy Valley, a twin to the more famous Yosemite Valley. The main route up the steep slope was the New Priest Grade, with its numerous switchbacks. This road climbed less precipitously than the Old Priest Grade, used primarily by locals and those with four-wheel drive. Not by me, though. It was a bit too steep for my taste.

At the Big Oak Flat entrance at the northern boundary of Yosemite National Park. I showed my national parks pass at the entrance and stopped nearby to use the rest room. I wasn't going to the Valley, the magnet for most of the park's visitors. I continued east on Highway 120. It was only sixty miles or so to Lee Vining, but one didn't hurry on this narrow strip of asphalt. Tioga Pass Road, as it was now called, twisted and turned through Yosemite's spectacular scenery. It closed in autumn with the first snowfall and sometimes didn't reopen until late May or early June.

The highway climbed steadily. Huge boulders, carved and deposited by glaciers, lined either side of the road, and I glimpsed a waterfall to my left. At Olmstead Point, I parked, and got out of my car. I was 8300 feet above sea level and the sky was clear and blue. To the south was Clouds Rest, the peak towering nearly 10,000 feet. Nearby I saw the familiar granite profile of Half Dome, photographed many times by Ansel Adams, and climbed by people far more adventurous than I. A ranger had set up a telescope trained on the peak. I peered through the lens. The hikers making their way up Half Dome's sheer granite looked like ants climbing a huge pickle.

Thinking of pickles made my stomach growl. It was after one and I hadn't eaten since breakfast. I returned to my car and opened the trunk, taking out my cooler packed with water and provisions. I made myself a pastrami sandwich and I ate my lunch, sitting on the wide rock railing that edged the parking lot, watching people hike the short trail out to the boulders beyond the parking lot.

Refreshed, I took another swig of water and walked back to my car. Coming down from Olmsted Point I drove along the rim of Tenaya Lake, its cold glacier-fed water a deep blue. At the eastern edge of the lake picnickers walked along the sandy beaches and waded in the shallows. A yellow-bellied marmot, a big rodent common in the park, sunned itself on a boulder near the road as I entered Tuolumne Meadows. I finally left the park at the eastern gate near Tioga Peak. From Ellery Lake, it was downhill, twelve miles of steep road and switchbacks, a road I didn't want to drive at night or during inclement weather.

I was now at the western rim of the Great Basin, which encompasses most of Nevada as well as parts of California and Utah. It's an arid region, the largest North American watershed that doesn't drain into an ocean, and the stark landscape has a beauty all its own. Ahead of me was Mono Lake, which doesn't drain anywhere. This ancient body of water, about seventy square miles, is estimated to be over a million years old. Fed by Eastern Sierra streams that wash in salt and minerals, the lake's fresh water evaporates, and the water becomes become more salty and alkaline than the ocean. It has no fish. Instead it has brine shrimp and alkali flies. Along the lakeshore and rising from the water are picturesque limestone formations called tufa towers. Millions of migratory birds visit the lake each year, feeding on the shrimp and flies, and the large islands in the lake are nesting grounds for California seagulls.

Mono Lake used to be larger. Back in 1941, the Los Angeles Department of Water and Power began diverting water from the tributary streams feeding the lake, depriving it of fresh water. The lake's level dropped drastically and its ecosystem began to collapse. The islands became peninsulas and predators devastated the nesting sites. The exposed lake bed sent particles into the air, damaging the region's air quality. By 1995 the lake level was almost forty-five vertical feet below its pre-diversion level. Mono Lake had lost half its volume and doubled in salinity.

People who love Mono Lake, the stark, eerie landscape surrounding it, and the wildlife it supports, lined up with David and Sally Gaines, who formed the Mono Lake Committee in 1978. They began litigating, winning an important California Supreme Court decision in 1983 and finally, in 1994, a State Water Resources Control Board ruling that set limits on water exports and mandates a water level twenty feet above the lowest level. The water in Mono Lake is rising, slowly. It's not where it should be yet, but the ecosystem is slowly healing.

Highway 120 leveled out as I reached the bottom of the canyon and the junction with US 395. I stopped, watched for an opening in traffic, then turned left and headed north into the small unincorporated town of Lee Vining. The old mining camp has a population of a few hundred people, but that number increases in the summer. Lee Vining is a major hub for recreation on this side of the Sierra Nevada. Visitors are drawn to Mono Lake, Yosemite and the remote ghost town of Bodie, on a high plateau to the northeast. Hikers and campers explore the canyons and there are plenty of places to fish and boat. Some businesses close when winter blankets the Sierra, opening in spring and shutting their doors with the first snowfall. But this is also a popular spot for winter sports, with ski runs at June Lake and Mammoth Lakes, both to the south. Photographers love the area in any season, with its many moods.

And Mono Lake itself is a prime location for birders, a major stopover on the Pacific Flyway. In fact, my father was here for the Mono Basin Bird Chautauqua. I'd left a message on his cell phone to let him know I was on my way over the mountains, but he hadn't yet returned the call. I wanted to see him, of course, but there was also the possibility that the assembled birders had booked all the available lodging in Lee Vining. Maybe I could stay with Dad. It was either that, or the sleeping bag and air mattress in my trunk.

It was just after four in the afternoon when I parked on Third Street, just around the corner from the old dance hall that housed the Mono Lake Committee Information Center and Bookstore. The front steps were crowded with people, many wearing T-shirts with Bird Chautauqua or Audubon Society logos, binoculars and cameras hanging around their necks. Inside the center was stocked with books and souvenirs. The cash registers were doing a brisk business. I waited my turn, leafing through a photo book showing the lake during all four seasons. Then the woman behind the counter finished ringing up a customer and turned to me.

"I'm looking for Pearl Bishop," I said. "I understand she sometimes works here."

"Pearl?" the woman said. "She's not here today. But I did see her awhile ago, over at the Latte Da."

"Thanks." I stepped outside the bookstore and walked back across Third Street. The Latte Da Coffee Café was attached to the El Mono Motel, and it was busy as well. I went inside, queued up to order a latte, and looked around. Then I spotted a couple of likely prospects near the back, four senior citizens, two women and two men, at a table, its surface decorated with red, white and blue poker chips.

I walked toward them. The dealer, a big, grizzled man with a tonsure of gray hair around his balding head, had his back to me. He flexed his fingers and growled, "Down and dirty," dealing the last card in a hand of seven-card stud. He set down the deck without looking at the card he'd dealt himself. He had a pair of tens showing on the table. He glanced at the woman on his left. "Bet your aces, Ida."

Judging from the smile that tweaked her lips, Ida liked the last card she'd been dealt. She tossed a blue chip onto the pile in the middle of the table, sat back, and reached for her coffee cup. The man next to her, bald and skinny, bet his pair of queens, saying nothing as he added his blue chip to the pot. Now the other players looked at the white-haired woman on my right. She had an eight, a nine, and a jack showing, all diamonds, a possible straight or flush. She let them wait as she took a sip from an insulated metal coffee mug with a Mono Lake logo.

"Up to you, Pearl," the dealer said.

Pearl Bishop set down her mug. "Yours, and another one like it," she said in a voice that was equal parts gravel and whiskey. She tossed two blue chips onto the pile as though she were tossing pebbles into a pond.

If her Internet Movie Database bio was accurate, Pearl was pushing ninety, and she looked pretty good for her age, a medium build in green slacks and a striped shirt. Her short white hair was swept back from her wrinkled face and she had bifocals perched on her nose. She had a pretty good poker face, too.

"In or out, Elmer?" Pearl asked the dealer. He grumbled as he took a look at his cards. Then he shook his head and turned his cards face down. Ida and the skinny man called Pearl's bet.

"Read 'em and weep." She chuckled as she displayed a straight flush. Then she pulled her winnings toward her and arranged her already substantial pile of poker chips according to color.

"Got time for another hand?" Elmer asked, shuffling the cards.

Ida consulted her watch. "I can't. My daughter's driving down from Bridgeport and she'll be here in half an hour."

"I gotta go, too," the skinny man said.

"Well, if George is out, we might as well settle up," Pearl said. The poker players tallied their chips. This was a game of nickel-dime-quarter. Pearl was the big winner. At six dollars and seventy-five cents, she'd more than doubled her initial buy-in of three bucks. She stowed her winnings in her purse, a grin on her face. "Pleasure doing business with you."

Ida brushed cheeks with Pearl and tossed her empty coffee container in a nearby trash can. She and George headed for the door. The dealer put a rubber band around the cards, then scooped the poker chips into a flat tin box. He slipped both of these into the canvas tote bag hanging at the back of Pearl's chair. "See you tomorrow?" he said, patting her on the shoulder.

"I'm game. Call me."

He walked slowly toward the front door. I took a step forward. "Pearl Bishop?"

She looked up at me, sharp blue eyes twinkling over the rim of her bifocals. "Who wants to know?"

I smiled at her. "My name's Jeri Howard."

Pearl's eyes widened and she tilted her head back with a raucous laugh. "Jeepers Creepers! It's Jerusha, by damn. You're named for her."

"Now how did you know that?"

"Your grandma once sent me a picture of you. The famous private eye. She used to write me about your exploits. She was so proud of you, said you know your onions. Besides, you look a lot like her. That red hair comes from your Grandpa Ted, though. What in the blue blazes are you doing in Lee Vining?"

"Looking for you."

"Well, you found me." She patted the seat recently vacated by the dealer. "Sit down and we'll beat our gums."

I pointed at her coffee mug. "May I get you a refill?"

She shook her head. "No, one's my limit. Why are you looking for an old relic like me?"

I sat down. "I've been going through Grandma's letters from the years when she worked in Hollywood. They make interesting reading."

"Your grandma always did write good letters. I never did, but she made the effort to stay in touch, and I appreciated that." Pearl sighed. "Now she's gone, and so is Anne. I'm probably the last one standing."

"Mildred's still alive," I said. "I talked with her yesterday."

"She is? Do you have her number? I'd love to talk with her."

I'd jotted Mildred's phone number in my notebook. Now I wrote it on the back of one of my business cards, and gave it to Pearl. "I was trying to locate you. I even called the Screen Actors Guild. Then Anne's daughter connected me with Mildred, who gave me some clues. She said you were from Lone Pine."

"Movies in my blood," she said with a laugh. "Back in the early twenties they filmed a silent picture in Lone Pine. It was called *The Round-Up* and it starred Fatty Arbuckle. My father was an extra in that one. Pa worked the pictures every chance he got. Ma, too. They needed every dollar, especially during the Depression. I went off to Hollywood in 'thirty-seven, same year as your grandma. But I stayed."

"Yes, I've looked at your credits on the Internet Movie Database. I even watched those three episodes you did for *The Fugitive*."

Pearl chuckled. "Ah, David Janssen. Now there was a good-looking man, and such a pleasure to work with. I had fun in the movies and television. And I made a living at it, which was more than a lot of starry-eyed youngsters did. But there comes a time when the parts aren't there for an old gal like me, even if I am spry and have most of my brain cells. Jeri, I'm delighted to see you. We have a lot to talk about. Where are you staying? I think every motel in town is full. It's tourist season. With the Chautauqua this weekend, we're up to our butts in birders."

"I'm not sure just yet. My father's due here for the Chautauqua, and he's staying over at the Lakeview. If he's got room in his cabin…"

"You're bunking with me," Pearl declared. "I live with my son and daughter-in-law. They added on an apartment when I gave up Hollywood and moved north. You can sleep on the sofabed. Can you give me a ride home? I walked over here. It's just a few blocks. Everything in Lee Vining is just a few blocks. I don't drive anymore, you see. At my age I've got no business behind the wheel of a car."

"Thanks for the offer of a bed," I said. "I'll take you up on it."

I looked up just as several people entered the Latte Da and approached the counter. The two middle-aged women in front were talking about Western tanagers. More birders. The tall man was Dad. He didn't see me. He had his nose in a copy of a slim book, *Sierra Birds*. He turned to the younger man next to him and showed him a page in the book. Dad's companion was very attractive, I thought, my gaze lingering. Like my father, he was tall, and his rangy frame filled out a pair of dark khaki hiking pants and a green T-shirt. His hair was dark and curly. He had a nice smile as he nodded, flipped to another page in the birding book and pointed at something.

"There's my father." I stood and waved both hands to catch Dad's attention.

Pearl turned to look at the counter. "Well, I'll be jiggered. He's with my grandson." She upped the volume. "Hey, Danny!"

The dark-haired man spotted her and grinned. Dad waved back, looking surprised to see me. They stepped up to the counter and ordered. Then, with coffee containers in hand, they walked over to join us. As they got closer, I saw that they both wore the same green T-shirt, with a legend that read, LIFE IS GOOD. EAT. SLEEP. BIRD. I'd given Dad the shirt for his birthday, along with a matching baseball cap.

Pearl's grandson leaned over and kissed her. "Hey, Grandma," he said in a pleasant baritone. "Did you clean 'em out at poker?"

"Got a queen-high straight flush. Had more chips than I did when I started."

"What are you doing here?" Dad asked me.

"You haven't checked the messages on your cell phone," I said. "Dad, this is Pearl Bishop."

"Pearl Bishop?" he repeated. "Mom's friend?"

"The same," Pearl said. "Danny, this is my friend Jeri Howard and the fella you're with is her dad."

"Dan Westbrook," he said with a smile and a firm handshake. He and Dad pulled out chairs and joined us at the table.

Pearl beamed as she gazed at Dad. "Timmy Howard. I'd know you anywhere. You look so much like your father. You were about twelve the last time I saw you. Jerusha and Ted drove down to LA with you and your kid sister, Caroline."

A slow smile spread over Dad's face. "I remember that vacation. You took us to Disneyland and Knott's Berry Farm."

Pearl nodded. "And the Santa Monica Pier. You're about four years older than my son Carl, Danny's dad. I live with him and his wife now. He's a ranger at Mono Lake."

"Your father told me about you," Dan said. "He says you're a private investigator."

"Yes, I am. And you?"

"I bird and hike, and try to make a living at it. I do some writing. I'm here to lead some of the Bird Chautauqua field trips. Your father and I ran into each other over at the bookstore and got to talking."

"Wait a minute," I said. "Dan Westbrook. Did you write a hiking guide to Point Reyes National Seashore?"

"That's me."

He smiled again. Such a nice smile. He was about my age, with laugh lines around his blue eyes and some silver threading his dark brown hair. Get a grip, Jeri, I told myself. He's probably married. I didn't see a wedding band on his left hand, though.

"I have a copy of your book on my shelf," I said. "I love Point

Reyes. In April, I hiked the Tomales Point Trail. The wildflowers were spectacular."

"It's one of my favorite hikes in the spring," Dan said. "I have a place over there, near Point Reyes Station. It's just a cabin, really, for weekends. I live in Berkeley."

"I'm in Oakland."

We talked about some of his other favorite hikes, in the Bay Area and the Eastern Sierra. This was his fourth year leading field trips at the Bird Chautauqua. His first outing was to Rush Creek, one of the streams feeding into Mono Lake. Dad was signed up for that trip and he and the other birders were scheduled to meet Dan at 6:30 A.M. tomorrow, at the Lee Vining Community Center.

"Are you coming to the dinner tomorrow night?" Dan asked Pearl.

"Wouldn't miss it." She squeezed his hand.

Dan explained that the Chautauqua tradition was a kick-off dinner on Friday night. "If you'd like to join us, I can arrange it," he added.

"That would be nice," I said. "But if you can't, don't worry about it. I don't know how long I'll be here."

"Where are you staying?" Dad asked. "My cabin's just one room, but we could improvise. Did you bring your sleeping bag and mattress?"

"I did, but Pearl has invited me to stay with her."

"That's right," Pearl said, glancing at her watch. "And we'd better get going. Dan's dad will be home from work soon and we're having barbecued chicken. Tim, you're coming for dinner. No arguments."

Dad grinned. "You'll get none."

~ 25 ~

OUTSIDE THE coffee shop Dan and Pearl got into a green Subaru wagon parked near my Toyota. I followed his car to a rambling one-story wood frame house a few blocks to the west. The old house looked as though it had been added to several times over the years. I parked and took my overnight bag from the trunk. Dan, with Pearl on his arm, waited near the front door. He shepherded us inside, to a spacious, comfortable living room with a fireplace, shelves on either side holding framed photos, books, pottery and baskets. More pictures were lined up on the mantel.

A medium-sized mutt greeted us with a wagging tail. Her rough coat was a mixture of black, tan and rust, and she had one ear pointing up, the other flopping over, giving her a rakish look.

"This is Tinkerbell," Pearl said. "She's a good dog."

Tinkerbell agreed, chiming in with a friendly woof. She nuzzled my hand. I scratched her behind the ears and her tail wagged even faster. Then I set my overnight bag in the hallway leading back to the bedrooms.

"That you, Pearl?" a voice called from the back of the house.

"Me and Dan," Pearl said. "And we've got company."

Tinkerbell trotted ahead of us through a dining room, into a big kitchen. An older woman, her shoulder-length black hair threaded with gray, stood at a work island, spreading cream cheese frosting on a two-layer carrot cake. The news of me as houseguest, and two extra people for dinner didn't faze Loretta Westbrook. She wiped her hands on a dish towel and said hello, a smile on her strong-featured face.

Dan's index finger hovered over the frosting and she moved to intercept him. "Don't you stick your finger in that bowl. You can have it when I'm done, but not until."

"My favorite," Dan said with a grin.

"You'd eat a roof shingle if it had cream cheese frosting on it," his mother told him. "We'll have garlic bread and salad to go with the chicken." She waved her spatula at the stainless steel double sink, where a head of romaine lettuce, already rinsed, sat waiting in a colander, with salad vegetables and an avocado. There was a loaf of sourdough bread on the counter. "Your dad's on his way home and he's bringing Holly. Better fire up the grill."

"Okay," Dan said. He went outside. Tinkerbell noisily lapped water from a big bowl. Then she curled up in a thick plush dog bed in one corner of the kitchen.

"May I help?" I asked.

"You could set the table." Loretta put the last flourish on her cake and set the spatula and bowl at the end of the counter. She pointed me toward a cupboard. "Dishes above, and silverware in the drawer below, and placemats in the drawer next to that. There will be seven of us."

"Tim and I will make the salad," Pearl said. She pointed at the cupboard above the refrigerator. "Tim, there's a big wooden bowl up there. I can't reach it without a step stool, but maybe you can."

Dad removed the bowl and carried it to the kitchen table. I found what I needed and set the oval oak table in the dining room. When I returned to the kitchen, Dad and Pearl were talking a mile a minute while they made the salad. Loretta minced fresh garlic, mixed it with softened butter, and spread it between the slices of sourdough bread.

Dan leaned against the counter, bowl in hand, scraping out the remnants of the frosting with his index finger. He caught my eye and grinned, looking for all the world like a kid. "Want some?"

If I'd been at home, I'd be right there with him. Instead I shook my head. "I like a little cake with my frosting. You go ahead."

"Just as well. It's all gone." He licked the last morsel from his finger and moved toward the sink, where he washed the bowl and set it in the dish drainer. He dried his hands on a nearby towel, took a foil-covered pan from the refrigerator, then grabbed tongs from a crock on the counter. "Jeri, would you get the door?"

"Sure." I opened the screen door and followed him out to the covered patio. Two hummingbird feeders filled with sugar water hung from hooks on the longest horizontal beam. A picnic table stood in the center of the patio, near a large propane gas grill, its lid open, with shelves extending on either side. Dan set the pan on the right shelf and held his hand over the grill itself, feeling the heat.

"How long have your folks lived in Lee Vining?" I asked.

Dan folded back the foil, revealing chicken pieces marinating in a thick, dark red sauce. With tongs, he transferred chicken to the grill. "Mom was born and raised here. This house belonged to her parents and grandparents. My Grandma Nelly, Mom's mother, was Northern Paiute. Her people, the Kutzadika'a, have lived around Mono Lake for thousands of years."

I'd heard of the Kutzadika'a, also called the Mono Lake Indian Community, the remnants of the group that had summered at the lake, moving to the forested regions in the autumn. When gold and silver were discovered on the high plateaus to the north, the lives of the Kutzadika'a were forever altered. The forests that sheltered them in winter were logged for mining timber, and their food supply dwindled, dispersing the community. There weren't many Kutzadika'a left in this area, but those who remained sought federal recognition of their tribe.

"Your father grew up in Hollywood because of Pearl's acting career," I said. "How did he get from there to Mono Lake, and meet your mother?"

Dan smiled. "When Dad was a kid, he spent most of his summers with Grandma Pearl's folks in Lone Pine. So he's always liked the Eastern Sierra. After high school he did a tour in the Army, in Vietnam. When he got out he went to college on the GI Bill, at Sacramento State, studying biology and geology. One summer he had a job here at the Inyo National Forest, at Mammoth Lakes. He met Mom and discovered she was at Sac State, too. So here we are, nearly forty years later. Dad's been with the Forest Service most of that time. Mom teaches at Lee Vining High School."

"You must have moved around quite a bit when you were growing up."

Dan nodded. "At national forests all over Northern California. When Dad was at Shasta-Trinity National Forest, we lived in Redding, which is where I graduated from high school. That's how I come by my love of the outdoors. We were always going hiking and camping. Mom and Dad were glad to get back to this side of the Sierra, at Inyo where he started out. Now he's at Mono. They'll retire here in Lee Vining, because of the house. I'm going to get a beer. Want one?"

"I'd love one, thanks."

Dan went inside. I heard the distinctive buzz of a hummingbird and looked up just as the tiny green bird swooped in and landed at one of the feeders. It was a male Anna's hummingbird, with a distinctive iridescent red gorget. I watched as it stuck its long beak into the feeder, then zoomed off.

I walked out to the backyard, covered with native grasses rather than a lawn. Mono Lake was visible to the east, flat and blue in the afternoon sunshine. To the south, ancient volcanic cones rose, stark and bare, silent and inactive now, but looking as though they could erupt at any moment. The Mono Craters had been quiet for thousands of years, but Panum, close to the lake's south shore, had erupted about 500 years ago, blowing out debris and leaving a huge crater surrounding the collapsed lava dome. The most recent volcanic activity had been about 250 years ago, when a series of eruptions on the lakebed brought Paoha Island to the surface and then higher.

Near the fence line, posts held bird houses and feeders, the latter hosting an assortment of birds. Half barrels and plastic containers held colorful flowers, while a vegetable garden had been fenced to prevent deer and other critters from munching the plants down to a nub.

At the back of the lot, several Jeffrey pines lofted skyward. One low branch of an oak tree held a swing, two lengths of rope attached to a wooden seat smoothed by generations of bottoms. I sat down and pushed off with my feet. The rope creaked as I swung back and forth. A makeshift ladder had been affixed to the oak's thick trunk. I leaned back and spotted a tree house nestled in the tree's higher branches. It looked as though it had been there for a long time.

I heard a rapping sound and looked for the source. On a bare branch near the top of the oak I spotted the red cap on the head of a black-and-white acorn woodpecker. Then a twig snapped behind me. I stopped the swing's motion, and stood up. Dan had returned, a bottle in either hand. He handed one to me. I examined the label, Mammoth Brewing Company's Double Nut Brown. I took a sip. "Nice," I said.

"Yeah, it's one of my favorites."

"That, and cream cheese frosting." I pointed upwards. "Who built the tree house?"

"Mom and her brothers, when they were kids." Dan took a swallow of beer. "It's been well-used by several generations, on both sides. Right now the grandkids like it." The back door opened and closed with a creak and a slap, and Tinkerbell loped across the back yard, flushing birds from the feeders. "There's Dad."

Carl Westbrook's face was tanned and seamed from many years spent in the sun and he had eyes like his mother, blue and twinkling with good humor. He was tall, his gray hair still thick, though receding from his high forehead. He had changed into faded jeans and a T-shirt.

"Great to meet you and your dad," Carl said as he shook my hand. "Mom's talked about your grandmother a lot. They kept in touch over the years. And I remember her and your father from that summer they visited us."

The chicken on the grill sizzled and popped. It smelled delicious and it had been a long time since lunch. Dan set his beer on the table and picked up the tongs, turning over the pieces. "This chicken is almost ready. Hope you've got an appetite."

Carl took a sip of Dan's beer. "I do indeed. I'll go wash up and help your mom."

Dan and his father went into the house, followed by the dog. Dan returned a moment later with a platter. He removed the chicken from the grill and turned off the gas. The rest of the meal waited on the dining room table. Tinkerbell hovered in the doorway, hopeful of cadging a bite, but Loretta sent her back to the kitchen. Carl said grace, blessing the food and the company, and we sat down to eat.

As the food was passed around, I helped myself to a chicken breast, garlic bread and salad. Dad and Dan were on the opposite side of the table, talking about birding and the field trips scheduled for tomorrow. I sat between Pearl and Carl's guest, Holly McGinnis, who was about my age, with short, curly blond hair and brown eyes in a tanned face. She was a state park ranger, at Bodie State Historic Park, the largest and best-preserved ghost town in the American West.

I'd visited Bodie several times and the place had cast a spell on me, because of its fascinating history and current state of "arrested decay," a description coined by the State of California when it took possession of the town in the early 1960s. Bodie, isolated on a high plateau, had sprung to life in 1861 with the discovery of gold. Another rich vein of ore had been located in 1874. At the height of the boom, the town had 10,000 residents, some respectable, others less so. Bodie had sixty-five saloons, numerous brothels and opium dens, and reportedly one murder a day. As happened with many mining towns, the gold ore that had been so plentiful finally dwindled and the gold-seekers moved on to other strikes. Fire took its toll, and remaining buildings were abandoned as people left the area. The last residents departed in the 1940s, leaving behind houses and stores that still had furniture and goods on the shelves.

When I thought of Bodie, I pictured weathered, empty buildings inhabited only by barn swallows and ghosts. But that wasn't really the case. Plenty of tourists made the thirteen-mile trek off Highway 395 to visit Bodie. Rangers assigned to the park lived there as well.

"What do you do all winter?" I asked. "I'm sure you get most of your visitors from spring to autumn, but I can't imagine braving that road in the winter. Even in good weather you've got to take it slow on that last stretch." The last three miles leading into the park are unpaved, with ruts that are hard on a car's undercarriage, particularly if traveling faster than ten or fifteen miles an hour.

Holly grinned. "The park's open, but you've got to be able to get in, with snow transportation, because the snow's too deep for even a four-wheel drive. We do get visitors, though. Photographers just love Bodie with all that snow. Me, I find plenty to do. I read a lot. And play Scrabble. One of the other rangers is a Scrabble nut. I've gotten pretty good at it. I got tired of being whupped."

"In her later years, my mother was quite the Scrabble player," Pearl said. "She and her sister, my Aunt Katie, would get into arguments and accuse one another of making up words. My land, you should have heard them when they were going at it hammer and tongs. Now me, I never was much good at Scrabble. Poker's my game."

"Yeah, Mom." Carl winked. "I hear stories all over town, people talking about you taking quarters off folks down at the Latte Da."

"Keeps me off the streets." Pearl winked back. "Maybe we can play a few hands after dinner."

"I've got a pocketful of change," I said, wiping barbecue sauce from my fingers.

"I'll pass," Dad said. "You always beat me at poker. Besides, early to bed for me, what with that birding trip tomorrow morning."

Dan nodded. "For the next three days. Early morning's the best time to bird. You said you're going on the June Lake field trip Saturday morning. There's a bald eagle's nest with an eaglet, in a dead tree on a hill above the lake."

Dad's eyes lit up. "Wonderful. What a treat to see that."

Loretta speared a wedge of avocado and looked across the table at Carl. "Someone at the market said a bear was spotted over at the county park."

"Does that happen often?" I asked.

"We get a few every year, come down out of the mountains,

looking for food," Carl said. "Black bears don't usually range in the Eastern Sierra. You're more likely to see a mountain lion, but they tend to stay out of sight in the high country. Now, you might see a bear up the canyons, Lee Vining or Lundy, closer to the mountains, and the forested areas. Bears typically eat plants, roots, insects and small mammals. The only reason a bear would come down this far out of the woods is human food, garbage, or something a camper has left out."

"We don't have much of a bear problem here," Dan said. "Now, Yosemite or Lake Tahoe, that's a different story."

"I've seen the damage up close," I said. "A couple of years ago I was in Yosemite Valley, staying at the Lodge. Despite all the signs warning not to, some people left a cooler full of food in their car. The bear peeled the door off."

Holly chuckled. "Oh, yeah. A five-hundred-pound bear can go through a car windshield or the door of a house in nothing flat."

The conversation turned to the state's budget woes, and the threats to close state parks to save money. Everyone in the room thought that was a bad idea.

"Hell, it's a bonehead move," Carl said. "It won't save that much money. If the state parks close we'll have poachers killing the wildlife and the damn pot growers will move in, creating all sorts of environmental damage. It's already a big problem on national forest land. Closing the state parks will just worsen the problem."

"We're already stretched," Holly said. "We need more park rangers and more fish-and-wildlife wardens."

"You're preaching to the choir," Loretta told them. She pushed back her chair and picked up her plate. "Who wants a piece of carrot cake?"

She got a unanimous "yes" vote for that suggestion. We all pitched in to clear the table. While Carl and Loretta loaded the dishwasher, Dan started the coffeemaker. Pearl cut wedges of cake and transferred them onto plates. We talked as we ate the rich dessert, washing it down with coffee.

The clock on the mantel in the living room struck nine, and Holly consulted her watch for verification. "Is that the time? Goodness, I've got to go. I'm spending the night with a friend, then heading back to Bodie first thing in the morning."

"Would you mind dropping me off at the Lakeview Lodge?" Dad asked. "I'd like to get to bed. I have to get up early for the birding trip."

"Oh, sure thing," Holly said. "Just let me get my uniform and bag, and we'll go."

"See you bright and early at the community center," Dan said. "I should probably go to bed, too."

I kissed Dad and walked with him to Holly's Jeep. She started the vehicle and headed toward town, taillights glowing red in the darkness. I heard a series of hoots, and saw a great horned owl perched atop a nearby telephone pole, silhouetted by moonlight.

I called for Tinkerbell, who had come outside. "Come on, Tink. I don't want you to be dinner, whether it's a bear, a mountain lion, or that owl." She woofed at me and we both headed for the front door.

Inside the house, Tinkerbell made a beeline for Dan, who sat on the arm of the sofa. She leaned against his legs, tail wagging as he bent over and scratched her ears. Then he straightened and yawned. "Don't think I'm in the mood for a poker game tonight, Grandma."

"Oh, shoot," Pearl said in mock annoyance. "That's just how I like my opponents, with their guard down."

He laughed. "Some time this weekend, I promise." He kissed her and his mother, gave his father's shoulder an affectionate squeeze, and headed down the hall toward the bedrooms.

"I'll play a few hands with you, Mom," Carl said, "soon as Loretta and I finish in the kitchen and lock up."

I helped Pearl set up the poker chips and cards on the dining room table, then I looked around the living room, at the photos I'd noticed earlier. At first I thought one picture was a younger Dan, but then I realized the planes of the face were different. Pearl came up beside me and tapped the picture frame. "That's Seth, the youngest. He's an engineer, works for the California Department of Transportation in Sacramento." She pointed at another photo.

"This is Elaine. Looks just like her mother, doesn't she? She's the middle child, works as an operating room nurse in Carson City."

At the end of the mantel I saw a snapshot of Dan with two young children, a boy and a girl. Well, that answered the question that had been in my mind since I'd first laid eyes on him and had noticed he wasn't wearing a wedding ring. The children in the photo certainly looked like their father. It was ridiculous for me to feel disappointed. I'd just met the man. "So Dan's married."

Pearl gave me a speculative look. "Dan's divorced. The kids live with his ex and her second husband, in Fresno. What about you?"

"Divorced," I said. "No kids. Just cats."

"Dan likes cats. Almost as much as he likes Point Reyes."

Carl appeared in the doorway. Beyond him I saw Loretta at the dining table, shuffling cards. "Let's play poker."

Pearl winked at me. "Sometimes it pays to draw to an inside straight."

We played poker for an hour or so. I had a few good hands, but Pearl was a formidable player. It was after ten when Carl threw in his hand and said he was going to bed. He let Tinkerbell out one more time, then he and Loretta retired. So did the dog, curling up in her bed as I followed Pearl to her quarters, an apartment with a living room, kitchenette and bedroom. The bathroom had a walk-in shower, and grab bars had been installed throughout the apartment.

"I move pretty good for a woman my age," she said, using the bars to steady herself as she showed me around the place. "But I also believe in an ounce of prevention. Too many old gals fall and break a hip or a leg, and then never get back on their feet. If you can't walk, that's the beginning of that long downhill slide. I walk every day, whether it's downtown or just around the yard, or here in the house when we're snowed in during the winter. And I hold on, every chance I get. I aim to get to a hundred, by damn. Got the genes for it. My ma was a hundred and three when she went."

Pearl opened a closet opposite the bathroom and took out sheets and a blanket. I removed the sofa cushions and pulled out the sofabed. Together we made the bed. A crocheted afghan, blue and white with a daisy pattern, hung over the back of a nearby platform rocker. She picked it up and deposited it at the foot of the sofabed. "This and the blanket should keep you warm enough. It does get chilly at night. We're pretty high in elevation, even if we aren't in the mountains. I'll get you a pillow."

Pearl went into her bedroom. I unzipped my overnight bag and stripped off my clothes, putting on my sleep shirt and striped seersucker robe. I glanced at the nearby bookcase. The shelves held an assortment of large print library books, mostly mysteries and women's fiction. Mixed with these were books about Mono Lake, California history, and the natural history of the Sierra. A framed photograph on top of the bookcase showed Carl, Loretta, their three adult children, and Pearl. Next to this, a small frame held a black-and-white snapshot, its white borders faded to cream, showing cracks, nicks and a torn corner. A man and a woman stood close together, smiling at the camera. From the dress the woman wore, I guessed the photo had been taken in the twenties.

"That's Ma and Pa. I must have been six or seven years old when that was taken." Pearl had returned from the bedroom, wearing a blue cotton nightgown with a matching robe. She tossed a pillow onto the sofabed and approached the bookcase, touching the frame that held the old photo.

"Pa was a farmer in the Owens Valley. His family had been there since the eighteen-eighties. Then Los Angeles built the damn aqueduct in nineteen thirteen and started taking water out of the river, just sucked it dry. Stole it, Pa used to say, hornswoggling people into selling their water rights. Owens Lake dried up and turned into an alkali flat. They still have dust storms to this day. Dad's farm blew away. He and Ma had to work in town, doing what they could to put food on the table and keep a roof over our heads. Let me tell you, Los Angeles Water and Power isn't very popular on this side of the mountains."

"At least water is flowing into both lakes now," I said. "Though it took years of litigation. Thank goodness for people organizing to fight the water grab."

"The birds have come back to Owens Lake. Lots of them, Dan tells me. I haven't been down to Lone Pine since the last of my siblings died. I'm the only one left." Pearl sat down on the platform rocker and fixed me with a sharp gaze. "Now, suppose you tell me why you were looking for me. I've got a feeling it has more to it than nostalgia."

I sat cross-legged in the middle of the sofabed. "Does the name Ralph Tarrant mean anything to you?"

"It sure as hell does." Pearl scowled. "The whole sorry business. What in the world brought that up?"

"A chance encounter with someone who told me Grandma had a relationship with Tarrant and was questioned by the police after he was murdered."

Pearl snorted. "Jerusha didn't have a relationship with Tarrant. They barely knew each other. Who told you such nonsense?"

"A strange old man who calls himself Henry Calhoun, but I doubt that's his real name. He's not what he seems." I described my initial encounter with the man at the movie memorabilia shop. "I wasn't even sure Ralph Tarrant existed, but I found information about him, and his murder, on the Internet. Then I looked for some sort of connection between Tarrant and Grandma. That's why I started reading her letters. Her sister, my Great-aunt Dulcie, kept hundreds of them. They're fascinating. I got drawn in, all the stories about the roommates: Grandma, you, Anne. And Sylvia. Eventually I found a letter mentioning Tarrant. He sat down at the table where the rest of you were eating lunch, in the commissary at Metro."

"I remember," Pearl said. "And I devoutly wish he'd sat at another table. Maybe none of it would have happened. But it did, and we can't play what-if games. Sylvia was a charity girl—that's what we called them in those days—not too particular who she slept with. She took up with Tarrant right after we met him."

"And when he was murdered, the police questioned Grandma. I was in Los Angeles recently and I arranged to look at the case file. Someone gave the police a tip and said Grandma was there."

Pearl sighed. "It was one of those damned anonymous calls.

Whoever made the call told the cops that Jerusha had been dating Tarrant, said she was at his house the night he was murdered, and that she drove off in a Model A Ford, just like the Gasper. But that was my car and I had it that night. Anne was out, too, so Jerusha was home alone, with no one to vouch for her during the time Tarrant was killed, except our neighbor."

"The police interviewed all three of you," I said. "I read your statements."

"That's right. Anne and I went with Jerusha to the police station. I told the cops about me having the car. Jerusha couldn't have gotten over to his house unless she walked or took a bus. I waited in the hallway, pacing up and down, while they talked with her. I was so relieved when she came through that door. The detective who was in charge of the investigation decided he'd been given a bunch of hooey, and your grandma didn't have anything to do with the murder."

"So who gave the police a bogus tip?" I asked.

"I always figured it was Sylvia and that rapscallion brother of hers."

"Why would they do that?"

"Pure cussedness," Pearl said. "And revenge. Because we filed a police report after what they did."

~ 26 ~

Los Angeles, California, January and February 1942

"IT'S GONE!" Jerusha fought back angry tears as she stalked from the bedroom into the living room. "My locket, the gold and amethyst locket Ted gave me. And the rest of my jewelry, and some cash and clothes. Damn Sylvia! And damn Binky, too!"

Anne came out of her bedroom, her face furious. "My jewelry, too. Plus the cash I had hidden in my underwear drawer. She went through my closet and bureau, took my best dresses, my beaded evening purse, and my lace shawl."

"Same here. Clothes, jewelry, my silver picture frame. Everything that was portable." Pearl looked glum. She walked to the kitchen and returned with the coffee tin that had held the grocery money. "Empty. That's probably the first thing they took. I had a feeling something like this would happen, after what Binky said when we kicked them out."

"And the phone calls," Anne said.

The phone calls had started a few days after the housemates had packed up all the Jaspers' things and moved them out of the bungalow, aided by Pearl's cousin Floyd and several others. That was two weeks ago. Now they dreaded the ringing of the phone in the middle of the night. The first few times they answered, they heard a low voice spewing obscenities. Equally disconcerting were the hang-ups. It got to the point where they'd take the phone off the hook before going to bed. Jerusha was planning to go to the phone company, to get their number changed.

Now this. The landlord had changed the locks on the bungalow. Sylvia and Binky no longer had keys, but they'd simply broken a window on the back porch and entered that way, to take their revenge.

All three housemates were working. Pearl was at Fox, filming *This Above All* with Tyrone Power and Joan Fontaine. Anne was at the same studio, in *Moontide* with Ida Lupino and Claude Rains. And Jerusha was shooting *Her Cardboard Lover* at Metro, once again appearing in a picture with Norma Shearer. They'd left the house before dawn. It had already been a long day and now, on Friday evening, they'd come home to chaos. The front door was wide open and an ominous trickle of water dripped over the sill onto the small porch. Inside the little bungalow, the destruction left them temporarily speechless. Slashed sofa cushions leaked stuffing. Pictures and knick-knacks lay in heaps in the middle of the living room. The dishes in the kitchen cabinets were smashed, pieces littering the floor and counter, along with the cutlery from the drawers. Pages ripped from cookbooks were set afire and left smoldering in the kitchen sink, filling the air with smoke. A bottle of milk had been taken from the icebox and hurled at the wall, along with eggs, butter, and a bowl of leftover soup. All four kitchen chairs were tipped over, and two had broken legs and slats. Makeup smeared mirrors in the bedrooms and bathroom. Cosmetics had been dumped into the bathtub and toilet. Both taps in the tub had been turned on and water overflowed. The resulting flood had soaked the rugs in the hall and living room. Anything that was available and easy to carry—jewelry, cash, clothing—was gone.

"Water under the bridge." Anne looked at the towels they'd put down to soak up the flood after they'd turned off the taps in the bathtub. She picked up a fork, its tines bent, and the now-empty box that had held oatmeal. "Let's get this mess cleaned up."

"First we call the police," Jerusha said. "We can't let them get away with it."

"I'm with you," Pearl said. "But they've pulled the phone out of the wall. I'll go next door and use Mrs. Ellison's phone. After I call the cops, I'll call our landlord."

Mr. Collier arrived about twenty minutes later, accompanied by his teenaged son Albert. At first the landlord stood in the middle of the living room, shaking his head in amazement. Albert fiddled with the camera he'd brought with him, sticking a flash bulb into the attachment. Then he started taking pictures. A few moments later, two Los Angeles police officers came up the walk.

It was late when the officers finished taking the report. "Sylvia and Byron Jasper, after you kicked them out, any idea where they would have gone?" one officer asked.

"When they left, my cousin drove them to a boarding house, I don't know which one," Pearl said. "And I don't know if they stayed there. Sylvia is friends with an actor named Ralph Tarrant. Good friends, if you know what I mean."

The cop nodded. "Yeah, I get your drift. You think they're staying with him?"

"Someone at the studio told me they were living with Tarrant," Pearl said. "Just a rumor. But I know Sylvia's been seeing Tarrant on a regular basis. And where Sylvia goes, so does her brother. It's like the two are joined at the hip. I heard Sylvia just started a picture at Columbia. I think Binky might be working at RKO. You can catch up with them at the studios."

"We'll pick them up," the other officer said. "Maybe we can get some of your stuff back. They've probably sold or pawned it."

When the officers left, Jerusha sighed, her hands on her hips. "Now we clean up this mess."

They started with the kitchen. Meanwhile, Mr. Collier and Albert pushed the living room furniture back, picked up the sodden living room rug and dragged it out the front door and around to the back of the house, where they hung it on the line to dry. They came back for the hallway rug. Then the landlord fetched his toolbox and nailed some plywood over the broken window on the back porch. He checked the locks on the front and back doors. "They're okay," he said. "Me and Albert, we'll come back in the morning with some boxes. We can haul all this trash to the dump."

"You're a peach, Mr. C." Pearl smiled. "I'm sure sorry about all this damage. We'll pay for repairs."

"It ain't your fault people are idiots," he said. "You've been good tenants. We can work somethin' out."

It was close to midnight before they got to bed. Early Saturday morning Pearl went out to fetch coffee and doughnuts. After a quick breakfast, they spent most of the morning setting the house to rights. Just before noon, Mr. Collier and his son showed up in a battered Ford pickup truck. The sofa could be reupholstered, they decided. But two of the kitchen chairs were broken beyond repair, so those went to the dump along with the smashed dishes. Mr. Collier said he'd replace the chairs with others from one of his rental houses.

Saturday afternoon they took a break and made the rounds of secondhand stores in the area, looking for a new set of dishes and other kitchen crockery. Mr. Collier returned on Sunday with four chairs that matched and a new rug for the living room.

It was Tuesday before they could get the phone fixed. Late that afternoon, as they arrived home, the phone rang. It was the two policemen who'd taken the report, asking them to come down to the Hollywood station. They piled into the Gasper and Pearl drove the old Model A Ford to the station. Inside the station they were greeted by one of the cops who'd taken the report. "They pawned your jewelry," he said. "One of the pawnbrokers tipped us off when we put out a list of the stolen items. We figure they sold your clothes to a secondhand dealer."

"The money they took is long gone," Pearl said. "But we should be able to get the rest of our stuff back from the pawn shops."

Anne wrinkled her nose. "If Sylvia's been wearing my clothes I don't want them back. But my jewelry, that's a different story."

"We'll lean on them," the policeman said. "They'll cough up the pawn tickets. My partner's got them down the hall."

They followed the policeman to a dingy interview room, where the second officer waited, a bulky man standing near the door. Binky slouched against the wall on the other side of the room. Sylvia paced the floor, wound tight as a spring in her gray skirt and black sweater, a black leather purse clutched under one arm. She held a cigarette, sucking in smoke and blowing it out through her nostrils. Then she stopped and stared at her former housemates, her blue eyes full of venom.

Jerusha spoke first. "My amethyst locket. You stole it. I want it back."

"I don't know what you're talking about." Sylvia tossed her head. She ground out the cigarette in a nearby ashtray.

"Don't give me that bushwa," Pearl said.

Then Anne chimed in. "You're a thief, plain and simple. You took all my cash and jewelry. You ought to go to jail."

"You can't prove anything," Sylvia said. She looked at Binky for support, but he shrank back against the wall, his dark eyes narrowing as the bulky policeman loomed closer.

The cop leaned over Sylvia and spoke in a rough voice. "I got a witness says you pawned that amethyst necklace in a shop on Vine. I ought to lock you up, you and your brother both, after what you did to the house. You two and that limey you been running with, I hear you've been using hop at a nightclub on Sunset. I'll forget I heard that story, so long as you give up those pawn tickets. Better do it quick, before I change my mind."

Sylvia's mouth tightened. Then she reached into the black leather handbag and took out a handful of pawn tickets. She held them for a moment. Then she hurled them at Jerusha's face. "Bitch! I hope you choke on them."

"Get out," the cop growled.

Sylvia tilted her head back and quickly walked out of the room. Binky moved toward the door, stopped and looked back at Jerusha. A malicious smile teased the corners of his mouth. Then he was gone, followed by the big policeman.

Pearl exhaled in a gusty sigh. "Whew, I'm glad that's over."

"I want my locket." Jerusha picked up the pawn tickets. There were seven of them, from different shops in Hollywood and Los Angeles. "Come on. Let's find these places and get our things."

The cop took the pawn tickets from Jerusha. "I'll take care of this. Call me tomorrow. I should have your stuff." They thanked him and returned home, getting back most of their belongings the next day.

~

Jerusha hoped that the matter was closed, but it wasn't. She heard about Ralph Tarrant's murder one rainy Saturday night in February. In the first few days after the story hit the news, there was much talk and speculation making the rounds at Metro. On Wednesday of that week, she completed her bit part in *Her Cardboard Lover*. She was finished with her Hollywood career, finished with all of it, ready to marry Ted.

But Hollywood wasn't quite finished with Jerusha. She got a phone call on Thursday, another invitation to the Hollywood police station, this time for questioning about the Tarrant murder. It was a subdued group that made the trek in the Gasper.

The older detective, a stocky, florid man with thinning gray hair, introduced himself as Sergeant Mulvany. His tall, thin partner was Detective Partin. They asked Jerusha what she was doing the evening Ralph Tarrant was killed.

Jerusha took a deep breath and willed herself to stay calm. "I was at home all evening."

"You were alone?" Mulvany asked.

Jerusha nodded. "It was raining. It seemed like a good night to stay in."

"What did you do all evening?" he asked

"I listened to the radio and mended a dress. And I read for a while before going to bed."

"Can anyone confirm that?" Partin asked.

"Anne and Pearl were out," she said. "But Mrs. Ellison, our next-door neighbor, came over. About seven, I think it was. Some of our mail, a letter for Anne, wound up in her mailbox, so she brought it over. We talked for a bit. Then she went home."

The two detectives looked at each other. "How well did you know Ralph Tarrant?" Mulvany asked.

"I didn't," Jerusha said. "Well, I knew who he was. We both worked at Metro. But I've never made a movie with him."

Partin leaned closer. "What would you say if we told you we got a phone call from someone telling us you were his girlfriend?"

Jerusha's eyes flashed. An anonymous phone call, no doubt, and she had a pretty good idea who'd made that call. She squared her shoulders and lifted her head. "I'd say you were badly misled. I met Ralph Tarrant exactly once, last summer, in the commissary at Metro. My friends and I were eating lunch. He sat at our table and introduced himself. That's all. I saw him from time to time at the studio. I've never had a relationship with that man, not even a friendship." She held up her left hand, where the diamond ring sparkled on her finger. "Besides, I'm engaged to a sailor. His name is Ted Howard and he's in training down in San Diego. He and I have dated steadily since last June."

The two detectives exchanged looks again. "That'll be all for now, Miss Layne. Please wait outside while we talk with Miss Bishop and Miss Hayes."

She left the room and walked out to the hallway, where Pearl and Anne waited, sitting on the benches. They stood up as Jerusha approached. "You're as white as a sheet," Pearl said. "What did they want?"

"They got an anonymous tip that I was involved with Tarrant," Jerusha said.

"Son of a bitch," Pearl said.

"Or just bitch," Anne said. "I know who made that phone call."

Before Jerusha could answer, the detective appeared and beckoned to Pearl. She walked into the interview room. Sergeant Mulvany took out a pack of cigarettes and offered one to Pearl. She shook her head. He fired up a smoke and told Pearl they'd gotten a tip that Miss Layne had used Pearl's car to drive to Ralph Tarrant's house the night he was murdered.

"Your tip is jive," Pearl said. "I was driving my car that night. Had a date, dinner and dancing. I left the house at half past six and got home around ten. So my car was parked outside a chop house and a nightclub all evening. The only other person who has a key to the car is my cousin Floyd, out in San Pedro."

"Who were you with?" Detective Partin asked.

"A soldier. His name is Chuck Ferris. But don't bother looking for him. He was on leave between duty stations and he shipped out Monday morning, headed for Hawaii. Maybe the parking attendant at the nightclub remembers us, but I doubt it." She smiled at the two detectives. "Come on, Model A Fords are as thick as flies in this town. Somebody gave you the hooey about Jerusha and my car."

"You know this guy Tarrant?" Detective Mulvany asked.

"I'm an actress, he was an actor," Pearl said. "I knew who he was. He introduced himself once, in the commissary at Metro. I don't even remember when, except it was last summer. I saw him at the studio. That's about it. I do know he was dating another actress named Sylvia Jasper. She used to live with us, but she moved out in January. I heard a rumor she and her brother, Byron, were staying with Tarrant. Have you talked with them?"

"We heard that rumor, too," Mulvany said, with a slight smile. "Miss Jasper and her brother are on our list. Why did she move out?"

"We asked her to leave," Pearl said. "And when she wouldn't, we made her go. She was pretty angry about it."

"Why'd you boot her out?" Partin asked.

"She was a lousy roommate," Pearl said. "Messy, late with the rent, stole things, you know the drill. We got browned off."

The two detectives exchanged looks, then Mulvany nodded. "I get the picture. You can go now, Miss Bishop."

~ 27 ~

"THAT LOCKET is mine now," I said. "Grandma gave it to me several years before she died."

"Your grandpa gave it to her the fall of 'forty-one. It was really special to her. That's why she was so upset when it turned up missing."

I took a folder from my overnight bag and removed the photographs I'd taken of Henry Calhoun and Chaz Makellar the day I'd seen them unloading merchandise from the SUV. My cell phone's digital camera wasn't the best, and not wanting to be seen, I hadn't been close to either man. But I did have two decent shots of the old man, one in profile and the other revealing three-quarters of his face. I showed the photos to Pearl, pointing at the image of the man I knew as Henry Calhoun.

"Could this be Binky Jasper?" I asked.

Pearl took the photos from me and stared at them. Then she sighed. "I don't know. I just don't know. It's been a lot of years since I saw him. I sure don't look the same as I did in 'forty-two, and he probably doesn't either. Binky was a chameleon. He could take on the coloration of his surroundings. He looked like everyone, and no one. I can't even remember what color his hair was, or his eyes."

"The way I figure it, Henry Calhoun must be Binky Jasper. How else would he know that Grandma was questioned by the police in connection with Ralph Tarrant's murder?"

"Good point." Pearl riffled the edges of the photos with her fingers. "Tarrant wasn't famous. He wasn't even well known. He was just another British expat actor holing up in Hollywood for the duration. Oh, there was plenty of newspaper coverage right after the murder, because of the way it happened, him getting shot and the house set on fire. But the war shoved everything else off the front page. And Sylvia's murder, well, she dropped out of sight that spring. Binky reported her missing in May. She must have been killed right around then. When they found her body in August, she'd been dead awhile. That cop who handled the vandalism situation back in January, he came around again after Sylvia was reported missing. He wanted to know if we'd had any contact with her since then. Jerusha and Anne had left Hollywood by then. I told him that I'd seen Sylvia, from a distance at whatever studio we were working at, but not to speak to, not close up. Not since that day in the police station when she threw those pawn tickets in your grandma's face."

"I wonder if the two murders were connected."

"So did I," Pearl said. "I still do."

I speculated about what could have happened. "Sylvia and Binky are at Tarrant's house, one of them shoots Tarrant and sets the house on fire to cover their tracks. Then they call the police and tell them Jerusha was at the house, that she was dating Tarrant, when it was really Sylvia he was involved with."

"I think Binky was what we called swish, a homosexual," Pearl said. "And I'm betting Tarrant swung both ways, for all that he was dating Sylvia. I saw Tarrant with Binky one night, at that nightclub the cop was talking about. It was a place where people used hop, and by that we meant all kinds of drugs, cocaine and reefer. I didn't like the place, but the sailor I was with that night wanted to stop there. I was heading for the ladies' room at the back and saw Binky and Tarrant coming in the back entrance. I'm just going on body language, but those two didn't look like a couple of buddies out for a drink, if you know what I mean."

"I get the picture," I said. "More like a tryst in the parking lot. So Tarrant's relationship with Sylvia was just camouflage?"

"For all I know, Tarrant was involved with both of them," Pearl said. "He certainly came on to every female he met. He tried to put the moves on Jerusha that day at the commissary. Then Sylvia came along, twitching around like the bimbo she was, and Tarrant took the bait. He was practically drooling. Maybe he was covering the bases, putting on a front for public consumption. That was the Hollywood Code era and contracts had morals clauses in those days. There's something else, though. Jerusha saw Tarrant and Binky together, too, coming out of a hotel. She was naïve about things like that and she told me about it when she got back to the bungalow. She was bothered by it, because Binky saw her. He looked right at her with a nasty expression on his face."

"When was this?" I asked.

Pearl thought for a moment. "It was a few weeks after the scene in the cop shop, and just a week or so before Tarrant was murdered."

"So maybe Binky was the anonymous tipster, getting back at Jerusha."

"Could have been either Sylvia or Binky," Pearl said. "Retaliating for us kicking them out and then calling the cops. What a pair. There was something unsavory about their relationship."

"In what way?"

Pearl shook her head. "Sometimes the Jaspers' behavior toward each other was what I'd call inappropriate for siblings. There was a sexual undertone that made me uncomfortable. Binky came to see Sylvia one night after he got to Hollywood, and the way he kissed her hello, it sure didn't look like a brotherly greeting. But I know Sylvia was crazy about Tarrant. She bought him some expensive presents, a tie and a scarf. I always figured it was the fella who should buy presents for the girl, not the other way around. And her working only as a bit player. He was on contracts, so he was definitely making more money. Later she turned up wearing his ring on a chain around her neck. She said he gave it to her, like it was some kind of engagement present. But knowing how light-fingered she was, I figured she'd stolen it from him. That ring was gold, must have been valuable. Tarrant was wearing that ring the day we met him. There was an inscription inside. Sylvia showed it to me, to prove it was his. *RT from EO 9/1/39.* I remember the date because that's the day the Nazis invaded Poland."

"I'm guessing Sylvia was the same age as you and Grandma, early twenties." Pearl nodded. "How old was Binky?"

"When he showed up at the end of 'forty-one, he claimed he was eighteen. Had to be, to get jobs. But I think he was younger. In years, anyway. At times he seemed really wet behind the ears. But there were other times when he was way too grown-up and cynical. A chameleon, like I said."

"So maybe he was sixteen or seventeen. He'd be in his eighties now." Like Henry Calhoun, I thought. Tarrant, Sylvia, and Binky—that was one strange threesome.

"Think back to nineteen forty-two, later that year after Sylvia disappeared. You said you had seen Sylvia from time to time at the studios. Did you see Binky at all?"

Pearl nodded. "Binky was working as a bit player and extra, all that year. In fact, we were both in a movie at Metro, shot in November and December of 'forty-two. I ran into him on the set shortly after we started shooting. I told him I'd heard about Sylvia's death. He didn't say much about her. After that I spoke with him a time or two, nothing much, just hello."

"What about nineteen forty-three?"

She frowned, and then she brightened. "I remember something. It was right before Christmas in 'forty-two. I overheard Binky talking with someone on the set. He said he'd been drafted, had to report in January. He was going to training at Camp Roberts. I remember the name of the camp, because that's where Anne's husband, Lem, was stationed before he shipped out to the Pacific."

Camp Roberts was a California Army National Guard base now, located a dozen miles or so north of Paso Robles, in the Salinas Valley. I knew that during World War II it had been a big training camp. There was something else about Camp Roberts, I thought, that lingered in the periphery of my mind, something more recent. Maybe I'd read a news article about it. If that were the case, I couldn't remember the substance. It'll come to me, I thought, turning back to the matter at hand.

"If Binky was in the Army, I should be able to find something in the military archives. Maybe the trail's not so cold after all."

Pearl yawned and got to her feet. "I'm all in. Time to hit the hay. I'll see you in the morning."

~

I woke to sunshine streaming through the white curtains on Pearl's living room window and the smell of coffee. Pearl was at the kitchenette counter, filling a mug from a coffeemaker.

"Good morning." I stretched my arms over my head and sat up, looking at my watch on the side table. It was almost seven.

"Same to you," Pearl said. "Hope you had a good sleep." She reached for another mug and filled it. I got out of bed, put on my robe, and crossed the living room as she turned and proffered the mug. I took a sip. The brew was hot, strong and black, just the way I like my coffee.

"I slept very well, thanks."

"Sometimes I do, sometimes I don't," Pearl said. "One of the perils of getting older. I've had my shower and I'm on my second cup. Loretta tapped on the door just a little while ago. She's making waffles if you're interested."

"I'm always up for waffles."

I took another sip of coffee and grabbed a change of clothes from my overnight bag. One quick shower later, I was dressed. Pearl and I went to the kitchen, where Carl, in his ranger uniform, was frying bacon in a cast-iron skillet. Loretta dipped batter from a bowl into a waffle iron. We sat at the kitchen table and ate waffles as fast as they came out of the iron, crisp and brown, with plenty of butter and maple syrup.

Finally I pushed back my plate. "Oh, my, that was good. Nothing like homemade waffles. I'll have to go for a nice long walk to work off all these calories."

"I recommend the Lee Vining Creek trail," Carl said. "You can pick it up across from the Lakeview Lodge, and it goes all the way to the visitor center."

"Are you going to stay for the Bird Chautauqua dinner?" Pearl asked.

"I don't know. It's Friday," I said, thinking out loud. "I don't have anything so pressing that I need to do back in the office until Monday."

"It's a shame to come all this way and head back the next day," Carl said. "Especially when there's so much to see around here."

"Might as well stay awhile," Pearl said. "I'm enjoying your company."

"And I'm enjoying yours," I said. So I stayed another day. I took Carl's suggestion of a long walk on Lee Vining Creek trail. Later I went to the South Tufa area with Dan, walking and talking as we watched seagulls waddle through the clouds of alkali flies with their beaks open.

~ 28 ~

EARLY MONDAY morning I unlocked my Franklin Street office in downtown Oakland and made a pot of coffee to go with the chocolate croissant I'd purchased from a nearby bakery. I checked my messages, returned some phone calls and switched on the computer. I spent the next hour or so working on reports for current cases.

Then I took a break from paying clients and turned my attention to my own personal investigation into the mystery surrounding Jerusha and events in Hollywood, back in 1942. I renewed my search for information on Byron Jasper, known as Binky. When his name first came up in Jerusha's letters to Dulcie, I'd done a background search. With all the interest in genealogy these days, there are plenty of resources. Through one of my many subscriptions, I was able to access United States census data. The seventy-two-year privacy mandate on these records meant that records for the 1940 census were not yet available. I had looked at the 1930 files and found that the Jasper family in Mobile, Alabama consisted of two adults—Earl, occupation businessman, and Martha, occupation housewife, plus four children, two boys, two girls, including Byron Cade Jasper and Sylvia Lucille Jasper, both born in Mobile. The records didn't tell me whether Earl was Sylvia's birth father or stepfather, just that six people with the last name of Jasper had lived as a family unit in 1930.

Byron Jasper arrived in Hollywood late in 1941. During 1942, he worked briefly in the movies as a bit player and extra. After that,

I had nothing. If he were still alive, he'd changed his name, but he wasn't using Byron or Cade or any other variation of his birth name. Binky's paper trail was as empty as that of Henry Calhoun.

Now I had another clue. Late in 1942, Pearl overheard Binky talking about his draft notice, saying he was due to report to Camp Roberts, the big training base in central California. On the National Archives website there's a searchable database of World War II–era Army enlistment records from 1938 through 1946. The disclaimer notice on the web page says the database is by no means complete. And it contains only Army records. If Binky's draft notice had prompted him to join another branch of the service rather than the Army, his name wouldn't be here.

I typed Byron Jasper's name into the space provided for a search. I got fourteen hits. Some of the people whose names came up had Byron as a first or last name, and several had joined the Army while living in Jasper County, Missouri. There were two men with both names. Byron A. Jasper had enlisted in January 1946 in New York City, his race listed as Negro. The other, Byron C. Jasper, white, had enlisted in Los Angeles in January 1943.

This had to be Binky, I thought. Here, then, was a small paper trail, and I could think of one reason why the trail had stopped and I couldn't find anything more recent on Byron Jasper. What if he'd died during the war?

I looked through the resources available on the National Archives website and found state summaries of casualties from World War II, listing service personnel from the states, territories and possessions of the United States. These documents from 1946 had been scanned and put on the website, two pages at a time. First I looked at the Alabama listings, since Binky had been born in that state. I clicked my way through web pages showing a county-by-county listing of casualties, but I didn't find the name Byron Jasper. Then I looked at the California listings. Binky had been living in Los Angeles at the time he enlisted in the Army. There were twenty pages of names for Los Angeles County alone. I clicked through more web pages, looking for the last names beginning with J.

Jasper, Byron C. The name was followed by his Army serial

number. Then came a three-letter abbreviation, PVT, for private. There were three more letters in the last column, reading DNB.

I clicked the back button on my browser, which took me to the list of counties. At the top of the list were links to an introduction and the document's foreword. As I read through the foreword, it cautioned that the names of people listed were those who had died in the line of duty only. I found the abbreviations and their definitions. KIA meant killed in action. M was for missing. Of the others, DOW translated as died of wounds while DOI meant died of injuries. FOD was finding of death. DNB meant died, non-battle. This category included deaths due to sickness, homicide, suicide, and accidents outside combat areas, including training or maneuvers.

I sat back in my chair, frowning. My hunch that Henry Calhoun was Binky Jasper had just run into a very large roadblock. It appeared that Binky was dead, possibly since 1943, the year he went into the Army. Died where? And how? The casualty roster didn't list the dates or location of deaths.

My cell phone rang. I looked at the readout. It was a number I'd recently added to my contact list, while I was in Lee Vining. I flipped open the phone, said hello, and heard Pearl Bishop's voice.

"Jeri, I found a clue. It's a picture. I mailed it to you this morning."

"A picture of what? Tell me about it."

"Me, on the set of the TV series *Lou Grant*," Pearl said, "with the star, Ed Asner. It's a publicity still. I was working on an episode of that series back in 'seventy-eight or 'seventy-nine. I had several scenes, a speaking role. Anyway, I was having a memory fest. I got rid of lots of things when I moved up here to Lee Vining, since I've got smaller digs. But I have a few file boxes with personal memorabilia, I guess you'd call it. I was looking through things from that World War Two–era, remembering living in that house with your grandma and Anne and Mildred, and this picture caught my eye. It was misfiled, you see. The stuff in the boxes is in chronological order."

"What is it about the picture that made you send it to me?"

"The folks in the background," Pearl said. "You see, one day during that *Lou Grant* shoot I saw a bit player who looked familiar. The more I looked at him, the more I thought I knew him. Finally it came to me. He had a lot of years on him, but Jeri, it was Binky Jasper."

"I found Byron Jasper's name in an online list of World War Two casualties," I told her. "He may be dead."

"No way," Pearl said. "The man I saw in the late seventies was Binky. How did this Byron Jasper supposedly die?"

"The casualty list says died, non-battle, which means he could have died in any number of ways, such as an illness or an accident. I don't have a date of death or any details, but he was on the California casualty list."

"Maybe the list is wrong and he didn't die at all."

"It's possible. There's a disclaimer saying the list may not be accurate."

"Jeri, when I saw that picture I was so sure. I had such a flashback, remembering him on the set."

"You shot that *Lou Grant* episode in nineteen seventy-nine." I was on the Internet Movie Database website now, looking at Pearl's credits. I found the episode with Pearl and the year it was made. "You saw Binky on the set at Metro late in 'forty-two, and again in 'seventy-nine. That's thirty-seven years, Pearl."

"I know that. But it was Binky, or someone who looked a lot like him."

"Tell me everything you remember."

"I kept looking at this guy," Pearl said, "thinking his face was familiar. Finally it came to me. It was Binky Jasper. I said to myself, he'd aged well. It was the end of the day. As soon as I could, I walked over to where I'd seen him but he was gone. We were supposed to do some retakes the next morning but he didn't show up for work, even though he was supposed to be there. I asked around and found out he was using a different name, similar to my first husband's last name, Galvin, which is why I remember. Binky was calling himself Hank Calvin."

I clicked on the episode title and read through the names in the credits. "I'm still on the IMDB, looking at the cast list for that *Lou Grant* episode. He's here, Hank Calvin, playing a parking lot attendant."

"That's right," Pearl said. "It was an exterior shoot in downtown LA. In the picture I sent you, I'm talking with Ed Asner in the foreground. In the background you can see Binky handing over some car keys to Nancy Marchand, another cast member."

If Hank Calvin was really Byron Jasper, had he recognized Pearl at the same time she had recognized him? Was that why he hadn't come back to the set?

"Thanks for the lead, Pearl. I'll look into this."

"I want the picture back when you're done with it," she said. "Ed Asner autographed it to me, bless his heart."

I ended the call and sat for a moment staring at the computer screen. I definitely needed a copy of Byron Jasper's death certificate.

I went to the website for the National Personnel Records Center, which contained death records of service members, and read through the information there. Unfortunately access to the files was limited and required authorization. Unless I was a relative or a researcher, forget that route. As a citizen I welcomed the new emphasis on privacy and safeguarding personal information, particularly in this era of electronic records. On the other hand, it made investigations more difficult.

I had to start with Binky's last known whereabouts. What if he'd died at Camp Roberts, where he'd gone for training after being drafted into the Army? I was basing that theory on the definition of "died, non-battle," a category that included accidents during training or maneuvers. I could be wrong, but it was a logical place to start.

If Binky Jasper had died in California, the Department of Health's Office of Vital Records in Sacramento would have his death certificate on file. I did an Internet search for that website and read through the information there, considering my options. Getting an informational copy of a death certificate from the Office of Vital Records involved filling out a form, mailing that and a check, and waiting eighteen weeks for a response. To fill out the state's form, I needed information I didn't have—city and county of death, a date of birth, and a social security number. I also needed a date of death—or a range of dates when the death may have occurred.

The Clerk-Recorder's office in the county where he died would have the information on file. I consulted an online map and realized I had a problem. Camp Roberts was huge, straddling southern Monterey and northern San Luis Obispo counties. In fact, the county line ran right through the middle of the cantonment, the main site for the administrative buildings. So if Binky died at Camp Roberts, which county would have his death certificate? It looked as though most of the streets on the map were on the north side of the line. There was one way to find out. I searched online for the Monterey County Clerk-Recorder's office, which was located in Salinas. I found a number and picked up the phone. While I listened to several voice mail options, I probed the site. The county form for requesting a death certificate was less specific than the state form, but it still required a city and date of death. The county had also contracted with a third-party provider for online orders of vital records, but again, I needed a date of death and a city where the death occurred. All I had were maybes—the year 1943, and Camp Roberts, which didn't come up in the online list of cities.

After wending my way through voice mail, I was given the option to punch a number that led me to a real live person, a helpful clerk in the vital records office. She confirmed that, for administrative purposes, Camp Roberts was in Monterey County.

"Suppose I need a death certificate and I don't know the date of death?" I asked.

"We've got a computerized index here in the office," she said. "It lists the name of the deceased and the date of death, nothing more. Whenever you come in, we'll give you a password for one of the computers. Then you can do a search on the name. When you've got both the name and the date of death, you can get an informational copy of the death certificate."

I thanked her for her help and ended the call. Salinas is about ninety miles from Oakland, two hours down and two hours back. I looked at my calendar for the coming week. It was crowded with commitments. I really didn't have time for a road trip. Who did I know in Salinas who could search through the death records index at the Clerk-Recorder's office and obtain a copy of Binky's death certificate?

I pulled open a desk drawer, took out a small box and sifted through the collection of business cards I'd collected while working on cases. I filed them by location rather than alphabetically, just in case I needed help in a situation like this. Some of them were sadly outdated, though. Behind the tab marked SALINAS, I found a card for Guadalupe Hernandez, a paralegal at a law firm in downtown Salinas. I'd met her a few years ago while working on a case down in Monterey County. I reached for the phone. She was still at the firm and she was in her office this morning. We chatted, catching up on our lives and work, then I told her why I was calling.

"Oh, sure, Jeri. We're on Main Street, just a couple of blocks from the county offices on Alisal. I'm over at the Clerk-Recorder's office all the time. I'll look at the index. If this guy's name pops up with a date of death, I'll get an info copy of the death certificate. Could you spell the name, so I've got it right?"

"That's Byron Cade Jasper." I spelled it out.

"Got it," she said. "I've got your card here somewhere, but give me your contact info. When I've got the certificate, I'll fax it to you, and then mail it."

"Thanks, Lupe. I appreciate your help." I rattled off my address and numbers, then said good-bye. I'd been sitting too long, so I stood up and stretched, working out the kinks in my shoulders.

Camp Roberts. Something about Camp Roberts. What was it? I sat down and stared at the screen on my computer, willing the memory to come.

Of course. Now I remembered. My fingers moved over the keyboard as I did another Internet search. The newspaper article had originally appeared in the *Los Angeles Times*, then it was picked up by several news outlets, including the *San Francisco Chronicle.* When I'd read it, I thought the story was an interesting curiosity. Now it was more than that, possibly a clue.

Several years ago, while demolishing outdated barracks at Camp Roberts, workmen found wallets in the heating ducts of several old buildings. The wallets had been stripped of money, but were still full of personal effects and keepsakes—social security cards, driver's licenses, letters, snapshots, religious medals. Authorities at the camp figured the wallets were stolen from recruits—probably by other recruits—during World War II and the Korean War, emptied of cash, and tossed into the heating ducts, where they'd been remarkably well-preserved. An Army National Guard staff sergeant took on the task of restoring the wallets to their owners. He'd located some of them, still alive after all these years, and in other cases, the heirs of those who had died. Just a few wallets remained unclaimed.

Stealing someone's wallet is one way to appropriate a new identity. The typewritten social security cards of that time could be easily altered. That could explain why Binky Jasper, whose name appeared on a list of World War II dead, could turn up in Hollywood over thirty years later.

I'd learned about the wallet thefts from the newspaper. Now I wondered about newspapers in the Camp Roberts area. Surely they had covered the camp's wartime activities. In Monterey County there were two big newspapers, the Salinas *Californian* and the Monterey County *Herald*. But Salinas was about ninety miles from the camp, and Monterey even farther. King City was closer. And in San Luis Obispo County, the town of Paso Robles was only nine miles from Camp Roberts. Farther south was Atascadero and the county seat, San Luis Obispo, and its newspaper, the *Tribune.*

Camp Roberts probably had a newspaper, I thought, turning once again to the Internet for research. During World War II, the base had been the size of a small city. What was once agricultural land, part of the Nacimiento Ranch, an old land grant, had been turned into a major training site built to accommodate the large number of wartime draftees. By mid-1944, more than 43,000 troops were stationed at Camp Roberts, and that didn't include support personnel. During the war, about 430,000 troops went through training there, an intensive cycle of seventeen weeks, nearly four months. The camp had a Main Garrison, where most of the buildings were located, including the main administrative offices on what was called Headquarters Hill. A smaller East Garrison was located on the heights above the Salinas River. The camp had two training centers—infantry and field artillery—plus a 750-bed hospital and internment camps for German and Italian prisoners of war. When the war ended and the soldiers came home, Camp Roberts became a ghost town, until the Korean War began in 1950.

I explored the website of the Camp Roberts Military Museum and found an article about the Soldier Bowl, the camp's large outdoor amphitheater. Midway down the text was the name of the newspaper, the *Camp Roberts Dispatch*. Where could I find some copies? Other than the museum itself, I could think of one place that might have the newspaper.

The University of California library system is enormous, containing millions of items. It's a useful resource for any investigator. And I'm a Cal alum, a paid-up member of the alumni association, so I had a library card and access to all those books—and periodicals. I pointed my Internet browser to the UC Berkeley library's website. The main building, Doe Library, houses the Newspapers and Microforms collection, which has over 200 newsprint subscriptions and another 900-plus archived on microfilm, with microform reader-printers that have software for scanning articles to a USB flash drive. The newspapers from Salinas, Monterey and San Luis Obispo were there. But the *Camp Roberts Dispatch*, five volumes of newspapers from the years 1941 through 1946, was in the nearby Bancroft Library.

Historian and writer Hubert Howe Bancroft began collecting books and manuscripts back in the 1860s and eventually wrote a thirty-nine-volume history of California and the American West. Because so many of the figures he was writing about were still alive, he'd accumulated original documents, transcribed portions of original archives, and interviewed the people who'd made the history. Bancroft sold his vast collection to the University of California in 1905 and it was now one of the largest and most valuable collections in the United States, containing among other treasures Mark Twain's papers, the university archives, a pictorial collection containing everything from drawings to photographs, and an oral history project full of recordings. The Bancroft also has old newspapers like the Gold Rush–era *Alta California*, and more important to the case at hand, an Army camp newspaper published during World War II.

The online catalog listing told me that five volumes of the *Camp Roberts Dispatch* were stored in an off-campus location. I had to put in a request for the materials and I did so online, asking specifically for the volume that contained newspapers from 1943. A short time later I received an e-mail from a librarian telling me he wasn't sure which volume held 1943, so he'd requested all five, and they'd be available at the Bancroft around three o'clock the following afternoon. The library closes at five, so I made plans to be there before three. That way I'd have a couple of hours to search the newspapers.

For now, it was noon and I had just enough time to grab some lunch before keeping a one o'clock appointment with a new client.

~ 29 ~

LUPE HERNANDEZ called Tuesday morning as I was getting ready to leave my office for an appointment. "Jeri, I found that death certificate. Byron C. Jasper, died March 20, 1943. It says he died in a fire. I'm putting it on the fax machine now."

"Thanks, Lupe. I appreciate your getting to this so quickly. How much do I owe you for the certificate?"

"Call it a favor, and next time I need something in Oakland you can get it for me."

I hung up the phone and heard my fax machine buzz and whir. A single sheet of paper slowly emerged from the machine. I picked it up and examined the copy of Byron Jasper's death certificate. The cause of death was listed as injuries due to fire. I was hoping the fire had merited a story in the *Camp Roberts Dispatch*. At least I had a date to bring the incident into sharper focus. I quickly looked up a 1943 calendar on the Internet. March 20 fell on Saturday that year.

I left the office for my appointment. A couple of hours later, I drove to Berkeley. Parking near the University of California campus is always problematic. I found a public lot on Channing near Telegraph Avenue and walked two blocks north to the campus, heading across Sproul Plaza, site of so many demonstrations, from the Free Speech Movement and the anti-war protests in the 1960s to the current protests about lack of state funding. At Sather Gate, a bridge leads over Strawberry Creek. Though it was late June, the campus was crowded with students attending summer sessions. I angled up the hill past Wheeler Hall and took a path between that building and South Hall, one of the oldest campus buildings. A couple of well-fed squirrels were chasing each other around the trunk of an oak tree. When they saw me, they skittered up the trunk to a branch and looked down at me, chattering a warning. The Bancroft Library fronts on a green space looking east toward Sather Tower and the Campanile, its bells now chiming three. Inside the building I stowed my belongings in the lockers provided for that purpose. Because of the fragile nature of the items in the Bancroft, nothing can be taken into the Reading Room except paper and pencils, and I'd brought an ample supply of both. I showed my ID at the desk on the first floor, then climbed the stairs to the second-floor Reading Room. At the registration desk I was issued a one-day pass, then I went inside the Reading Room. I'd printed out the e-mail I'd received yesterday from the librarian, so now I showed it, then took a seat at a nearby table, waiting for the materials. A short time later, the librarian carried five oversized bound volumes to the table. I stood over the table, the better to see the pages as I opened the first volume, finding a yellowed newspaper dated 1941. It was like holding history in my hands.

I leafed through the first few issues of the newspaper, which had been published weekly, on Fridays. I glanced at headlines on articles and the advertisements, some of which were illustrated. Here was an ad for Muzzy Marcelino and the Fanchon Marco "Girl Revue," set to appear at the Paso Robles Auditorium, and another from a used car lot where one could acquire a 1929 Model A Ford Coupe for the sum of $35, which sounded like pocket change now but was probably a lot of cash in the early forties.

It was tempting to linger, but I needed to find some information about the fire that supposedly took the life of Byron Jasper. I quickly determined that volume three of the *Camp Roberts Dispatch* ran from May 1942 through May 1943.

There was a date and cause of death listed on Byron Jasper's death certificate. But had the fire that claimed his life occurred the same day? He could have been injured days or weeks before that, lingering until he died. I carefully examined the yellowed newspaper, turning the pages dated January and February 1943. I learned that for a buck-fifty, I could get a "ranch dinner" at the Paso Robles Inn, the "Waldorf Astoria of Paso Robles," according to the ad.

The camp really was like a small city. Here was a photo of a singing group comprised of several of the camp's "Negro soldiers," and an article about Tuesday and Thursday music and drama workshops at the Paso Robles USO. There were four movie theaters and the listings changed every week. Each week held a photo and a caption describing a "Roberts Rose," a civilian woman who worked at the camp. Some of these roses had joined up as well, trading civvies for uniforms. And there was a Ping-Pong tournament underway at the recreation halls.

In a February issue, I found an article about Second Lieutenant Emmet E. Heflin, otherwise known as actor Van Heflin. His latest real-life role was a training officer in Battery D, 53rd Field Artillery Training Battalion. In early March I learned that a big Hollywood show was due at the camp, and so was the Broadway play *Claudia*. The newspapers for the following weeks contained an article and photo from a sham battle conducted by the 88th Infantry Training Battalion. The March 19, 1943 edition told me that Bing Crosby and the Clambake Follies had packed them in at the Soldier Bowl the previous Sunday.

In the next issue, dated Friday, March 26, I saw photos from the Crosby show—and a headline that read SOLDIER DIES IN FIRE.

On Saturday, March 20, 1943, a late-night fire had consumed a tool shed located northwest of the Main Garrison at Camp Roberts. Firefighters had extinguished the blaze. On Sunday morning, daylight revealed a burned body in the rubble. The military police had been called in, along with the camp provost marshal, the military police detachment commander, and two special investigators, both sergeants.

The victim had been identified as a recruit at the camp for training—Byron Jasper, from Los Angeles. A second man from Jasper's company was missing, listed as absent without leave. His name was Harold Corwin, from Oakland, California.

So Binky had died. Or had he? I stared at the old newsprint, trying various scenarios. What if Byron Jasper hadn't died in that fire? The man Pearl saw in 1979, the one she was sure was Binky, had been using the name Hank Calvin. The name of the soldier who'd supposedly gone AWOL—Harold Corwin—could easily migrate to Hank Calvin. Or maybe Binky really was dead and this was an exercise in futility. But the prospects intrigued me.

I searched for more information about the fire in subsequent editions of the *Camp Roberts Dispatch,* and found one more article, dated in early April 1943, some two weeks after the fire. The Camp Roberts investigators had determined that arson caused the fire. Did that mean the dead soldier had been murdered, with the missing soldier as the probable suspect? Was fire really the cause of death? Or was the victim dead before the fire consumed his body?

How had the bodies been identified? Did they use dental records back in 1943? Or were there items found on the body that told the investigators the dead man was Byron Jasper? Had the Army investigators, with a missing soldier and a body, simply assumed which was which?

I reached for my index cards and pencils, listing every detail I could find about the fire and the death. I added my own questions, and I had plenty. Had Harold Corwin and Byron Jasper been reported missing from their barracks Saturday night? Were they considered absent without leave until Sunday morning, when the fire's ashes revealed the grisly remains? Why were those recruits together in that shed, after hours?

A fire set to cover one's tracks—I'd read that scenario before, in the LAPD file on Ralph Tarrant's murder. The actor had been shot and his house torched in an attempt to cover up the murder. But a neighbor saw the flames and called the fire department. My theory was that Binky and Sylvia Jasper had killed Tarrant and set the fire. Had Binky, at Camp Roberts, killed the other soldier and set another fire? Or was he really dead? Was I letting my feelings about what was a very personal case get in the way of my judgment? Maybe I wanted Binky Jasper alive, living in Alameda under the name Henry Calhoun.

I shook myself out of this funk. I was finished with the newspapers, so I used a computer terminal to search the Bancroft catalog for Oakland city directories. The library had them, back to the nineteenth century, and including volumes from 1921 to 1941. A note said that no issue had been published in 1942. I requested the volume for 1941 and looked up the name Corwin. I found a listing for Arthur Corwin, his wife Ruth, two sons, Stanley and Harold, and two daughters, Donna and Thelma. Corwin's occupation was listed as cannery worker, and the address was on Brookdale Avenue in the East Oakland district known as Fruitvale. Back in the late nineteenth century, the area had been full of orchards, mostly cherry and apricot, and by the time World War II broke out, Oakland with its major seaport and rail terminus, had a huge canning industry, with food processing plants like the Oakland Preserving Company, the precursor to the now-famous brand Del Monte.

I left the Reading Room, retrieved my belongings from the locker where I'd stashed them, and went next door to the Periodicals Room in Doe Library. There I looked through microfilmed copies of the Salinas *Californian*, Monterey County *Herald*, and San Luis Obispo *Tribune*, searching for more details about the Camp Roberts fire. I didn't find much beyond what had already appeared in the *Camp Roberts Dispatch*. Then I got a roll of microfilm from the *Oakland Tribune* and looked at the newspapers for late March 1943. Sure enough, I found an article, a brief column that said Corwin's parents resolutely denied that the eighteen-year-old private would have deserted.

Were any members of the Arthur Corwin family still living in Oakland? The Fruitvale District had changed quite a bit since World War II. Before the war the population was primarily white. After the war, African Americans moved into the district, but now the majority population was Latino. I rewound the roll of microfilm and returned it to the desk. Ranged along the walls of the Periodicals Room were computers with access to library catalogs and the Internet. I used one of these to log onto the Alameda County Assessor's Office website, which had a searchable online database for property tax information. I typed in the Brookdale Avenue address I'd found in the 1941 Oakland city directory. When I clicked the "submit" button, the tax records came up with a parcel number. The amount of taxes owed on the property made me guess that it had been sold since Proposition 13 capped real estate taxes in 1978. I went to the Clerk-Recorder's website, clicking on the link for real property sales and transfers. Electronic records were available back to 1969. If the property had been sold prior to that, I'd have to go to the county offices to look at microfilms of actual documents, which often had information useful in locating a person, such as the name of the realtor involved in the purchase.

I typed in the last name Corwin and selected "deed" as the document type, then clicked on "submit." My search returned more than a hundred records. There were lots of Corwins in Alameda County. I searched on the name Arthur Corwin. The database didn't return any records. But the name of Stanley Corwin, Arthur's older son, did come up. He and his spouse, Marlene, had owned the property until the late seventies, when it had been conveyed to Joel and Shelley Corwin. The most recent deed, dated just a few years ago, listed the owners as Ramón and Elsa Torres.

I looked at my watch. It was late in the afternoon, after five. I resisted the impulse to go home. Instead I walked back to the parking lot, retrieved my car, and drove to East Oakland. Maybe I could find Ramón and Elsa Torres at home on Brookdale Avenue. The address I sought was just below Thirty-fifth Avenue, where houses were close together on deep lots. I drove slowly along the street, looking at numbers. Then I spotted the house, a classic one-story California bungalow, of a type built in large numbers in the 1920s and 1930s. This one had stucco siding painted pale blue, with orange trim around the double-hung windows. The front porch had thick, square columns and was decorated with clay pots full of succulents and bright red and orange geraniums.

I found space at the curb opposite the house and parked my Toyota. Then I crossed the street and climbed the steps to the porch. When I rang the bell, I heard a dog bark inside the house. But no one answered. I glanced at my watch and saw that it was nearly six. Maybe the people who lived here weren't home from work yet, or they'd stopped for an errand. I took out one of my business cards and scribbled a note, leaving it stuck at the edge of the door.

I went down the steps, car keys in hand, waiting to cross the street after an oncoming car passed. Instead, the gray sedan pulled into the driveway of the blue house. Two people got out, a stocky man in khaki work clothes and a woman wearing jeans and an oversized red-and-white striped shirt. He opened the trunk and took out two canvas bags full of groceries, while the woman reached for a third sack. I turned and intercepted them as they approached their front steps.

"Mr. and Mrs. Torres?"

They stopped when they saw me. I guessed his age as mid- to late-forties. His wife was a few years younger. "Can I help you with something?" he asked.

I had another business card out, ready to hand over. "My name's Jeri Howard. I'm a private investigator. I'm looking for the Corwins, the people who used to own this house. Do you know where I can find them?"

"Why are you looking for them?" Mrs. Torres asked.

"I'm trying to trace a member of the family. His name was Harold."

Mr. Torres shrugged as his wife stepped past me and went up the front steps. She plucked the card I'd left and glanced at it before unlocking the front door. The dog that came barreling out was a medium-sized black-and-tan mutt with some terrier antecedents. He barked at me and sniffed my shoes.

"Stop that, Patch," Mr. Torres said. The dog paid no attention, instead wagging his tail as I stroked his ears. "Never heard of a Harold Corwin. The man who owned the house was Joel Corwin, and before that it was his father, Stan Corwin."

"Stanley Corwin would be Harold's older brother."

"Ramón, the groceries," Mrs. Torres said from the porch.

"Let me get these inside." Mr. Torres hefted his sacks and carried them up the steps and into the house.

I lingered on the porch with Patch and smiled at Mrs. Torres. "It's a nice house. I love these California bungalows."

"We like it, too." She returned my smile. "We rented this house for several years before we bought it. We paid rent to a real estate company that managed the property, so we didn't actually have much to do with the Corwins."

"We did see Joel now and then," Mr. Torres said, returning to the front door. "Like the time that pine tree in the backyard fell over during a storm and hit the back of the house and caused all that damage."

His wife nodded. "Oh, yes. What a mess that was. It broke a window and poked a hole in the roof. We had rain coming in, and pine needles and cones everywhere."

"Joel came over to take pictures of the damage and again when the roofing company people gave the estimate for a new roof," Mr. Torres said. "Another time he had his father with him. The old man was in failing health. Cancer, I think."

"Old Mr. Corwin died. I remember reading his obituary in the newspaper." Mrs. Torres looked at the house's pleasant lines. "When Joel decided to sell, I'm glad he gave us the first opportunity to buy. He told us his grandfather bought the house when it was first built, back in the twenties. The grandfather was a cannery worker, back when there were lots of canneries here in East Oakland. My daughter is a history major at Cal State down in Hayward, so she looked up all sorts of stuff on the neighborhood in the history room at the Oakland library."

"Small world," I said. "My dad taught history at Cal State Hayward. Professor Tim Howard. He's retired now."

"I'll have to ask Laura if she took a class from him. She's going to graduate next year. Right now she has a summer job at the state archives in Sacramento."

"I think I've got Joel's card somewhere," Mr. Torres said. "Let me see if I can find it. He and his wife live in Orinda and he works in the City. I can give you the name of the real estate agent that handled the transaction for us. I'm sure she could put you in touch with him."

He disappeared into the house while I chatted with Mrs. Torres, then returned a few moments later and stepped out onto the porch, carrying a business card. "Found it right away," he said. "Here's his work address and phone number, and that number written on the back is a cell phone number. Now, he gave me this card several years ago, when we bought the house. So I don't know if any of this information is current. I'd guess he's in his early sixties, probably still working."

"It's helpful, and a place to start." I jotted down the information. Joel Corwin worked for Wells Fargo Bank, at their offices in the San Francisco Financial District. Maybe he was still there, and if he wasn't I could get a lead on his whereabouts. I thanked Mr. and Mrs. Torres and gave Patch one last ear scratch. Then I headed for my car, where I took out my cell phone and punched in Joel Corwin's cell phone number. I got voice mail, no name, just a recording advising me to leave a message of my own. So I did. Then I started my car and headed home.

~

Pearl's photograph, an eight-by-ten-inch color glossy, arrived in Wednesday's mail. Ed Asner, who played the lead role of the crusty Los Angeles newspaper editor in the television series *Lou Grant*, was in the foreground of the picture. To his right was a younger version of Pearl Bishop, in a tailored business suit. Both had smiles on their faces as they talked. It looked as though they were sharing a joke. At the top of the photo Asner had scrawled a short note to Pearl and signed his name. To Asner's left, in the background, was actress Nancy Marchand, playing the newspaper publisher. She stood at the driver's-side door of a car. With her was a short man wearing nondescript clothes, the bit player as parking attendant. He held a set of car keys over her palm. I could see most of his face, but the image was small.

I took my digital camera from a drawer and used it to photograph the face in the picture, zooming in as much as I could. Then I uploaded the photo to my computer and enlarged it. The result was grainy and slightly blurred but I could see the man's face clearly enough. I opened the digital photo of Henry Calhoun, taken while he and Chaz Makellar unloaded the SUV in front of the shop. I arranged the photos so they were side by side on the screen. Thirty years separated the images and Calhoun was in his eighties. Was he also the anonymous-looking man, middle-aged and ordinary, in Pearl's photo? There was a resemblance, but it was slight. Because of the age difference, I couldn't be sure.

Pearl said Binky Jasper was a chameleon, taking on the coloration of his surroundings. I wouldn't have given the man in the photo a second glance, unless I had a reason to do so.

After Pearl's phone call on Monday I had done some online research about Hank Calvin, the name Pearl said the actor had been using when he'd played the parking attendant in that episode of *Lou Grant*. I saw a list of credits that encompassed thirty-five years, starting in 1946, the year after World War II ended, and extending to 1981. In the forties and fifties it was mostly movie work. I'd even heard of some of the films, a couple of fifties noir movies directed by Samuel Fuller, and the rousing Western *The Jayhawkers*, starring Jeff Chandler and Fess Parker. From the early sixties on, Calvin's credits were primarily television work, episodes of long-ago shows like *Gunsmoke*, *The Big Valley*, *Mannix*, and *Dallas*. Sometimes the character he was playing had a name, but at other times he was identified merely as janitor, clerk, mailman, bartender, farmhand, or simply "(uncredited) bit part." It looked as though Calvin had worked steadily enough to earn a living at it.

Then he'd stopped working in movies and television. I wondered why. If Pearl was mistaken, and Hank Calvin was not Binky Jasper, maybe Calvin had retired, or died. If he was Binky, maybe he'd taken on another persona. I looked at the photos again. From Calvin to Calhoun wasn't that big a stretch. Maybe Binky *was* Henry.

I called Liam Cleary's cell phone number. When he answered, I asked if he could talk and he said, "Sure, I'm in my office doing paperwork. Any excuse for a break. What's up, darlin'?"

"When I was in LA two weeks ago, looking at the Tarrant file, you said you'd check to see if Henry Calhoun had ever come up on the radar down there. Anything come up?"

"Not a thing, sorry. Been meaning to call you about that, but I got busy on a double murder."

"Thanks for checking," I said. "If you get a chance, could you check the name Hank Calvin? I have a witness who claims she saw the man I'm looking for, back in nineteen seventy-nine. He was working as a bit player on a television show using that name. I'm looking at the Internet Movie Database and I see credits under that name from nineteen forty-six through nineteen eighty-one. When I ran a background check on Henry Calhoun, I found information back to the early eighties, but no further."

"Hank Calvin," Liam repeated. "Sure, I'll take a look. Might take me a few days to get to it."

"Thanks, I appreciate it."

After ending the call, I rinsed cold coffee from my mug and left my office. I walked to the Alameda County Courthouse and waited outside the Twelfth Street entrance, where the security checkpoint was located. A moment later, my client, a defense attorney, came out. We walked up Oak Street toward Lake Merritt, the large lake in the middle of downtown Oakland. A nearby gaggle of Canada geese waddled across the grass, honking and eating. A mother with a toddler in tow held onto her little girl, who seemed determined to chase the geese. Workers from the county offices and nearby businesses sat on the grass eating their lunches, or joined the crowds of people who walked or ran around the lake's three-mile perimeter. When we were finished conferring about the case, the attorney went back to the courthouse and I walked in the direction of my Franklin Street office, stopping at a deli to buy lunch, turkey and provolone on an onion roll, instead of my usual pastrami on rye.

My cell phone rang as I left the deli. I answered, straining to hear the caller over the noise of traffic and people on Twelfth Street. "This is Joel Corwin," a man's voice said. "I'm returning your call from yesterday. I must say, you've got me intrigued. Why is a private investigator looking for information about my Uncle Harold?"

"Your uncle being reported missing may have something to do

with a case I'm working on. Or it may just be a coincidence. At this point I'm not sure. I can't discuss details due to client confidentiality." I rounded the corner onto Franklin Street and headed for my office building in the middle of the block. "What can you tell me about Harold?"

"Not much," Corwin said. "My father, Stan, never talked about him. Dad was a Marine. He fought in the Pacific and got wounded at Okinawa. He had all sorts of medals. And Gramps was in the Army in France during World War One. So Uncle Harry being a deserter was a sore subject for both of them. They were ashamed of him. To tell you the truth, I never heard the deserter story until I was in college. I knew Dad had a younger brother but my impression was that Uncle Harry had died when he was a kid. Come to think of it, he was a kid, just eighteen when he left home."

So many of them were so young, I thought, fighting and dying in Europe and the Pacific, like my own grandfather, and Stanley Corwin and Pearl's first husband. "What about the rest of the family? Your grandmother and your aunts? Any theories as to why Harold would go missing?"

"The women in the family always said the Army must have made a mistake," Corwin said. "They were sure Harold died in that fire and the other guy went AWOL. Granny said if Harold had left Camp Roberts alive, he would have come home to Oakland. Now that you bring it up, I wonder if there's a way to find out if it really was Harold that died. Exhume the body, you know. These days you hear about DNA testing and all that."

"Probably there is. I'm not sure where the soldier who died was buried. The testing is expensive."

"And it happened so long ago. Gramps and Dad are gone. So are Granny and Aunt Donna. But my Aunt Thelma is still alive and kicking. She'll probably outlive us all."

"Then I want to talk with her. Where can I find her?"

"I'll give her your phone number," he said. "She'll find you."

"Thanks. I'll look forward to hearing from her." I hung up the phone and entered my building, taking the stairs up to my third-floor office. I ate my lunch at my desk, then I switched on the computer to work on a report for a client. I'd just sent the document to the printer when the phone rang.

The woman on the other end of the line had a brisk, no-nononsense voice. "This is Thelma Darwell. My nephew Joel tells me you're asking questions about my brother Harry."

"I am. Do you have some time now?"

"I'm on my way out the door," she said. "But if you get yourself over here to Alameda, I'll be happy to talk with you in about an hour, at the tennis courts at Lower Washington Park."

"I'll meet you there," I said.

~ 30 ~

WE SHOULD ALL age as well as Thelma Darwell, I thought from the bench where I sat, watching the woman hustle around the tennis court. She was short, about five feet two inches, and she wore a brace on her left knee, visible below the hem of her blue shorts. She must have been past eighty. She and her doubles partner, a trim man with silver hair and glasses, trounced their opponents in straight sets. After the match ended and the four players shook hands over the net, she walked toward me. I stood and noticed the logo on her T-shirt, from the National Senior Games.

"How did you do at the Games?" I gestured at the shirt.

"Two gold medals, one in mixed doubles and one in women's doubles. I'll keep playing as long as I'm able. My daughter says, in the end they'll carry me off the tennis court." She removed her sun visor, revealing short, tousled white hair above a tanned, wrinkled face and a pair of friendly blue eyes. "You must be Jeri Howard."

"I am." We shook hands and I gave her my business card. "Thanks for agreeing to talk with me, Mrs. Darwell."

"Call me Thelma," she said. "Well, I had to, when Joel told me it was about Harry. Why are you asking questions about him?"

"It relates to a case I'm working on," I said. "But I can't discuss the details."

"I suppose not." She zipped her tennis racquet into a red nylon bag and took a sip from a water bottle. "I'll tell you straight out, my brother never deserted. Harry was proud to be in the Army. He was wild to go, especially since our older brother, Stan, had already joined the Marines, right after Pearl Harbor. That's all Harry talked about the whole first year of the war, trying to convince my folks to let him join up. But my parents said no, he had to wait until he was eighteen. He enlisted that very day, his eighteenth birthday, the sixth of January, 1943. Does that sound like someone who would desert?"

"No, it doesn't." But he could have, said the devil's advocate in my mind. What if Harold had arrived at Camp Roberts and found out the Army wasn't his cup of tea?

"The Army got it wrong," Thelma said, shaking her head as though reading my thoughts. "I wish there was a way to prove it. That whole business just broke my mother's heart. And it drove a wedge between her and Papa. Mama never believed Harry had deserted. She insisted till the day she died that if he went AWOL, he'd have come home and at least explained. Papa said that if Harry was a deserter, he would have been afraid to come home because he knew Papa would turn him in, or make him go back, face up to it somehow. But Harry never came home. Mama figured he died in that fire and someone else took his identity. That's what I thought when I saw that newspaper article a few years back, about all those wallets at Camp Roberts, the ones that had been stolen and thrown into the heating ducts."

"I read the article, too." And it had me thinking the same thing. "When was the last time you saw your brother?"

"I was twelve when Harry left home," Thelma said. "A month or so later, we drove down to Camp Roberts to visit him one weekend, Mama, Papa, me and my big sister, Donna. Stan was already in the Marines by then. We visited missions along the way and stayed in an auto court in San Miguel. Harry was glad to see us, and he seemed to be happy. He said he liked the training and he'd made some new friends. We went to church that Sunday, then a dinner at the USO. That was the last time I saw him." She sighed. "I still have the letters Harry wrote to Mama from the camp."

"Do you? May I read them? To see if he mentions any of his Army buddies."

"You mean that guy who died in the fire? Yes, he does." She

shouldered her tennis bag. "Come home with me. I'll let you read the letters."

Thelma and I walked out to the parking lot next to the tennis courts. She stowed her tennis bag in the trunk of a blue Volvo. I followed her to a well-kept Victorian house on San Antonio Avenue. She had a pitcher of iced tea in the refrigerator and poured glasses for both of us. She directed me out to the deck at the back of the house, warmed by the late afternoon sun, and went into one of the bedrooms. She returned with a fabric-covered box containing her brother's letters.

Harold Corwin, age eighteen and newly enlisted in the Army, went to Camp Roberts in January 1943. He had vanished the night of the fire, March 20, 1943. The packet of letters he'd written to his mother during those two months was pitifully thin and lovingly preserved, tied with a blue ribbon. I counted ten envelopes and two postcards. I wiped my hands on a napkin, wanting to make sure I didn't damage the paper, and opened the first envelope. I was guessing Harold's accounts of Army life had been edited for his family's consumption, but the impression I had as I read this letter was of a fresh-faced, naïve young man, away from home for the first time in his life, and nervous about the prospect of going out to the Pacific to fight the Japanese. It was really different to sleep in bunks surrounded by all those other guys. The fellow in the next bunk snored like a buzz saw, he wrote. It was hard to get any sleep those first few nights, and the company got up so early. The chow was all right, and there was plenty of it, but of course it didn't hold a candle to Mama's home cooking.

In his second letter from camp, Harold talked about day-to-day life in Company A of the 78th Infantry Training Battalion. Then he mentioned that there was another guy there from the old neighborhood—Salvatore Bianchi—in the same company. "You remember Sal," Harold wrote. "He was on the basketball team. His father works at the same cannery as Pop."

I looked up from the letter "Did you know Salvatore Bianchi?" I asked Thelma.

"Sal? Oh, yes. He was Harry's age, and his younger sister Adelina was one of my classmates. We were friends later, in high school. I still see her from time to time."

"Is Sal still alive? Your brother says he was at Camp Roberts at the same time, and I'd like to talk with him."

She set down her glass. "You know, I'd forgotten Sal was there for training. He was wounded in the war, got a Purple Heart. He stayed in the Army, made a career of it, then retired after thirty years and came back to Oakland. But yes, he's still alive. At least he was the last time I talked with Adelina. She said his wife died. He sold his house and moved into a retirement home. Let me see if I can find out where."

She went inside the house. A moment later I heard her talking on the phone. I glanced at a postcard showing a scene of the Camp Roberts Soldier Bowl, with a note saying that there was talk that Bing Crosby was going to perform there. I opened the third letter. Harold wrote about the training he was going through there at the camp, learning how to use a rifle and throw a hand grenade, how to crawl under wire and read maps. He added that he saw Sal from time to time, at chow or in one of the camp's recreation halls. In the fourth letter, toward the end, he mentioned meeting a guy from Colorado, Will Kravin. The two had met while playing Ping-Pong at the San Miguel USO. There was going to be a rodeo there at Camp Roberts, and Will, who'd grown up on a ranch in southwestern Colorado, could ride steers. The fifth letter contained more information about the training Harold was going through, and also said he'd been playing cards at the recreation hall with Will Kravin and another guy from Colorado, whose name was Vidal. I wasn't sure if this was a first or a last name.

Harold wrote the sixth letter in the stack after his family visited him at the camp, in mid-February 1943. Following that was a second postcard, showing a Paso Robles street scene. Then, in the seventh letter, came the name I was looking for. Harold, writing to his family in the last week of February, roughly a month before the fire, said he'd become friends with another guy in his company, Byron Jasper, who used to be an actor in the movies before he'd been drafted. There was a hint between the lines that he didn't quite know what to make of this exotic fellow from Los Angeles. From the next two letters, the eighth and the ninth, I gathered that Harold, Will, Vidal and Byron became pals, playing cards on the weekends in the recreation halls on the base, or Ping-Pong at the San Miguel USO, which had everything from a soda counter to a library.

Thelma returned to the deck and handed me a piece of paper. "Sal's still living in Oakland, that big retirement home just off Piedmont Avenue."

I looked at the address. "I know the place."

Now I reached the tenth, and last, letter in Harold Corwin's meager correspondence. The envelope was postmarked March 18, 1943, two days before the fire, and it felt thicker. I opened the envelope and pulled out the letter. Tucked inside the sheets of paper I found a small black-and-white snapshot showing four young men in civilian clothes, looking as though they were ready to go into town on a Saturday night. I flipped over the photo. On the back, in fading pencil, was the legend *L–R, Harry, Will, Vidal, Byron, 13 March 42.*

I had been eager to find a photo of Byron Jasper from the 1940s. Now here it was, in my hands. I held it closer, examining every detail of the young man on the far right side of the picture. Binky was partly hidden by the bulkier form of the man next to him, and something in his manner suggested that he'd shrunk back from the camera, not wanting have his picture taken. But I could see his face and his left side. He was wearing the loose-fitting pants of the era, a long-sleeved shirt and a tie.

"I need a copy of this picture," I told Thelma. "I have a digital camera with me. May I take some shots?"

"Have at it," she said. "From the look on your face I can tell it's important."

I pulled my digital camera from my purse. The photo was small to begin with. I focused on the figure of Byron Jasper and zoomed in, taking several shots. Then I read the letter that had contained the snapshot. Harry had heard Bob Hope was coming to the camp with a USO show later in the spring, and he hoped he'd still be there to see it. By the middle of March 1943, Harold had been at Camp Roberts for two months. He and his company were due to finish training in May, and then they'd get into the war, he wrote. There was much speculation about where they'd go. The bloody fighting on Guadalcanal had ended with the Japanese defeat but there was still a lot of war to be fought.

"There was a dance Saturday night at the USO in Paso Robles," Harold wrote. "We hitched a ride into town with Sal and his buddy Tito, who is from Paso. His mom cooked us a great dinner. We went to a dance. Sal took this picture of me and the guys. He gave it to me soon as he got it developed at the PX. So now I'm sending it to you."

I put the letter back in the envelope and returned the correspondence to the box, feeling the specter of Harold Corwin's unfinished life looming over me. "So that's all."

"That's all," Thelma repeated. "Does it sound like my brother Harry deserted?"

I shook my head. "No, it doesn't. Unless something happened that night to make him feel he had to leave. But I'm inclined to agree with you. I think your brother died at Camp Roberts and someone took his identity. Proving that theory will be another matter."

"Well, if you do, let me know," she said. "It would mean a lot to me."

~

When I left Thelma Darwell's home I drove downtown and parked a block away from the Alameda Theatre. I strolled past Matinee, the movie memorabilia shop, and glanced inside, looking past a display featuring posters and lobby cards showing Bette Davis. Raina Makellar was behind the counter, which suited my purpose.

I walked to the Peet's on the corner and bought a latte. Then I returned to the shop, opened the door and raised my cup in inquiry. "Okay if I bring this inside?" Then I echoed Raina's earlier words, spoken when I'd eavesdropped on her and the other woman a few weeks earlier. "I really need my caffeine fix in the afternoon."

"Oh, sure, come on in." Raina looked happy at the prospect of some company. The shop probably didn't get much foot traffic on a weekday afternoon. She pointed at a coffee cup near the computer. "I know what you mean about the caffeine fix. I'm Raina. Are you looking for anything in particular?"

"Hi, Raina. I'm Jeri. I'm not really looking for anything specific. I was walking past your shop and I saw the display of Bette Davis posters. I love her movies. My favorite is *Dark Victory.*"

She smiled. "I really like *Now, Voyager.* And then there's *All About Eve,* which is wonderful. I met Bette Davis once, when I was just a kid."

"Really? How did that come about?"

"My Aunt Dolores," she said, leaning her elbows on the counter. "She was a bit player way back in the forties and fifties. Do you know what a bit player is?"

"Yes, I've heard the term." I sipped my coffee.

"After she gave up acting, Aunt Dolores worked in publicity at Metro and Paramount. Sometimes I'd visit her at the studio, and that's how I met Bette Davis."

"Is that how you got into this business?" I waved my hand at the posters on the wall behind her. "Because of your aunt?"

"She certainly helped. My father collected movie memorabilia," Raina said, "and Aunt Dolores would bring him posters and stills and all sorts of stuff. After awhile he had so much, he opened a shop in Los Angeles."

I sipped my latte. "I walked past here a week or two ago, and saw an older man behind the counter. Was that your father?"

She shook her head. "Oh, no, my father died last year. The man you saw was Henry Callan. He worked for my father, and now he works for me and my husband."

Callan. She'd used the name Callan instead of Calhoun. I wondered why.

She stepped back from the counter, through the doorway that led to the back of the shop, picked up something from the desk and returned bearing a framed-eight-by-ten inch photograph. "This is my father." Her voice was sad, as though she missed him still. The picture was a group shot and she pointed at the man in the middle, tall and lean, with white hair brushed back from a high forehead, with his left arm around a younger Raina and his right encircling the waist of an older woman who resembled him. Next to Raina was Chaz Makellar, raising a beer bottle to his lips.

"This was taken about six years ago," she said. "On the Fourth of July. We were in the backyard at Aunt Dolores's apartment building. There's me, next to Dad. And my aunt on the other side, and the rest of the people are my aunt's tenants. There's my husband Charles, though we weren't married yet. We'd just started dating, as a matter of fact. And the man talking with him is Henry Calhoun, the man you saw here."

It was indeed the man I'd encountered here in the shop, standing just to the right of Aunt Dolores, wearing a long-sleeved shirt, the light glinting off his cufflinks. Long sleeves in July? "I'm a little confused," I said. "Just a moment ago you said his last name was Callan and now you say it's Calhoun. Did I hear you wrong?"

Raina laughed. "I do that all the time. I keep mixing up the names. Henry worked for my father years ago, when I was a kid, and he lived in my aunt's building. I guess I must have heard his last name as Callan and it just stuck in my head. I went off to college and then I was out on my own. I came back to help Dad run the shop. He was getting very elderly, forgetful, and Aunt Dolores had died. Henry was still living in her building. He and a friend of his lived in one of the apartments on the top floor. They were both scouts, looking for memorabilia for my father's shop, working odd jobs. I don't remember the roommate's name, if I ever knew at all. He died, though. Tripped and fell down the stairs. I told Henry I'd always thought his name was Callan. He said it was Calhoun, but that was an easy mistake to make."

Or maybe there had been a Henry Callan, I thought. It was worth investigating. I pointed at Henry's image in the photo. "Odd for him to be wearing long sleeves in July. Now July can be cold here in the Bay Area, but I imagine it's hot down in LA."

"He wears long sleeves all the time," Raina said. "I asked him about it once, but before he could answer my mother said that was rude. I figure he has a scar or something like that. Maybe it's to show off his fancy cufflinks. He has a ring that matches, with a Celtic cross. I know several times when he's been down and out, he's had to pawn his gold ring and cufflinks. He told her that they were special to him, a gift from his sister."

The sister who wound up dead on a beach in Santa Monica? If Henry was in fact Byron Jasper, I suspected he'd killed Sylvia.

"It sounds like you're very fond of Henry," I said.

"I guess I am. He's a link to the old days, with Dad and Aunt Dolores." She picked up the photograph and took it back to the desk.

When she returned to the counter I looked at my watch. "Oh, wow, I've really lost track of time. I have to go. Raina, it's really been nice talking with you."

And productive, I thought as I exited the shop. I tossed the coffee cup in a nearby trash receptacle and headed for my car. Before starting the engine, I took out my cell phone and called the number Thelma had given me, for Salvatore Bianchi. I got voice mail and left a message.

When I got back to my office I downloaded the photos I'd taken of the snapshot showing Harold Corwin and his buddies, including Byron Jasper. I wished I'd been able to take similar photos of the picture Raina had showed me, that showed an older Henry Calhoun. But this would have to suffice. I enlarged the image of Byron Jasper's face and printed several copies, intending to show it to Salvatore Bianchi. I hoped to arrange a meeting with him when he returned my call.

I began searching online for any records I could find on a man named Henry Callan, who had lived and worked in Los Angeles a few years ago. I also called Liam Cleary and left a message on his cell phone, asking him to check the name Henry Callan as well as Hank Calvin. I did the same kind of search on Raina's aunt, Dolores Simms, who had also been a bit player. Perhaps she'd married and was using a different name when she'd owned the apartment building where Henry Calhoun—or Callan—had lived.

Then I sat back in my chair and thought about something else I'd learned from my brief conversation with Raina. When she showed me the photograph taken at the Fourth of July party six years earlier, she'd said that she had just started dating Chaz Makellar, the man she married. Mike Strickland had purchased posters from Wallace Simms, Raina's father, twice, nine years ago, and twelve years ago. So if Chaz wasn't in Raina's life when Mike bought that merchandise, maybe it wasn't Chaz whom Mike recognized before he was murdered. Maybe it was Henry Calhoun.

~ 31 ~

I HAD A DATE with an old soldier the following morning. Salvatore Bianchi called me back, and when he heard why I wanted to talk with him, he invited me over for a chat. He lived in a high-rise complex for senior citizens, on a side street just off Oakland's Piedmont Avenue. He greeted me in the lobby, a wiry old man with a gravelly voice and a few wisps of white hair. He was medium height, but stooped with age. He led the way to one of the common rooms, walking slowly, using a three-legged cane for balance. We sat at a corner table and I showed him the enlarged version of the snapshot Harold Corwin had sent to his mother, showing all four men.

"Yeah, I took that picture," Sal said, positioning the photograph on the table surface. "I'm a pretty good photographer, been taking pictures all my life. Even won a couple of awards. Got my start back then. Mom and Dad gave me a Kodak for Christmas in 'forty-two. Had it with me most of the time. I was always taking pictures, right and left. Some pretty good shots, too. One of 'em was in the *Camp Roberts Dispatch*, right before I shipped out. I still have the picture, and the newspaper. I have a photo album, pictures I took at Camp Roberts. I sent it to my mother before I went overseas and she gave it back after the war."

"This particular picture," I said, pointing at the shot of Byron Jasper and his three companions.

"We were going to a USO dance in Paso Robles, with a guy in my company named Tito. He was a *paisan*, Italian American like me. His folks lived in Paso and his mom cooked us a feast. I took that picture in their living room. That Tito, he was a good kid. I heard later he got killed on Guam. Anyway, that's Harry Corwin on that end." He tapped the figure on the left side of the photo. "The other guys were Will Kravin and Vidal Castillo. And Byron Jasper, on the other end." He said the last name as though it left a sour taste in his mouth.

"You didn't like Byron? Why not?"

"Nope. Sure didn't. He and Harry were both in my company, and Byron was in my platoon. Second Platoon, B Company, 78th Infantry Training Battalion. Byron had the bunk right across from me. Why didn't I like him? I don't know. I just didn't. There was something off about that guy. You know how it is. You don't have to like everybody. And you get a feeling."

I nodded. I'd had those visceral feelings before, reacting to something in a person's manner or behavior. "What do you remember about Byron?"

Sal laughed. "I can't remember what I had for lunch yesterday, but I remember those days, training at Camp Roberts. It was tough, hard training, being away from home, living in barracks, thrown together with all sorts of guys. But what came after makes it all seem like a picnic. The war. Yeah, I remember the war like it was yesterday. Got a piece of shrapnel in my hip that reminds me of Okinawa to this day."

He rubbed gnarled fingers against his chin, which showed silver whiskers here and there, missed by that morning's shave. "So… Byron… He was an odd bird. Claimed he was an actor who'd been working in Hollywood. Well, let me tell you, we had actors aplenty. Robert Mitchum, William Holden, Red Skelton, all of 'em went through basic training at Camp Roberts. Byron Jasper I never heard of. I figured if he was an actor, big *if*, he was low on the food chain."

"He worked as an extra," I said. "And something called a bit player, in a few scenes, with a few words of dialogue."

"Bit player, is that what they call it? Well, he was too slick by half. Later I wondered if he was maybe homosexual. I got nothing against those folks, now anyway. Hell, I got a grandson that's gay. But back then, me a cocky kid, just barely eighteen, trying to prove how tough I was. And people were prejudiced. It was the times we lived in, you see. There was a lot of feeling against the Japs, because of Pearl Harbor. And against the Negroes. The Army was segregated back in those days. People even had hard feelings against the Okies from the Central Valley. Mexican American kids like Vidal. And the Italian Americans like me. You know, they had Italian POWs at Camp Roberts. Some of 'em liked it so well they came back to the States after the war."

"Yes, I read that on the Internet," I said. "So if you were in the same company, you, Harry and Byron must have arrived at Camp Roberts at the same time."

"Second week in January, nineteen forty-three. They had guys reporting for training every day, lots of recruits, so it's funny that two guys from Oakland who went to the same high school wound up in the same company. After we'd been there a week or so, Harry hooked up with Will." Sal tapped Will's face in the photo. "Will was a hell of a Ping-Pong player. There was a Ping-Pong tournament going on and Will was right in the thick of it. And there was going to be a rodeo, with soldiers and local boys from the area around the camp. Will and Vidal were going to ride steers. They were both ranch kids from Colorado."

I nodded. Harold Corwin had mentioned the rodeo in one of his letters to his mother. "Any idea how Harold became friends with Byron?"

"Playing cards, I think," Sal said. "I remember the four of us playing poker in the recreation hall one weekend and Byron won a big hand drawing to an inside straight. It seemed strange to me that that Harry would hook up with Byron. They didn't have much in common. But Harry really liked the guy. Basic training had a way of throwing all sorts of people together. Camp Roberts was huge. They kept us busy with training but we had all kinds of activities. Two USOs, in San Miguel and Paso Robles. The camp had recreation halls, sports teams, clubs for all sorts of hobbies, and four movie theaters. We had dances and touring shows, with big bands, or even plays and musicals."

I steered the nostalgia train back toward Byron Jasper. "So Byron had the bunk across from you. That meant you saw him every day."

"Sure as hell did. First thing in the morning, all through the day, and last thing at night. Saw him dressed and buck-naked in the shower."

"Did he have any distinguishing marks, like a birthmark, a mole, a scar?"

"Funny you should mention that. He did have a scar, a really bad one." Sal held his hands apart. "Maybe six, seven inches." Then he moved his left hand and traced a line down the inside of his right arm. "Right here, on the underside of the right arm between the elbow and the wrist."

"Was it like a cut, or a surgical incision?"

Sal shook his head. "Looked more like a burn. It was maybe half an inch to an inch wide in places. He was really sensitive about the way it looked. First time I saw that scar we were in the shower. Byron saw me looking at it and he draped his towel over his arm to hide that scar. I was going to ask him how he got it but then I figured he'd had an accident of some sort. And it really wasn't any of my business."

A scar on Binky's arm. I thought of the photograph I'd shown Sal, with the four young soldiers, and Byron wearing long sleeves. Then the photograph I'd seen of Henry Callan—or Calhoun— taken six years ago with Raina Makellar and her father. A Fourth of July backyard barbecue, and he'd been wearing long sleeves. And more recently, on that hot June afternoon when I'd seen him helping Chaz Makellar unload the SUV at the shop. Long sleeves again. To hide a scar?

"How was Byron doing, as an Army recruit?"

Sal shook his head. "He wasn't cut out for it, being a ground-pounding infantry man. Of course, he'd been drafted, like so many other guys. So what choice did he have? Though he was the kind of guy that it wouldn't have surprised me if he didn't report for training. He was trying, I'll say that for him. He was never going to make it out in the field. He was company clerk material, or supply, something like that. But give that guy a rifle and send him into battle? Not a good idea. Now if you'd told me Byron had gone AWOL instead of Harry…"

"Maybe he did," I said. "You know, Thelma Darwell says her brother Harry never would have deserted. She thinks he died in that fire at Camp Roberts and Bryon went AWOL."

"I wondered the same thing myself. I knew Harry Corwin. He was a good kid. I never thought he would have gone over the hill. But they found Byron's dog tags on the dead man," Sal added, talking about the metal identity tags issued to military personnel. "I suppose that's how they identified the body."

"No other kinds of testing?"

"Not that I know of, but I wasn't part of the investigation. Now that I think about it, I guess when the MPs found those dog tags, they took 'em at face value."

"The night of the fire, were Harry and Byron missing at lights out?"

"Harry's bunk was in a different part of the barracks," Sal said. "I didn't see him. But Byron was in his bunk. He must have sneaked out later. He wasn't the first and wouldn't be the last."

"So what were those two doing in that tool shed after hours?"

"That's a good question," Sal said. "I never heard an answer. I did hear lots of rumors. Any Army camp I was at, all those guys together in one place, you got all kinds of things going on and all sorts of stories, most of 'em bushwa. One story making the rounds was that Harry and Byron had a still in that tool shed, making hooch, and somehow they set the place on fire. Another story going around was that they were playing craps or poker for big money, smoking and joking, and that's how the fire started. But both of those theories are assuming the fire was an accident. The official version was arson, deliberate. But why would anybody torch that shed, with people inside? That's murder. I have a hard time getting my mind around that."

He shook his head. "As for why those guys were there in the first place, I don't know that I buy the story about a still. It could have been gambling. They liked to play poker. So did I. We played poker, pinochle, blackjack, bridge, gin, you name it. But hell, none of us had any big money. We were boot recruits on Army pay, and not much of it. We played bridge for a penny a point, and when we played poker, it was nickel-dime stuff. Whether those guys were gambling or making hooch, it's a mystery to me. Why would they be doing it in civvies?"

"Civvies? Why do you think they were in civilian clothes?"

"Because Byron's uniform was still at the barracks." Sal wagged his finger at me. "Remember, I had the bunk across from him. And I was the one the corporal grabbed a couple of days later, after the powers-that-be decided he died in the fire. The corporal said we had to inventory the stuff in Byron's footlocker. He handed me some paper and a pencil, and told me to write down everything he found in that footlocker. The corporal jimmied the lock, so I was right there as he took Byron's stuff out. I noticed right away that all his uniforms were there. And some things were missing. Byron had a pair of gray pants and a blue shirt he liked to wear out in town of a Saturday night. Those were gone, along with his civvy shoes. The jewelry was gone, too."

"What jewelry?" I asked.

"A pair of fancy gold cufflinks, with a ring to match," Sal said. "You can't really see them in this picture I took the night of the dance. But Byron was wearing them. He always wore them in civvies. First time I saw them I thought they must be worth a lot of money, and that he was crazy to bring something valuable like that to camp, where somebody might steal them. Things got stolen all the time. He kept that ring and those cufflinks in a little wooden box at the bottom of his footlocker. The box was there, but it was empty. That fancy gold jewelry wasn't with the rest of his stuff, the pockets or the bottom of the footlocker, when we took that inventory of his things. I figured he must have been wearing them. I remarked on it to the corporal, but I don't think he paid me any mind. I wondered if that jewelry melted in the fire." He frowned. "But the dog tags didn't melt, so how do you figure that? Hmmm. Maybe that's how they knew it was Byron, because of the jewelry. But something doesn't make sense."

"What did the ring and cufflinks look like? Round, square? Were they plain, did they have initials?"

"They looked heavy," he said. "The design, it was a cross with a circle, and engraving inside the arms of the cross. A Celtic cross, that's what they call it. I remember because my granddaughter had a necklace with the same kind of cross. She got that on a trip to Ireland and she told me what it was."

Henry Calhoun had been wearing a gold ring and cufflinks the first time I'd seen him, at the shop in Alameda, with a Celtic cross design, the arms of the cross slightly wider at the ends, with a Celtic knot engraved inside. And he'd been wearing them in the six-year-old photo Raina Makellar had at the shop. But were they the same gold ring and cufflinks that Byron Jasper had at Camp Roberts? I needed something that linked Byron to Henry, and I didn't have it yet.

"You mentioned a photo album, with pictures you took at Camp Roberts," I said. "Any chance that you might have another picture of Byron Jasper somewhere, wearing the jewelry?"

"You know, I just might. Let's go look."

Sal and I took the elevator up to his apartment on the seventh floor. It had a dining-kitchenette area with a small refrigerator and microwave, and beyond that a long living room with bookshelves and a large-screen television. Through a doorway I glimpsed the bedroom. On the walls I saw framed photographs, some of them taken in familiar locations. Here were Half Dome and El Capitan at Yosemite National Park, and a view of Mount Shasta in Northern California. I paused in front of a shot of some craggy rocks. "This is very good."

"Thanks. I took that at the Pinnacles, down by Hollister," Sal said. "Even printed it myself. I had a darkroom at the house, way back when. These days with digital photography, it's really different."

He was standing by the bookshelves, squinting as he looked at their contents. "Here it is. I cleared out a lot of stuff when I moved to this assisted living place. But this I kept. Lots of memories here." He picked up the photo album and carried it to the round dining table, where he pulled out a chair and sat down. I joined him. The album was brown imitation leather, cracked and worn. His gnarled fingers caressed the edges. Then he opened it. I saw black-and-white photos affixed to the beige pages with adhesive photo corners, some loose. Sal leafed slowly through the pages. He pointed at a picture of a dark-haired young man with his arms around a girl, both carrying Ping-Pong paddles. "That's Tito, the guy I was telling you about. We were at the USO in Paso Robles. That's his girl, his sweetheart from high school." He turned the page. I saw three young men with goofy smiles, dressed as women. Sal chuckled. "And that was a talent show. These fellas are supposed to be the Andrews Sisters. As I recall, they did a pretty good 'Don't Sit Under the Apple Tree.'"

As Sal turned the pages, he commented on the pictures he'd taken. Among them were photos of training, of young soldiers in fatigues, with helmets and rifles, crawling under wires. Here were some shots taken at USO touring camp shows, one showing singer Frances Langford, and another with comedian Jack Benny. He'd also taken photographs of the scenery of Camp Roberts, the coastal mountains to the west, and the banks of the Salinas River. Mostly, though, they were pictures of the guys, the soldiers going through training at the camp, playing volleyball or Ping-Pong at the USO or the recreation halls, drinking sodas or dancing with local girls, queuing up for a movie at the post theater.

Sal turned over another page and pointed. "There. That's Byron. I took this at the recreation hall. We were playing cards, but it's a close-up, so you can't see the table or the other guys."

I pulled the album closer and examined Byron Jasper, circa 1943. He looked like the chameleon Pearl said he was, nondescript, the guy you wouldn't give a second glance. His hair was neither dark nor light, just in-between, and he had an expression on his thin face that was somewhere between a smile and a frown. He held a bottle of Coca-Cola in his right hand, as though saluting the camera. His left hand was raised as well, in a loose fist, with the thumb pointing over his left shoulder, as though he were hitching a ride. He wore a long-sleeved shirt fastened with square cufflinks, both visible, and a ring on his left hand. I could see that there was a design on the jewelry. It looked like a Celtic knot. But the photograph itself was small, about three-by-five inches.

"Is there any chance you have the negatives?" I asked. Sal had been an amateur photographer most of his adult life. He just might have retained the negatives from the pictures he took at Camp Roberts, but it was an extreme long-shot. Even now he was shaking his head.

"Back that far? I doubt it. But I'll have a look."

"I would appreciate it. In the meantime, let me take some digital photos of this picture." I got out my camera and framed a few shots, taking in Byron's face, arms and hand. Sal said he'd look through the negatives that he had to see if he could find this one, and that he'd contact me if he remembered anything else about Byron.

I thought about the scar on Byron's right arm as I drove back to my office. After I'd downloaded the photos onto my computer, I enlarged them, hoping I could see the design on the jewelry Byron was wearing when the photo was taken at Camp Roberts. The ring had a pattern of Celtic knots. And the cufflinks, roughly square, had a Celtic cross in the center. But it wasn't enough only to prove a link between Byron Jasper and Henry Calhoun. I wanted a link between Byron Jasper and Ralph Tarrant as well. I remembered the crime scene photos taken at the actor's home the night he was murdered in 1942. He had been dressed to go out, wearing a long-sleeved shirt, but his cufflinks had been removed, so hastily that the cuffs themselves had been torn.

I logged onto the Internet and did a search through the directory of one of my professional organizations and located a private investigator in Mobile, Alabama. His name was Barry Taft and he was happy to take on my assignment.

"The name is Byron Cade Jasper," I told him. "He left Mobile late in 1941. He was seventeen or eighteen at the time. The census data from 1930 shows him living in Mobile with his parents and three siblings. I want to know if Byron was injured in a fire in Mobile and if so, the details."

"I'll check the city directory first," Taft said. "Then I'll go over to the University of South Alabama. They've got the *Mobile Press-Register* on microfilm back to the eighteen-twenties. I should be able to find something."

My next call was to Pearl Bishop. "I hope I haven't interrupted a poker game," I told her.

"I'm getting ready to go to Bridgeport for a doctor's appointment," she said. "At my age I have to get my body parts checked out from time to time. Did you get my picture?"

"Yes, I did. I found out Binky supposedly died in a fire at Camp Roberts, but I don't believe it. There are a couple of photos of Binky taken at the camp, by a man who was in his company. He says Binky always wore long-sleeved shirts, frequently with gold cufflinks that had a Celtic cross design. Binky also wore a matching ring. He's wearing the ring and the cufflinks in the photos. One of my grandmother's letters mentions Sylvia buying cufflinks for Tarrant. When we were talking last week, you said when you and the girls met Tarrant, he was wearing a ring. Later, Sylvia had the same ring on a chain around her neck, and she claimed Ralph Tarrant had given to her. Do you remember what the ring looked like?"

"I just remember the inscription inside the ring, with Tarrant's initials and the date," Pearl said. "The ring was wide and it had some kind of design on it, I don't remember what, but I thought it was kinda busy. Not something I would have picked for myself. But a man's ring, definitely. I'm not familiar with the Celtic cross, but I'll look it up on the Internet so I can picture it."

"My source, the man from Camp Roberts, says Binky had a burn scar on his inner right arm. Do you recall ever seeing a scar?"

"I don't," Pearl said. "But he did wear long-sleeved shirts all the time."

"What about a fire? Did he or Sylvia ever say anything about a fire in Mobile? I'm wondering how he got the scar."

"No, I don't think either of them said anything about a fire. But when they trashed the house after we kicked them out, they did start a fire in the kitchen. They tore out pages from cookbooks, put them in the sink and torched them."

"It's pure speculation on my part," I said. "But the fire is a re-curring motif. The fire at the house after you and the others moved them out. Whoever killed Tarrant tried to cover up the murder by starting a fire. And now there's this Camp Roberts fire."

"Binky's not dead," Pearl said. "That was him I saw on the set of *Lou Grant* in nineteen seventy-nine."

"The authorities found Binky's dog tags on the body. At the same time, a soldier named Harold Corwin disappeared. If Binky didn't die, he took Corwin's identity, and turned up years later, using the name Hank Calvin, which is close enough to Harold Corwin. I'd like to find a picture of Ralph Tarrant wearing the ring and cufflinks. Maybe a publicity shot would show them in detail. Do you still know anyone in Hollywood?"

"I sure do," Pearl said. "He's retired now but he used to work in publicity at Metro. I'll call him later. But now I've got to get going to my doctor's appointment."

I'd just hung up the phone when it rang again. I discovered Sadie Espinosa, Roberta Cook's neighbor, on the other end of the line. "Jeri, you've got to come up to Petaluma. I've got a witness for you."

~ 32 ~

A COUPLE OF hours later I was in the living room of Sadie Espinosa's Victorian house on Liberty Street near downtown Petaluma. Sadie passed around a plate of homemade oatmeal raisin cookies to go with the iced tea she'd already poured. Her two cats were very much in evidence. Poppy had claimed Sadie's lap, and Ducks had designs on my cookie. "I don't think cats are supposed to eat cookies," I told him as I shooed him away. He snuggled next to me on the sofa and purred.

"That cat will try anything once," Sadie said. "Now, Melita, you tell Jeri what you told me."

Melita Wong was short and sturdy, and she wore khaki shorts, a white T-shirt and tennis shoes. She swallowed a mouthful of cookie and washed it down with some iced tea. "I clean Sadie's house twice a month. Usually on a Thursday, like today. But in March I was here on a Friday, the same day that lady next door died. Not my usual day. I had to change my schedule in order to go on a class field trip with my son."

"I didn't remember that," Sadie added. "Then Melita came to clean earlier this afternoon. After she was finished, I took the calendar off the wall so I could write down the date of our next appointment. And Melita said something about needing to change the date, like she did back in March. So I looked at that page and realized she was here the day Roberta was killed. After I heard what Melita had to say, I called you and asked her to come back so you could talk with her."

250 ~ Janet Dawson

"I can't stay long," Melita said. "I have to pick up my son. He has a soccer game tonight."

"Tell me what you remember about that Friday," I said.

Melita reached for another cookie and took a bite. "It was raining off and on all day. I got to Sadie's house about two o'clock and finished cleaning around three. I was taking my gear out to my car." She pointed out the front window at the blue hybrid SUV I'd seen parked at the curb when I drove up. "I bring all my own equipment when I clean houses, it's better that way. Sadie's car was parked in the driveway, and my car was behind her, hanging over the sidewalk just a little bit. Anyway, I saw the mailman go by. Then I noticed this dark red sedan parked down the street." She waved her hand in the direction of downtown Petaluma. "Maybe two houses down. It had one of those Fas Trak toll gizmos on the windshield. There was a man inside, just sitting there."

She finished off the rest of the cookie and took a sip of iced tea. "After the mailman went by, that man got out of the car and walked up the street, past me. I got a good look at him because my vacuum cleaner was kinda blocking the sidewalk and I apologized and moved it out of the way. He said, think nothing of it, and kept going. He was whistling. So I finished loading the vacuum cleaner into my car and then I looked back and saw him climbing up the steps to Mrs. Cook's front porch. He rang her doorbell. Just then it started to rain really hard. So I got in my car, backed it out and drove away."

"Do you remember what time it was?" I asked.

"I know exactly what time it was," Melita said. "A quarter after three. I looked at the clock on my dashboard because I didn't want to be late for my next appointment, which was at three-thirty out west of town."

"What did the man look like?" I asked. "How was he dressed?"

"He was about as old as Sadie." Melita looked from me to Sadie and I recalled that she'd told me she was eighty-one. "A few inches taller than me, and I'm five three. He was wearing a tan raincoat and a hat. And gloves. Brown gloves. The hat was covering his hair but I got a really good look at his face."

Sadie chimed in. "It sounds like that man I saw at Roberta's, one of those dealers, the one I saw later at Copperfield's bookstore downtown. Did you bring those pictures you showed me?"

"I did." I reached for my purse and took out the photos I'd shown Sadie on my earlier visit, the ones I'd taken with my cell phone camera, of Henry Calhoun in front of the movie memorabilia shop. I handed the printouts to Melita.

She examined the pictures, frowning, looking from one shot to the next. Then she nodded. "That's him. I'm pretty sure that's him."

"Tell me about the sedan," I said.

"Wow, I'm not sure what I remember about that. Just the color, dark red, maroon, I guess. I couldn't tell you the make. Late model, though." Melita looked at her watch. "I really have to go now, and pick up my son. I hope this helps. Sadie seems to think it's important."

"I do, too, very important. Thanks. I appreciate you taking the time to talk with me." I gave her my business card. "If you remember anything else, call me."

Melita gathered up her oversized purse and made for the front door. Then she turned. "You know, that sedan had vanity plates. Something that started with an R."

I smiled. Raina Makellar had a maroon Lexus with vanity plates that read RNAMAK. And I wouldn't be surprised if Henry Calhoun borrowed it from time to time.

Sadie insisted that I stay for dinner, so I did. Then I drove back to Oakland, missing the worst of the evening rush hour traffic, and mulling over what I'd learned. I now had a witness who could place Henry Calhoun at the scene of Roberta Cook's murder. He'd made it look like an accident—the elderly woman had fallen down her front steps—and most people assumed it was an accident, except Sadie. Henry's motive for killing Mrs. Cook was evidently to gain access to her collection of movie memorabilia, purely financial.

But why would Henry kill Mike Strickland? I remembered what Mike had said when we talked about the dealers who were constantly trying to purchase his Hitchcock collection. The two men who'd visited him the Wednesday before, observed by Mike's granddaughter, were Chaz Makellar and Henry Calhoun. Mike thought one of the men looked familiar.

It'll come to me, he'd said that night at the gallery. *I never forget a face.*

At first I'd thought Mike recognized Chaz. But now it seemed that he'd recognized Henry. But why was that important? I was missing something. There had to be an intersection somewhere. If Henry was, as I suspected, Binky Jasper, was there something in the long-ago past that connected him to Mike Strickland?

~

I had just arrived in my office Friday morning when my cell phone rang. The readout told me the call was from Liam Cleary down in Los Angeles. "Well, darlin', you've hit the jackpot."

"LAPD had something on Hank Calvin or Henry Callan?"

He laughed. "On both. They were roommates back in the late seventies and early eighties. They shared an apartment on the top floor of a building in Hollywood, owned by one Dolores Cirillo."

"Wallace Simms's sister," I said. "A former bit player who later worked in publicity at Metro and Paramount."

"The very same," Liam said. "Both Calvin and Callan were making a living any way they could, working off and on as bit players and extras, scouting merchandise for Wallace Simms, even doing odd jobs around the apartment building for reduced rent. It's a three-story building, old place, built in the twenties. Henry Callan showed up in our files because he died in October of 'eighty-one. Fell down the stairs and hit his head."

That sounded exactly like the way Roberta Cook had been killed in Petaluma. "Any chance Callan had help falling down the stairs?"

"The question came up, but there was no evidence to support it," Liam said.

"And Hank Calvin?"

"That's where the fun begins. Callan was in his sixties and he was collecting social security. He was also getting residual checks from a number of television gigs. He didn't have any family, so after he died, nobody told the Social Security Administration to stop sending those checks. The checks kept coming, and Hank Calvin, who conveniently had Callan's driver's license and social security card, cashed all those checks. He kept cashing them until early in nineteen eighty-three, when someone noticed and called the cops. At which point Calvin disappeared."

"And resurfaced later as Henry Calhoun," I said. "But he didn't go far. He kept working for Wallace Simms, and whenever Wallace's daughter Raina called him Henry Callan, he just told her she'd made a mistake about his last name."

From Harry Corwin to Hank Calvin to Henry Callan—then Henry Calhoun. The same man. Binky shed personas like a snake sheds skins.

After my phone call from Liam, I checked my e-mail. I had a message from the private investigator in Mobile, Alabama. He'd sent me some scanned documents to go with it. I opened the files and learned that there had been a fire at the Jasper house in Mobile, early in 1941. Binky was injured, a bad burn on the inner side of his right arm.

What's more, it appeared that Binky had set the fire.

While I was chewing on this, thinking about Binky and his predilection for setting fires, my cell phone rang again. I looked at the number on the screen as I reached for it. Tory Strickland Ambrose, calling me from Santa Rosa.

"Dad's neighbors—the Millers—they're back," she said. "They got home last night."

~ 33 ~

I MET TORY later Friday morning, at her father's house in Healdsburg. The house next door was about sixty feet away, the property line marked by a four-foot-high row of manzanita bushes with dark red bark and light pink flowers. Tory and I walked through a gap in the bushes to the Millers' driveway, where two vehicles were parked, one a silver SUV and the other a green sedan. A pop-up tent camper with a trailer hitch had been backed onto a concrete pad next to the open double garage, where a stocky blond man was stowing camping gear on shelves along the garage walls. The sleeping bags were already lined up on one shelf, waiting for the next trip, while a camp stove sat at his feet.

Ryan Miller greeted Tory, then he led the way into the house. His wife Ginny was in the laundry room just off the kitchen, transferring clothes from a washer to a dryer. She was short and plump, with curly brown hair, looking rumpled. She enveloped Tory in a hug. "Oh, it's so good to see you. How are you holding up?"

"As well as can be expected," Tory said. "This is Jeri Howard."

Ginny smiled at me, then turned her attention back to Tory. "We got back late last night. Just fell into bed, and figured the unpacking and the laundry could wait until this morning. How did you know we were home?"

"Bobby sent David a text message," Tory said.

"Of course." Ginny switched on the dryer and beckoned us into the kitchen. "Come on in. I just made a fresh pot of coffee and there are some banana-nut muffins left over from breakfast."

"This isn't really a social call," Tory said. "We'd like to talk with Bobby."

Ginny was reaching for the coffee carafe. She stopped and looked up at Tory. "Bobby? Why?"

"I'm a private investigator." I handed business cards to both the Millers. "Tory has asked me to look into her father's murder. I'd like to ask Bobby some questions about what he may have seen the Wednesday before, when Tory's kids were here and Bobby was playing with David and Jason. Two men stopped to visit Mike Strickland that afternoon. I'm wondering if your son saw them or heard any part of their conversation with Mike."

Husband and wife exchanged glances. Then he nodded. "Certainly, anything to help. We were shocked when Mike was killed. This is normally a safe area. To have something like that happen, it's just unheard of."

"Mike was such a good neighbor. I miss him. Neither Ryan nor I was here when it happened. Ryan was at work. I'd gone into town with Bobby. He had a dentist's appointment. And Carly was off shopping with her friends." Ginny opened a cupboard and took out some red ceramic mugs. "Sounds like coffee all around."

The sliding screen door that led to the backyard opened and a teenaged girl came in. She was blond like her father, wearing sandals, khaki shorts and a skimpy yellow tank top that showed off the tan she'd acquired on vacation. "The garden looks okay," she told her mother. "I deadheaded the roses. We're gonna have lots of zucchini."

"We always have lots of zucchini," Ginny said, pouring coffee. "Jeri, this is our daughter, Carly. Where's your brother?"

The girl tucked a strand of hair behind her ear. "Out back, doing something with the recycling. Want me to get him?"

"Yes, if you would, please." Ginny finished pouring coffee and handed mugs to Tory and me.

"Let's go into the living room," Ryan said.

He and Ginny sat side by side on the sofa, while Tory and I took chairs opposite. A moment later Carly returned, accompanied by her younger brother. Bobby Miller was twelve, the same age as

Tory's son David, and he had his mother's round face and curly dark hair. He looked at the assembled grown-ups and frowned. "Am I in trouble?"

"No, son, you're not in trouble," Ryan said. He patted the sofa. "Come and sit by me. This lady would like to ask you some questions."

Bobby complied and looked at me. Carly perched on the arm of the sofa, next to her mother.

"Bobby, my name is Jeri. I'm a private investigator."

Bobby gave me the same wide-eyed reaction I'd received from Tory's sons. "Really? I never met a private eye before."

"I want you to think back. It's about three weeks ago, that first Wednesday in June, when David, Jason and Serena were here visiting their grandfather. They went on a picnic to Lake Sonoma that day. When they got back, you and the boys were together."

Bobby nodded. "They saw an osprey. I have a bird book, so I went and got it. We were looking at pictures of raptors and I was telling them about this bald eagle I saw at Point Reyes. Then I was showing them our camper and telling them all about our trip."

"Two men came to visit Mr. Strickland that afternoon," I said.

"I saw them," he said. "They were driving a brown SUV. I think it was a Ford but I'm not sure."

"Where were you when they got there?"

"I climbed up on top of the camper." Bobby ducked his head and his sidelong glance at his father told me he probably wasn't supposed to be climbing on the camper. "I was showing David and Jason how it opened up on the top. I saw that brown SUV come up Mr. Strickland's driveway. I was up high, so I saw them pretty good. One of them was really old. He had white hair. He was on the passenger side. The other guy, the driver, he was, like, Dad's age or maybe older. He was really tall and skinny."

"What happened then?" I asked.

"Those men went to Mr. Strickland's front door and they rang the bell." Bobby furrowed his brow. "Mr. Strickland came to the door. He stepped out on the porch and they talked for a while."

"Did you hear any of the conversation?"

He shook his head. "No. I was too far away. They didn't stay very long. They were leaving, walking away, toward their SUV. Then Mr. Strickland followed them and said something to the old guy."

"Just to the older man, not the driver?"

"Right," Bobby said. "The driver, he was already around the side of SUV and he had the door open, ready to get inside. Mr. Strickland was talking with the old guy."

Tory's daughter had overheard part of that conversation. Mike Strickland told one of the men that he recognized him. I'd thought it was Chaz Makellar, but it appeared Mike's words were directed at Henry Calhoun. I had the photos of both men with me. I took them from my purse and showed them to Bobby. "Are these the men who visited Mr. Strickland that day?"

He held them in his hands, a serious expression on his young face. Then he nodded. "Yes, those are the men." He set the pictures on the coffee table.

"Thanks, Bobby. You've been a big help." I took a sip of my coffee.

"Who are these guys?" Ryan asked. He'd been growing restive as I asked his son questions. "Does this have something to do with Mike's murder?"

"The younger man is a dealer in movie memorabilia," I said. "The older man works for him. They were asking Mike Strickland if he wanted to sell some of his Hitchcock collection. As to whether it has anything to do with the murder, I'm not sure."

Carly, the Millers' daughter, was older than her brother, about sixteen or seventeen. She was sitting on the arm of the sofa, listening with interest to the conversation, and she'd examined the photos that I'd showed her brother. I looked at her now. "Did you see anything that day?" I asked.

"Oh, Carly wasn't here." Ginny glanced at her daughter. "You borrowed my car and went into town with your friends. That was the day you packed a lunch and went to the beach on the Russian River. I'm a stay-at-home mom," she added, turning to me. "But I was in the backyard working in the garden. I didn't see any of this."

"But I did see them," Carly said. "I was just getting home. I'd turned off Dry Creek Road and I was slowing down to make the turn into our driveway when that brown SUV backed out of Mr. Strickland's drive. So I stopped to let them pass. I saw this older man in the passenger seat. As the SUV backed into the road he was right in front of me."

She leaned over and picked up the photo of Henry Calhoun that her brother had left on the coffee table. "Then I saw him again, a few days later. The same day Mr. Strickland was killed. He was getting out of a car parked on the other side of the road. A maroon sedan with vanity plates."

Ginny's mouth widened into a shocked O. "What? You never said anything about that. Not even when that sergeant came over to ask us questions. I thought you were with your friends."

"I didn't think it was important," Carly said. "At the time it was just a guy parked by the road. I didn't connect it with Mr. Strickland's murder. The girls were late picking me up, that's why I was still here. When we came out of our driveway, I saw that car. It was almost across from Mr. Strickland's driveway. I did think it was odd to be parked right there. I mean, if he was going to visit someone, why not park in the driveway? I guess that's why I really looked at it. I saw one of those electronic toll-taking things on the windshield. Then I got a good look at the driver and recognized the man who had been there before. Besides, I don't know when Mr. Strickland was killed. Tory found his body that night, didn't she? This must have been around one-thirty in the afternoon, because the girls were supposed to pick me up at one."

That jibed with the coroner's estimate of the time of Mike's death. I steered the focus back to the maroon car. "You said the car had vanity plates. Do you remember what was on the plates?"

Carly shut her eyes, as though trying to visualize the car. "Started with an *R*," she said, "and ended with a *K*."

Just like Raina Makellar's car, with the vanity plates that read RNAMAK. I was betting it was the same maroon sedan seen parked near Roberta Cook's house in Petaluma shortly before she died. A car that was probably driven by Henry Calhoun.

Ginny had been following this conversation, her gaze moving from my face to her daughter's face, as though she were watching a tennis match. The import of what Carly was saying hit her. "My God, do you mean that old man killed Mike?"

I did, but I hedged my response. "This is circumstantial, of course. But what your daughter just told me places him in the vicinity the same afternoon Mike was killed."

"But why?" Ryan asked.

"Because Dad recognized him," Tory said. She had been silent through all my questioning, drinking coffee and watching. "That's what Serena told us. She was in the tree above the porch and she heard the conversation that Bobby saw. Dad somehow knew that man. But that doesn't explain why that man would kill Dad."

If Henry Calhoun was indeed Byron Jasper, as I suspected, he didn't want anyone to know that Byron was still alive. He'd had the means and the opportunity to kill Mike Strickland. But what was the motive? The fact that Mike had recognized him? But what was the intersection between the lives of Mike Strickland and Byron Jasper?

Then the last piece of the puzzle clicked into place. I knew what it was, a twisting trail that led all the way to a movie set—and a dinner table.

I stood up and Tory did the same. "Thanks so much," I told the Millers. "You've been very helpful."

"What is it?" Tory asked as we walked back to her father's house. "You've thought of something. I can see it on your face."

"I need to use your father's computer," I said.

She unlocked the house and disarmed the security system. We went back to Mike's office and I switched on the computer. As soon as it powered up, I went to the Internet Movie Database and typed in Byron Jasper's name. He had worked as an extra and bit player in the movies from late 1941, when he'd arrived in Hollywood, until early January 1943, when he'd reported to Camp Roberts for Army training. His list of credits was short, just a handful of films. I clicked on each title and scrolled through the complete cast list.

Byron's name was at the bottom, as a bit player. Pearl Bishop told me that they had worked together on a film at Metro, in November of 1942. That's when she overheard him say he'd been drafted. I found the film, a forgettable opus starring nobody in particular. It had been released in 1943. And there was the intersection. In addition to Pearl Bishop and Byron Jasper, the bit players included Molly Strickland, Mike's older sister.

She'd started working in the movies in 1942, her brother had told me, right out of high school. She lived at home and she would bring her fellow bit players home for dinner. Her eleven-year-old brother Mike remembered them. "We always had a few of them around the table," he told me. And he'd recognized one of them, after all these years.

I took out my cell phone and called Pearl Bishop. She answered the phone with her characteristic good cheer. "Hey, Jeri, my buddy in publicity found a picture of Ralph Tarrant wearing those cufflinks. He said he'd send it FedEx yesterday, so you should have it today."

"Thanks, Pearl. Listen, do you remember a bit player named Molly Strickland? She was in the movie you were making at Metro in November of 'forty-two."

"Molly Strickland? Hell, yes, I remember her. We did several movies together. And we both volunteered at the Hollywood Canteen, starting when it opened in the fall of 'forty-two. We both met Marines and married 'em. She left Hollywood and I didn't keep up with her."

"She's dead now. Her brother Mike is the man who was killed in Healdsburg."

"The Hitchcock collector? Oh, my God. I remember her brother, too. Well, she had several, but the youngest, that was Mike. He was a sweet kid, a real movie buff."

"How did you meet Mike Strickland?"

"Why, Molly took a bunch of us to her house for a home-cooked meal. The bit players, I mean. Molly lived at home, you see, right there in Hollywood. Her uncle was a stuntman, worked on *Gone with the Wind*. Anyway, Molly's mom would cook up a batch of spaghetti and meatballs and we'd have a feast. That happened two or three times while we were shooting that movie."

"Think, Pearl. Did Binky ever go to one of those dinners at Molly's home?"

"Yes, he did. Twice. I remember him sitting next to Mike at the table. Binky was paying a lot of attention to Mike, including him in the conversation."

"And Mike never forgot a face," I said. "That's what he told me the night of the gallery opening. He recognized Henry Calhoun as Binky Jasper. So Henry came back the following week, and killed him."

Tory was hovering over me as I ended the call. "What next?" she asked.

"Back to Santa Rosa," I said. "To pay a call on Sergeant Toland at the Sonoma County Sheriff's Office."

~ 34 ~

JUST AFTER NOON on Saturday, I opened the door to Matinee, the movie memorabilia shop, and strolled in, holding the door for the young couple following a few steps behind me. They were casually dressed in khakis, both wearing lightweight jackets over T-shirts, as though they were killing time before the next matinee at the Alameda Theatre across the street. Once inside, the man stopped at a bin containing lobby cards and began flipping through them. The woman headed for the books, pulling a hardback from a shelf.

I walked toward the back of the shop, where Raina Mackellar stood behind the counter, talking with a trim, silver-haired woman in a green print ensemble. Raina glanced at me and smiled. "I'll be with you in a moment," she said.

I plucked a photograph of Carole Lombard and Clark Gable from a nearby bin of movie stills and held it up by the edges of its protective sleeve. As I looked past Raina toward the doorway that led to the storeroom, I saw someone back there, but it wasn't Henry Calhoun. Instead Chaz Makellar walked through the doorway, his bright yellow T-shirt a splash of color over his tight-fitting jeans. He carried a framed poster, an insert from *Decision at Sundown*, showing Western star Randolph Scott in a blazing orange shirt and blue pants, cowboy hat on his head and his hand on the six-shooter in his gunbelt.

"Here it is, Mrs. Jeffries," he said, turning up the wattage on his charm as he set the bottom of the insert on the counter. "Isn't this a beauty?"

"Oh, it's wonderful," Mrs. Jeffries said. "My husband just loves old Westerns, and Randolph Scott was his favorite."

"I really like the colors and composition in this one," Raina said.

"And it is a good price," Chaz added. "Excellent condition, no tears or folds."

Mrs. Jeffries laughed, already reaching for her wallet. "It's just perfect. He'll love it. I'll take it."

"Good choice," Chaz said with a grin. "And since your husband likes Randolph Scott I'll keep an eye out for other posters. I'll wrap this up for you." He disappeared into the storeroom while Raina took care of the credit card transaction. Then Chaz emerged with the woman's purchase encased in bubble wrap, secured with tape. "Let me carry this to your car. Where are you parked?"

"Thank you so much. I'm just down the street, near the produce market."

Chaz hoisted the package and followed the woman out the door. Raina stepped away from the counter, as stylishly dressed as she had been the first time I'd seen her, in slim black slacks and a long lilac blouse, large silver hoops dangling from her earlobes.

"Can I help you find anything?" she asked.

"I'm just looking right now," I said. I put the photo of Gable and Lombard back into the bin and shifted my attention to a title card from *The Buccaneer*, starring Yul Brynner.

Raina approached the man and woman who'd entered at the same time I had. The man had left the bin of lobby cards and joined the woman on the other side of the shop. Together they were looking at an oversized book of photographs from movie musicals. "Just browsing," the man told her.

She went back to the counter and took a sip from a take-out coffee container, another one of her caffeine fixes. Chaz returned and joined her behind the counter. "We will definitely have to look for more Scott posters," he told her. "Mrs. Jeffries is a good customer. Say, where's Henry? I thought he was going to be here at noon. We need to get over to Walnut Creek and pick up that lot of film noir stuff we just bought."

"He's on his way," Raina said. "I talked with him just before Mrs. Jeffries came in."

That answered one of my questions. I'd been concerned when I didn't see Henry Calhoun in the shop. And if he and Chaz were planning to leave, I needed to make my move, and soon.

Chaz pointed a finger at the coffee container Raina held. "I'm gonna walk down to Peet's. You want a refill?"

She smiled at him. "Sure. My usual."

Chaz stepped away from the counter, taking a few steps toward the front door. Before he got more than a few feet, I intercepted him. "I'd like to talk with you, Mr. Makellar. Both you and your wife."

Chaz Makellar smiled at me. "Of course. Can we help you with something?"

"Yes, you can," I said. "Back in April you purchased a collection of Joan Crawford movie memorabilia from a man named Lewis Cook. He was the executor of the estate of his mother, Mrs. Roberta Cook in Petaluma, who died in March."

Chaz nodded and went into salesman mode. "Yes, we did. That was a good-sized lot containing some rare and collectible posters. Are you interested in Crawford memorabilia?"

"Mrs. Cook had a three-sheet poster from *Rain*, very valuable because it's in mint condition. You're selling that poster for ten thousand dollars. You paid Lewis five thousand dollars for the entire collection. I'd say that was a steal."

Chaz's expression turned cagey. "Wait a minute. Are you saying there's something wrong with the sale? Mr. Cook was relieved that I took the stuff off his hands."

"He wouldn't have been relieved if he'd known how much it's worth. I saw the inventory you did for him. You undervalued everything."

Raina looked alarmed and spoke to her husband. "Is there a problem with that lot? I told you I didn't want any trouble."

"No, there's not a problem. There's no trouble." Chaz's tone was placating as he shifted his gaze from his wife to me, raising his hands as though to forestall any further questions. "That's just business. With the collectibles market, we have to consider what the merchandise might be worth, and what we might get for it. The asking price on that *Rain* three-sheet may be ten thousand, but unless we can find a buyer to pay that, the poster doesn't have any value."

"Let the seller beware, is that it? You saw him coming and took advantage."

"What business is that of yours?" Chaz said, his tone turning hostile. "If you're not interested in buying, why are we having this conversation?"

"We're having this conversation because I think there's a good chance Mrs. Cook was murdered."

Raina blanched. She set her coffee container on the counter, so hard that it tipped over. Brown liquid trickled onto the counter. She pulled a box of tissues from under the counter and mopped the spill. She tossed the wad of wet paper and the now-empty container into a trash can as she stepped out from behind the counter.

The lines around Chaz's mouth tightened. "What? What the hell are you talking about? That was an accident. That's what it said in the newspaper. She fell down the stairs and hit her head."

"Why would you, a businessman in Alameda, read a newspaper article about the death of an elderly woman in Petaluma?"

That stopped him short. Then he shrugged. "That? Well, I… Someone showed me the article."

"Would that someone be Henry Calhoun, your employee?"

"You haven't answered my question," Chaz said. "Who the hell are you?"

I handed him my business card. He looked at it and swore. Then he passed it to Raina. She put her hand on his arm.

"A private investigator?" Raina looked from him to me. Then she cast an anxious look at the man and woman who were still looking at books near the front of the shop, apparently oblivious to our conversation. She lowered her voice. "I'd think you'd better tell me what's going on."

"About three weeks ago, Chaz and Henry went up to Healds-burg to talk with a man named Mike Strickland, who owned a large collection of Hitchcock memorabilia. He wasn't interested in selling any items from that collection. Five days after you visited him, Strickland was murdered."

"Murder?" Chaz ran a hand through his graying hair as Raina stared at him with alarm. "I don't know anything about a murder."

"You knew Strickland was dead," I said. "You called and left a message on his answering machine, a message saying you were interested in buying his collection, just like you did with Mrs. Cook."

"Yes, I knew he was dead. I read about it in the *Chronicle*. I figured it was an opportunity, just like the Cook woman. But murder? I've got nothing to do with that. I'm a businessman. I look for people with collections and I try to buy the merchandise, that's all. I've been doing it for years, ever since I hooked up with Raina and her dad."

"Tell me what happened the day you visited Mrs. Cook."

Chaz was sweating now, moisture beading on his upper lip. "That old woman in Petaluma? She had some great stuff, all Joan Crawford. Once I saw that three-sheet from *Rain*, I knew that one item alone was worth a lot of money, that we could move if we found the right buyer. I tried to convince her to sell me some things from her collection. She didn't want to sell. But she did say something about needing to get an inventory done, because her son didn't have any idea how much it was worth. I told her I'd be happy to do the inventory. She said she'd think about it. That was it, we left."

"Did Henry say anything during all of this?"

"He said she'd come around. That's all he said. I didn't think anything else about it. Then later, Henry came to me, said the woman from Petaluma was dead. He showed me her obituary from the Santa Rosa paper. He reminded me what she said about her son, that he didn't know what the stuff was worth. Henry said I should contact the son and offer to take the stuff off his hands. It was a good idea, so that's what I did."

"I suppose it never occurred to you why Henry was reading a newspaper from Santa Rosa." I turned to Raina. "Tell me, does Henry borrow your car?"

"Sometimes," she said. "If he needs to run an errand. He's very careful and he fills it with gas after he's used it."

"Did he borrow your car the first Monday in June?" I asked, naming the date.

"He told me he was going to the doctor."

"A maroon Lexus sedan with vanity plates was seen parked across the road from Mike Strickland's house in Healdsburg the day he was murdered. The witness says the car had vanity plates, beginning with R and ending in K. You drive a maroon Lexus sedan, Raina, with license plates reading RNAMAK. Another witness saw a maroon Lexus with vanity plates starting with an R, in Petaluma the afternoon Mrs. Cook died. That was in March, a few weeks after Chaz and Henry visited Mrs. Cook."

Raina clutched Chaz's arm, her fingers leaving white marks where they dug into his skin. "A Friday in March? He borrowed the car on a Friday, I don't remember when. Another doctor's appointment, he said. We were going out to dinner that night, in San Francisco, and we had to drive the SUV, because Henry didn't get back in time. He apologized later, said it was raining, he said there was a lot of traffic."

"It was raining that afternoon. And I'm sure there was plenty of traffic. It was rush hour and he was driving all the way back from Petaluma." I heard the front door of the shop open and glanced in that direction.

Henry Calhoun looked as dapper and spry as he had the first afternoon I'd seen him, slender in a pair of gray trousers and a long-sleeved, cream-colored linen shirt. He paid little attention to the young couple browsing through the books near the door and walked toward us, his hand raised in greeting. I could see the gold cufflinks fastening his cuffs, heavy and square, decorated with a Celtic knot and in the center, a large distinct Celtic cross.

The cufflinks Henry wore were exactly like the cufflinks in a couple of photographs I'd seen recently. One photo had been in the FedEx package from Pearl's friend, waiting for me when I returned to my office Friday afternoon. The black-and-white publicity still of Ralph Tarrant was taken in January 1942, according to a notation on the back, a month after Sylvia Jasper gave him the cufflinks as a Christmas gift, a month before his murder. In the photo he held a cocktail in his right hand and a cigarette in his left, and the cufflinks he wore were clearly visible. The same cufflinks, or a pair just like them, were worn by Byron Jasper in the photo Sal Bianchi took at the Camp Roberts recreation hall.

"Henry Calhoun," I said. "Or is it Binky Jasper?"

He stopped and looked me over with his dark, stony eyes. "You were in here a few weeks ago. You're the woman who bought the Norma Shearer lobby cards."

"That's right," I said. "Jerusha Layne's granddaughter. You told me a yarn that day, about an unsolved Hollywood mystery involving the murder of an actor named Ralph Tarrant. You picked the wrong person. I don't like unsolved mysteries. I'm a private investigator."

"So you investigated," he said.

"I did. I think you killed Tarrant back in 'forty-two."

I didn't know why, though I had some theories. Anger, revenge, jealousy—perhaps all of these had combined into the fury that led him to shoot Tarrant at close range. There may have been some truth to what Pearl had told me, about a possible sexual relationship between Binky and Tarrant. If that were the case, Binky had a rival for Tarrant's affections, his own sister Sylvia. She, too, had a relationship with the actor.

"Sylvia was with you that night," I said. "After you shot Tarrant, you set a fire, hoping to cover your tracks. You took something off the body." I pointed. "Those cufflinks, a present from Sylvia to Tarrant. Then you made an anonymous phone call to the police, implicating someone else."

Henry's smile was malicious. We both knew it was my grandmother he'd tried to tar with that brush.

"Sylvia threatened to expose you," I said. "You killed her, buried her body on a beach in Santa Monica, and reported her missing. Later that year, you got your draft notice. You reported to Camp Roberts in 'forty-three. The Army didn't appeal to you, so you started looking for a way out. You killed Harold Corwin, put your dog tags on his body, and set another fire. Then you went back to Hollywood with a new identity, as Hank Calvin. That worked until someone who knew you as Binky Jasper recognized you. Pearl Bishop. Remember her? So you needed a new identity. You were sharing an apartment with someone who had a similar name. That was Henry Callan, who worked for Raina and her father."

Raina gasped and I glanced at her. "You weren't mistaken about the last name, Raina. The man who lived in your aunt's building and worked for your father as a scout really was Henry Callan. This man calls himself Henry Calhoun. He helped himself to another man's name and social security checks after Callan died very conveniently by falling down the stairs. Maybe that was an accident, maybe not. He died the same way Roberta Cook did, by falling down some stairs. That was so Chaz could buy her collection, especially that valuable poster."

"You can't prove any of this," Henry said.

"You were seen," I told him. "Getting out of Raina's car parked just down the street from Mrs. Cook's house on the afternoon she was killed. And again in front of Mike Strickland's house, right before he was shot. That wasn't about the collection. It was because after all your efforts to bury Binky, Mike recognized you. He wasn't sure of your name but he was sure he'd seen you before. He never forgot a face. That's what he said to you the day you and Chaz talked with him. So you killed him."

The young couple who'd entered the shop after me moved closer, coming to stand on either side of Henry. Both of them had their shields out. They were plainclothes detectives from the Alameda Police Department. I'd spent the morning with them, outlining my evidence, with Sergeant Marty Toland of the Sonoma County Sheriff's Office and Detective Kevin Harper of the Petaluma Police Department participating in the conversation by speaker phone. The man took out a pair of handcuffs while the woman invited Henry down to police headquarters to answer a few questions.

"You've racked up quite a body count," I said. "By my count, you've killed six people."

His smile was brittle. "More than that. I'll leave it to you to figure out who you've missed. The first one was hard. But it gets easier."

~ 35 ~

THELMA DARWELL and her doubles partner were running their opponents all over the tennis courts at Lower Washington Park. I sat on a bench outside the fence and watched them, enjoying the breeze blowing off San Francisco Bay on this fine summer morning. When the tennis players finished the set, Thelma walked to the fence and set her tennis racquet on top of her bag. She pulled off her sun visor and ran a hand through her white hair. As she unscrewed the lid from her water bottle, she saw me and waved. A moment later she joined me outside the courts, sitting beside me on the bench.

"I thought I might find you here," I told her.

"Every chance I get. At my age, exercise is what keeps me going." Thelma sipped her water. "Do you have news for me?"

I nodded. "I'm almost certain the man who died at Camp Roberts was your brother Harold. The dog tags found on the body after the fire belonged to a recruit named Byron Jasper. I believe he lured Harold to that tool shed, killed him and set the fire. Then he took Harold's identification and went AWOL. I found out the body is buried in a cemetery in San Miguel, near the base."

A shadow passed over Thelma's face. "I knew it. So did my mother. We were so sure Harry would never desert. What happened to the man who killed my brother?"

"Byron Jasper is still alive. He's about the same age your brother would have been if Harold had lived. As far as I know, your brother is his third victim," I added. "Jasper is responsible for a string of deaths going back to Los Angeles in nineteen forty-two. He's about to be charged with two recent murders in Sonoma County."

A lot had happened in the few days since Byron Jasper, aka Henry Calhoun, had been taken into custody. After questioning by the Alameda police, he'd been transferred to Sonoma County. I called Nacio Lopez, the LAPD detective who'd inherited the file on Ralph Tarrant's murder, and told him what I'd learned. Lopez was pleased at the prospect of finally closing the decades-old case. So was the Santa Monica detective who had the file on Sylvia Jasper's murder. And my friend Liam Cleary had been in touch with the investigator who'd initially looked into the death of Henry Callan, Byron's roommate who died in a fall back in the early eighties. He was interested in clearing that case, if there was enough evidence to show that Binky had killed Callan. Closer to home, the district attorney in Sonoma County thought the evidence was strong enough to convict Byron Jasper for the murders of Roberta Cook and Mike Strickland.

There was one more loose end, the murder of Harold Corwin, and that was why I was here this morning. I knew it was important for Thelma to clear her brother's name, to remove the stain of Harold having been listed as a deserter. With the evidence that Byron Jasper was alive, not buried in that cemetery near Camp Roberts, she could set the wheels in motion to correct the Army records. And she planned to claim her brother's body, she told me, to bring Harold back to Oakland, the city he'd left so many decades ago, to have a proper memorial service and inter his remains in Mountain View Cemetery, near those of his mother and father.

When I left the tennis courts I drove to downtown Alameda. The movie memorabilia shop was closed, even though it was Wednesday, when it would normally be open. It was a legitimate business, built from the enterprise started by Raina's father. But Chaz Makellar was facing some hard questions about his purchase of Roberta Cook's collection. Lewis Cook, chagrined to learn that his mother's "junk" was worth a lot of money, was threatening legal action against the Makellars. "Serves him right," Sadie

Espinosa said when I told her the news. "I knew Roberta had been murdered."

I went back to my office and worked on my final report for my client, Tory Ambrose. She was relieved to have some closure concerning her father's death, pleased that his killer was in jail.

When I finished the report I closed and locked my office door, walking down the hall to the law firm where my friend Cassie is a partner. I said hello to the receptionist and headed back to Cassie's office, where she sat, leaning back in her office chair, feet propped up on a stool. She looked up from the document she was reading and patted her pregnant abdomen. "Baby is being really active today. Thumping and jumping. Two more months to go. You look cheerful."

"I am. I just closed the case of the Hollywood murders from nineteen forty-two, and helped find a killer responsible for two murders up in Sonoma County."

Her eyes widened. "You're kidding."

"Have lunch with me and I'll tell you all about it."

She swung her feet off the stool and rose from her chair. "Let's go over to Le Cheval. I'm craving Vietnamese food."

We walked to the restaurant, a few blocks from Franklin Street, where our building was located. Over Singapore-style noodles with chicken, I told her about Binky Jasper and his homicidal ways.

"You pieced together quite a puzzle." Cassie picked up broccoli with her chopsticks. "He would have been better off if he'd never said anything to you that day at the shop."

"But he couldn't resist one last dig at Grandma. That's what started all of this." I scooped up chicken and chopped bell pepper. "It was Grandma's letters that really gave me the bigger picture. They're fascinating. I'm so glad Aunt Dulcie kept them. The other result of all of this is that Dad is now reading the letters. He's decided to write a book. I knew he wouldn't stay retired long."

After lunch we walked back to our building. I worked in my office a couple of hours. I was getting ready to leave when my cell phone rang. The number was in the 510 area code, the East Bay.

"Jeri, this is Dan Westbrook."

I smiled. Pearl's grandson, the man I'd been attracted to when I met him a couple of weeks ago in Lee Vining. I'd given him my phone number, hoping he'd call.

"I talked with your grandmother this weekend." I had called Pearl to let her know that I'd finally run Binky to ground. Pearl's assistance had been crucial, especially her memories of what happened back in the forties. She had provided physical evidence, the photo of Binky working as a bit player using the name Hank Calvin in the late seventies. And she'd contacted her friend in Hollywood, who'd provided the publicity still of Tarrant wearing the cufflinks before he was murdered. I liked Pearl a lot, not only because she was a link to my grandmother. I wanted to see her again, and I was contemplating another trip over the Sierra to Lee Vining and the stark and beautiful landscape around Mono Lake.

"I know," Dan said now. "Grandma is excited about you finding that guy Binky. She told me about that old murder case. I'd like to hear more details."

Would he? And I'd like to see Dan. I was attracted to him when we met in Lee Vining earlier in June and I thought I'd picked up a hint that the feeling was mutual. "Well, maybe we can get together," I said.

"That's why I called. When I saw you a couple of weeks ago, you said you really like Point Reyes. I'm going over there on Saturday, to hike the Coast Trail. I'd like some company, if you're interested."

"Yes, I am. Very much."

My smile stayed on my face the rest of the afternoon. I left my office an hour or so later and drove home. I had one stop to make first, though. I parked at the curb on College Avenue and fed a few coins into the meter. Then I walked half a block to a shop where framed posters and photos hung on the walls. Inside, near a rack holding frame samples, a woman looked up from a work table, where she was fitting a blue mat around a color photo of a field full of lupine blooms.

"I'm here to pick up an order," I said, handing her a slip of paper.

She glanced at the notation and nodded. "Oh, yes, those. They really turned out great." She turned and picked up two frames that were leaning against the wall and propped them on the work table. No more buyer's remorse, I thought, looking at the title cards from *The Women* and *We Were Dancing*. No matter how much they cost, the purchase was worth it. I'd been right about the colors, yellow and red, to go with the yellow backgrounds on the cards and the red lettering. I had picked out the yellow mat for the wider outside edge, with a narrow red edging inside, just for contrast. Both frames were bronze. I held each frame up in turn, looking at the faces of Norma Shearer, Joan Crawford, and Rosalind Russell in *The Women*, then gazing at Shearer in her red satin gown from *We Were Dancing*.

"Yes, they look wonderful." The picture framer gave me the invoice. I looked it over and took out my credit card, thinking about the afternoon I'd bought the title cards and how they'd sent me on a journey into my grandmother's past.

~

Julia Turner

ABOUT THE AUTHOR

Janet Dawson's creation, Oakland PI Jeri Howard, has sleuthed her way through ten novels. *Kindred Crimes* won the St. Martin's Press/ Private Eye Writers best first PI novel contest, also earning Shamus, Macavity, and Anthony award nominations. Dawson has also written a number of short stories, including a Shamus nominee and a Macavity winner. She lives in the East Bay region of the San Francisco Bay Area, and welcomes visitors at www.janetdawson.com.

MORE MYSTERIES
FROM PERSEVERANCE PRESS
🙂 *For the New Golden Age* 🙂

JON L. BREEN
Eye of God
ISBN 978-1-880284-89-6

TAFFY CANNON
Roxanne Prescott Series
Guns and Roses
*Agatha and Macavity Award
nominee, Best Novel*
ISBN 978-1-880284-34-6

Blood Matters
ISBN 978-1-880284-86-5

Open Season on Lawyers
ISBN 978-1-880284-51-3

Paradise Lost
ISBN 978-1-880284-80-3

LAURA CRUM
Gail McCarthy Series
Moonblind
ISBN 978-1-880284-90-2

Chasing Cans
ISBN 978-1-880284-94-0

Going, Gone
ISBN 978-1-880284-98-8

Barnstorming *(forthcoming)*
ISBN 978-1-56474-508-8

JEANNE M. DAMS
Hilda Johansson Series
Crimson Snow
ISBN 978-1-880284-79-7

Indigo Christmas
ISBN 978-1-880284-95-7

Murder in Burnt Orange
(forthcoming)
ISBN 978-1-56474-503-3

JANET DAWSON
Jeri Howard Series
Bit Player
ISBN 978-1-56474-494-4

KATHY LYNN EMERSON
Lady Appleton Series
Face Down Below
the Banqueting House
ISBN 978-1-880284-71-1

Face Down Beside
St. Anne's Well
ISBN 978-1-880284-82-7

Face Down O'er the Border
ISBN 978-1-880284-91-9

ELAINE FLINN
Molly Doyle Series
Deadly Vintage
ISBN 978-1-880284-87-2

HAL GLATZER
Katy Green Series
Too Dead To Swing
ISBN 978-1-880284-53-7

A Fugue in Hell's Kitchen
ISBN 978-1-880284-70-4

The Last Full Measure
ISBN 978-1-880284-84-1

MARGARET GRACE
Miniature Series
Mix-up in Miniature
(forthcoming)
ISBN 978-1-56474-510-1

WENDY HORNSBY
Maggie MacGowen Series
In the Guise of Mercy
ISBN 978-1-56474-482-1

The Paramour's Daughter
ISBN 978-1-56474-496-8

DIANA KILLIAN
Poetic Death Series
Docketful of Poesy
ISBN 978-1-880284-97-1

JANET LAPIERRE
Port Silva Series
Baby Mine
ISBN 978-1-880284-32-2

Keepers
*Shamus Award nominee, Best
Paperback Original*
ISBN 978-1-880284-44-5

Death Duties
ISBN 978-1-880284-74-2

Family Business
ISBN 978-1-880284-85-8

Run a Crooked Mile
ISBN 978-1-880284-88-9

HAILEY LIND
Art Lover's Series
Arsenic and Old Paint
ISBN 978-1-56474-490-6